Magicae: Book Two
The Storm of Garmr

By Bo Luellen

Becky

Thank you for making my smile brighter.

Enjoy!

Copyright © 2020 Bo Luellen

All rights reserved.

ISBN: 9798633539646

DEDICATION

This book is dedicated to the role players who gamed in my Paranormal vs. Spy campaigns. The Agents of AEGIS was a concept I came up with after binge-watching Archer, James Bond and X-Files. I went to my tabletop gaming group and pitched them the idea, and instantly they were in. We dived into weeks of adventures, pitting the 1970's period MIB-style shadow agents against the powers of the unknown. During those games, we came up with memorable characters that we still talk about today. Some of these friends have been by my side in life and at the gaming table for over two decades.

I dedicate this book to:

Larry Fennel
Mitch Langston
Lucy Langston
Sean West
Henry Cribbs
and
Christian Miller aka Roger Quinlynn

"I would rather walk with a friend in the dark, than alone in the light."
— Helen Keller

Contents

DEDICATION iii
ACKNOWLEDGMENTS vii
Prologue 9
Chapter 1: Amanda VI 13
Chapter 2: Henry VI 29
Chapter 3: Richard VI 47
Chapter 4: John VI 63
Chapter 5: Henry VII 81
Chapter 6: David I 97
Chapter 7: Shoshannah I 113
Chapter 8: Amanda VII 129
Chapter 9: Richard VII 149
Chapter 10: John VII... 169
Chapter 11: David II 189
Chapter 12: Shoshannah II... 205
Chapter 13: Edward I 223
Chapter 14: David III.. 239
Chapter 15: Amanda VIII 251
Chapter 16: John VIII... 267
Chapter 17: Shoshannah III 285
Chapter 18: Richard VIII.. 297
Chapter 19: Edward II 307
Chapter 20: Amanda IX.. 321
Epilogue.. 337

ACKNOWLEDGMENTS

This first step into the world of Magicae couldn't have happened without some key people. Thank you to the test group who read my book one chapter at a time, giving me honest feedback. Without your truth, the book wouldn't be what it is. Thank you: Misty Moore, Cindy & Trevor Messner, Johnny McLain, Alicia & Taj Murphy, Gabriel & January Rider, Sarah Walters, Mary Jane Whisnant, Larry Fennel, Samara Hamby, Susan Melton Turner, & The Magicae Series Book Club

To bring some validity to the subject matter of this work of fiction, I enlisted the help of several experts in their field. The following individuals spent their time helping me to flesh out the details to give the story as much authenticity as possible:

Thomas Lee Harris, Jr, Consultant – Druid, Arthurian Legend
Johnny McLain, Consultant – Biblical

My thanks to my editor, Henry Cribbs. His hard work and dedication to the spirit and theme of my books has helped safeguard my vision.

Cover Art by Christophor Volk. Cover Graphics and Promotional Media by Francessca's PR & Design. Interior Art by Steve Standeford (Steve's Instagram - @incompletesaint)

Finally, I would be remiss if I didn't give thanks to the master authors Bram Stoker, Mary Shelley, Robert Louis Stevenson, and H.P. Lovecraft. Your stories continue to inspire and terrify.

Prologue

New York City, New York - Tuesday, October 23rd, 2018 – 11:31 a.m. EST

His grandson pushed open the reinforced door to their apartment carrying a bag of groceries. Basten Van Helsing turned up the TV in hopes it would draw Nicolaas's attention. The young man locked up behind him and dropped the door bar horizontally into brackets bolted to the frame.

This was Basten's fifth day in his recliner, watching the ongoing news coverage of the crisis in Oklahoma. The 80-year-old man only got up to use the bathroom and get food. The Crimson Brotherhood captivated him and kept him locked, stone-faced, at the screen.

Nicolaas unloaded the groceries and started lunch for both of them, "Grandpa, you need to get out. It's not healthy for you to just sit there."

Basten ignored his grandson, as a TV reporter announced, "The dead are now counted at 15 law enforcement, 176 unidentified bodies and 46 alleged members of The Crimson Brotherhood. With the apparent suicide of one of the surviving ringleaders, Tom Chapman, the police are running out of leads. The only alleged cultist still alive and in custody is the comatose Henry Jekyll. This puts the FBI in the hot seat, back to you Bill."

The screen faded back to the anchor who continued, "Thank you, John. Today, Tulsa stands paralyzed, with many parents refusing to let their children attend school without armed guards present. With the President calling this 'the worst example of homeland terrorism in United States history,' it's understandable why the fear level is on a high. The people of the Sooner State are clamoring for swift justice, and some are losing faith."

Basten clicked onto another station, "... Jekyll is still in St. Francis Hospital under 24-hour guard. This is the third attempt on Henry Jekyll's life since he was admitted. According to sources, the nurses found Tulsa Sheriff's Deputy Thomas Carter holding a pillow over the face of the suspected serial killer. Deputy Carter is the uncle of one of the dead found in The Preserve. The FBI has restricted the Tulsa police from access to the suspect…"

Nicolaas slapped a tomato slice on some bread, "Well, you can't blame Carter for trying. The Crimson Brotherhood is pushing that city to the edge."

The elderly bald man grunted, "You're too quick to judge. Truth is a relative state. Time can reveal its secrets and cloud the mind to actual events. A keen mind can unravel its mysteries while assuming the intelligence of those involved. A real detective… "

The younger man put some slices of ham on the sandwiches and sighed, "… puts evidence first and opinion second. Yes, grandpa, I know."

The old man's face lit up as he yelled at the TV, "Ahh, ich habe dich erwischt!!"

The young man dropped his plate on the counter and rushed next to his grandfather, "You caught who? What are you talking about?"

On the screen, a video was playing footage of a break-in at a funeral home in Broken Arrow, Oklahoma. The text at the bottom read, "Embalmer Present During Brotherhood Break-In." A picture of a shorter woman with dark hair emerged in the corner of the screen. The banner under her face read, "Mrs. Willow Young".

The station played the grainy video from the night in question. It clearly showed Willow filming from the back of a vehicle with tinted windows. Two men stood over the corpse of a local Tulsa restaurant owner, Lewis Turner. One of them jammed the dagger into the body, and then stood back. The handle of the knife had an octopus looking design that contrasted to the dark surroundings.

A young blonde reporter faded into view, "Funeral home staff member, Willow Young, initially withheld this evidence in fear of Crimson Brotherhood reprisal. Charges were dropped against Ms. Young when she agreed to testify in the trial of Henry Jekyll in exchange for immunity. in return for her cooperation. Prosecutors have passed a stay on the statute of limitations pending Henry Jekyll's emergence from his coma. If and when Mr. Jekyll awakes, he will be arrested for his suspected involvement as a ringleader in the Crimson Brotherhood. She, along with Professor Amanda Lanyon of Eastland College, David Keller, Thomas Booth, millionaire philanthropist Josh Dyer, and Detective John Utterson will be called to testify. Back to you, Tom."

The screen faded back to the anchorman who reported, "Another layer of tragedy emerges, as the ME report of Larry Lanyon was disclosed this morning and revealed some disturbing details. The cause of death was a combination of blood loss and a broken neck. The report says that the victim had two stab wounds on his throat that were caused by an icepick. Larry Lanyon is survived by his wife, Amanda Lanyon, and two daughters

April and Nancy. The whereabouts of the Lanyon daughters are still being investigated and the FBI has officially connected the kidnapping to the Crimson Brotherhood."

His grandfather showed off his white partials with a wide grin, "Did you hear that?"

Nicolaas took a bit of the sandwich, "Hear what?"

Basten pointed at his neck, "Two puncture wounds! Then the neck snapped like a twig!"

He rolled his eyes and sighed, "Grandpa, the ME said it was an ice pick. Don't go into this whole vampire business again. I don't think it's ... "

His grandfather slammed the tip of his cane down on the floor, "No! I've seen enough evil to know what it looks like. Where you find darkness, you find the creatures of the night. Go get our car out of storage, and I'll start packing!"

Nicolaas didn't move from his spot, "Grandpa, you have to stop doing this. You sit and talk about conspiracies like you're Quincy Hunt. How many times have we went on a road trip to vanquish some dark evil, only for me to die of boredom in a hotel room. All the while, you skulk around the city, until you get bored. Then we come back here and wait for you to get fixated on yet another stupid adventure. How about we go to Disneyland instead?"

Basten stood up and puffed out his chest, "While I'm still alive, we go where I say we go! Maybe after, we go to Disneyland."

The young man shook his head and smiled, "Okay Grandpa. You win. We are going. I only ask that you keep on your meds and not hit the sauce too much. The All-State Jiu-Jitsu Tournament is next week, and I'd like to be back by then. Do you think you could resolve your imaginary monster hunting by then?"

The withering man stood up as straight as he could, "Kleinzoon, I've worked hard to prepare your mind and body for what is to come, but you can't see past the phone that is constantly in your face. It is time for me to stop coddling you! It is time for you to understand what it truly means to be a Van Helsing!"

The older man reached over and grabbed an onyx colored walking cane with a silver handle. He adjusted his stance to face his grandchild and tapped the stick hard on the floor. The young man rolled his eyes and took the sign that he needed to get moving. As he gathered their things, the elder took out a white handkerchief and polished the gleaming handle until the initials "AVH" shined in the New York sunlight.

Basten admired the initials of his ancestor and announced, "Today, I tell you all Nicolaas . It's time to join the family in the hunt."

Chapter 1: Amanda VI

Tulsa, OK - Friday, October 19th, 2018 – 1:10 a.m. CST

She held the pistol on the intruder as he gave a calm, "Please, Mrs. Lanyon, let's not lose our composure. I'm not here for this, I simply want to know..."

Amanda opened fire on the Brotherhood member, putting four holes in his chest. The blood showered onto the wall behind him, and his body shook from the impacts. The noise from the shots deafened Amanda, leaving only the sound of a high pitched whine in her ear. She waited for the man to fall as he staggered in place for a moment, but then the drunken swaying suddenly stopped. Marcus lifted his arms like he was a puppet on a string and systematically straightened each of his limbs as if someone was controlling him. To her horror, he stood straight up and regarded her with a serene expression on his face.

Amanda turned from shock to terror as she realized he wasn't going down from the slugs. She screamed and unloaded eight more 9mm rounds into Marcus. A messy collection of holes accumulated on his chest and discarded shell casings bounced off the kitchen counter next to her.

The large black man stayed motionless until the gun clicked empty and then sang softly to her, "I've got no strings to hold me down, to make me fret, or to make me frown. I had strings, but now I'm free. There are no strings on me."

The man's hand flashed upwards and snatched the gun from her. The motion was quick, powerful and precise, with brute force hidden within the blur of speed. Her hand felt the cruel bite of his iron grip, as the weapon was stripped from her.

Marcus put the pistol back in his shoulder holster and warned, "Now, Mrs. Lanyon, that was foolish and costly. My clan has a rule, blood for blood. You owe me a debt, and as much as I adore your passion, I am compelled to collect."

The smell of gunpowder was thick in the air as she watched his eyes turn to a golden sheen. The bullet wounds in the chest stopped flowing with blood, and the skin healed before her eyes. On the kitchen wall behind him, the crimson spray fell away and landed as dirt on the floor. As she tried to inch away along the counter, she watched the blood at his feet transformed into dark earth.

She heard the front door open, and the voice of her husband rang out, "Honey, it's us. We heard a noise. Are you okay?"

Larry Lanyon burst into the kitchen, trailed by their daughters Nancy and April, and yelled at Marcus, "Who the fuck are you?"

Amanda's heart sank, and she gave a desperate shout, "Get out! Get the kids and leave, now!"

Marcus looked at the three new arrivals, as they appeared in the kitchen and bemused, "Now things seem to be getting messy indeed. My name, Mr. Lanyon, is Marcus Holmes, and I'm a member of the Crimson Brotherhood. Your wife has put you in a very precarious position I'm afraid. You see, I need information from her, but she has decided to be difficult. That will cost someone."

Larry let out a bellow that filled the room and charged at the black man. The overweight, aging former linebacker hit Marcus with his entire body weight. Both of their children screamed as they saw their daddy slam into the stranger that had invaded their home. Larry managed to move the intruder no more than six inches across the slick linoleum floor. He seemed to be unable to drive his target to the ground with his practice tackle that had served him so well in college. Holmes grabbed the back of the big man's neck and pulled him off his waist, like a cat with a kitten. Her husband made a howl in pain, while the skin on the back of his shoulders was bunched up into Marcus's grip.

The Brotherhood man held Larry up off the ground, and Amanda flew to his defense. Before she could reach them, the powerful assailant struck her in the chest with a crisp open palm. The blow felt like a car wreck, slamming Lanyon back against the cabinets, and knocking the air out of her.

Larry thrashed against the iron grip as Marcus turned to Amanda and beamed a wicked grin. The upper canine teeth grew downwards and extended out slightly. The elongated fangs fit perfectly over his lower cuspid's and looked inhumanly white. His mouth was dripping with yellow mucus as he turned back to his captured prey. With a lion-like snarl, Holmes plunged his teeth into the thick round neck of Amanda's husband. She gave a blood-curdling shriek, as Larry's eyes rolled back into his head and April and Nancy wailed for their dad. The skin complexion of the vampire's victim turned to a pale opaque, and his arms fell slack to his side.

Marcus drew away from his meal and let out a satisfied moan. With a flick of his wrist, he broke the neck of her dying husband then flung the large man across the kitchen. Larry's wrecked body struck the same wall that had once been covered by the vampire's blood. As Amanda's husband crashed down into the mystical dirt that covered her floor, a collage of wedding photos bounced off the wall and crashed to the ground. The father of her children stared blankly at the ceiling, as a pool of blood poured onto one of the broken pictures. The red liquid leaked past the shattered glass and covered a photo of the two of them eating wedding cake.

Marcus moved with astonishing speed and grabbed both of her children by the backs of their necks. Her daughters stopped screaming and fought against the pain and tightness in their throats to continue breathing. Amanda cautiously worked her way around the counter and held her aching chest. Marcus turned the girls towards their mother and kneeled down between them.

He wrapped his murderous arms around her daughters and granted, "You've lost a husband, but those can be easily replaced. Now, daughters, on the other hand, oh, those not so much. I will allow them to continue living, and all you have to do is tell me everything, from the beginning, leading up to tonight. Come now, Mrs. Lanyon, haven't you done enough damage to your family? It's time to do something to save what you have left."

She held her hands up in surrender and recounted everything that had happened up to that moment. Marcus stayed transfixed on the story, with his hands around her daughter's throats. Amanda spoke about Henry Jekyll, her meeting with Utterson, becoming a member of the task force, and the raid on the Preserve. Marcus requested specific details about the incident with Mr. Purple and the Athame Dagger.

When she was done, he observed, "My, you have been through it. I appreciate your delinquent, yet straightforward retelling. I had initially intended to let you live, but now things have become much more complicated. I will hold onto these two lovelies... "

She beseeched, "No! I did what you wanted! Please!"

Marcus stood up, yanking the girls off their feet by their necks and continued, "...As long as you offer no further assistance to any law enforcement, they will be returned to you in one year. That's one month for each bullet, Mrs. Lanyon." He hugged her daughters close to his chest and told them, "Say goodbye to your mother, girls."

Nancy gave a petrified whimper, and The Vampire shot out towards the front door in an impossible flash of motion. Driven by fear and paternal instinct, Amanda clutched her chest and forced herself to move through the pain to go after him. Only seconds behind him, she chased Marcus into the living room and saw the front door was wide open. The cold wind was blowing hard in the night, and fallen leaves from her maple tree were tumbling into her house. Amanda gripped the oak door facing and look out at the empty lawn. Marcus, April, and Nancy were gone from sight, and only the barking neighbor's dog was evidence of something alive on her block.

She wondered out into her lawn and screamed frantically for her absent kids. Amanda called Josh Dyer, and he phoned the police. Within minutes a cruiser was in her driveway. A half-hour later, Detective Michaels and Cobb were on site, along with five other patrol cars. She sat in the back of an EMT truck and gave a statement, while the medics checked her out. Amanda had avoided any broken bones, but she had deep bruising where the Vampire had struck her.

News vans got there just as she was being driven away towards the police station. John Utterson had stayed with her as Amanda gave another full statement to the FBI. As she talked, Agent John Hamilton walked in, sat in the back, and listened intently to the hours of interrogation.

Amanda told the agent that the intruder identified himself as a member of the Brotherhood, but she had never seen his face. She lied and told them he wore a ski mask and that she never learned his name. When they asked what had been used to kill her husband, she said the assailant had used an ice pick. That part she knew wouldn't stick, but it was all she could think of. The safety of her children depended on her being of no further help to the police.

When she went to leave, John Hamilton informed the room that she was now being taken into protective custody by a specialized branch of the CIA, called AEGIS. The Texan would occasionally pepper her with questions about the night Larry was killed, in an attempt to find a crack in her story. What was more unbearable than the hounding by her protector, was waiting for the inevitable confirmation that her lie didn't pan out.

By Sunday, she was told that the Police ME, Amy Howard, had

determined that the cause of death was from two sharp puncture wounds to the carotid artery. The murder weapon was determined to be an ice pick, which astounded Amanda when Agent Hamilton told her. It corroborated her story, but she knew the evidence shouldn't line up. The wounds on Larry's neck were savage, and Marcus had ripped the flesh with vicious abandon.

A day later, she found a note slid under her hotel room door that read, "You did fine. I'll need a favor before this is over. The girls send their love. Yours - Marcus"

Tulsa, Oklahoma – Friday, October 26th, 2018 – 9:02 a.m. CST

The Oklahoma sunlight poured into the hotel window and warmed her tear-stained face. It was the first time she had enjoyed a moment of pure silence since Thursday. Amanda Lanyon watched a crow bouncing along the pavement outside and pecked around at a discarded piece of bread.

Her solitude was shattered as Agent Decker burst in the room and bellow out, "Mrs. Lanyon, it's time."

Amanda sighed and requested, "It would be nice if you knocked."

Patrick Decker spoke into his wrist microphone, "I'm with her now." He did his usual sweep of the room as he responded to her, "Mrs. Lanyon, we agreed not to have an agent in your room, but we need complete access at all times. With the death threats made on the Mayor and city officials, our Agency needs your complete cooperation to keep you safe."

Amanda whirled around in frustration and asked, "What does the CIA care about me anyway? Shouldn't I be under the protection of Detective Utterson's…"

Decker swept the room with a device as he interrupted, "Again, we are not the CIA, Mrs. Lanyon. We are a special branch that has been tasked to provide you protection."

She threw up her hands and raised her voice, "What branch is that exactly? I know next to nothing about you people. You come in, flash a badge, and drag me from one safe house to the next. Who are you?"

The straight-laced Agent replied, "Our unit is called AEGIS, and all you need to know is that we take your safety as of paramount importance. You are one of a handful of witnesses that survived the Preserve. More importantly, you have a unique connection to Henry Jekyll and the new leader of the Crimson Brotherhood, your 'Mr. Purple.' While the cult is hunting you, the international news agencies are continually trying to track you down for the story. Ma'am, I know this isn't easy, but our methods are for your own safety."

On TV, a rerun of the previous night's *Real Time with Bill Maher* played and the comedian's monologue filled the small hotel room, "Look, Amanda Lanyon is a hero, no doubt about that. She helped bring to light these murderous thugs and prevented the loss of more innocent lives. No one is debating that, but let's be honest. Did her actions play a part in what happened to her family? I can't say for sure, but the police were already mobilizing to the Preserve. The good professor decided it wasn't good enough, and that decision had consequences."

The agent mercifully hit some buttons on the remote control and switched to a news station, whose reporter announced, "… ongoing identification of the dead continually being discovered in the wake of what is being called 'The Battle of the Preserve.' Investigators have revealed that the homeless who were kidnapped by the Crimson Brotherhood had migrated in from other States. Some of the bodies are over five years old, which makes a positive identification problematic at best. Families of the victims whose names could be ascertained have started flowing into Oklahoma from all over the country to claim their lost loved ones. Overnight, Tulsa has become a national tragedy that dwarfs the Oklahoma City Bombing. The cultists left no survivors, no need for blood drives, no prayers for hope, there is only the knowledge that the Crimson Brotherhood still lives among them. The name Cthulhu has become a household word that represents dread and panic."

As she put on her coat, Decker observed, "There is a new development that you need to be cautious of. The police raid on the Brotherhood's compound has galvanized the people of Tulsa into a type of religious hysteria. Churches preached the militarization of their congregations and ignored the FBI's pleas to allow the police to do their jobs. The looming threat of a secret cult, embedded in the city, has sent shockwaves of fear through the citizens. Oklahoma has gone from just under 300,000 concealed carry permits to 600,000, doubling in a week. Gun shops are staying open 24 hours a day, and ammunition costs have spiked to take advantage of the sudden demand."

She sat down on the edge of the bed, "I've seen the reports on TV. What does that have to do with me?"

The agent checked his watch and then revealed, "The college at Eastland has a televangelist program that airs every Sunday and Wednesday."

Amanda gave him a perplexed, "Yes, The Eastland Worship Hour. Brother Dunn has been doing that show ever since I started teaching at the college."

Patrick leaned on his elbow and gave an unempathetic, "Greyson Dunn is the son of one of the influential members of the Southern charismatic movement in the Mid-South. Greyson stands as a Pentecostal leader of enormous influence in the Christian community. The Saturday after the raid on the Preserve, he bought time on the cable networks to start broadcasting nightly."

Amanda remarked, "Well he is a spiritual leader."

The agent raised his eyebrow, "On the following Sunday, during the highest watched program in the history of The Eastland Worship Hour, he announced the creation of The Tulsa Christian Crusaders. In front of a live studio audience, the good Brother Greyson lifted a 9 mm pistol above his head, and quoted Ephesians 6:11, 'Put on the full armor of God, so that you can take your stand against the devil's schemes.'"

Professor Lanyon's brow wrinkled as she repeated, "The Tulsa Christian Crusaders?"

The agent pulled out his phone, "The next day, Eastland's courtyard was full of armed followers answering the call of Brother Dunn's Pentecostal Crusade. Greyson divided the city into sections, and patrols were assigned. By Monday, the streets were being continuously monitored by groups of Christian Crusaders, as a type of armed neighborhood watch. Your boss, Greyson Dunn, has declared war on the Crimson Brotherhood and made the college a battle camp."

He turned his phone around to show her a photo of a burning body on a stake, "A clerk at a PetSmart discovered her manager had concealed some personal articles behind a false wall. The worker jimmied the lock and found three robes with the Cthulhu symbol on the chest. Instead of calling the police, she called the Tulsa Christian Crusader Hotline set up by Brother Dunn. Three hours later, the police found the manager tied to a stake, and her body burned. The pet store had been spray-painted with the words, "Cthulhu Worshipper!" The vigilantes were never found, and no one from the strip mall was willing to testify."

Amanda covered her mouth at the sight of the image and lamented, "That is repugnant. How awful! They are burning people at the stake, like witches. Can't the cops stop them?"

He put away his phone, "The police and FBI openly discussed with reporters the idea of bringing in the National Guard to quell the rising Crusader's version of mob justice. Within a few days, the public found their law enforcement to be a toothless tiger, as your Oklahoma's Governor, Katherine Hill, refused to deploy the Guard. It seems she is a supporter of Mr. Dunn."

Amanda felt nauseas at the sight of the charred woman, "Governor Hill has been to Sunday service more than once."

Patrick shifted to more images of the burned body, "More than a few of the Oklahoma military said that if they were ordered to initiate Martial Law, they would deploy on the streets of Tulsa but stay in the service of Brother Dunn. By Friday, people knew who the real law was. 47% of the nearly four million people who live in this State are Evangelical Protestants who are falling in line with the Tulsa Christian Crusaders."

She shook her head and rebuked, "This is awful! Rumors will turn into facts, and suspected people will be executed on a hunch. Someone has to do something!"

Standing up, Decker remarked, "Once again Mrs. Lanyon, you seem to be square in the middle of yet another element of this mess. You work at Eastland, so you should be prepared in case anyone asks you questions about your boss or his Crusaders. We can't tell you what to say, but it is my suggestion that you refrain from commenting. Denouncing the TCC will pull their crosshairs onto you. A strong number of the population of Oklahoma believes you have some level of involvement in the Crimson Brotherhood, simply because of your coincidental association with Jekyll. If they heard you speaking against them, it might spark a mob response, and you might find yourself on the next burning stake."

She shook her head in disbelief and looked at herself in the hotel mirror. Amanda straightened the wrinkles in her black dress that had hung in her closet for the last five years since she had attended a funeral. She picked up her purse and peered down at her wedding ring with a feeling of guilt eating at her stomach.

Decker opened the door to her room, checked out the hallway, and ordered, "Okay, Ma'am, follow me."

As they walked, she felt anxiety over the impending circus she was headed towards. This day wouldn't be easy, and dealing with the forced pageantry wasn't going to help her grieving process. With Decker in the lead, the pair walked out of the back door and made for her AEGIS provided white Nissan. Parked next to it was a black Sedan with Patrick's partner, Agent John Hamilton, sitting in the driver's seat. Decker checked the perimeter as Amanda got in her car and started it. She rolled down the window and breathed in some fresh air to calm her nerves. Taking a moment to collect her thoughts she suddenly became lost in a wave of self-hatred.

A burst of motion erupted from behind a dumpster, as a man sprinted towards her car. A lanyard that read "PRESS" flopped around his neck, and trash floated off his body while he ran. He had a Go-Pro camera on his head and a microphone in his outstretched hand. Before she could react, the person grabbed her arm and put his helmet camera in her face.

The man burst into a question, "Mrs. Lanyon, Quincy Hunt from "The Hunt for the Truth!" Can you tell us what the police are doing about your kidnapped daughters?"

Behind her, the agents were launching out of their car. Her mind raced as she felt a degree of shock, as it was the first person she had spoken to outside of the AEGIS detail. Instinctively, she shook with fear at the sudden reminding of her children's absence.

The reporter glanced up and rushed to his next question, "Mrs. Lanyon, do you feel responsible for your husband's death, and how do you respond to the accusations that you're a secret Brotherhood member?"

As Hunt's final words exited his mouth, Agent Hamilton speared him hard to the ground. She heard the air rush out of the reporter's body, as the large Texan's 250-pound frame pancaked on top of him. Her car door flung open on the passenger side, and the firm grip of Agent Decker latched onto her wrist.

Decker gave a controlled command, "Get out towards me. Move!"

She barely had time to grab her purse before he pulled her over the console. She slid into the passenger seat and then out of the car door. He nearly picked her up entirely while he lifted Amanda to her feet. Across the car hood, she could hear the reporter being told to stop resisting and the clicking of handcuffs being applied.

Hunt was barking at the Agent, "The Press has a right to know! I have a First Amendment right!"

As she was walked to the black Sedan, she heard Hamilton's twang yell, "You have the Constitutional right to feel my boot in yer ass! Give me those hands!"

Agent Decker put Amanda in the passenger seat of the Sedan and moved quickly to the driver's side. She trembled in her seat as she watched Hamilton slam the reporter on the hood of the Nissan. Decker raced out of the parking lot and reported their situation to someone named 'Control.'

She faintly heard an old man's voice reply back, "Continue to the graveside. We have support agents in place, and be aware that the Dutchman is on site."

Decker hung up the phone as she asked, "Who is the Dutchman?"

The agent glanced over and requested, "Ma'am, put on your seat belt, please."

The sedan maneuvered through the streets of Tulsa towards the cemetery as they passed thousands of people who were lining the streets on the way. Hundreds of hand-made signs were being held up for those entering the graveyard to see. Some offered support to the families who had loved ones that were being laid to rest today. Others were a mixed bag of anti-Crimson Brotherhood and pro-Christian Crusaders. She sat up straight as Amanda caught sight of her husband's plump face on a giant billboard that was attached to a shop wall. She recognized the photo from his Facebook page. The image stabbed deep into her chest, as she read the words below it, "Remember The Hero Who Saved Two Officers and Killed By The Crimson Brotherhood. We Love You, Larry!"

The memory of her husband's death jarred her mind, as she saw her car join a line of vehicles on the way into the Oaklawn Cemetery. Thousands of people surrounded the outer edges of the fence of the graveyard. They stood in respectful observance of those being laid to rest. She saw hundreds of armed Tulsa Crusaders, wearing black armbands with the gold lion symbol of Eastland College mixed in with the mourners. People yelled support towards her car and threw roses as they passed through the front gates, and news crews stood on top of their vans to get a better camera angle.

Agent Decker pointed out, "The city banned reporters from Oaklawn out of respect to the dead."

Patrick parked the vehicle, radioed in their position to Control, and walked Amanda to her chair. Dozens of caskets lined up next to each other, and Lanyon was seated directly in front of her husband. The family photo she had provided the city was framed and placed on top of his dark wood coffin.

John Utterson and Terry Johnston, both in wheelchairs and in their dress blues, rolled over to her. Terry had gauze wrapped around his arm, and the elderly black woman she had seen in the waiting room was pushing him along. John was muscling through the grass but was keeping pace.

Utterson stopped and consoled, "Professor, I'm so sorry about Larry."

She nodded solemnly and replied, "So am I."

The bagpipes played, and everyone stood to salute the flag-covered caskets of the fallen police. John and Terry returned to their spots as Brother Dunn took to the podium and started the ceremony. Each of the officer's names was called out in turn, and a 'thank you' was given to the surviving family members. A shock of energy went over her when her husband's name was listed at the end. She knew it was coming, but it didn't make the moment any easier to digest.

Governor Katherine Hill took to the podium, "We cannot easily reconcile the evil in people's hearts to commit these unspeakable acts. It was only due to the courage and tenacity of our law enforcement that more deaths were prevented. These fallen heroes displayed incredible bravery in a time when Oklahoma needed them most."

Slowly, the mourners lined up to give sympathies to each of the grieving families. She shook the hands of friends, family, and colleagues, as they took turns to offer their respects. After five minutes, a numbness came over her as she was subjected to a broken record of sympathy. Familiar faces would tell her how sorry they were, hug her, and the cycle repeated. Some would praise her courage; others would remind her not to lose faith in God. She looked over at Decker, hoping to figure out a way to get him to let her leave early. Instead, she only saw the stalwart agent frisking people as they waited to see her.

Looking back to the next person in line, she saw the face of Eve Lanyon glaring back at her. It was the first time that she had encountered her mother-in-law since the night her husband died. Amanda started to speak but was stopped by a stiff slap to her face that cut her bottom teeth into her lip. The sound of the strike drew gasps from the people still in the line, and Agent Decker quickly launched in between the two women. James Lanyon grabbed his wife's shoulder and pulled her back away.

Eve spun around, hugged her aging husband tightly, and wailed, "I want my son back! I want my granddaughters! Harlot! She leads the Devil to them!"

All around, people's cell phones were coming up and recording the scene. The taste of blood hit her tongue as she held her mouth and stared dumbfounded at the irate Eve Lanyon. Decker radioed in something on his wrist communication piece. Still, Amanda couldn't seem to focus enough to make out what he was saying.

James Lanyon wrapped his arms around his wife and bellowed, "My son spoke to me the night you and Josh Dyer became the so-called heroes of the Battle of the Preserve. He said how he tried to talk you out of getting mixed up in this any further. I told him to pack up the kids and come over. He did. The three of them were safe with us until you called. Because of that, he decided to bring his family back home and stand by you. We begged him not to, but he did it because he loved you. Now he is dead, and our granddaughters are in the hands of his murderer. These people might call you a hero, but you're just as bad as the Crimson Brotherhood. You put your family in harm's way because of what? A love affair with a college fling? A need to feel important? Our only child is dead because of you. If our grandchildren are found, we will do everything in our power to get them away from you!"

Agent Decker pulled Amanda away and warned, "Okay, that's enough. Ma'am, are you hurt?"

She shook her head no, replying, "I just want to leave."

He nodded and radioed that they were exiting. As he escorted her from the funeral, Amanda felt the heat on her skin from the slap. She wasn't angry at Eve; she understood the maternal feeling all too well. Right now, her daughters were with a supernatural madman, and the only thing she could do to help them was to stay silent for a year in the hopes Marcus followed through on his promise.

As they approached the black sedan, a familiar set of faces were bunched up and regarding her somberly. Jessup House, Thomas Booth, and David Keller stood side by side in front of a worn pickup. Keller was wearing a pair of wranglers with a black pair of dress boots, with a white shirt and a black necktie. House had his wild white hair slicked back and was sporting a veteran's vest that was filled with medals from his days in the Marine Corps. Booth had on a dark tan colored poncho with a hood, which looked suspiciously like a cloak to her, and was leaning on his gnarled wooden staff. Jessup gave a little wave and flashed an innocent grin towards her.

Amanda stopped and told the agent, "I need to go talk to some friends of mine, can you give me a moment?"

He eyed the group of men and stated, "Okay, you have five minutes, but stay within eyeshot. Please make it quick, Mrs. Lanyon. We are out in the open here."

She walked towards them, as the grey-bearded Jessup lumbered his portly frame towards her and opened his arms, welcoming, "Come here, girl."

She received a bear-sized hug from the old man and then another one from Keller. Amanda felt a kinship that could only be brought about by living through a life and death situation. It made her ignore the bold aroma of Old Spice from Jessup and Booth's aura of stink.

House put a hand on her shoulder and said, "How're ya holding up?"

She adjusted a stray hair nervously and responded, "I'm not sure. My children are in the hands of a psychopathic killer, my husband's dead because of me, and the world just saw me get slapped by my ex-mother-in-law. My job is likely going to fire me because I haven't been to work, and Brother Dunn has been leaving me messages demanding that I openly support the Tulsa Christian Crusaders. People in town either think I'm a hero or the whore who is looking for attention. I'm numb."

Keller cleared his throat and asked carefully, "We don't mean to pry, but what happened at your house? The news says a cult member killed your husband with an ice pick and then kidnapped your daughters."

She looked towards the news trucks with their high powered microphones and cameras, wondering, *How sensitive is their equipment? I can't risk it.*

Amanda looked back and robotically replied, "That's what happened."

David uncrossed his arms and chuckled, "One guy killed your husband, took your kids right out of your home? All while you, the person that outran me towards an armed cultist, stood by and couldn't do anything. No description, no license tag, and then you disappear with those MIB looking bastards. I call bullshit. What really happened?"

She shook her head and admitted, "It's complicated."

The big man made eye contact with her, "The newspapers said that Larry's head was twisted around backward. A friend in the sheriff's department told me he was thrown into a wall like a rag doll. Your husband was a large man. Lifting him off the ground isn't something the average person could do. You know what I think? I think that the superwoman I fought in the woods came to your house. She killed your husband and kidnapped your kids. Amanda, I fought her. I know that thing looks human, but it isn't. I've had nightmares every time I sleep about what I experienced. You see, I get why you're reluctant to share those kinds of details with the police. If I told the cops that some tiny woman was yanking full-grown men off the ground by one arm, they would lock me up or worse. You can't stand by and do nothing. That woman needs to be stopped. All of us agreed that we will help you."

Her face twisted in anguish when an old grizzled voice came from the opposite end of the road, "Indeed, she does need to do something Mr. Keller, but your theory is off a bit I'd say. Yes, there was a supernatural element to that night in your house, but this superwoman wasn't who came to visit you. Was it Mrs. Lanyon?"

The tapping of his black cane accompanied the crooked stride of the old man. The weathered face of the aging gentleman twisted into a grin, showing off a perfect set of false teeth through his shaggy white beard. The approaching stranger was dressed in a two-piece black suit, with a long grey scarf around his neck. At his side was a younger man in his twenties who was in black slacks and a dress shirt. She could see some resemblance in their features and thought she caught a hint of a European accent in the man's voice.

Booth pushed his thick glasses up on his nose and gasped, "An old person, gross!"

Amanda had enough surprises for one day and retorted, "It's none of your business. Whatever newspaper you are writing for can kiss my…"

The well-dressed visitor held up a hand and pleaded, "Please forgive me, Mrs. Lanyon. The journey to Oklahoma has caused me to lose my manners, and, certainly, you have been through a lot. My name is Basten Van Helsing, and this is my grandson Nicolaas . It isn't everyone that comes face to face with a vampire and lives. The newspapers said that your husband was stabbed in the neck by a man with an ice pick, but that's not what happened, is it, Mrs. Lanyon?"

Amanda felt anger swell up inside at the thought of Marcus biting Larry's neck and then ending his life. The sound his snapping bones made as he died haunted her. Amanda glanced at the AEGIS Agent, who was staring intently at her and knew she only had a small amount of time. She couldn't risk endangering her children, but she dared a tiny shake of her head.

Keller grabbed his head and whispered, "Holy shit!"

Jessup let out an incredulous laugh and asked, "Wait, what are we talkin' about here? Ah, vampire? You got to be kiddin' mister."

The younger man entered the conversation with an artificially deep voice, "The vampiric undead have been recorded in the oral and written traditions of most cultures on the planet. There are dozens of different types, and each has its own strengths and weaknesses. Some will live no longer than a few years, while others saw a time before Jesus Christ hung from the cross. All of them are deadly. They are beings of darkness, kin of Satan, and liars."

Amanda put her hand across her face to hide her mouth, then whispered, "I don't know what to do. If I stay silent and out of their way, I've been promised my daughters will be returned to me in a year."

The stranger leaned on his cane and said, "If you wait until that year is up, I'm sure your children will be lost to you. Even if you do get them back, they will be strangers and reborn of evil. If you have the means, get out of the State, or better yet out of the country. With you gone, the one who has them will lower their guard around your Nancy and April. My grandson and I will find them and free them."

Amanda lost her cool, grabbed the interlopers collar, and hissed, "Why should I trust you, old man?"

He patted the top of her hand, "Our family has been hunting monsters like this for generations. I saw the footage from the funeral home and heard about the way your husband died. So, the Helsing's answered the call, as my ancestors have done over the many years. Mrs. Lanyon, if you must stay silent to fulfill this dark agreement, then why not do it elsewhere. Let me go to work and save your children."

She studied his face for a moment, then let out a tearful, "Okay."

Basten took her hands in his own and asked, "I will need but one thing from you; the name of the vampire who has your children."

Amanda hugged the old man and whispered in his ear, "Marcus Holmes."

Chapter 2: Henry VI

The Mind of Hyde – Unknown Date – Unknown Time

Henry Jekyll wandered about the Study, as Hyde told him, "The mortals are working to revive our body with their crude devices and methods. Their science can't begin to understand what is happening, so we will take advantage of their ignorance and bide our time wisely. The coming metamorphosis will activate the divine DNA in your genetic code."

Henry looked towards the dark figure and asked, "So, I'm still in a coma?"

The Demon nonchalantly explained, "It's more akin to being in a cocooned state, but to your understanding, yes, you are still in a coma. The process is tasking your frail body and draining it to the point of death. Over time, we will gradually change into a Nephilim, and our two beings become one. In the meantime, we must use the pending months to re-train your mind to accept what is coming."

The young man gave a shocked, "Months? We can't stay like this for that long. Those lunatics will get to us by then!"

Hyde had pity in his eyes as he relayed, "Calm yourself, my child. Time is a function of the universe that you barely understand. While we hibernate, the flow of time moves very differently. To simplify this for you, one hour of time in your world is equal to one month here in the Study. Your mind is entwined with my consciousness, which means reality bends to Hyde."

Henry examined an onyx bust of a man he didn't recognize and inquired, "I thought Nephilim were created when one of you has sex with one of ours?"

The Devil fluidly sat down on a brown leather love seat, "Your species is just now discovering how to clone and selectively alter the genetic markers. Yes. In its most basic form, a Nephilim can be created through impregnating a human woman. The idea that coupling is the only way to create a new lifeform is the primate thinking that keeps your kind looking for caves when the storm comes. What we will experience will be spiritual, physical, and mental unification. The strongest and best elements of each of us will be kept, while the more undesirable shall be discarded."

The man shook his head and objected, "The Bible never spoke of this."

An emotionless Devil responded dryly, "Do be still my heart, it didn't? Well, let's go on a little faith, for now, shall we?" Henry gave a sour look at the jest, as Hyde plowed along, "It's forbidden to create a Nephilim, even among those that fell with Lucifer, for the blended offspring have strange powers and abilities. The transformation will purge disease and imperfections from our body, and we will cease to age. Unfortunately, we will retain most of your human physical characteristics, but take heart. My more exceptional celestial features and traits will shine through. We will experience some degree of increased strength and agility, but that will pale in comparison to the deep well of magical energies we will be able to draw from. Our new body will be both the human and divine, giving us the skill to use both of the arcane talents of angels and mortals. Only a few rare creatures have dared to embrace this path, and were hunted down and killed by jealous gods and envious beings who wanted that power for themselves."

Henry walked around the bust and lamented, "Wait! If we are changing physically, won't the doctors and nurses notice?"

His host played with a lock of his black hair and said, "I'll stay the more pronounced physical changes until we are close to our rebirth. We will be at our most vulnerable until then. I wouldn't fear for us too much, as the mortals have us sequestered under armed guard. They hope to put us on trial when we revive as a leader of the Crimson Brotherhood. You humans and your witch trials. Alas, I can't judge them too harshly, as I've done enough to warrant such a tribunal, but my justice will come from a more exalted court. In any case, hours before we awake, our face and body will be altered. When we rise a stranger to this world, you will no longer resemble the pathetic man you once were. The law bringers will find only an empty bed, and Henry Jekyll will have vanished from existence."

Henry sat down across from his ancestor and pondered, "Does that mean I won't be me anymore?"

Hyde rested longways on the couch, "The melding into one being will cause both of our personalities to go dormant inside the genetic coding of the new body. In essence, we will become the parents to a new life form, a construct of blended physiognomies."

Henry took a deep breath and revealed, "I have to admit, the idea of a new beginning sounds exciting, but I don't like the idea of being out of control. This thing we will become has the potential to be a great force for good or a creature of evil."

The Demon propped his head up on hand and examined, "My child, think back to your roots on that dull, miserable ranch in the country. Consider how your mother's influence carved your soul into several dysfunctional pieces, all of which were woefully ill-prepared to deal with the pressures of life. You thought leaving for college would free you of a tortured existence full of regret, guilt, and cowardice. Still, you've only floundered, as you try desperately to fit into ordinary society. You have only been at peace when coiled inside the dream state of an opiate, which only offered a brief reprieve from the hurtful memories. The end to your wretched path is upon you. Embrace the notion of becoming something that doesn't tremble in the dark. You will be a new being, that will cut away the fear. The demons of your past will slink away from the beast you will become."

Henry digested Hyde's words as the Demon mused, "Really, it's a small matter. It is the same method that God used when he transferred his essence into the Jewish child. The difference is we're not Mary, a married teenager, and no one is running out on the newborn afterward. We shall enjoy the spoils of this world and feast in the forbidden temple of Solomon."

While the days past in the Study with Hyde, he poured into the books. Henry discovered it was nothing more than a collection of life experiences from the Demon's victims. Each person he possessed was represented in a single tome that expounded on the individual's failures and successes. Hyde taught him how to attune himself to the books and absorb their knowledge. The content of the pages transferred into his mind, as the memories of its subject became his own.

Hyde told him with a sneer, "Angels are talented at conveying information, just as humans are formidably incapable of hearkening. Now that your Angelic qualities are surfacing, you will absorb the essence of these Vessels' life experiences."

Over time, Henry realized that the thoughts weren't merely implanted there as a reference point, but intimately connected to him. The process came with an emotional joining, and he would feel their life and death as if it was his own. The benefit was that he would absorb some new skill or trade with each book consumed.

One morning he read about a Brazilian fisherman Hyde had possessed.

When he was done, Henry could sail, knew how to deep-sea fish, and spoke fluent Portuguese. Just as with each of these magical downloads, he felt the deep sadness of the Vessel's death when Hyde abandoned the fishermen after the cartel killed him for moving in on their illegal ventures. There was always a give and a take with the Demon's sorcery.

When he was done processing the emotional ramifications of the day, Henry thought, *This is like living in a real-life version of Quantum Leap. I'm Sam, Al is a Demon, and Iggy is a long line of nightmarish books.*

In the weeks to follow, Henry lost his sense of time as one day bled into another. He was consuming dozens of life experiences each day, and finding his outlook on life was changing. While he was gaining new skills and languages, he was also having nightmares from Hyde's impact on the possessed victims. As usual, the Demon had a tendency to only jump into damned sinners who were already bound for hell. When he became bored or needed to run from Miniel, he generally made sure the Vessel died in some stimulating way. After living through hundreds of demises, Henry had a series of psychotic episodes and anxiety attacks. The Demon could see he was on the verge of insanity, which would result in a disastrous union. If Henry went crazy, the new creature would become wild and prone to chaotic violence.

Hyde told him sympathetically, "Do you remember where you were when your people experienced the attack you call 9-11?"

Henry nodded and recalled, "They rolled a TV into the classroom so we could watch, and then let out school."

The Angel placed a comforting hand on his shoulder and continued, "Just like your parents remember where they were when John F. Kennedy was assassinated. Just like how your grandparents remember when America entered World War II. Your species uses a tragedy to define each generation. Most benevolent races take inspiration in great accomplishments and let it renew their culture's hope and unity, but not humanity. You only find the noblest parts of yourselves when you are deep in blood. As I inhabited the filth called 'Man,' I consumed those moments with an intensity you couldn't comprehend. It was a drawback to my cohabitation and caused me no end of problems. Unfortunately, I still feel the grieving, the love, the lost family members of all those I've possessed, with complete accuracy. That is the curse of my perfection. You remember everything as if you were still in that instant. Your kind has a saying, 'Time heals all wounds.' It is not so for Angels. We remember the love and slights as if the prick of the pin never stopped."

Henry felt his anger rising and replied, "You kill and lie with no regard! How dare you judge our ..."

Hyde held a hand up and attempted a degree of diplomacy, "Why do you speak as if you are one of them? You have been granted a divine gift of knowledge that you are not fully human, and therefore have some hope of a greater existence. Henry, you must accept the pact you made and, therefore, no longer need to make excuses for your behavior. Humans are naturally sinners who walk the earth devoted only to their own destruction. God forgives them eternally, while we, the Angels, have no such reprieve. Relish in the freedom that you will never need acceptance from your creator again. You will be immortal and, once we are strong enough, free to roam the cosmos for all eternity. These humans and their failings are beneath you, never forget that."

Henry's hands trembled as the stress of the conversation initiated an anxiety attack. He leaned on the oak center table and held onto the edges to steady himself. The core of his mind was starting to rip apart, and for a brief moment, his body flashed for a few seconds, then solidified again.

Hyde took him by the shoulder and explained, "My child, you are on the precipice of discovery, but your mind is rupturing." The Demon held a book out in his left hand with the title, *Post Traumatic Stress Disorder for the Lower Lifeforms*.

He glanced up at the dark entity and scowled, "You have a sick sense of humor."

Hyde pushed it towards him with a calming, "You won't be able to endure this process unless you learn how to manage your human flaws. Inside are the memories of Master Sergeant Aiden Lowe, a veteran of fourteen tours in the Middle East in your United States military. Read it."

Henry felt another wave of horrendous images from the books assaulting his mind again. It wouldn't be long until he cracked up completely. Hesitantly, he reached out and took it out of the Demon's pale hand. The cover had a picture of the laughing Marine, as he held his rifle and posed on a sand dune. Henry opened it and was thrust into the soldier's body. He found himself sitting in a small office, facing an older woman in a gray pants suit with a notepad on her lap. The lady had dark hair and wore a white lab coat with a name tag that read, "Dr. Katie Shaw,

MD." She was taking notes and glancing back up at the soldier as he spoke.

She put down her pen and ordered, "Aiden, I want you to start retaking your medicine. These violent outbursts you are having at work aren't going to help your situation and are a sign that you are backsliding. Starting Monday, I want you in a group again."

The image flashed forward in time to Aiden sitting with other vets in a circle of chairs. Each was telling their stories from the war and sharing what it was like adapting again to civilian life. Henry soaked in all of the violent encounters the soldiers were sharing and felt the anxiety set in.

When it became Sergeant Lowe's turn, he stood up and related, "This morning I couldn't get a thought out of my head from a skirmish we had in Iraq. We crossed paths with a convoy of Army tankers transporting JP8 fuel. The lead truck ran over an IED and was disabled. They were pinned down by enemy fire and taking causalities. There was only one soldier from the convoy that was returning fire, and the contacts were starting to move in. We gave support and forced the enemy into retreat. I was in charge and ordered our medic to assess the wounded.

"The front truck's driver was a twenty-three-year-old woman from Fort Smith, Arkansas. The explosive had splashed her with acid, and the left side of the private's face was burning away. Pieces of the woman's flesh were just melting away and dripping onto the sand. She was screaming in pain and losing it. Our corpsman gave her some morphine. It kept the woman comfortable while we waited for an evac helicopter to take her.

"I chewed out the transport for not returning fire. They had been denied ammunition by the commanding officer. When I asked why, they said it was because the CO was having their company take on missions that were never officially ordered. Three dead and one woman irrefutably scarred for life, all for one incompetent officer's attempt to get a promotion. I never found out what happened to the Arkansas woman. Whether she lived or not is a mystery, I think about all the time. Regardless, she wasn't going to come back the same person she left."

Henry felt the anguish in the man's heart and could see the damaged private first hand through his mind. The jelly-like flesh that slithered off her cheekbone and her inhuman shrieks of agony were now in his head. Henry was starting to feel his grasp on reality slipping away again, as another anxiety attack battered his consciousness.

In the darkness of the sergeant's mind, Henry thought, *Why are you doing this Hyde! I can't take this anymore!*

The image shifted back to a time when Sergeant Lowe was alone in his house in Houston, Texas. On his nightstand were a bottle of pills and a half-empty glass of water. He felt the antidepressants kick in, and soon the veteran was fast asleep. In the peaceful, dreamless slumber, Henry followed along with Aiden's consciousness. The nightmares never came, and Henry was able to get a full night's rest. After some time, he opened his eyes to find he was in the Study, and his mind was refreshed. Hyde sat cross-legged across from him in a crushed velvet black three-piece suit and drinking his usual Bourbon.

The Demon gave a bored expression, "Did you rest well?"

Henry sat up and took a moment before, answering, "Yes. Very well. The awful memories from those poor souls have faded but not gone. I feel different but more in control."

Hyde poured himself some more liquor and revealed, "That memory you absorbed will act as an anchor. Re-read that same book for the next few nights, and eventually, you will have balance and no longer languish in an ocean of pain. Instead, you will dwell in harmony with the memories of the past and be equipped to harness your potential."

Jekyll threw his hands up, shouting, "Why didn't you have me read that at the beginning? Why make me suffer?"

The Angel didn't rush to answer and gulped down his drink before replying, "There is a price for everything."

Henry glanced back at the book on the floor and asked, "What happened to Sergeant Lowe?"

Hyde answered swiftly, "He damned himself by putting a gun in his mouth and pulling the trigger."

Jekyll replied with confusion, "Damned? For what? He was a soldier doing his duty, and because of that sacrifice, he couldn't live with what he had been forced to do. After feeling all those battles personally, I get it. God wouldn't damn a person for being a patriot!"

Hyde's eyes widened, "He took his own life, my Child. God has rules and didn't want him. Lucifer might have him, though. You can rejoice, as Hyde has found a use for him, and now you're better for it."

The Demon shifted in the chair, rubbed his head, and said, "To be forthright, I'll be happy for this cessation. I've been forced to hide inside cages of dwindling potential and boundless sin for far too long. It has made me bored and weary. Though, fear not for your beloved ancestor and savior, for when our new body dies, I will be free once again."

Henry took a step towards him, red-faced, "What of me, Hyde!? What happens to my soul if we die?"

The dark-haired creature smiled wickedly and replied, "Nothing that you didn't agree to when you made the pact. You will be judged by God. So, let's do hope for your sake our union is a long and successful one."

One evening he wearily went to take down yet another book and saw something sticking out from under Hyde's long backed chair. Henry glanced around to find the Demon was off on one of his many recesses and then leaned over to take a closer look. Staring back at him was a gray bound tome with a draped confederate flag embossed on the cover. The spine had silver letters that read *The Story of Edward Tallman*.

As he opened the book, the all too familiar flash of strobes assaulted his eyes, and he was once again transported into the subject's life. Henry found himself standing in a field of dead Union and Confederate soldiers on a freezing morning. He could smell the gunpowder and defecation coming from the bodies around him. His left foot was ankle-deep in horse manure, and Jekyll suddenly felt a sharp pain in his right arm. He wanted to check his arm for injury, but just like all the rest of the memories, he was only a passenger in the story.

The flood of life experiences sank into his psyche from Edward Tallman and momentarily overwhelmed his senses. He came out of it with the realization that this was the aftermath of the Battle of Fredericksburg, and the date was December 13th, 1862. He was standing in a cold Virginia field as the fog burned away in the noon sun. The battle casualties had been the highest of any campaign he had seen yet. The Union Army of the Potomac, led by General Burnside, had repeatedly tried a frontal assault on General Lee's Confederate Army of North Virginia. Lee had placed his troops in a superior position that caused the Union casualties to be three times that of the Confederate.

Under cover of a mixture of fog and smoke from the gunpowder, Ed walked among the dead. While his arm had been grazed by a musket ball, he had come away with only a few bruises. His face was covered in a layer of black powder from firing at the enemy. The Vessel was a decent soldier and could pull off up to three shots a minute with his .54 caliber Harpers Ferry rifle. Henry had never been that good of a marksman, until today.

Now he possessed the same skill as the soldier with that rifle.

As he walked among the dead, Henry was imbued with the battle experience of the Confederate soldier. He learned that most of the conscripts who had lost their lives on the field battle were hit with random shots made by the terrified common folk. Unlike the uneducated farmers who signed up for this war, Edward Tallman was a West Point-trained professional soldier. He had grit and a steady hand in a fight. Opposite to those patriotic souls who were willing to die for their convictions, he was only ready to kill because it paid well.

Henry settled into the macabre scene and thought, *Tallman is the typical Hyde target; a villain with an agenda.*

As he strolled through the freshly slain patriots of two unlike ideals, Ed would stop and pilfer through the pockets of the dead, taking anything of value. He knew it was a crime that could get him court marshaled or worse. The man had every intention of living through this bloody war, and he had made plans to be wealthy in his military retirement. In his knapsack, there were dozens of gold watches and a large roll of Greybacks and Greenbacks that numbered in the thousands. He decided to be well provisioned, regardless of who would win in the end.

Soon, his pockets were stuffed with new loot from a dozen of soldiers that had been killed in dreadful ways. The bloodstained currency bulged in his grey trousers, and a collection of gold wedding rings topped off his shirt pocket. The fog was starting to lift, and his cover would be gone soon. Taking a breather, he pulled off his gray hat and ran his dirty fingers through his sweaty long black hair. He hadn't shaved or bathed in weeks, but he knew it would be worth it one day.

He felt a hand grab around his ankle, which caused him to instinctively pull away with his rifle raised and ready to strike. As he moved to come down with the butt onto the crimson face of the prone Union soldier, he stopped in horrified recognition. The man under the caked-on blood was his younger brother, Roy. He dropped his gun into the cold mud and fell down to his knees next to his mortally wounded sibling.

Ed sobbed and put his hands on the man's chest as he screamed, "Roy! Roy, what are ya doing here? You damn coot! You're supposed to be back in Kentucky, helping momma!"

His brother began a coughing fit that caused more blood to seep out of his belly wound. Ed ripped open Roy's muddy blue coat and saw a bullet hole that entered just below the navel. The injured man screamed as Ed rolled him to his side to examine the exit wound. His little brother's cries pierced the fog and echoed on the field, while steam rolled out of the open hole in his back. A fist-sized patch of flesh, muscle, and bone was missing from just beside his spine. Through the chewed up tissue, Ed could see the mangled internal organs of his kin. A void of hopelessness filled his heart as he noticed the large birthmark he had made fun of in their youth was completely missing. Ed rolled him to his back and took out his canteen. Slowly he gave him a few drinks until it all came back up in a spray of blood and mucus.

Ed sat down on the cold ground in defeat and broke the news, "Roy yer not going to make it long. The wound on yer back is gonna kill ya. They won't be able to patch ya up."

His brother blinked hard and cried, "I can't feel ma legs. I can't get up. Stay with me, Ed."

Ed shook his head and asked, "Bub, what are ya doing in that Bluebelly uniform? Why aren't you looking after our farm?"

His brother's face wrinkled up in pain as a spasm hit him, and then he found his words, "Mama died of the dysentery last summer."

The Confederate soldier cussed at the hard news, and it put him on his heels. His mother had raised them both after their dad passed away, and the woman's tenacity was the only reason they both survived their youth. The lady was rigid and was free with the lash, and brought them up to be the same.

His little brother took a labored breath and continued, "I married Mary that same month on the account that I put ah child in her."

The news snapped him out of his melancholy, and he let out a little chuckle, as he confirmed, "The pig farmer's fat daughter. Ya always doted on that smell."

The shared smile faded after a moment, and Roy informed him, "By August, the Union army took our cattle and horses for the war effort. Our home was used to house some of the sick and dyin'. They burned it afterward."

Tallman looked away in disgust from his dying brother and asked, "Jesus Roy, why didn't you two move away?"

Trembling from pain, he replied, "Couldn't do it. Mary's folks disowned her on account of her getting pregnant without being properly married first. She is living on the outskirts of town in the old abandoned farmhouse that the Millers used to own. I've been sending her my pay every month to keep her and the baby alive. Ed, she'll starve to death before the baby is born if the money stops!"

Roy started another violent coughing fit that Ed thought would finish him. His skin was white, and his bowels released in his mangled trousers. When the attack was over, Roy's breathing was shallow, and he grasped his older brother's hand. Their mother had never cottoned to the idea of showing affection, and this was the first time the two had consoled one another.

Ed pulled up close to Roy and exclaimed, "Balderdash! Now you listen close. My nephew ain't gonna die. I'm gonna head on back now. I'll get to them and take care of them. I'll be a deserter, so I will have to leave out of Kentucky once I've got 'em. We'll head west towards California and set up there."

His brother agreed, and the two squeezed one another's hands. Ed said the Lord's Prayer before leaving his sibling on the cold ground to die. He used the fog while it lasted to get clear of the battlefield without being noticed. Luckily, he found a horse, and he commenced his hard ride towards Louisville.

The memory sped up, and he saw Ed finding Mary, the birth of his nephew, and the long, harsh trek into the West. On the trip, Mary was murdered when a war party of Comanche attacked the wagon train. Ed paid one of the women in the caravan to look after the child and feed him.

Every night while Ed slept, Hyde would take over his body and watch over the infant. To Henry's amazement, he felt Hyde had genuine affection for both Ed and the man's newborn nephew. When they reached California, the Confederate soldier bought a gambling hall with his stolen loot. He quickly married one of his prostitutes and put her to work taking care of the infant.

As the years passed, the Demon continued to watch over Ed's new family. If there were trouble, Hyde would solve it by morning in his own vile fashion, but always to the benefit of his wards. When the child grew to manhood, Ed watched as the nephew took a wife. At the wedding, the Fallen Angel exited Ed peacefully. For the first and only time, the story ended without a horrific death. This puzzled Henry, as this was a lone Vessel in a sea of shipwrecked lives the Demon had ruined. What was it about this man that caused this devil to transform into a protector?

He closed the book, and he was once more in the Study. He jumped as he saw Hyde standing behind the high backed chairs, looking cross and seething with anger. Henry wondered what fresh hells the Demon could bring upon him for seeing this obvious outlier from the rest of his training.

Henry decided to be the first to make a move, "I found it under your chair. Why did you do that for Edward Tallman? What was so special about him?"

The Angel tapped his glass, answering, "We've done enough mental training, I think. Time is short, and we need to get you moving along. The Study will now allow you to relive my training in the magical arts of the Angels."

Henry felt the dismissal of his question, "So you're just going to ignore me?"

Hyde took a drink of his Bourbon, then replied, "You will learn the divine Enochian language, celestial combat techniques, and how to soar among the clouds. Unlike the memories this Study offers, you will be in complete control of the experience. Our first lesson will be on learning how to use divine spells. I'd like to say the worst is over, but I would never lie to you, Henry."

Henry cocked his head and replied sarcastically, "Oh, I trust you completely."

The Demon stood up, pulled out a square of chalk from his pocket, and drew strange symbols on the hardwood floor. The markings looked more like geometric symbols, rather than a language. Hyde finished and then etched a circle around his work. Carefully he placed black candles down along the edges and then lit them.

Henry stood up and asked, "What are these? I don't recognize the language."

The Demon sat down in the circle and replied, "No human would. It's Enochian, the magical tongue of the Angels."

The young man questioned, "What do you mean, magical tongue?"

Hyde stood up and drew glowing lines in the air, "My child, each race has their own way of accessing the magical realms. Modern humans speak the dead language of Latin to use the arcane, while the Angelic use Enochian. When we emerge from our cocoon, we will have access to both Celestial and human pools of magic. Our amalgamation combines the spellcasting abilities, speaking in Latin, and use the hand gestures of the Enochian. This is what will make us so unique. Now come, sit, and take my hands."

Henry guardedly stepped into the circle and felt a tingle come over his feet. Crossing the threshold, the true form of Hyde was revealed. The Demon's salt-and-pepper wings were folded behind him, and he was dressed in a tunic made of black chain mail. His fingers were slightly elongated, and his hair was braided with leather and silver. On top of his head were a pair of onyx colored horns that curled like a ram. His skin was pitch black, matching the color of his eyes. The Angel stuck out his talon-tipped fingers in a gesture to join hands.

In a moment of courage, Henry clasped hold of Hyde, "What do I do?"

Hyde closed his eyes and muttered in a language that seemed both musical and rhythmical. The room around Henry went dark, and only the candles flamed in the icy blackness. He started to say something when the Demon let go of him and put his right index finger on the center of Henry's forehead. The darkness vanished and was replaced by a snow-covered landscape. Henry was alone and dressed in a long-haired red fur coat. He ran a hand down the jacket and felt the softness of something akin to rabbit skin. When he pulled his hand away, he noticed it wasn't his own. The flesh was a pale white, and his fingers seemed unusually long. In a flash of recognition, he discovered he was in Hyde's pure Angelic form, from before his fall from grace.

Hyde's voice resonated from thin air, "This is the planet Ioarus in the galaxy your people call Messier 82. It once played host to a thriving civilization two million years ago. The Ioarusians stripped it of all its natural resources and left to conquer other worlds. Since that time, the remaining inhabitants evolved to survive in the harsh climate. Vegetation only grows in rare places, and the ecosystem is based on a cycle of carnivorous predation. Small larvae feed themselves through photosynthesis and, in turn, are consumed by a multitude of smaller predators. The result is some of the most successful species of hunters in the galaxy. The apex predator emerged and rules the tundra. To you, they would most closely identify as bears, but they are a sophisticated and intelligent race."

An impending sense of danger-filled his belly as he said, "Hyde, why am I in your body, and why are you telling me all of this?"

The Demon's voice shifted around him, "Because my child, I've added a few additional incantations to the Study. From this moment on, everything will feel real to you. Anything you experience here will happen to your body back in the Study. If you die here, our body dies too. I will transition back into the spiritual form of my Angelic perfection while you will simply pass on. You should focus because you are being hunted right now."

Henry's heartbeat quickened as he looked around, "What? From where? I don't see anything!"

Only the whipping wind over the tundra could be heard for several minutes before Hyde responded, "You'll have to do better. The Ioarusian beasts have a nasty habit of using the whiteout effect to blur your vision. They've learned to ride the mirage and become almost invisible."

Henry caught a glimmer from the reflection of a tooth tipped bone spear as it sailed from the nothingness towards his chest. He stepped to one side with astonishing speed and grace. As the weapon sailed past his face, Henry's reflexes and mental acuity were so tuned in that he almost reached out and snatched the traveling spear. The massive shaft buried in the snow and he grinned at the sensation of having the Angelic abilities.

The Demon's voice whispered in his ear, "They are testing you, to see how you move, how fast you are, and whether they view you as a threat. I don't think you impressed them that much."

Henry took a step back and picked up the white spear and said, "Okay, so I'm here to learn magic. So what next? Do I cast a fireball at them? Magic Missile? Do I wave my hands? Hyde! Talk to me!"

The snow behind him exploded upwards into a fountain of ice, and an 8-foot tall humanoid sprang up. The creature was holding the jawbone of some large dog-looking animal in its hand as a weapon. The monster was covered in white fur that Henry couldn't decide was a coat or its skin. The hands had no fingers, but highly articulating claws that seemed to bend around its weapon. It growled and bared its sharp teeth at the Angel. Henry sprang back and put his hands up. To his surprise, the creature turned and ran off into the snow. After two bounding strides, it dived headfirst into the white powder, disappearing from sight.

Henry screamed, "What the fuck, man! What... the... fuck!"

The Fallen Angel's calm voice whispered in his ear, "They are testing your courage, and again, it seems they are not awestruck. I would guess their next attack will be in mass. Though they have evolved into a complex culture, their tribal society still holds onto some of the feral traits. One such characteristic is they have a tendency to eat their prey alive. Bears on earth do the same thing. Did you know that, Henry?"

Jekyll turned and ran, shouting, "I'm going to die, Hyde! Show me one of those spells, or I'm going to die!"

The Fallen Angel didn't reply, and fear took over Henry. He turned and plowed through the snow at a full run. He had never moved this fast in his life, but it still didn't feel quick enough.

As he sprinted over the packed snow, the Demon replied, "You're attempting to escape them on foot? Tisk, tisk. They will run you down."

In the blinding white powder, Henry heard a chorus of yells from behind him. The voices sounded like a cross between a lion and a bull. The howls sent a surge of fear into his borrowed body. Looking back, three massive six-legged cats stepped out of the blur of white and sprinted towards him. On their backs rode more Ioarusian hunters, who were sitting on leather saddles and spurring their mounts onward. The felines were no less than fifteen feet tall and had solid white coats. As they ran, their oversized footpads kept them on top of the snow. Henry looked down at his own feet, noticing he was sinking a foot down with each step. The aliens were gaining on him fast, and he was feeling his muscles burning.

Henry sucked in the cold air and let out a yell, "Hyde! What do I do?"

The dark mentor's advice echoed out around him, "Why not start by taking off your coat?"

Just then, the answer hit him, and he skidded to a halt. He pulled off the heavy fur jacket, while the angry roars of the snowcats heralded their approach. Henry was unaccustomed to this body, and the enhanced strength caught him by surprise. He ripped the hide jacket into two pieces before he knew what was happening. He threw the rest of the coat and flexed outward with his wings that were hidden beneath the parka. He looked to each side, as new muscles displayed his entire 16-foot wingspan. The black and white feathers thrust against the cold wind as Henry struggled to work out how to operate them. He thrust his wings and buffeted a vast blanket of snow at the approaching hunters.

One of the cats penetrated the snow flurries and jumped towards him. Henry tried to thrust upward, but only managed to toss himself hard to the left. The beast skidded past where he had been, its teeth dripping with saliva and giving a frustrated grunt. As the rest moved out of the white cloud he had created, Henry's right-wing jabbed into the ice, and his left continued to move around chaotically.

Henry grabbed at the ground to stop himself and thought, *Great! I'm going to die on Hoth, looking like a dying pigeon!*

He looked up just in time to see a massive paw swiping at him. Instinctively, he brought his right hand up to protect himself from the 12-inch white claws. Just like a puppeteer, his right-wing followed the path of his hand, and hit the side of the cat's upper body and knocked the feline over. The Ioarusians rider went flying in the opposite direction and landed headfirst into the snow. Both creatures were groggy from the attack and struggled to find their feet. Jekyll let out a nervous laugh and whooped in victory, as he admired the feathered appendage. As if the planet was answering his war call, the two remaining riders strode out of the icy mist and locked eyes with him.

With slush caked-on half of his face, Henry yelled, "Shit!"

Their charge was wild and accompanied by Ioarusian howls of challenge. Both threw their bone spears with deadly accuracy at the Angel. His increased reflexes allowed him to roll out of the way of one of the projectiles. With the grace of a cat, Edward attempted to catch the other in his hand. Again, his wings mimicked his arms, and the massive wing slapped away the spear before he could grab it.

Pushing the frustration aside, Henry realized a connection, *The wings are controlled through my back and shoulder muscles.*

With a flex of his back, Henry felt the wings respond, and he floated off the ground a few feet. The gusts from the buffets threw ice and snow at the approaching cats hard enough to slow them down. Henry rocketed upwards at an astonishing speed and leveled out at 30 feet off the ground. He smiled at the thrilling feeling of flight and the powerful sense of being free of earthly bonds. He looked down at his enemies, who were enraged and spoiling for a fight.

His mind went to the long hours he spent watching Lewis Turner's old Indiana Jones movies and yelled, "Nice try Lao Che!"

The lead cat lunged with a massive push from its muscular hind legs, bounding it upwards. Henry made a high-pitched scream and flapped frantically to gain altitude. The enormous animal missed his foot by inches, and Henry soared up towards the clouds. The Ioarusian and his steed hit the ground with the grace of a dancer. Henry watched as they shook their fists in a fury and attempted to follow him from the ground.

He righted himself in the air and worked out the nuances of flight. Within a few minutes, he had discovered how to glide, turn, and even hover. He laughed to himself and streaked out over the horizon. He broke through the atmosphere. To his amazement, his body was unaffected by the vacuum of outer space. The celestial wings caught the cosmic currents and were thrust into an unbelievable velocity. He put one fist out in front of him, as if he was Christopher Reeves in Superman and let out a triumphant howl.

Hyde's voice chimed, "My child, your wings are no different than a hand or a leg to an Angel. They allow you to move about on planets with relative ease, but in the void of space, they can propel you to distant planets in just a few hours. They are also essential for some spell castings, and an integral part of the celestial aerial martial arts. Learning to use your wings was your first lesson."

Pivoting towards the purple Ioarus moon, Henry yelled, "You told me you were going to teach me magic first!"

Hyde gleefully replied, "I lied."

By Bo Luellen

Chapter 3: Richard VI

Tulsa, Oklahoma – Thursday, November 1ˢᵗ, 2018 – 6:24 p.m. CST

The heat from the hot lights was causing Richard Enfield to sweat through his undershirt. Brother Greyson Dunn showed no signs of having any issues as his broad grin and charismatic demeanor reflected only measured control. He nervously took a sip of the water sitting next to him as the preacher finished his question.

He cleared his throat and stated, "Pastor, it wasn't an option to do nothing. When I found out a Crimson Brotherhood member had infiltrated my law firm, it threw me into doubt. How many cases had I worked alongside Tom Chapman? Who else in the office was he in league with, and how could I feel safe being there? I knew if I was going to serve my community and fight this malevolence, I was going to need help."

The golden-haired televangelist nodded in approval and replied, "Who did you turn to?"

Richard looked at the camera and back at the host, "God. He was the only person I could."

Brother Dunn rang out, "Praise Jesus!"

A round of "praise Jesus" came from the audience as one unified voice. The Eastland worship center was packed to capacity, with over eight thousand Evangelical Christian followers of Brother Dunn in attendance. Walking the edges of the hall were armed members of the Tulsa Christian Crusaders, who displayed their rifles with pride. They wore black armbands that sported the shining golden lion of Eastland College. Most of those attending had been encouraged to bring in their firearms, and they hadn't disappointed.

The televangelist turned back to Richard, "After you turned to the Almighty, what happened?"

He lifted his open hands to the sky and testified, "The spirit spoke to me. It said my direction was clear. I needed to dedicate my life to the Christian Crusaders."

Dunn got a serious look on his face, "God delivers to those in need. While the police department remained impudent, our congregation was taking action. It was then that the city bureaucrats and politicians tried to stop us from protecting our flock. They called our patrols "unlawful" and attempted to disarm us. Our attorneys did what they could, but they said their hands were tied. It was then that Richard Enfield took a knee before the glory of God and asked for divine inspiration in this very church. On that spot, he heard the voice of The Almighty.

"In just two days, Richard had beaten them at their own game. He filed no less than 23 separate lawsuits, put body cameras on each of our patrolling Crusaders, and hired off-duty officers as campus security. The Chief of Police was forced to stop wasting the department's time fighting the good Samaritans of the Tulsa Crusaders and put their attention back on rooting out the disgusting Crimson Brotherhood!"

The applaud sign came on, and the crowd responded with cheers and clapping. A bell rang, indicating that the segment had ended, as the house lights came up. An announcement was made that there would be a 20-minute intermission, and the audience talked in a low rumble.

Richard got up from his chair, "Pastor, I'm going to step out for some fresh air. All of this has been overwhelming, and my head is spinning."

Greyson stood up and replied, "Of course. Use the back door, but hurry back. The night's not over for you. We still have a surprise to come."

Richard gave a broad smile and exclaimed, "I can't wait! Whew, okay, see you in a minute."

He turned and marched off stage towards the rear of the studio. As he filed past the TV crew, he approached the guard at the back entrance. The security officer was a barrel-chested Crusader in his late 40's that had an AR-15 slung against his chest.

Richard flashed him his visitor's badge, "Stepping out for some air."

The man's deep voice returned, "I'll have to escort you, Sir."

Richard nodded, "Of course."

As the two exited, and the soldier radioed in their excursion to the back parking lot. Richard put his hands in his pockets and took a deep breath. The night air filled his lungs, and he gave a little shiver, as he walked towards the metal fence that separated the church parking lot from the adjacent residential neighborhood.

Samuel's ghost hovered just on the other side and asked, "Have they made the announcement yet?"

Richard looked back at the guard, who was smoking a cigarette and then shook his head. Eastland's Worship Center and the TV studio were both sanctified ground. Samuel couldn't cross the threshold to the building, a fact that irritated the spirit to no end.

Richard didn't dare speak out loud, *Not yet. I'm confident he's about to.*

Samuel clasped his hands behind his back, "Richard, I need you to focus and remember to watch what you say."

He wrinkled his forehead indignantly and thought, *My actions have always been measured and led us down a path to Cthulhu's favor!*

The spirit's face drooped in defeat, "Of course it has. Let's just hope that tonight pans out as expected. Cthulhu knows we've donated enough money to this church to build half of Eastland College twice over."

For the benefit of his guard, Richard lowered his head and acted as if he was praying, *Are the Pearce Brothers on schedule?*

The ghost stuck his chin out in pride, "Yes. They are at the grotesque monument as we speak."

The guard stepped towards him and announced, "Mr. Enfield, it's time to get you back."

He left the spirit and walked back inside to the warmth of the Eastland studios. Richard was shown back to his chair in time for the broadcast to restart. Brother Dunn had received a fresh application of makeup on his shiny face.

He noticed a long table had been wheeled out on stage. It was covered with a white cloth that had the Eastland gold lion insignia embroidered on the surface. Two of the highest-ranking Tulsa Crusaders were standing at attention at each end. The applause sign lit up as the audience welcomed them back on the air.

Brother Dunn put a hand on Richard's shoulder and announced, "Let us pray! Father, we ask for protection on this child of God and the faithful protector of his flock. We come to you humbly and ask you to anoint this man with your divine wisdom. In Jesus's name, amen."

When the prayer was over, Brother Dunn looked at the cameras, "I have been searching for a soul of profound leadership and grace to aid me in my plight against the vile Crimson Brotherhood. I'm happy to say God has shown me such a person. Richard, stand up please."

He came off his chair and did his best to keep a controlled face. Richard enjoyed moments like this when his guile and planning settled him closer to his goals. The eyes of the Christian world, as well as the Brotherhood, were on him, and he reveled in what was to come.

Brother Dunn pulled the cloth from the table to reveal a bulletproof vest, a ball cap, and a silver Glock 9 mm, all of which sported the Tulsa Crusader's logo. A cameraman walked up on stage to give the audience a close up of the table's contents. The crowd went silent as a twenty-person choir sang softly, *Onward Christian Soldiers*. Richard was guided over to the table by a Crusader, as Brother Dunn mumbled in Tongues for several minutes.

Once the prayer was over, Dunn announced, "Brother Richard Enfield, you have taken up the fight against evil and defeated attempts to stop our Crusade against Cthulhu. You were able to protect the flock because God has blessed you with quick action and a sharp mind. The Lord has placed an anointing upon you. As a former Army Reserves officer, a community leader, and an ability to blaze a trail for the Crusaders, I have faith in the path God has put you on. Brother Enfield, I'm asking you to take up the calling to lead the Tulsa Christian Crusaders and stomp out the evil that is the Crimson Brotherhood. Will you accept this tremendous responsibility?"

Without hesitation, Richard reached up and grabbed Dunn's hand, replying, "Yes!"

The crowd sprang to their feet and shouted praises to God. The two guards carefully placed the silver pistol on his belt, the body armor on his torso, and the hat on his head. The cap and the vest both said, "Major Richard Enfield, Commander of the Tulsa Christian Crusaders."

The horde erupted with applause as the sounds of heavy footsteps came from off stage. Appearing from behind Brother Dunn was a seven-person squad. Each was dressed in blue army fatigues, the gold lion of Eastland on their chests, and had parade rifles resting on their shoulders. They marched in unison and came to attention facing the audience.

Brother Dunn put a hand on Richard's shoulder, proclaiming, "Major, you are now in command of the twelve thousand Tulsa Christian Crusaders. Behind you are the seven Captains in charge of the seven patrol districts of our city."

Just like he had practiced in rehearsal, he turned and saluted the Captains. He had already spent several hours with each of them, going over their patrol routes, tactics and leads to possible Brotherhood movements. They were each highly trained soldiers and war veterans who operated their districts with precision. This worked out in Richards's favor, as he was able to feed his operatives in the Crimson Brotherhood precise patrol times and routes. This would allow the Pearce Brothers to complete their mission with decreased risk.

After a lengthy speech from Dunn urging for more dedicated souls to volunteer for the Crusaders, he reminded members to keep the tithing dollars coming. Richard was shuffled off stage after the show and was led into the pastor's private dressing room. After a brief wait, the leader of Eastland burst in the door and roared in triumph at the show's success. As an assistant removed the layers of makeup from the pastor's face, Richard took a seat in the corner of the room and watched as Eastland staffers filed in and reported ratings, what topics generated the most donations, and the current congregation numbers.

After ten minutes, Dunn dismissed the analysts and shut the door, saying, "Well, Major Enfield, what is your first move?"

Richard played the game and said, "Prayer. That will be my first step. While I wait for His inspiration, I'm going to let the Captains do their jobs. My main focus is going to center on the Tulsa Police and hold them accountable for their lack of cooperation with the Crusaders. They should be welcoming the help instead of trying to block us. I suspect they are getting direction from our Governor."

Brother Dunn tilted his head and said, "Kathrine Hill? She is a strong Christian."

Enfield lifted his eyes towards him, "A strong Christian who didn't lift a finger to help us when the Chief of Police tried to stop our anointed patrols. She might have spoken at the mass funeral, shook your hand off-stage, but Governor Hill hasn't come out in support of our movement. In this war, a neutral party withholds vital resources from the righteous and gives the followers of Cthulhu more places to hide. Without the assistance of the Governor, our efforts could be stopped at the presidential level. Hill needs to be more than just sympathetic; the office needs to wear the colors of Eastland."

Greyson's eyes lit up at that, and he replied, "Yes. Oklahoma needs spiritual leadership now more than ever. If we are to defeat this evil, we cannot have a lukewarm Governor."

Richard blinked as if he had just thought of something, "Brother Dunn, if she refuses to join the Lord's cause, I believe it will be time to look into other options."

Dunn sat back in his chair, "We can't let the Devil in our door, Brother Enfield. If she doesn't join us, then…"

The door burst open, and a red-faced intern wearing a grey sweater said, "Brother Dunn, come quick!"

The two men jumped up from their chairs and ran along behind the young lady. As the group reached the control booth, they found everyone was watching Channel 6 News on TV. Gasps and sobs were coming from Eastland production staff as they fixed their gaze on the monitors. The video feed showed a giant statue of a man in a hardhat that was set ablaze. Fire trucks had just arrived and were attempting to get the flames under control. The fires were centered on the monument, and the cameras zoomed in on an outlined symbol of Cthulhu on the statue's chest.

The news reporter said, "… the Golden Driller has been engulfed in flames. Reports started coming in twenty minutes ago. The fire department has just arrived on the scene. Tom, witnesses say they saw a flash of light. Then the symbol of the Crimson Brotherhood started burning in the center of the statue's chest and quickly spread over parts of the monument. As the statue is made of a mixture of concrete and plaster, it is naturally fire-resistant. I've been told by firefighters that some kind of chemical agent was used to create the blaze. The police have backed people away, as parts of the famed Driller have started to melt."

The desk anchor replied, "Tragic. Again for those of you who just joined us, the Golden Driller has been vandalized, apparently by agents of the Crimson Brotherhood. So far, the police have made no official statement and …"

Dunn pounded his fist on a nearby desk and yelled, "That is right off of 21st. In plain sight of passing traffic. How? How did this happen? Where were our patrols?"

Richard stepped forward, "Brother Dunn, I think I can answer that."

Tulsa, Oklahoma – Friday, November 2nd, 2018 – 8:11 a.m. CST

The next morning the press was gathered around the steps to the Worship Center. News trucks from all the local stations, as well as CNN and FOX, filled the parking lot. An empty podium had dozens of microphones clustered behind the logo of Eastland. Rope barricades kept the eager reporters at a distance, while hundreds of the college campus students surrounded the stage to hear the announcement.

Richard sat in a chair just behind the podium, wearing a two-piece suit that still let the chill in. The temperature had dropped significantly, and the freezing wind was turning everyone's face red. He looked out over the crowd and saw Daniel's grimacing mug. The thief was bundled in an old sailor's peacoat and wore a black beanie over his balding head. Richard had ordered him to be present in the throng to gauge the audience's reaction to the press conference. Polls were one thing, but he liked to get the first blush response from the loyalists of Brother Dunn.

After a few more minutes, Dunn approached the microphones wearing a grey suit and coat. His thinning bleached blonde hair was perfectly styled and impervious to the pulsing gusts. He reached inside his vest pocket and pulled out a collection of notes. Reporters sat eagerly in the front row, while campus security flanked each side of the dais.

The pastor announced, "Good morning. I appreciate everyone coming out on this cold November day. Last night our good city suffered yet another attack. The Golden Driller statue was vandalized in what our scholars at Eastland are calling an offering to the pagan god Cthulhu. This is an act of intimidation that sends a clear message: The Crimson Brotherhood is still an active threat, and they are on the hunt.

"I ask, where were the police and FBI when this happened? They were busy making sure the lawful patrols conducted by the Tulsa Christian Crusaders stayed marginalized. The Tulsa Chief of Police Blake Kelly and Mayor Walker made it perfectly clear that they had the backing of Governor Hill. Last evening could have been avoided, but the city said, "trust us." Well, we trusted you, and this was the result.

"Governor Katherine Hill, the people of Oklahoma, are demanding that you exercise your emergency powers and give the Tulsa Crusaders the ability to patrol our streets as agents of the State. You have the ability to secure our town and to root out these terrorists. The over three million Christians in Oklahoma await your response, Governor."

Brother Dunn took a step back from the podium as reporters surged forward, yelling questions. Richard got up and followed him to a waiting black SUV. Crusaders were flanking them on both sides as bodyguards opened the armored vehicle's door. The warmth of the heaters was inviting, as the long hour wait for the pastor's arrival had taxed his patience.

Richard removed his gloves and asked, "Do you think she will do it?"

Greyson signaled the chauffeur to drive and answered, "Only God knows."

The vehicle worked its way towards the main street and quickly put the college behind them. As they drove, Richard rolled his eyes at the old southern hymns that were piped into the cabin and grimaced at how Greyson tapped his foot to the music. He glanced outside the window in disgust and saw his old mentor flying next to the SUV.

The ghost smirked, "Oh, do sing along, Richard."

Having no refuge from irritation, Enfield trained his eyes on his phone and did his best to stay calm. Ten minutes later, they pulled up to the charred remains of the once magnificent Golden Driller statue. Both arms had fallen to the ground, and the head had melted off at the neck. The once-great figure had been a symbol of the oil prosperity of the city. Now its blackened head lay at the feet of the mangled statue. Richard took stock of the Pearce Brothers handiwork and did his best to play dumb.

As Dunn was being prepped for the camera, Samuel floated over and ribbed, "Have you prayed to Jesus today, Oh Master? Do remember to sober up your wife enough for church this Sunday. I hear they are having a potluck. Considering the bulbous cows I saw coming out of the meeting hall, I'd venture to say they know their way around a kitchen."

Richard shot him a glare and thought, *This must be unsettling for you. Sitting outside the Eastland buildings because you can't walk on hallowed ground. Relying on me to make the decisions, while you keep your place.*

The spirit landed and walked next to him, "I had some reservations about you. You are rash and bull-headed, but I must admit, you are picking up a few things from me."

The crew whirled the camera lens at Brother Dunn as he stood in front of the lopsided head of the statue. Cars that passed by were honking and yelling loving encouragement towards the evangelist. Pedestrians were gathering around at an alarming rate. This caused the producer to double-time his staff in fear the speech would show up on YouTube before they had a chance to air it.

The camera started recording, as Dunn went into action, "My fellow Christians, I come to you with a heavy burden. I've been deep in prayer, and the Lord has told me that the devil has a hold of our political system. I've just asked Governor Hill to do her duty and let the Christian citizens of this town defend themselves from the lackeys of Cthulhu. It should have never come to this, but here we are. If the Governor doesn't commit to the Tulsa Christian Crusaders in one week, I will run against her in the Governor's race as a write-in candidate on November 8th. Governor Hill, there will be a reckoning against the followers of Cthulhu, and we are determined to defend our families from those heathens. I hope this is a wake-up call for you. The Christians of Oklahoma await your response."

The camera cut off, and Samuel remarked, "Our good Brother Dunn, how well he seems to be adapting to the national spotlight. I must confess, his message was to the point. He covered the bases and ensured Governor Hill would be cornered into not complying or risk being labeled a puppet. Ironically, he persecutes the actions of the Crimson Brotherhood and manipulates his followers to take up arms for their Hebrew God. A stranger to this world might have a hard time telling us apart."

Richard bit his upper lip and thought, *There is an off chance Governor Hill might actually say, 'Yes.'*

Samuel semi-transparent grin shimmered in the sunlight, "She could. If she did, then the Crusaders could march in the streets, the Crimson Brotherhood could savage the town, chaos would rise, and Governor Hill would be to blame. The Aeon is coming to a close, and the Herald will be with us soon."

Richard regarded him suspiciously, *The Herald?*

The ghost raised an eye at his former Apprentice, "Oh my boy, did you ever pay attention to anything I taught you? One month before Cthulhu can be awakened, the Herald will rise from the grave and visit the plagues upon man's most powerful nation."

He sent a text to his driver to pick him up and thought, *A Herald, huh? Rising from the grave no less. I suppose after everything I've seen, it shouldn't surprise me. Does this Herald have a name?"*

As Daniel Harris pulled up in Richard's black Lexus, Samuel replied, "Imhotep."

Richard nodded, oblivious to who or what an Imhotep was, and quickly got in the vehicle. Daniel was sporting a black chauffeur's hat and sunglasses. It was a thinly veiled disguise for the former institutionalized criminal, as the tattoos on his neck poked up over his collar.

He slammed the door and ordered, "To my estate."

The short, balding man darted the car out into traffic and quickly pulled a U-turn. The tinted windows of the vehicle did little to filter the morning sun as Richard attempted to sleep during the drive. The long night had been filled with prepping for today's announcement. He had set up new patrol routes for the Tulsa Crusaders and filtered the information back to his Sect of the Crimson Brotherhood. Richard was now carrying the responsibility of leading the cult and the Tulsa Christian Crusaders at the same time. Juggling two opposing forces was taxing, and the fatigue was starting to show on his face.

Samuel appeared in the seat across from him, saying, "You need to start trusting your subordinates and delegate some of these responsibilities. You're not doing any of us any good if you pass out."

Richard squinted his eyes at the annoyance, *I can't slow down, not now. When the Preserve was raided, and the national news reported that an active cult of Cthulhu was responsible, it was like ringing the dinner bell. Crimson Brotherhood members have started arriving from all around the United States to fill up our ranks. Our safe houses and even the Library are at capacity with murderers, arsonists, and anarchists eagerly waiting their turn at distributing mayhem. Now's not the time for me to slow down.*

The ghost leaned back in his chair, "You're in a better position than you give us credit for. I've been preparing for this day and provisioned the Howard Estate with enough explosives, guns, and ammunition to arm a thousand followers of Cthulhu."

Before Richard could respond, sleep overtook him, and he drifted off. In his dreams, he saw a tanned figure standing on top of a sand dune surrounded by servants and retainers. The figure was dressed in gold finery and had strange symbols decorating his chest and face. Standing to his side was a beautiful woman, dressed in a cheetah hide. Overhead a falcon cried out and snapped him out of the dream

The squealing sound of the garage door closing mimicked the bird's cry, and he found himself leaning at an odd angle against the car's glass door. He wiped some drool from his face and looked out of the window to see Amy Howard standing at the doorway to the garage.

Richard got out and gave his coat and gloves to Daniel as he told her, "Good Morning, Miss Howard. Report, please?"

Amy followed him into the house, as she replied, "The cops have nothing. The Pearce Brothers avoided the security cameras, and there weren't any witnesses. They got away clean."

As they entered the main study of the estate, Samuel sat staring at them from a brown leather chair. The house was sanctified to Cthulhu and was magically prepared by the ghost in the event of his death. Here he looked almost solid and could interact with the environment with little effort. Richard noticed the ghost's magical abilities were also enhanced while in the house, and his spells could have some small effect on the living. Thanks to a few enchantments, his daughter Amy was able to see and hear her father.

The spirit stood up and replied, "That is what worries me."

Richard flung his suit coat onto a chair and asked, "Explain?"

Samuel reached out and took a book off the shelves titled *The Art of War*, saying, "An enemy that is starved of success cannot be guided to their defeat."

He turned, stating, "Ahh, Sun Tzu."

The ghost dropped the book onto a table and snapped, "No, I made that up just now. You assumed it was Sun Tzu because you're attempting to look smarter than you are. We must make the enemy believe they are on the right path to keep them in our trap. If all they receive is failure, then they will change their tactics. Right now, you are the spearhead against the Crimson Brotherhood. If you look inept, they will replace you. Do you get the point?"

Richard went red-faced as Amy giggled at his expense. He kicked a chair out of the way and walked over to the cherry wood bar. He loaded up a glass with ice as he considered the wisdom of having these meetings in front of Amy.

He kept his back to the ghost, and calmly asked, "So what are you suggesting? Let them raid one of our strongholds?"

Samuel looked exasperated, "No. That would only weaken us with no benefit to our cause. Sacrifices will need to be made for sure, but what I suggest is something more elegant. Every action we take needs to be centered towards the awakening. If we do that, Cthulhu will strengthen our spells and grant us guidance. I believe we could find an opportunity in the town that has lingering confidence in their police department, the FBI, and the politicians that run Oklahoma. If they were to prove incompetent, such as if Henry Jekyll were to be liberated, then support would die on the vine. I think it is time to put our new Angelic friend to work."

Richard took a long drink then asked, "Just where are we on delivery of the golem?"

Amy leaned on a cherry wood desk and answered, "There's a problem with that. Shoshannah Feinstein sent a message this morning saying she won't be able to produce the golem until next year. She says there are some security concerns she is dealing with, and she is about to go underground."

Samuel looked out the window at the beautiful Oklahoma sky. "We shouldn't wait. Hyde is staying in Jekyll for a reason, and it shouldn't be allowed to finish whatever game it's playing. We can still house Hyde in another Athame dagger, but we have to get to him. The police have his room surrounded. Without Miniel leading our forces, we would have no chance of getting inside. No, Shoshannah Feinstein will have to postpone her sabbatical. Without her creation, Miniel is a ticking timebomb waiting to go off. Once we have her inside that golem, nothing can stop us."

Richard turned to Amy and ordered, "Send the Pearce Brothers to her. Inform Feinstein we have a contract, and if she fails her obligation, we will be the security concern. I want them on her doorstep in the next 24 hours."

From the east end of the room came a knock, and Emilia Nores nervously announced, "Señor Enfield, your eleven o'clock appointment is waiting for you in the sitting room."

He waved her off with one hand and gulped down the rest of his rum. After she closed the door, he reached over and grabbed his laptop. His calendar had quickly filled up with meetings since his appointment as leader of the Crusaders had been announced.

Richard grunted as he stabbed buttons on the computer, "Dunn expects me to not only run the patrols with efficiency but to promote the Crusader's hotline. The people of Tulsa are already calling Eastland with tips on the Brotherhood more often than the police. I have to authorize another hundred staff members to take in all the tips, then filter them back to the Library. It's a house of cards. One wrong move and the whole operation falls in on itself."

Samuel balked, "Once we have the new recruits in place inside the Crusaders, the burden will be lessened. We know precisely where the patrols are at any time, and if a tip comes in that could identify us, we take care of it. You wanted a seat of real power, and now you have it. Did you imagine this would be easy?"

Leaving the Howards behind, he walked out into the hallway of his house to the sound of his guards snapping to attention. Richard was assigned a considerable Crusader security detail to monitor the grounds and two personal sentries to stay at his side at all times. Unbeknownst to Brother Dunn, both of the men were freshly trained Leviathans. They had replaced the missing Marcus Holmes and the purple-robed man he killed in the woods at the Preserve. The soldiers were hand-selected by the Pearce Brothers and seasoned killers.

The towering guards followed him through the house to the sitting room. He stopped for a moment and composed himself before opening the double glass door. With a wide grin, Richard marched at his guest with an outstretched arm towards an older man, who was sitting in a chair made of bamboo. The odor of old spice and cheap whiskey hit Richard's nose.

The room had a traditional oak floor and a broad set of glass windows on the ceiling that let the sunshine pour in. It was adorned with maritime memorabilia and ships in a bottle. In the center was a ship's helm that was lying flat and had been reworked into a table.

Richard clasped the older man's hand and firmly pulled him up out of his chair, "I do apologize for the wait. I was in prayer. This matter with the Golden Driller has us all very worried. My captains are understandably troubled. Tell me, what brings the Tulsa Police to my doorstep? It isn't another complaint about our patrols, is it?"

The man steadied himself with his cane, "Hi, Mr. Enfield. My name is Detective John Utterson. As a matter of fact, yes. I do want to talk about the patrols and the hotline you have."

A flush of red came over Richards's face as suddenly he recognized Utterson from the Preserve. He did his best to steel himself and let out a little laugh. His heart beat faster at the excitement of coming face to face with the cop who took Jekyll from him. He smiled at the irony that the Detective had no clue he was Mr. Purple.

Richard waved his hand, interjecting, "Please, call me Brother Enfield. We're both children of God fighting together to rid our good city of this evil. So, please, tell me your concerns. The Crusaders are always ready to cooperate with law enforcement."

John nodded and replied, "Well, Brother Enfield, it's that spirit of cooperation that I'm hoping to build on. My task force has been hitting some roadblocks. Our official police hotline has been dead for days, and we are only getting hoaxes and bad information. The people are calling Eastland when there is suspicious activity, and your Crusaders are responding before the police have had a chance to get there."

Richard settled into a brown leather chair, "We are a servant to our community and respond when they are in need. We send you all the tips we get at the end of each day. Is that not cooperation enough?"

John adjusted his right leg, "Sending Crusaders to interview the witnesses is seen by many in the FBI as an impediment to the investigation."

He pursed his lips and asked, "We have over thirty thousand Crusaders helping to patrol and run the hotlines every day. That is a direct reflection of the way Oklahoma takes care of their neighbors and not a statement against the police. Detective Utterson, I'm careful not to interpret your words as a threat against Eastland."

John ran his hands through his hair, "No. Not what I meant at all. This is a mess. Brother Enfield, can we speak off the record?"

He stifled a smile and answered, "Of course. What we say here is for God and us. Speak your mind, Brother."

The detective leaned forward and continued, "The Chief wants the Eastland call centers taken down, and is considering pressing charges against Brother Dunn for obstruction of justice."

Richard put a hand on the table and asked, "I take it that you are risking your career telling me this because you want something different?"

John tapped his cane on the ground nervously and replied, "Your network is the best chance we have of stopping the Brotherhood. The people trust their spiritual leaders more than the cops. If those get taken down, the citizens will hate us for it, and the Crimson Brotherhood will have another victory. In all frankness, Governor Hill has issued orders to Chief Blake. 'If the Crusaders succeed in capturing members of the cult before the police can, it will set a dangerous precedent for the Oklahoma government.'"

Richard shook his head in mock disgust, "They play their politics, all while the people of Tulsa sit in fear. They are so worried about their careers and their egos that they can't see the glory of God's plan. We would happily work closely with them if it meant our Crusaders would be a partner with the police. Now, I fear that it can never happen when selfish men and women sit in positions of power in this great State."

John said plainly, "Brother Enfield, your organization is being investigated right now by a secret internal task force, headed by Detectives Michaels and Cobb. They are looking for anything the FBI can use to shut you down, and they are both very good at their jobs. All they need to do is find, or concoct, one thing, and it will spark a Federal investigation. They want you stopped at all costs."

Richard's cheeks went red from anger, but he said calmly, "And what is it that you want? Surely your superiors wouldn't like you tipping us off. I believe what you are doing is considered obstruction of justice, as well. As a lawyer, I do know a thing or two about the system."

John leaned to one side and replied, "I think our best chance is to work together. This witch hunt into Eastland is a waste of resources. I believe it is unethical and illegal."

Richard smiled and calmly asked, "Detective, have you ever heard of the Whistleblowers Protection Act?"

By Bo Luellen

Chapter 4: John VI

Tulsa, Oklahoma – Monday, November 5th, 2018 – 8:15 a.m. CST

It was cold in Veterans Park, and John Utterson's ankle ached more now than it had when he first broke it. Standing at attention in his dress uniform on the uneven ground was causing sparks of pain to shoot up his body. He cursed silently to himself, wishing the ceremony would hurry up and start.

Aggravated, he whispered, "Why are we holding this out on the grass. I'm freezing."

Captain Andino stood to his left in his own dress uniform, "Tulsa is under attack, and the city workers refused to build the ceremonial stage. Death threats from the Crimson Brotherhood had flooded the Tulsa Christian Crusaders hotline over this award ceremony. They promised swift reprisal if honors were placed upon the murderers of those faithful to Cthulhu. So, the Chief wanted this held outdoors. He said it would minimize the chance of someone hiding a bomb."

John scoffed, "That is idiotic. There are a dozen places a sniper could be hiding. Oh, well. At least the city isn't backing down. I just wish Terry could be here."

The Captain adjusted his collar, "Detective Johnson has plenty of work to do getting up to speed. Considering our losses at the Preserve, we need as many good people on the streets as we can get, injured or not."

The Detective bragged, "It's not everyday that someone can ace a Detective's exam from their bedside. He's always been a natural at investigative work. It would take time for him to be able to be on active duty again, but I'm happy having him behind a desk and helping the team."

He looked over at Terry's mother Evelynn and then at the TV news cameras, *Having the mother of my dead partner at my side to collect an award for Terry will look good for me. The Johnston family might hate me for what happened to David, but Evelynn will have to stand with him in the spotlight publicly. Terry and David will always be my brothers, but after being despised by the Johnston's for so long, they've earned some return on their judgmental negativity. Mrs. Johnston will have to shake my hand and smile at the cameras.*

Chief of Police Blake Kelly finally walked up to the podium and announced, "Thank you for coming. We're here today to honor and recognize the men and women who have made the ultimate sacrifice to keep Tulsa, and their families, safe. We're also here to honor family members of the fallen officers here today. My prayers go out to you, and I hope this day brings some comfort. I want to welcome and recognize Governor Katherine Hill for joining us in honoring these brave Oklahomans."

The names of the dead officers were read off, their families recognized for their loss, and medals given to the wives, husbands and mothers. The sounds of sobbing spread as the ceremony continued. John was starting to sweat badly from pain, and felt the pill bottle in his pocket.

He licked his lips and thought, *If this doesn't end soon I'm going to pass out.*

After a few more minutes, the Chief turned to them, "Officer Terry Johnston was injured during a terrorist blast in a Tulsa apartment building. He was pulled out by a local hero, Larry Lanyon, whose life was tragically taken. Officer Johnston went through hours of surgery to remove shrapnel and to treat burns. When I spoke to him this morning, he said there was no question about returning to work and came back off of medical leave early. He's absent today because he is at the department and working hard to protect Tulsa lives. Giving him the Medal of Honor and the Purple Heart is the least we can do."

John bit back some tears at the speech as a round of applause started. Terry's mother walked up and received her son's award with a smile. John had become even more determined not to let his injuries be for nothing.

He gritted his teeth and thought, *The Crimson Brotherhood will pay for this.*

After pinning a medal on Captain Andino, the Chief turned to John, "Detective John Utterson pursued more than just the truth, he relentlessly upheld the law in the face of overwhelming adversity. His actions led to the discovery of the heinous murders of over two hundred souls, the terrorist organization known as the Crimson Brotherhood, and he was the first to find their hideout. At great personal risk, and working with injury, he helped save lives and apprehended one of their ringleaders, Henry Jekyll. When I asked why he didn't accept the paid medical leave he told me, 'My job isn't done.' Detective John Utterson, awarding you the Medal of Honor and the Purple Heart is the least the city can do."

A rousing applause blasted out from the audience as the Chief pinned both of the honors on his coat. At that moment he felt no pain and lavished in the admiration of his fellow officers who had once belittled him as a drug addict. His Captain slapped his back with his white gloved hand and Mrs. Johnston was forced to pucker a smile for the cameras. He leaned in and gave the elderly woman a kiss on her cheek and enjoyed the anger she was compelled to contain.

He looked out into the crowd and saw his brother Karl standing next to his wife Sarah and his two nephews, Charles and Alex.. He hadn't spoken to his sibling since the Preserve, mostly due to the pressures of the task force. Karl brought up his cell phone and took a picture of John shaking the Chief's hand.

The moment was everything he had hoped for, *The newspapers will make the name John Utterson into Tulsa's own Elliot Ness. The town will watch as I hunt down the Crimson Brotherhood. People love a comeback story.*

Reporters snapped photos as he displayed his new honors. The flashes of the cameras and the applause of the crowd was the validation he had so wanted. He was a shooting star, thanks to the Brotherhood.

He looked at his brother's approving face and thought, *Maybe life isn't as awful as I thought. Maybe Dad was right, good things do happen to those that put in the time and effort.*

As the Chief made his way back to the podium, "We have one more medal to give out."

John's brow scrunched up in confusion at the statement, as everyone who was involved in the Battle of the Preserve had been recognized. He repositioned his cane for better support and did his best to maintain a fake smile. From the side of his vision, he saw David Keller walk out from behind the line of those honored. All the cameras whipped around to focus in on the animal that was sitting in a red wagon the big man was pulling. The three-legged, one-eyed German Shepherd named Charlie was resting its chin on the wooden guard rails and looking inquisitively out over the crowd. The dog had on his old police vest that John had found him in back at the Preserve.

The Chief turned to the K-9 and announced, "This officer lost his leg in the performance of his duty on a drug raid some years ago. He was retired and handed to a new owner named Nancy Bell. Bell and Charlie worked together at a homeless shelter in downtown Tulsa, providing support and guidance for the less fortunate. Bell was abducted by the Brotherhood and Charlie refused to let her be taken. They both found themselves captive on the Preserve and in mortal danger. Because he wouldn't cooperate, they took his eye and tortured him. Nancy Bell's life was taken from us, but Charlie was with Detective Utterson's team as they apprehended Henry Jekyll. He sustained life-threatening wounds in defense of Detective Utterson and it is clear that this brave dog was a key factor in the apprehension of the Crimson Brotherhood ring leader."

John saw that every audience member had their cell phones out to record the moment. His jaw dropped, and he reeled at the way his Chief was giving a dumb dog his moment. Anger turned his face a beet red.

He thought to himself, *Fine. The dog gets an award. Who cares. The Chief wants a PR moment. Let him have it.*

The Chief brought out a brand new police vest for the animal and announced, "We have lost precious blood and with it, outstanding officers. During his time in the force, Charlie was one of the best drug and explosive-sniffing K-9's in the unit. I'm officially re-instating him to reserve status. Most of you might know Mr. David Keller as one of the brave civilians that helped apprehend Henry Jekyll. I should note that David Keller has requested to aid the department by volunteering to keep Charlie until he is fit to return. Since K-9 units live with their handlers and operate as partners, the Tulsa Sheriff Patrick Lloyd has made Mr. Keller a reserve deputy sheriff."

The crowd let out a sound of approval as the dog looked around, slightly confused but happy. Keller carefully took off the K-9's old vest and replaced it with the new one. John gripped his cane tightly, as his temper boiled up.

The Chief held up Charlie's old vest, "This will be hung up in the station as a symbol that Oklahomans persevere and never give up. They have desecrated our monuments, taken our loved ones but fueled our resolve."

Those in attendance stood up and applauded. Keller had a broad smile on his face and shook the Chief's hand. The big man wheeled the dog's cart to the side and stood there as several police officers gave Charlie a warm welcome back to the force. Utterson looked out at the crowd who was fawning over the crippled mutt. His family had stopped recording him and were now taping the animal. He instantly hated them all for belittling what he had achieved.

John felt a nudge on his arm and heard Mrs. Johnston's tiny voice, "Why John, if you don't clap, people might start wondering about you."

He shot a look towards her and glared at the elderly woman's sarcastic grin. He wanted to leave, scream or do something, but he couldn't. He had to live through this indignity. Begrudgingly, he lifted his hands and robotically applauded, as a loud cackle came from Evelynn.

Tulsa, Oklahoma – Monday, November 5th, 2018 – 10:02 a.m. CST

John had said his goodbyes to his family after the ceremony and posed for several pictures. He had conducted three interviews with reporters, which lessened the sting of the insulting way the event had ended for him. He was talking to Captain Andino when he saw the Chief marching towards them.

Chief Kelly ushered them both behind a police vehicle for some privacy, "Pony show's over! Governor Hill and the Mayor Walker are all over me. Every four hours I have to call them and give them a progress report. I want you two taking the gloves off. Start shaking down every informant you have. I want arrests, gentlemen. We are looking like keystone cops compared to Greyson Dunn"

His Captain started to speak, but John interrupted, "The town believes in the Crusaders more than us. They are calling them with tips, leads, or suspicious activity. Hell, the dog catcher is getting more calls about cult tips than the task force. Our chances of catching a real lead to Brotherhood activity goes up exponentially if we agree to cooperate with the Crusaders."

His Captain stayed silent as the Chief shook his head, "John, the Governor has been clear on this. The Crusaders are not police officers, and, for the good of the Department, they never will. We are the law, and it is the Mayor's position that giving that privilege to a vigilante force of that magnitude is a recipe for disaster. That is an opinion I share and I expect you to as well."

Captain Andino's squeaky voice crept in, "We couldn't agree with you and the Mayor more. Our department doesn't need their help. You can count on..."

John blurted out, "With all due respect Chief, you're tying our hands and shoving them up our ass! There are ten thousand Crusader eyes on these streets every day watching on behalf of the citizens of Tulsa. The more we resist their assistance, the more the Robin Hood effect is setting in. Old people sitting on their porches, truck drivers, waiters and every average joe you can think of are keeping their eyes and ears open on behalf of the TCC. They all listen to the daily Eastland Worship Hour and believe in Greyson Dunn's message. His network is massive, willing, and dedicated to their faith. What I want to know is, how can you sit there and ignore that multi-million dollar resource? How many more terrorist acts will the Governor and Mayor allow to happen, while you order us to half-ass this job? I need to know, is this is a policy decision or is this a political one? If it's so people can stay in office, that's bullshit and you should know that!"

Chief Kelly tapped John's badge as it hung on his dress blues, "Detective, you will do as you are ordered. You will track down the hiding place of cultists, and you will do it within the guidelines I've provided. I'm willing to overlook your insubordination this time, John. Because if someone in authority over you judged your words as suspiciously erratic, they might ask you to piss in a cup. Do we understand one another?"

John looked over at his Captain who had his head down. He glared back at the stone-faced Chief, then nodded in agreement. It took all the self-control he could muster to comply to the threat.

The Chief slapped his arm, "Good. Get out there and get me results! The city of Tulsa is counting on you."

Tulsa, Oklahoma – Monday, November 5th, 2018 – 12:10 p.m. CST

John was back in plain clothes and at his desk next to the wheelchair-bound Terry Johnston. The pair were thumbing through a list of contacts they had made through the years, searching for an informant that could help them. As he cycled through his rolodex, he came to Amanda Lanyon's name and held it up.

Terry glanced up, "Amanda Lanyon? What about her?"

John flipped the card around, "I was there when AEGIS took over her security detail and promised she would be present at the trial of Henry Jekyll. To date, there are no suspects for the man that murdered her husband and kidnapped her kids. Something about her statement made me feel like she was holding something back. I think she knows more than she's letting on. I think it's time to pay the widow a visit."

The black man leaned back and asked, "How are you going to find her? Those agents have her tucked away and they ain't talkin'."

He pulled out a business card with the AEGIS Medusa logo on it, "Lucky for me, I lifted this off the desk of one of the Feds."

Terry smiled, "You slick bastard."

John forced himself to his feet, "Stay here and keep looking for leads. I'll talk with Lanyon. I'll see you soon, partner."

Tulsa, Oklahoma – Monday, November 5th, 2018 – 12:41 p.m. CST

One phone call later to the Texan and he was given the address of the hotel where the Feds were keeping her. As he entered the lobby, he saw Agent John Hamilton sitting in one of the chairs, reading the *Tulsa World*. The man had his boots up on a table and engrossed in an article.

The Texan looked over and beamed, "Well look at you, Detective John Utterson. I do say that having the Tulsa Police Department's decorated officer and hero of city come to visit is the highlight of my afternoon. Now, could I interest you in a cold soda or some sweet tea? They have the store bought stuff in here, but if you add some sugar it almost tastes like momma's."

Utterson joined the Agent in the lounge, "No thanks. I need to speak with Amanda Lanyon."

The man folded his paper and got up from his chair. At 6'4", John Hamilton towered over the detective. He wore a silver tipped bolo tie with a turquoise centerpiece that looked Native American in design.

Hamilton put on his black Stetson cowboy hat, "This is a safe house for the before-mentioned guest. We have to be careful." The Agent spoke into his sleeve relaying, "Headed to Sabriel with one. Stand down."

The man led the detective down a hallway to a room in the back of the hotel. With each step, Utterson listened to the heavy clomping of the cowboy boots of Hamilton as they noisily made their way down the narrow corridor. A blond haired agent was standing guard at the door when they arrived. After a pat down, Utterson followed the Texan into the room. He walked in and found the place had been lived in but was empty. The bed was used, with water bottles on the cabinets, but no Amanda Lanyon.

Utterson put up his hands and asked, "So, where is she."

Agent Hamilton plopped down into a desk chair and put his feet up on the disheveled bed, "Oh she is right here."

The detective glanced around, "Is this some kind of a joke?"

The black-suited agent wiped his forehead with a blue handkerchief, "If Widow Lanyon weren't right here in this room, then the poor thing would be a target for the cult. Now, as long as the Crimson Brotherhood thinks she is under our protection, ready to testify against Henry Jekyll, then that gives her some small degree of security… if she was elsewhere."

Utterson caught on and inquired, "Okay so if Amanda did choose to leave your custody, where might she have gone?"

The agent tipped his cowboy hat up with his index finger, "You know in all my five marriages, I've never once been able to accurately predict their mind. I suppose that is why they are exes. If I were you, I'd tell everyone in the department that asks, that you met with the Widow Lanyon and everything was okay. If someone did go off halfcocked and tell folks she wasn't here, well, that person could be arrested for treason under the Patriot Act."

Utterson's mouth went dry as Hamilton continued, "Amanda does thank you for your kindness in visiting, Detective. Do drive safely now."

He clinched his jaw, *This was the second time today I've been threatened for attempting to do my job.*

He considered his options and took the path of least resistance. Agent Hamilton followed him back to the lobby and watched him get into his car. The Texan tipped his hat, as John glared back at him and gingerly slid into the driver's seat. As he stowed his new black cane, his phone buzzed and startled him. Utterson winced in pain from his broken ribs and read the text, "I have something for you on the Crimson Brotherhood. - Moss Vickers."

He phoned Terry and reported, "Good news partner, I got a solid lead."

Terry sounded exhausted, "Is this a reliable source?"

He drove his car out of the hotel parking lot, "Moss Vickers. He's an informant your brother and I picked up when I first became his partner. We busted the man with almost a half a pound of mushrooms just outside of a Wendy's. Moss was a small timer who would have gone away for a long time, but we let him off in exchange for information on the big fish in Tulsa."

His new partner scoffed, "You've been letting this guy deal drugs in exchange for information?"

Utterson ignored him, "I'll let you know what I find out."

He hung up and drove down Highway 169 towards Moss's apartment complex. The pain was hitting him hard from his injuries, and he washed down two Oxycodones with the vodka from his flask. He waited in anticipation until the drugs kicked in and dulled his senses.

Ten minutes later, he pulled up to an apartment complex near Riverside Drive. It was a depressed area that was known for its drug trafficking and high crime rate. He parked at a nearby Burger King and sent a text to Moss letting him know he was at the usual place.

Eventually, a man in his late thirties came walking around the corner wearing a faded black Pizza Hut t-shirt. Moss Vicker's face was covered in acne, and his dirty blond hair was unwashed and oily. Utterson unlocked the car door, and the man slid in the passenger seat.

Moss looked at the cane and said, "S-s-s-sorry to hear about the f-f-f-foot."

The detective adjusted his leg, "Thanks. Do you have something for me?"

The pimply faced man pulled out a Ziplock bag of weed, "Oh yeah, J-J-J-John. I always b-b-b-bring something for ya."

Annoyed, he snapped the pot out of his hands and yelled, "How many times do I have to tell you! Don't give this shit to me out in the open. Wrap it up in a bag or something! Now, do you have anything on the Brotherhood!?"

Moss's anxiety tripled at the verbal thrashing, "M-m-m-my runner Leon t-t-t-told me that h-h-h-he..."

"For God sakes, smoke some weed, or we're going to be here all day waiting for you to mah-mah-mutter through a single sentence!"

Moss reached in his pocket and pulled out a vape pen full of marijuana. After a few minutes of smoking from the device, he seemed to calm down and relaxed. Utterson had learned that when the man was high, the annoying stuttering stopped.

Moss gazed at him with narrow eyes, "Leon told me he saw people dressed in black masks tagging the walls and buildings with Crimson Brotherhood symbols."

Utterson's annoyance mounted, "Yes, we know about that. It is the cult's way of letting the people know the Brotherhood is still out there. This isn't new information, Moss. You know our deal. You keep the intel coming and I look the other way."

The informant raised his hands and pleaded, "Just hang on, John. Right, but what your people don't know is *when* it is being done. Leon said the tagging isn't random or opportunistic. It's being done in sections of the town where the Crusaders are not patrolling. I've talked to two other of my suppliers, and they said the same thing. If you see tagging, you won't see Crusader patrols."

That caught the detective's attention as he asked, "You mean they are keeping away from Brother Dunn's people? Wait, but the Crusaders rotate their patrol routes each night to keep the Brotherhood from predicting their movements. How could the Brotherhood know the TCC routes?"

The man gave him a sleepy-eyed look and asked, "Don't the Crusaders tell the police department where their routes will be each morning?"

Utterson made the connection, "Yes. If the Brotherhood are being tipped off by someone in the department or someone in the Crusaders, then they could move around at will. It also means we could lay a trap for them. If the task force could coordinate with Dunn's people, we could create corridors of unpatrolled sections of the town where undercover cops could lay in wait. All we would need is one or two low-level members that we could interrogate. Hell, just announcing we had a living member of the Brotherhood in custody would let the people know the Department was making headway and send a message to the cult."

Moss took another hit from his vape pin, "What's your move?"

As he answered, Police Dispatch rang in on his phone, "Keep pushing for more information. Now, get out of my car, and watch yourself."

He answered the phone as the man exited. "Detective John Utterson."

The dispatcher said, "Detective, they need you at Rolling Oaks Memorial Gardens Cemetery at 91st and Yale. There has been a Brotherhood vandalism of one of the graves."

Utterson's heart sank at the thought of who was buried there. He started his car and drove like a bat out of hell. With his sirens blazing, John whipped past cars at 90 miles an hour on the packed city streets. His sweaty hands gripped the wheel so tight his wrists ached as his heart beat like a drum.

A few minutes later he squealed his tires as he turned into the cemetery. He beelined for the three patrol cars that were lined up on one of the side road between the graves. He saw the officers putting up yellow tape around a familiar plot. John screeched his tires as his vehicle slid to a stop. He endured the pain as he hopped out and pulled his bad leg along the road.

Hobbling along the paved path, he saw it. The grey granite tombstone of his dead partner, David Johnston, was in the center of the crime scene tape. As he shambled closer to his friends grave, one of the patrolmen saw him coming and rushed to intercept him.

The Hispanic officer stepped in his path, "John, hold on, we need to keep this clean. Let the investigators do their jobs."

Utterson's body began to shake as he took in the desecrated grave. The tombstone had the symbol of the Crimson Brotherhood spray painted over the front. A large mound of dirt was piled up on either side and a hole had been dug all the way down to the coffin. The concrete container was cracked open, and the coffin lid had been destroyed. Fragmented wood and rock littered the bottom of the hole. The body of his partner, the man who had died on his living room floor, was missing from its resting place.

He staggered and fell hard onto his backside. The soft earth and grass absorbed most of the impact, but his ribs blasted agony. The patrolman knelt down next to him, and put an arm on his shoulder. John's face felt numb, and his fingers dug into the cold turf.

The patrolman gave a comforting squeeze and said, "None of this would have happened, if you hadn't killed me, John."

The voice that came out of the officer's mouth was David Johnston's. The shock of hearing it caused John to snap his head up. He saw the uniformed officer next to him had the head and neck of his deceased partner. The decayed face had patchy black hair, and the flesh had turned to leather. The skull pivoted to one side and the jaw opened to reveal blackened teeth. A slime covered tendril made its way out of the undead mouth and past the rotted grin of the corpse.

John couldn't make his body move and froze with fear at the impossible sight. The olive color octopus-like appendage turned in the air and revealed suction cups on the underside. The thing slapped against the rotting flesh and dripped a green mucus down onto John's pants. It suddenly whipped outwards and latched onto Utterson's left jawline. The suction cups bit into the soft flesh of his cheek and gripped tight. The pin pricks snapped him out of the fear induced trance and he pulled back and screamed. He pitched himself backward onto on the cold ground and slapped at the tentacle.

His hands whipped around but found nothing but air. Forcing himself to open his eyes, Utterson looked up to see the Hispanic officer staring at him with confusion on his face. He had tears running down from a mixture of terror and sadness.

The cop tried to calm him down, "John, hang in there buddy. We'll find out what happened. Just take some deep breaths."

He sat up slowly and took some calming inhales. To his left the crime scene investigators' car pulled up and the driver stared at him. All at once he realized how ridiculous he looked sitting on the ground. With the help of the officer, he worked himself back up to his feet.

He patted the cop's chest, "Sorry. It's a lot to take in."

All the officers turned away and went back to their tasks. PTSD was commonplace in this line of work, and cracking under heavy pressure was just as normal. He had learned to let people vent, then keep on doing the job. These cops were no different and did their best to act like it didn't happen.

The detective gathered himself and then visited with the investigators. He ordered a few patrolmen to check the neighborhood to see if anyone saw something and sat in on the questioning of the groundskeeper who discovered the crime scene. All the while, the haunted vision of his friend's face on the officer's head filled his mind.

John sat down in his car to catch his breath, *Am I cracking up? It's got to be stress. Keep it together John! If these guys see you breaking, they will assume you are off the wagon. Keep your credibility, and keep your focus.*

His train of thought was broken as Detective Cobb tapped on his car window. He jumped at the sound, which shot pain down his side. As he rolled down the window, the craving to take more Oxys came over him.

The slender officer proclaimed, "Hey, sorry John, I didn't mean to scare you." He did his best to look normal as Cobb reported, "Okay so we took photographs of the area, checked for tracks and scanned the ground looking for any blood samples in case they hurt themselves while digging up the body. So far nothing, but we will take the casket into the lab to test for..."

As John listened, the investigator's voice faded out as he saw the corpse of David Johnston standing next to some squad cars 30 feet ahead on the road. Utterson stiffened up and tried not to react to the ghoulish image. David was in his police dress uniform, and the emaciated skin was covering the bones like Saran Wrap. The blue eyes of his old friend were replaced by empty black sockets that were transfixed on him. The cold wind flapped the folds of the dress blues he had been buried in.

Cobb's voice changed tone, "John! Are you hearing me?"

A layer of perspiration had appeared on Utterson's face, "Ummm, y-yes. That's fine. Send me a report."

He looked back towards the squad car to see the thing was gone and in its place was a patrol officer drinking a cup of coffee. Cobb left shaking his head in frustration. Utterson took some deep breaths and tried looking away, then back again to see if the phantom would return. It was gone, but he didn't want to chance any more encounters. He started up his engine and headed back to the station.

Tulsa, Oklahoma – Tuesday, November 6th, 2018 – 9:05 a.m. CST

John had managed to get some decent sleep with the help of some Ambien pills he got from Moss. When he arrived at the station, he was in no mood for the morning task force briefing. On the front desk was the a.m. newspaper which had Charlie and David Keller plastered on the front page. He flipped it open and saw his own smaller, less impressive black and white image on page seven. His nostrils flared, and he angrily folded the paper into his pocket.

As the briefing room filled up with plainclothes officers and specialized units, John drew down a map of Tulsa. On it were dots that indicated where Brotherhood related activity had taken place. If a location had been spray painted, structures damaged, or a terrorist act committed, it got a red dot. John begrudgingly put a red dot on the cemetery where David Johnston's grave had been robbed.

Captain Andino got up and started the meeting, "Good morning. As some of you know, the body of Officer David Johnston has been stolen. We believe that this is connected to the Brotherhood, as a message to John and the city. I'm assigning Michaels and Cobb to stake out at the cemetery in case someone comes back to inspect their handiwork. I'll turn it over to John for his assignments."

He limped up to the front and announced, "I received word from a reliable informant that Brotherhood members are avoiding areas patrolled by the Crusaders. This informant has provided credible intelligence that suggests the cult knows where Greyson's patrols will be. To test this theory, I want to avoid stakeouts and patrols in sectors where Dunn's men are working. Instead, tonight I want all of our resources spread out over the small sections that will not have any Crusader activity. This will create a corridor for us to lay several traps based on past targets the Brotherhood has hit. Traditionally they have gone after religious symbols, places of worship..."

Captain Andino got up, walked over to John and whispered, "What are you doing? We were told to keep a presence in all areas of the city. If the Crimson Brotherhood hits somewhere where the Crusaders are monitoring, the department will not be able to respond fast enough. This would be like handing over most of Tulsa to Dunn."

John replied in full voice, "This isn't cooperation, this is smart hunting."

His Captain lost his temper, "How would we explain leaving the majority of the city to Dunn if the Chief asks?"

From the back of the room, a voice bellowed, "You tell him that the safety of the people takes precedence over politics. You could say that you decided to serve and protect the people instead of worry about who gets the credit."

The fifty plus officers in the room turned to see Richard Enfield walk in like he owned the building. He had on a black Brooks Brothers suit and coat with an empty holster on his belt. Behind him were two of his personal bodyguards dressed in the blue Crusader's uniform.

Captain Andino held up his hands, "Mr. Enfield, this is an official police briefing. I would be happy to talk to you afterward."

Enfield pulled out an envelope from his jacket, "This is a list of Brotherhood targets we were given in the last three days. Some of these are public schools, hospitals, and libraries. Each day we give a similar list to this task force. Brother Dunn's resources are again being offered to you, but your Chief has inexplicably said 'No' at every turn. Now I'm asking you, Detective John Utterson; Put God on your side and give the Crusaders official status in this investigation. Will you let us work with you?"

Before the Captain could reply, John responded, "Yes. We need your help. I would be willing to..."

The room filled with murmurs as his Captain yelled, "No! We would not be willing to discuss this. If you really want to help, then let our officers have access to all of your resources. You're making a political attempt to divide my officers and take away their focus, Mr. Enfield! Get out or I'll have you arrested for interfering with a police investigation!"

Enfield pursed his lips together and looked at John. The detective remembered his meeting with Enfield and the part he had promised to play. He walked over and took the envelope from him.

Richard clasped his hands together and faced the officers, "God bless you all in your efforts tonight. May the Lord see you through and grant you success and safety. In Jesus name, Amen."

To John's surprise, almost half the room of police repeated, "Amen."

He opened the letter and looked at the list, as Captain Andino made a speech, "May I remind everyone that you work for the city and have sworn an oath to uphold the law. Brother Dunn is making a power play in this town and we can't let that happen. We lost good officers in the Battle of the Preserve, and we aren't going to lose anymore. You want to be a good Christian, fine, do it on your own time. What your town needs is a crack in this case. Go out there and do what you have to do. Bring me a member of the Brotherhood."

John interrupted, "Wait. This list says fifteen tips came in saying the Brotherhood is going to make a play at freeing Henry Jekyll tonight. That is more than we ever had on any single target."

He turned around to the map and pointed out the hospital, "Jekyll is in an area that isn't being patrolled by the Crusaders tonight. We could assign SWAT to the building, set up choke points by locking doors and stake out the area with..."

The Captain slammed his fist against a table, "To do that would leave the rest of the city thin! This could be the Brotherhood trying to draw us away from their real target. Only 2% of all the five-hundred daily tips that came from the Crusader hotlines panned out. That means...."

Detective Cobb got tired of waiting on the Captain to do that math, "2% of 500 is 10. So if those fifteen reports are the only ones in todays list that are accurate, then than means it represents 3% of the 500. John, that would exclude all other reports. Sure, it's statistically high, but we've seen multiple tips come in on the same target before. The probability that this is genuine is there, but slight."

The Captain nodded in agreement as John retorted, "It's not a coincidence. The Crusaders are doing their jobs; the Brotherhood is afraid of them. That's why they have waited until Dunn's men are away. This might be our best shot!"

His captain's face went red, "The matter is closed! This briefing is over. Everyone get out and go to work!"

Within a few moments, the room cleared out, leaving only the Captain and John. Andino locked the door, turned, and kicked a folding chair across the room. John didn't flinch, as it crashed into a desk and knocked it over.

Utterson said calmly, "This isn't the right call, Captain. We need them on our side. Hell man, we need to be on their side even more. They have twelve thousand members, we have just over 700 officers. We are working on a year's end budget, and they can bleed out millions of dollars a month without blinking. How can we look the public in the eye and justify our refusal to cooperate with Dunn?"

Captain Andino put his hands on his hips, "Because a single religion cannot be allowed to have that much power! If the city deputizes the Crusaders, then overnight Richard Enfield becomes the new Chief of Police. You see John, when you have authority backed by the kind of money Eastland can throw into the Crusaders, that makes the Department worthless. We don't have the manpower to oversee a force as large as the TCC. How do we ensure they will respond if a Jewish man is accosted? What if an Islamic family's house is broken into, or if a pagan business is vandalized? We can't guarantee they will follow the law because these people see the Christian faith first!"

John put Richard Enfield's list of leads in his pocket, "Right now you have lawmakers and politicians worried about keeping people dependent on civil services. They're scared citizens might discover they don't need a government to survive. You ask how can we be sure these Crusaders will be impartial? At least they are trying. You are just worried about your pension. The Mayor, the Chief, and the Governor are so eager to prove Dunn wrong, they refuse to do the best thing for the people. Today you had an opportunity to make a difference, Captain, and you decided to protect and serve your job, not Tulsa. You're a coward, and that will get more people killed. Lady justice is blind, but you can bet she sees your hypocrisy."

As he walked out, Captain Andino yelled after him, "Hypocrite? Who are you to talk! The drug addict that was too high to call 911 and let his partner OD on his living room floor. You're a real hero!"

John spun on his heel and landed a right cross on the Captain's jaw. The punch was flush and sudden, catching the shorter man by surprise. Andino went down like a bag of feed and sprawled out on the slick linoleum floor in an odd chaotic mixture of arms and legs.

He stormed out of the room, slamming the door behind him and left his superior unconscious in a heap. He grabbed his complaining ribs and clenched the letter in his other hand. He limped out of the building, and focused on what was next in the plan he and Enfield had concocted. As he drove through the streets, he picked up his phone and made a call.

Richard Enfield answered, "Hi, John."

He turned onto Boston Avenue in downtown Tulsa, "It went down just as you predicted. The damn fools. Is the offer still good?"

Richard sighed, "Yes, of course. It's sad to hear though. I wished they would have surprised me and made the right decision for Tulsa. Where are you?"

John parked his car at a news station, "I'm downtown at KOTV. Should I wait before I go in?"

Enfield responded quickly, "Yes. God told me to prepare for this. I have two attorneys that can meet you in fifteen minutes. Wait for them. The Whistleblowers Protection Act will work for you, but still, you must be careful. The Devil has many weapons, and your bravery will not go unchallenged. John, I have to ask you a question, are you sure about this? It's the end of your police career and your life will become a three ring circus of media and controversy."

Utterson looked down at the newspaper hanging out of his pocket. The headline read, "One Dog-Gone Great Cop," with a picture of Charlie. His mind flashed back to the humiliation he received at the awards ceremony. He recalled the threats from the Chief and from Agent Hamilton of AEGIS.

He looked up at the news station and answered, "I'm sure."

By Bo Luellen

Chapter 5: Henry VII

The Mind of Hyde – Unknown Date – Unknown Time

Henry Jekyll found himself on a black moon circling the ringed planet of Segradus, "This looks depressing."

The Demon's voice flowed from the ether, "It has a quality to it that produces a hardness to its population."

To his left, a baby's cry came out from behind one of the midnight black rocks. Henry moved gracefully inside Hyde's celestial body and peered around the large boulder. A crib made of dark wood was leaning to one side, and humanoid infant had spilled out onto the ground. The blue-skinned baby was wailing and confused. Henry flapped his wings and launched himself towards the helpless child.

Hyde shifted the memory and caused the baby to appear a little further away, "Saving the child won't be that easy. You see, the mother was my Vessel, but was attacked by one of the many predators that inhabit this moon. Miniel was close, so I jumped into the baby to avoid capture. As you will find out, it wasn't an easy day."

A thick, scaled, solid black snake slithered out from between two rocks, "The Segradusians call it a shell snake because it lives in the rock and has armor plating on its scales."

The serpent spotted the unattended child and stopped. A pair of tongues flicked the air, and the beast opened its mouth to display a double row of teeth. The alien creature poured out of the tiny cracks in the ground, and revealed its twelve-foot long body.

Henry muttered, "Jesus Christ!"

The Demon announced in a confident air, "I had no choice. If I had simply walked out of the body, Miniel and the Order of Virtue would have been on me in seconds. Now it's up to you."

He looked in the air and asked, "What's up to me? Hyde! I'm not going to stand here and watch some creature eat a baby! Tell me what to do?"

As the snake worked its way over to its meal, Hyde instructed, "Illusion is a powerful weapon if you know how to use it. Concentrate on the baby and repeat after me, 'Procidat Deceptioneum. You'd better act quick. That creature doesn't constrict its victims, it sprays it with acid."

Henry did his best to clear his mind, "Procidat Deceptioneum!"

An illusionary duplicate of the child appeared directly in front of the animal. The shell snake stopped and eyed the decoy. It flicked its tongue at the image and then slithered around it.

He exclaimed in a panic, "It didn't work!"

Hyde's voice was full of impatience, "Not good enough! You have to invest your emotions into the casting. The more hate and anger you put into the spell, the more substance the illusions will have."

By the time Henry completed his second attempt, the creature was only a few feet away. The duplicate baby appeared in its path, but this time the snake took its time. It made a violent hissing sound, as a spray of green liquid covered the doppelganger. In a shimmer of golden energy, the fake dissolved into thin air.

As the predator looked around in confusion, Henry pleaded, "What happened?"

The Demon chuckled, "You added substance to it, but that meant it could be hurt."

The snake coiled around the bawling child, and a drop of acidic saliva sizzled on the black stone. The acidic fumes wafted into the baby's face, causing it to start choking. The scales on the back of the serpent flexed upwards, making it look like it had spines.

Henry switched his mental focus and yelled the incantation in a rage, "Procidat Deceptioneum!"

An exact duplicate of Hyde popped into existence beside the animal. The snake's gaze shifted to the newly arrived angel and sent a spray of corrosive liquid towards the illusion. Henry mentally controlled the replica and dodged the attack. As a puppeteer, he worked the construct as the creature did its best to land a strike. It took a great deal of effort to maintain the spell, but after a few seconds, Henry had the hang of it. With a twist, he caused the image to take out his sword and slash the snake's head off.

A gallon of acid spewed out from the neck and doused the surrounding rocks. Henry looked down in horror as the small child melted away under the substance. The smell of burning flesh filled the air and caused him to lose his focus. The illusion blinked out. Hyde dissolved the memory and landed them back in the Study.

The Demon was once again in his black regal finery, "Don't concern yourself over the child. It was just a memory."

Henry was mentally exhausted and dropped down in a leather chair, "What really happened to the baby? I mean in the past that the memory is from. Did the kid survive?"

Hyde took a stiff drink and smiled, "Not at all."

He looked down, trying to reconcile both the spell he had learned and the horrific reminiscence he had just relived. After two months in "Hyde Time," Henry Jekyll had discovered dozens of incantations and how to activate them in Latin. The training was affecting more than just his mind, but Henry's entire being. With each arcane lesson, Hyde took him to a different planet to train in a specific spell.

His mind was able to deal with the trauma of seeing the horrors of Hyde's past. Still, the absorption of all the hundreds of life experiences had changed him. His posture, mannerisms, and even his diction were so altered that Henry barely felt like himself anymore. He felt what little innocence his abusive family had left him being taken by the Demon's education. Nevertheless, Henry clung to his values by cherishing the memory of his friends Juste and Lewis. He kept himself centered on why he had agreed to this covenant and the good he intended to do with that power.

Hyde sat down and peered into the burning fireplace, "The idea of being confined to a three-dimensional existence looms over me like a guillotine."

It was the first time Henry had heard him speak on this level, "What scares you about it? We will be powerful, nearly unstoppable, and the Order of Virtue will no longer be able to touch you. If our body dies, you continue on. This is a win-win for you. What's to fear?"

The Demon flung his glass into the flames, "Hyde fears nothing! What I feel apprehensive about is the idea of being dormant inside our body. What we are doing is a rare thing, and the long term results are a mystery. I could be lost forever."

Henry felt the creature become vulnerable at the moment, "Hyde, I'm just as uncertain. If what you say comes to pass, we won't be individuals, but a blended person. Our souls might be lost. What will happen to our minds? Will we be two individuals, riding along in the mind of a third? You can't tell me, and I don't think I'd believe you if you did. All we can do is learn to trust one another and follow through with this plan. The Crimson Brotherhood needs to pay, and this Miniel creature of yours, the one that killed Lewis and Juste, will pay."

Hyde rolled his beautiful eyes, "After all this, and you still think like them. The angelic legions stretch over multiple dimensions and hundreds of worlds. We act as the Almighty's messengers, warriors, and even his servants. We degrade ourselves for Him and communicate God's words and thoughts to the less evolved natives of the cosmos.

You see your friend's death as some kind of badge of courage, carrying you through our training. These things aren't worthy of your time or effort. Would you go out and avenge a cow or a chicken when the farmer harvests them for your dinner table? Humans are not worthy of your sympathy. They are delicious morsels of flesh and blood."

Henry winced, "You eat humans?"

A light flickered in the eye of the fallen angel, "God wishes humanity to take the sacrament and then be forgiven. There is no such luxury for angels. So, I seek my salvation in drinking the blood of mortals, but so far, I've not been granted a pardon."

He realized Hyde's game, "You do it to anger God? Why? Out of spite?"

The Demon sat up straight, "And why not? If a Vessel is evil by nature, do you think God really cares? Don't be so appalled. You earthlings give names to the animals you keep as food and show them degrees of kindness before you devour them. I spare those that are noble or righteous and get no glory for my merciful restraint.

I can see in your face there is disgust, but your perspective is going to change. You see, a colony of ants doesn't thank the shoe for sparing their lives when it passes over them. Just as the shoe doesn't stop to demand praise for its benevolence. Humanity is a social experiment at best. A pet caught in the center of a celestial war of egos between God and Lucifer. So when it suits me, I occasionally partake in human blood and flesh to mock God's sacrament. I vex Lucifer's plans for a lark and will never join his fallen angels in hell. While the Morningstar wishes to see the human experiment fail, I'm not interested in poisoning your culture. I believe the anthill needs its queen, the drones should continue their work, and I can hide among the insects. That is all they are my child, lesser beings undeserving of your attention."

Henry decided to stop short of inciting Hyde, *Is he trying to prepare or corrupt me? He said we would become a unified consciousness, with elements of each. If he taints my soul, then our combined mind would lean more towards Hyde's maniacal way of life. We would fill our endless days with carnage and maleficence. I must stay steady.*

That same day Hyde came to him announcing, "My Child, there is a book that I think it is time for you to read."

Henry grabbed the tome from him, "What is this Hyde? You said we were done with your memories and focusing on spellwork."

The title read, *Lewis Turner*. He took the book and moved his hand over the leather-bound cover. Each book had a different design based on what memory is held. During his delve into World War II memories, Hyde had possessed five Vessels, and all of them were German. One of those covers was bound in the leather jacket of a Gestapo trench coat.

Lewis's book was wrapped in the thick skin of an elephant. It had a beautiful recreation of the *Advanced Dungeons and Dragons Players Handbook* cover art neatly etched into the hide. It represented the memories of his games with Lewis, and the fun they shared through imagination and adventure.

His smile faded as he realized, *Being around Lewis was the opposite of his upbringing. I owe Lewis so much... or do I? Hyde was possessing Lewis the entire time I knew him. I wonder just how much of Lewis's generosity was due to Hyde's influence. Was Turner really that decent of a man, or was the Demon grooming me? If Hyde figured out I was one of his offspring, then all of this could have been orchestrated. Was this just a long con game?*

Wearily, he realized that this book had been saved for last. With some courage, he flipped it open and found himself outside a Chinese restaurant in mid-town Tulsa. Unlike all the other visions given to him by the Study, his spirit floated invisibly to those around him. Hyde, dressed in an all-white suit, stood beside him and took in the events. They watched the Asian man put together a lunch order for an elderly woman.

Hyde told him, "This memory begins as Miniel had once more tracked me down. This time it only took her five years to seek me out. She was getting considerably better at it. I spent the last two years inside this lowly man. His name was Woo, a sinner in his mid-forties and owner of a mediocre Chinese Restaurant. Unfortunately, Woo was also a small-time drug dealer who peddled meth, heroin, and marijuana out of his business. Many of his customers went down much darker paths because of his side vocation. Still, it helped him keep the store open so he could look legitimate to your law bringers."

Henry leaned on the outer wall, "I'm betting having you around made his life, oh so much better."

Hyde mocked pain at the insult, "Oh, be still your blade. This man was already dedicated to his path when Hyde crossed into him. Woo got his start by robbing his siblings of their father's inheritance, which gave him the start-up capital he needed for his dual businesses. This, of course, caused his soul to become bound for Hell. It was on that path in which I found him, and so I borrowed his body for a time. On this particularly fateful day, Woo and I were selling some drugs to a loyal customer that I believe you might know."

Henry shot his head around and saw Woo's greeting the overweight Lewis Turner with an exuberant smile. His heart sank at seeing his friend's face once again. He heard his familiar laugh from behind the glass, and it made a well of anguish swell in his heart.

Behind Lewis, a dark-skinned woman stepped out from a car in the parking lot. As she walked towards the restaurant, the lady shined with a light that hurt Henry's eyes, and a pair of ethereal wings trailed behind her. Woo instantly noticed her, but Lewis was oblivious to the presence of the masquerading Miniel.

Woo quickly stuck out his hand towards Lewis's. A look of surprise washed across his friend's face as he regarded the gesture with some trepidation. With a smile, he grabbed Woo's hand, and in an instant, the Demon jumped into Turner's body, possessing him. The black energy slinked across the arms of the two men and wormed its way into the eyes of his old boss.

Woo, dumbfounded by the sudden expulsion of the Demon, gripped the counter to hold himself up. The newly possessed Lewis waved his hands and cast a spell in Enochian. A black aura surrounded the elderly Asian man as he staggered back from the incantation. Hyde moved Lewis's body out the back and scampered into his friend's old Ford pickup truck.

A loud clank came from inside the restaurant, causing Henry to refocus his attention towards the lobby. Miniel was pummeling Woo to death with the hefty cash register. With each hit, money and change shot out onto the tiled floor, as blood splattered the walls a dark red. The Chinese man went down, and the angel beat his head into a pool of multi-colored liquid and bone shards. With her face spackled in crimson, she put her hand on her victim's chest and cast a restraining spell. Her eyes flared with divine energy as she bellowed in anger at the absence of Hyde's soul in Woo.

The image faded away, and they were once again in the Study, as Hyde remarked, "Miniel has lost her way. Her hurt stays hidden from her Order as she quests to return me to Heaven for judgment. Fortunately, I equal her ferocity with cunning. I left a curse upon Woo as I exited him. The black cloud of darkness fooled Miniel into thinking I was still there and caused Woo to become too confused to run. It was a ruse that has served me well enough on several occasions, but this was the first time she ever killed one of my Vessels. Her anger is unhinged, and she keeps her methods hidden by the Order of Virtue."

Henry lost his temper, "You got that man killed! You got Lewis killed! You say you don't poison humanity, but what do you call this?"

Hyde shifted the image to Lewis standing with his business partner Jeff and their friend Don, "Is the wolf a blight on the deer, or is it not a part of strengthening the species to cull the herd? When I came into your dear friend's life, he was a drunk, a drug user, and an adulterer. He was lost and set on his path towards the gates of Hell. I cannot possess a being that is pure of spirit, so I've spoiled no fruits. I've stolen nothing from the Almighty and only delayed the soul's journey to Lucifer. I took this wretch from poverty to a successful and productive member of the community. He was given purpose, something his child could look up to. All it cost him was a handshake with my divinity."

Henry watched as the vision showed him Lewis signing the lease agreement for Lewis's Hoagies and replied, "You gave him what? Money? From what I've seen, your help comes at a cost. I'm sure those things in my apartment didn't come from your divine credit card! Who suffered for your material wealth and appetites?"

Hyde dissolved the illusion into another vision of Lewis in a dark apartment, standing over three dead Hispanic men. Each one was shot dozens of times in the chest and head. On the floor were several kilos of cocaine, and on a kitchen table was a large suitcase filled with money. The possessed Lewis picked up the cash and calmly walked it back to his car, as a prostitute screamed in terror from the corner of the living room.

Hyde's voice dripped with satisfaction, "While I can't manifest the currency your kind uses, I do have dominion over the Seven Deadly Sins. The wicked feel the tickle of my tongue as I quicken their path to damnation. The unrighteous are powerless against the Fallen Angels, for they are outside of God's grace. With the Sins, I can call upon the unclean to do any number of things. These three condemned souls were profiting off the misery of their coworkers, friends, and even family. I called upon Cupiditas, and rid this planet of their infestation. Who benefited? Why your beloved friend Lewis, and in turn, his miscreant employees."

Henry shuttered a reply, "Cupiditas means greed. You called upon greed."

Hyde pulled them back to the Study and rejoiced, "Good, my child! Your studies have been going well, I see. Your Latin has improved, and so much, the better. The Sins will not be available to us when we become a Nephilim. Still, we will have access to the deeper mysteries of Solomon's magic. That mystical force your kind has chosen to forget will be ours to command. While your kind was fooled by religion to hate and forget the keys to that power, the magical well of energy never went anywhere. Unfortunately, earthlings have abandoned it, but the supernatural ability doesn't fit the control systems your religions use to manipulate the masses. Quite the opposite, practitioners are shunned and hunted by heathenistic hypocrites who are vain to know God's will. With the inclusion of the Internet, smartphones, professional sports, and the exclusion of the circle of nature in your daily culture, the number of mortals that have arcane potential is precious few."

Henry became intrigued, "Your contempt for humanity isn't as complete as you would like me to believe. What about Edward Tallman? You hid him from me. Why did you watch over him and his nephew, Hyde?"

Ignoring Henry's question, the Demon changed the scene to show the renovation of Lewi's Hoagies sandwich shop, the man's divorce, and his eventual meeting with Henry Jekyll. He watched as Lewis would stir from bed nightly with Hyde in control. The possessed man would use a phone the Demon had hidden, leave for hours on an errand of adventure or sometimes just stare out of his window in silent contemplation.

Hyde admitted, "I was content for the most part, but plagued by Miniel's relentless pursuit. You see, my child, on Earth, we divine creatures are forbidden from affecting the living. So God wove a failsafe into the magical fabric of angelic spells on this planet. When an Angel uses the Seven Virtues, or a Fallen invokes the Seven Deadly Sins, the Almighty can hear it. Because of his anger, God has turned away from the Fallen. So he chooses not to listen when we use our power. When one of us meddles too far into human affairs, we are visited by the Angelic Order of Virtue. These self-righteous genocidal zealots take great joy in destroying any Fallen they find. Miniel and I were once strong members of that Order."

As Henry continued to watch the life of Lewis flash in his mind, he deduced, "So, Miniel was looking to capture you in the Preserve?"

The image shifted to Lewis walking from the Halloween Party on the night of his death as Hyde said, "She longs to bring me through the gates of Heaven and place me before God."

Henry sensed there was more to the story, "Why?"

Once again, ignoring his question, "I would have never allowed my Vessel to be harmed if possible, but the assassin was magically blocked from my sight."

He snapped back, "The Vessel had a name! Lewis Turner!"

The vision shifted again to reveal Lewis traveling along the snowy bridge on the night of his death. From behind, a dagger flashed out from thin air and stabbed the portly man in the back. Slowly, the shimmering image of a grey-haired older man followed the blade into view from behind a spell that had blocked Hyde's sight. A bewildered Turner wobbled from the wound and held his back in pain.

Hyde's voice seemed to growl, "The human had a protection spell on him. Somehow this ant learned the High Magic of the ancients. I was blind to him until it was too late. The dagger he held was infused with a binding spell that held me helpless me inside your friend. I could do nothing to aid my Vessel or stop what happened next."

Just then, a vehicle that was about to cross the bridge slowed and drove towards the pair. It flashed its brightest beams onto Lewis and his assailant while blaring its horn. The sudden emergence of a witness startled the would-be assassin, and Lewis slipped on the ice, causing him to crash into the safety rail. Out of terror and confusion, Henry's friend pitched over the side, and free fell to the railroad tracks below.

The Demon remarked, "It wasn't an act of suicide, but a move of desperate survival. The Vessel was looking for an escape, not death."

Henry saw his friend's body as it lay shattered across the tracks. Red poured out from pressure tears in the skin. An opening made by a snapped bone that jutted out of his leg. Above, on the bridge, he saw the older man stuff the dagger in an open hole in the railing, cover it with snow, and run off into the night.

Henry felt a swell of anger, "Who was that man? Why did he do that?"

The Fallen Angel sighed, "It was a minion of a god named Cthulhu. At first, I thought it was Miniel in a Vessel, but her energy signature wasn't present, so I dismissed the notion."

Henry's attention went back to Lewis's struggled to lift himself off the crimson soaked snowy ground. He could hear the thoughts of his friend as he tried to make sense of where he was. The sound of crunching snow announced a figure walking towards the injured man from under the bridge. The mysterious person was silhouetted with the same glow he had seen Miniel display at the Preserve and at Woo's restaurant. As the stranger stepped out into the shine from the overhead streetlights, the vision revealed a possessed Juste Theriot smiling down at the fallen Lewis Turner.

Henry did his best to stay steady, "How long had he been possessed by your Angel friend? Juste only moved to Tulsa a year ago."

There was almost sympathy in Hyde's voice, "Hyde knows much, but not all, my child. She has changed her tactics and stopped following the rules of the Order of Virtue, which forbids them from possessing mortals. To do so is an act of a Fallen Angel, and punishment is banishment from Heaven. Miniel hid in Juste and orchestrated an alliance with Cthulhu. In return, she was given the leadership of his followers in Tulsa. With the Crimson Brotherhood in her pocket, she then stalked me for over a year without my knowledge. She has gone insane. Miniel believes she is serving God still, even as she defies his laws and hides from his sight."

Henry realized something, "Wait. The night Lewis was killed, Juste was at my house. He woke up the next morning, saying that Maisy had raped him. Was that Miniel talking, or did that even happen?"

Hyde's demeanor changed to one of melancholy, "She always did enjoy celebrating after a victory. Miniel used the Seven Deadly Virtues to seduce Maisy. In fact, both of them had sex against their will."

Henry focused back on the vision of a helpless friend laying on the snowy train tracks. The possessed Juste stood there, staring at him wordlessly. With considerable effort, Lewis was able to move away from the train rails. Henry's heart quickened as he rooted for his doomed boss to make it to safety.

Juste uttered one of the Seven Deadly Virtues, "Patientia."

Henry muttered the translation, "Patience."

As the train approached, Lewis stretched his neck across a track and begged, "Forgive me."

A few seconds later, the locomotive rolled over his neck, decapitating him. Lewis's body was thrown from the impact as the blare of the train horn filled the air. A few minutes later, the passing boxcars were gone, and Juste left with the head of his friend. The vision ended with blood pouring out from the mangled corpse.

Hyde drew them out of the image and back into the Study. Henry found himself sitting in the same high back chair that matched the one that the Demon enjoyed. His host seemed to be in a trance as the flames from the fireplace danced on the reflection from his long beautiful black hair. The angel wore an all-black suit, studded with silver and his standard glass of Bourbon in his hand.

Hyde took a deep breath and brought himself back into the moment, "Miniel's plan had worked, and I was trapped inside the dead body of my Vessel. Apologies, my child, inside Lewis Turner. There I was to stay, unable to break free and awaiting her minions to collect me. The mortal named Amy Howard is a member of the Crimson Brotherhood and had arranged for the Mages of the cult to extract me."

Hyde suddenly threw the drink into the fire, "She betrayed God and gathered new strength from the darkness she had opposed for so many millennia. It was brilliant, really, but risky. If the Order of Virtue had found out about her plan, there would be a reckoning.

I did have two strokes of luck. One was Miniel couldn't do the exorcism herself. It was an unfortunate drawback for our kind. Once possession has occurred, only a willing human can perform the exorcism. I suspect that is why she looked upon the cult of Cthulhu for the answer to her obsession. They are more than willing to do such a vile act, and, in her mind, she could use evil to fight evil. She had earned her prize, and all I could do was wait for her minions to collect me.

The second piece of luck was you, Henry. As a member of my bloodline, you were able to draw me out of the spell that bound me to Lewis Turner. Immediately, I noticed my divine DNA in your genetics, even while in my weakened state. I had fully recovered the evening you went to your game night. While you sat at the table, both Miniel and I discovered one another."

Hyde laughed at the irony, "Really though, an Angel of God, member of the Order of Virtue, playing Dungeons and Dragons! Blasphemous! Well, I suppose that would be the least of her crimes."

Henry reached over and took a bottle of Bourbon from an oak cabinet. With a degree of fascination, Hyde watched as Jekyll upended it, then threw the half-empty container into the fire. The broken bottle exploded into flame and shot a plume into the air.

He then turned to the fiend and said, "Juste and Lewis were the two closest friends I had, and now they are dead! I know why you showed me all that bloody history. You added the vilest memory to every lesson. You want to corrupt my spirit so it will be more like your own so that when we merge, Hyde will be in control. What you failed to realize is that you did your job all too well. You've prepared me to watch for your inevitable betrayal. Because of your Study, I've felt the birth and loss of hundreds of children, the ravages on the soul from war, and countless ways to have one's heart broken. I know there is more to your story! This Miniel, who was she to you, Hyde? Why did you protect Edward Tallman and then hide the memory from me!? Tell me now! If you truly want me prepared for what is to come, then grant me the truth!"

Hyde stood up, "Truth, then!"

The room in the Study went dark, as the fire around the hearth vanished. The pitch-black burst into a menagerie of pinholes of light, as Henry was suddenly floating in deep space. The celestial bodies that surrounded him swirled in colors and patterns he had never dreamed of. He was inhabiting Hyde's body again and soaring on the cosmic winds with his salt-and-pepper wings, traveling beyond the speed of light, streaking past the majesty of Orion's belt and soaking in the vibrant colors of the universe.

Henry marveled, "Is this how you travel to different galaxies?"

Hyde's voice filled his mind saying, "With the right spells, your wings can do so much more."

His eyes were caught in the infinite beauty of the void, "This is astonishing, Hyde!"

The voice of the Demon seemed to come from all around, "This is the galaxy in which you reside in. Our kind is responsible for executing God's will and keeping certain alien species from entering His domain. In your world, we are called Angels, but we go by many titles. In my beginning, Miniel and I both served in the Order of Virtue together, fulfilling God's promise to purge any meddling by our race into human affairs. You see, after Lucifer led one-third of the Lord's Angels into revolt, we found ourselves busy indeed. We traveled the cosmic winds, visiting distant worlds and purifying them of the ones polluted by the Morningstar."

Henry felt himself descend into the atmosphere of an inhabited world as Hyde continued, "On one such mission, we were on a distant world called Uvis III."

He interrupted, "We?"

Materializing beside him was the beautiful form of a female angel clad in silver chain mail. Miniel had long blonde hair that flowed back and licked her ankles as she flew next to him. At her side was a magnificent looking mace that was laced with silver and bathed in Enochian runes. The celestial woman looked at him and gave a smile that seemed to be made of the purest beauty he had ever seen or encountered.

The Demon continued, "Yes, Miniel and I were partners. During our visit, we happened upon a Demon inhabiting one of the planet's spiritual leaders. We gave inspiration to the local priests to discover the possession and performed an exorcism. When the Fallen Angel was banished from its Vessel, I saw it was Tabris, my former teacher and mentor. Tabris had trained thousands of our kind dating back to the beginning of our existence. He was one of the first generations of Angels that God created and bred for war. He was more than a teacher, he was my friend. Before my entrance into the Order, I fought in many battles for the Alpha and Omega alongside Tabris. He was a proud Angel, something not as discouraged as one would think. When Lucifer rebelled, Tabris fell with him. His reasons were his own, and he never asked me to betray my Order. During that war, I had the blood of my kin on my wings, but thankfully not his.

Now seeing him on Uvis III, the angel I had known looked like a husk of his former glory. Withered and darkened from the lack of divine grace, he had turned into a twisted amalgamation of himself. Unlike the other Demons, he never replenished himself from the nectar of human souls, nor enjoyed the blood and flesh of humans. Tabris had starved himself to the point of annihilation.

While I stayed my hand out of respect for my mentor, Miniel charged in and struck him with her mace. The blow was vicious and collapsed his chest inward. My old friend didn't have the strength to defend himself and seemed to almost welcome the end. As the last of his life eked out of his frail body, I knelt beside him and gave him comfort. In those final moments, he whispered in my ear and asked for a favor. The angel had sired an offspring on that planet before the rebellion in Heaven. Upon the child's birth, Tabris vowed to protect and raise his Nephilim son. The forbidden son had become a great chief among Uvis III, and, just like I have done with you, Tabris taught him the wisdom and magic of our race. I vowed to see to it that his son would live out his life, unharmed by the Order of Virtue. That act enraged Miniel as she was appalled by my compassion."

The vision showed Hyde and Miniel quarreling over Tabris's lifeless body, "She had plans for us, and my vow to my friend would bring us to ruin from the Almighty. Miniel demanded that I go to this Nephilim and destroy him personally as an act of fidelity. It was then I discovered I hated taking orders and hated what our kind had become. We argued, then we fought."

He trailed off, and Henry offered, "I'm sorry to hear that. What happened?"

Hyde looked up with tears coming down his perfect face, "I found the son of Tabris before Miniel. I told him of his father's death and attempted to hide him away. True to his bloodline, he refused and demanded to face his enemy. Standing on the same mountaintop where he earned the right to lead the people of Uvis III, the only son of Tabris met his end in combat with Miniel. After that, I went into hiding, and she started her descent into madness."

Henry felt sincerity from Hyde, "Edward Tallman. That is why you helped him and hid his sister-in-law and nephew. They were innocents caught in a war. Just like Tabris's son."

The alien planet melted away and was replaced by a new one. Henry found himself standing on a dry and cracked desert landscape. In the distance were two magnificent pink mountains with snowy peaks. The wind was hot on his face, and the breeze smelled like salt. He was once again inside the body of Hyde and sharing a memory of the past. He was completely nude with only an odd pair of leather shoes.

The Demon's voice resonated in his mind, "I didn't bring up Tabris to elicit your pathetic sympathy or to invoke your pitiful attempts to dissect my past! I wanted you to recognize his importance as a mentor. Since you never truly learned how to be a man, this will be a hard lesson indeed."

Hyde's voice sharpened to a razor's edge, "Our kind was created for many things, and war is one of them. This planet is called Hetoo Prime. It is used for several things, combat training being one of them. This memory is from my first meeting with Tabris, just after my creation. He will instruct you in the various divine martial arts, the weapons of our people, and in angelic battle tactics. This is your last lesson, my child. Once this is complete, I will move us into the final moments of our transformation process. Listen well to Tabris, and don't ever back talk him. It would be a shame to see you die so close to the end of our journey together."

On the horizon came a light purer than the twin red suns that burned in the sky. From its center, Henry could see an Angel dressed in golden armor, carrying a spear and shield. As the being soared overhead, he could feel the massive wings buffeting the hot wind against his face. Slowly, the 8-foot giant celestial landed gracefully a few feet away. The angel's skin was bronze and had sharp facial features just like his own. The creature's shield was covered in Enochian symbols and decorated with ivory. The hot wind flowed over his white cape that was pinned to his shoulders and waistline. His gold armor had an odd glow to it and did not give off a reflection. The auric helmet Tabris wore covered the top half of his face and was shaped like the head of an eagle. The spear he held was made of white wood, and the metal tip of the weapon was continually vibrating with energy. On the celestial's belt was a long sword, sheathed in a jeweled scabbard. The hilt of the blade was pure white with etched Enochian symbols decorating a vertical line.

Henry gasped, *This is what Tabris looked like before his fall? He's a mountain!*

As the massive being landed and roared, "My name is Tabris, the First Sword of His Forces in the Milky Way. God has seen something special in you and commanded that I teach you personally. It is your privilege to be under my wing. For you to survive my training is not my responsibility, but I will show tolerance if you give me devotion. Now, I have shown you my divine truth of self, and it's time for me to learn who you are!"

Henry buckled under the realization that he was in another life and death scenario from Hyde's past. The massive Tabris dropped his weapons and launched an attack at him. Before Henry could respond, the enormous fist of his teacher slammed into his face with blinding speed, breaking several bones in his jaw.

By Bo Luellen

Chapter 6: David I

Muskogee, Oklahoma – Monday, November 5th, 2018 – 8:23 p.m. CST

The images from David Keller's laptop reflected off his reading glasses as he dangled one hand down to pet Charlie. The "Hunt for the Truth" YouTube live stream was broadcasting coverage of a shootout between police and the Crimson Brotherhood at the St. John's Medical Center. The sounds of shots popped in his earbuds as police exchanged gunfire with the cult, who had taken up a defensive position at the front door.

Quincy Hunt's voice overlay the video, "The assault on the hospital started 30 minutes ago. A group of well-armed men and women wearing black tactical gear and sporting Crimson Brotherhood armbands stormed the front door. According to witnesses, the hospital security and police that were assigned to guard Henry Jekyll have been gunned down. The speculation at this time by the members of the police department is this is an attempt to free the cult ringleader, Henry Jekyll."

David looked down at the injured dog, "Yeah, we're not convinced he is their leader, are we boy?"

David thought back to the night at the Preserve, *Mr. Purple was so desperate to plunge that dagger into Henry Jekyll's chest. That seems like an odd way to treat your figurehead despite what the police want the public to think.*

The screen changed, and John Utterson's face appeared. He was wearing riot gear and had blood splatters on his face. He was busy reloading his clips from the cover provided by a SWAT truck.

Quincy Hunt shoved a microphone in his face, "Detective Utterson, has the Brotherhood freed Henry Jekyll, and what are you doing to keep that from happening?"

While shoving 9 mm bullets into a clip, he responded, "If there was ever any doubt that Henry Jekyll was an evil occultist who quietly led the Crimson Brotherhood from the shadows, that question has been answered. We've got five dead cops, one nurse with a headshot, and two civilians down."

Quincy centered the GoPro camera on Utterson, "Detective, alternate theories had surfaced online stating Henry is a government plant. They suggest the entire Brotherhood was a C.I.A. black ops program designed to cause anarchy. Others say that Jekyll is being held in a comatose state by operatives within the government. They suggest he could identify city officials and cops who are members of the Crimson Brotherhood. This is being seen as a rescue attempt, but couldn't this be just the opposite? Couldn't this be an assassination attempt by the Crimson Brotherhood to keep Henry Jekyll silent?"

John pocketed his clips and pushed the camera away, "Get back behind the yellow tape!"

He glanced up at the time, "Oh shit! I better get moving, Charlie."

David left the dog on his nest of pillows and went into the back bedroom. The big man knocked and then opened the door to his Uncle Enrich's room. Inside, the elderly German man reclined back in his bed wearing a light blue tracksuit that covered his fish gut-like midsection. His oxygen mask was attached to his face by a rubber band, and the beep from the heart monitor told David his vitals were doing fine. The man's skin had small blue bruises around his wrinkled arms, and Enrich's thinning white hair was cut short into a flattop. The smell of ointment and dirty clothes hit David in the face as he marched up to him. His uncle looked up from the old TV that was broadcasting the news and gave his nephew a yellow grin.

David checked the IV and said, "Okay, Onkel Enrich, ich muss ein paar Freunde treffen. Wenn Sie mich brauchen, rufen Sie an? "

The old man pulled his right hand from under his blanket to reveal a pearl-handled Luger pistol and waved it in the air. David smirked, pushed the gun down out of his face, and glanced over to the TV. A news channel was showing one of the middle floors of the hospital was now on fire. The ticker at the bottom of the screen read, "Standoff Escalates! Explosions Rock Hospital!"

He turned to his uncle, "Wenn jemand zur Tür kommt, antworten Sie nicht. Wenn ich zur Tür komme, erschieß mich nicht!"

Enrich laughed and replied, "Geh und hab Spass. Ich werde in Ordnung sein."

The old man patted his arm and went back to watching TV. David's uncle had come over from Germany when his mother was pregnant with him. Now he had the same kind of cancer that took his mom. There were certain aspects of the German he had adopted, but David was fully Americanized.

As he left his room, he pulled an old black climbing backpack from the hallway coat rack. He had repurposed it to house his everyday items and his gym equipment. Tonight, it was full of occult books he had checked out of the public library. As he went into his own bedroom for a fresh shirt and his running shoes, David flipped on the light to reveal his walls were covered in old cinema billboards. Every inch of the original wallpaper was hidden behind *Predator, Ghostbusters, Goonies, Masters of the Universe, Star Trek, Buckaroo Banzai, Army of Darkness,* and many other 80's and 90's movie posters. He threw down his pack and put on a fresh shirt that read, "go climb a rock" from *Star Trek: The Final Frontier*. He picked up his deputy sheriff's badge and put it on his belt opposite of his holstered 9 mm Glock.

Once he was ready, David sat with Charlie for several minutes, while watching the news coverage and waiting for the Van Helsings to arrive. The Channel 8 news ticker read, "Jekyll Has Escaped." An entire exterior wall was blown away from the hospital, and pillars of flame were shooting up towards the night sky. In the parking lot, several cars were flipped upside down and on fire from detonated grenades. Two dead officers were lying in several pieces on the wet concrete, and SWAT members were wandering around in a daze. Dozens of armed Christian Crusaders had flooded the area and opened fire on the entrenched Crimson Brotherhood. Within minutes, Brother Dunn's TCC had ripped apart the cultists' barricade with shotgun slugs and pushed them back into the hospital.

The TV reporter announced, "... Crusaders have broken through the Brotherhood line and saved the Tulsa Police. Tom, we can confirm that two Brotherhood members are on the ground and presumably shot by Crusaders. We can hear gunfire coming from within the hospital, as the fight continues."

The studio anchor broken in, "Mark, I'm sorry to cut you off, but I have something being handed to me. It's confirmed, Henry Jekyll has escaped. I can now report that the police have called for a citywide lockdown. We're not sure how this was accomplished, as the alleged cult leader was in a coma. Chief of Police Blake Kelly has called for an immediate curfew to be implemented for the city and says martial law options are now on the table."

The images of the hospital battle zone brought back memories of the night at the Preserve. Those thoughts still held sway in David's nightmares, as the killing of another human being weighed heavily on his mind. Yet no one single horror held such a high place of terror as his fight with the superwoman in the ski mask. The dark smile that inked out from the mouth opening in her covering still gave him panic attacks. Part of him wanted to think it was a hallucination, but the reality that someone that powerful existed plagued his thoughts.

A car honked just outside his house, and David patted Charlie saying, "Okay, boy, I'll be back soon. If anyone comes in the front door, go for their nuts first."

Charlie looked back with his one eye and blinked in confusion. His right leg was fixed in a cast, which allowed him only limited mobility. He helped the dog drag himself out of bed to use the bathroom one last time before leaving. He was an older German Shepherd, and the vet told David the dog would be lucky to heal fully. He gave the K-9 his antibiotics as he got him situated back in bed.

David pulled over a large burlap sack full of fan mail addressed to Charlie, "Here's some reading material while I'm gone. If you get any letters from lady dogs that include nudes, be strong and don't call them. Just start a scrapbook."

As he walked outside his front door, he saw a white 2016 Dodge Grand Caravan minivan waiting outside. His neighborhood was a mixture of Hispanic workers and their families. He knew them all, and most had lived in Muskogee for the majority of their lives. Anything new that showed up was viewed with suspicion, and several of his neighbors were on their porch, peering at the unusual collection of personalities inside the vehicle. The side door slid open, and Thomas Booth hopped out like a jack-in-the-box. He was wearing a new pair of cargo pants and a black t-shirt. His hair was wet, and his beard was trimmed.

Thomas yelled out, "Hurry up, we are late for soccer practice!"

Basten's voice bellowed from the passenger side, "Shut up, you damn hippie! Do you want to wake the neighborhood?"

David tossed his backpack into the vehicle as Thomas replied, "Four pasty white guys in a van, cruising around back streets at night. Yeah, no one will take any notice of that."

The side door rolled shut, and Keller greeted everyone in the car politely, then asked, "Where's Jessup?"

While Nicolaas pulled the van onto the road, the old man replied, "Mr. House has joined the Christian Crusaders and is currently patrolling the streets of Tulsa."

As the car accelerated down the street, David remarked, "No, shit. Really? Wow. Well, I guess that fits. He was always a very Christian man."

David noticed Thomas had a thick smell of Old Spice and shampoo as the druid replied, "He was fat. Although, I would have rather had him with us in case we had to run for our lives. Slowest person gets eaten by the bear and all that."

David sniffed Thomas's shirt, "You smell less... awful."

Basten laughed, "Yes. I brought him some new clothes and made him take a bath."

Thomas had a look of disgust on his face, "I only did it because I'm known for being considerate."

Twenty minutes later, they stopped at a Mexican restaurant for dinner. David noticed the contrast between the two Van Helsings. The younger man was in peak physical condition, while the elderly gentlemen looked as if he could fall over dead at any moment.

David stirred his tea as he asked, "So what's the plan?"

Basten patted his forehead with his napkin, "The 'plan,' Mr. Keller is simple, get Ms. Lanyon's daughters back. The minutia of that design is a bit more complicated. First, we must find out what kind of vampire we are dealing with. Once we know that, then we can assemble a strategy and then devise a tactic to pull our prey into a trap."

Nicolaas had a worried look on his face, "How can we know that? Is there some kind of test?"

David eyed the kid with suspicion as Basten responded, "There are tests, yes, but these creatures are notoriously uncooperative. You have to determine their clan by subterfuge or interrogation."

His grandson nervously asked, "Just how are we supposed to do that?"

David tilted his head in suspicion, "Shouldn't you know? You sounded like you knew your stuff back at the cemetery. Now you're asking questions like someone who's never done this before."

Nicolaas looked to the side as Basten replied, "He hasn't. This will be his first outing as a hunter of vampires."

Thomas choked on his chip as Keller exclaimed, "Oh, you got to be kidding me!"

The elder grinned, "Not to worry, Mr. Keller. I've been grooming young Nicolaas since birth to one day take over for me. Indeed, he has only recently become aware of our family's unique responsibility and heritage, but he has been well trained. The boy has a degree in history, has a black belt in several martial arts, is in good shape, an expert marksman, and has been schooled in interrogation and investigation techniques. I've kept him isolated from the rotting social circles of today's youth and centered on sharpening his mind. He might be green, but he is ready."

The druid spouted a mouth full of chips replying, "Kept him from social circles? You mean you didn't let him have friends?"

Nicolaas looked away, sheepishly as his grandfather proudly stated, "Today's youth is too chaotic and self-obsessed to allow Nicolaas to be around them. He has books instead of a cell phone. His destiny is to defend mankind against the vampiric plague that our family has waged war against for generations."

Thomas wrinkled his nose, "Oh, my god. What a horrifying childhood. You raised a child and didn't let him have friends. You put him through all of that and never told him what it's for? You're lucky he didn't turn out to be a serial killer! This kid sounds like he has abilities but no social skills. How is he supposed to serve mankind if he has no way to relate to it?" Before Basten could reply, Thomas pointed his fork at him, "Nicolaas has zero real-world experience, you look like a slight breeze will kill you, and we have no plan."

Nicolaas's face went red from embarrassment as his grandfather responded, "Oh, we have a plan, Mr. Booth. It is one I've used for decades to some great success."

David observed the old man as he pulled out his phone, thumbed the passcode "1897", and announced, "Here is where we shall lay our trap gentlemen."

The image on the phone was a Google Map of a section of land in Tahlequah. Thomas squinted at the screen through his thick glasses as David let out a loud guffaw. The elder Van Helsing dropped his phone on the table and gave the large man a scowl.

Thomas pulled the phone closer, "Where is this. I can't see that damn thing."

David leaned in towards Basten, "It's the Preserve, which is impossible to get to. That place is surrounded by armed FBI, police, and a small group of Christian Crusaders twenty-four-seven. The Feds are still digging up corpses, and the media is always looking to get in. We won't be able to get within 3 miles of that area without having to go through a checkpoint."

Nicolaas cut into his enchiladas and replied, "We were there just today."

The waitress refilled the group's water, as David exclaimed, "Bullshit! Prove it."

After a few minutes of looking through Basten's phone, David was shown dozens of photos the pair had taken from inside the Preserve. He cycled through images of the twin cabins, the burned sacrificial platform, and even the empty kennels. Thomas continued to chomp down on chips as he looked over David's shoulder at the phone at the battle-blasted clearing that had been the spot where a small war had been waged.

David handed the phone back, "How did you get these? The police were all over that place."

Basten gave a gnarled grin, "Yes, they should be, but they aren't, though. Oh, the FBI comes for a few hours during the day, salvaging up one or two bodies, then they leave. The gates have sensors, but the woods are thick enough to move around without being spotted. There are a few security guards, but they are easily avoided during the night."

David blurted out, "Okay, so why the Preserve? Wouldn't it be the last place some vampires would hole up?"

Queso dripped off Basten's grey beard as he replied, "Yes! Exactly, Mr. Keller! If this Marcus is a coven leader, as I suspect he is, then he will need a place to rest. Oklahoma isn't known for land sanctified to dark powers. A creature of the night would find a restful sleep on land anointed by Cthulhu, especially if that vampire had ties to the Great Dreamer."

Thomas dropped his fork, "Like I told those cultists, that ground is under my protection. If it's infested with vamps, then it needs to be cleansed."

The elder continued, "Yes, Mr. Booth, but not just yet, or we risk spoiling our chance to get back Amanda Lanyon's children. This Vampire Marcus is an agent of Cthulhu, and that means he will not travel too far from Tulsa. That is another clue that the Preserve is a viable place for them to lair."

David suddenly wasn't hungry, "Basten, exactly what will we be facing if we find this lair?"

The old man wiped his beard, "A layer of hell that can't be easily forgotten. You can expect corpses, scenes of feeding, and enthralled slaves. Their lair will be guarded by one or two spawn at most during the night. During the day, this particular clan of Vampire enjoys subterfuge in lieu of barriers. It's best to draw them out, Mr. Keller. If one did solve the puzzle of their resting place, you would be more likely to have stepped into one of their traps and become a servant of the devil."

David felt a cold well up in his stomach, "Great. So, your plan is to…"

Nicolaas looked up at his grandfather with an anxious expression as Basten boasted, "I say these creatures are hiding in plain sight, in graves at the Preserve. That area is where they rest, and that is where we set our trap!"

Thomas pulled David's plate over to him, stabbing a piece of chimichanga, "Okay, but afterward, I'm departing from your merry band of idiots and going to work cleansing the ground. I got one question though, what is going to make these vamps come out? I mean, you said they are really good at hiding."

Basten gave a broad smile, "We have some enticing bait, Mr. Booth."

David watched in disgust as Thomas ate his leftovers off his plate and asked, "What kind of bait?"

With a satisfied smirk, Basten replied, "The both of you to be precise."

Thomas muttered with a mouthful of food, "What did he thay?"

David gave Basten a hard stare, "He said he is going to use us as bait."

The druid swallowed his food and exclaimed, "Look you walking wrinkle, I might look like just another handsome face, but don't mistake me for some clueless bimbo. Cernunnos has shown me that Amanda Lanyon is a key part of my path, so I'm happy to help find her kids, but I'm not down with being a blood donor to some undead. You want to go vampire hunting with your grandson, then go play Castlevania! I'm not going to …"

Basten interrupted, "Mr. Booth, calm yourself. You are in good hands."

David opened his hands in confusion, "Why would we be of any more interest to a vampire than those Feds that are walking around out there? Why would they risk exposing themselves over Thomas and me??"

The senior Van Helsing shook his index finger at David, "Because something Amanda Lanyon knows is valuable to them. Something she has seen or heard has caused them to take her children hostage. Amanda has heeded my advice and left the country, which allows us to act. The last people she publicly spoke with were the four of us and Jessup House. Marcus Holmes has invested a great deal of his time and energy into maintaining a controlling hold on her. Thanks to Amanda's wealthy friend, Mr. Dyer, their travel plans to Scotland have been hidden from the general public. That means there is a good chance that Marcus wants to know where she is. Who better to know that secret than the two of you. You were the ones that fought alongside her at the Battle of the Preserve. You were seen speaking to her at Larry Lanyon's funeral right before she disappeared."

Thomas gave an expression of sudden realization, "You son of a bitch! You could have approached her at any time. You picked the funeral because all the cameras were on us. Now that's she's gone, it makes us the last people that could know her plans. You set us up!."

Basten grumbled, "Please, Mr. Booth, don't be so dramatic. The Crimson Brotherhood is a vengeful cult. They would have come knocking at your door, looking to take your life eventually. What, did you think you could walk into a hive of killers and not come away with a black mark?"

Thomas said flatly, "Yes."

A grizzled laugh spouted from Basten's gut, "Well, you're a bigger fool than I suspected. At least this way, if you die, it will mean something. You'll be doing your Cernunnos a service by helping Amanda get her kids back."

The druid threw his napkin on the table, "Well, that is a shit plan! So what are you two going to do if some superhuman vampire pounces on the two of us? One of you is going to instantly die of old age while the other one shows the monster his black belt. We're screwed! I request a new plan. You might have a death wish because you're dying, but don't put me in that coffin with you!"

David looked confused, "Dying?"

Basten lowered his head, glanced at Nicolaas , and confessed, "It's true."

The druid stabbed a piece of meat, "I think you're so desperate to get your grandson kick-started into the family business before you croak, that you're willing to risk our lives to do it.

The younger Van Helsing piped in, "My grandfather is a good man. He hid the horrors our family fought so he could protect me. It is my time to answer the call and become a defender of the weak and the meek. I shall be the stake to the night and ..."

A chip bounced off Nicolaas 's face, and Thomas interrupted, "Shut up, Justin Bieber! Did you memorize that in case you needed to make a speech? You sound like you're reading from an episode of Darkwing Duck!"

Insulted, Nicolaas stood up quickly from his chair and hit his head on the overhead lamp. Thomas giggled at the young man grabbing his stinging head and stabbed some food off the Van Helsing's plate. David took notice that the surrounding patrons were starting to take note of their conversation.

David reached up and steadied the light, "Okay, everyone take a breath. I get it. You needed an angle, but you need to be transparent with us from now on. That said, I'm still in."

David looked over at Thomas for his answer. The druid's smile went away when he realized David was serious. He downed the last of his margarita, belched, and nodded in begrudging agreement.

David returned his attention to Basten, "Just how do you plan on keeping the worms alive when the catfish come calling?"

Tahlequah, Oklahoma – Tuesday, November 6th, 2018 – 3:02 a.m. CST

The forest surrounding the Preserve was cold, and David's breath bellowed out of his mouth like a steam engine. He hadn't dressed warmly enough for an expedition like this, but he was determined and committed. Walking ahead of him was Thomas, dressed in his dingy brown cloak. The big man had to admit he was envious of the druid's forethought, even if he suspected the "cloak" was a repurposed poncho.

Thomas held sage in his right hand and was burning the incense as they marched. In his left hand was a cup of cider he was sprinkling about to anoint the ground. The druid walked a circle around the tree as he sang:

"Tha an soitheach seo air a dhèanamh naomh.
Na leig na h-uisgeachan àrdachadh,
agus na leig leam tinneas no baneadh
crois a-mach an èadhair, an talamh, an uisge no an teine seo."

David finally had enough and asked, "What is that song saying, exactly? You've been droning on for hours."

Thomas splashed the tree with cider, "It's Irish Gaelic, and the closest translation is:

"This grove is made sacred.
Let the waters not rise,
and let no ill will nor bane
cross this encircled air, earth, water or fire."

David pulled his hands out of pockets and rubbed them together, "You've repeated that dumb song so many times I think I know it by heart."

Thomas finished a tree and moved onto the next, as he replied, "You're face is dumb. These are ancient and important rites that need to performed to rid the forest of Cthulhu's influence. Too bad the same can't be said of you."

Behind him, David heard the dried leaves rustle as something stepped towards them. He whirled about and pulled his flashlight. Instinctively he unsnapped his service pistol and peered into the darkness. Thomas continued his chanting, oblivious to what was happening, as Keller kept the black Maglite centered on where the noise had come from. The branches and dried leaves caused the shadows to dance and play on a curtain of trees.

The noise happened again, but this time louder and closer. Thomas stopped his chanting and looked over at David, who jerked the light towards the new layer of sound. Slowly side-stepping, he made his way over towards the druid, while keeping his attention on the forest.

A sharp "crack" was heard behind Thomas, and the two spun quickly to face the new noise. The Maglite shined down on a young black girl, no older than 8 years old. She held two halves of a broken stick in her hand. She was smiling up at them with pure white teeth and a cherub-like face. The girl wore a light pink dress, her hair was long and flowing over her shoulders, and she had bare feet.

Keller inched his way around Thomas towards the newcomer, "Hey, honey. What are you doing all the way out here? Where are your mommy and daddy?"

The little girl took on a sad expression and shrugged her shoulders.

Thomas had a horrified look on his face, "Oh, no. I've seen this movie, man. Some creepy girl out in the middle of a haunted woods. Nope! Shoot her in the face."

David scowled at Thomas, squatted down, and asked the girl, "Honey, are you lost? Were you out hiking or camping with your parents?"

She shrugged, and David pulled out his cell phone, "I'm a police officer. I can find your parents and call them. What's your name?"

The little girl smiled, showing off her elongated canine teeth.

Thomas pinched his groin in fear, "Oh, shit! I knew it!"

The whites of her eyes disappeared into pure black, and she let out a hiss. The girl lunged, and in a heartbeat, had covered twelve feet. Her hands extended out towards David, and he braced for an impact that never came. He overcompensated and fell forward into the dead leaves and cold earth. Some of the apple cider the druid had been pouring soaked into the knees of his jeans, instantly bringing a chill. He scampered to his feet and looked back at Thomas, who was staring back at him with wide eyes that were magnified by his thick glasses.

David pulled his gun, looked around frantically, and then whispered, "Where did she go?"

The druid raised a trembling right hand and pointed at Keller's right shoulder. He instantly turned and aimed his Maglite at the area his companion had indicated, but no one was there. David glanced back, confused, as Thomas stabbed his finger towards the big man's shoulder. Turning his flashlight towards his chest, David saw a firefly crawling along his arm.

He relaxed his posture and took a deep, cleansing breath, "It's a bug, man. Calm down."

Thomas shook his head in disagreement as his frantic stare focused on the tiny insect. David brushed the bug off his shirt, sending it flying. In mid-air, a sucking sound popped, and David's ears felt like they had just depressurized. The firefly transformed into a monstrous version of the little girl and flew onto his shoulders. Her legs had become slimy and riddled with insect-like hairs. The girl wrapped around David's neck and locked into place. Her jaw unhinged and opened to reveal a long row of fangs that had ooze dripping. Globs plopped down onto David's shirt and ate through his clothes like acid. Her talon feet gripped his jacket, and she sported a hunched back that seemed to pulse in and out, suggesting something alive was under the skin.

David shrieked as he reached up in an attempt to detach the monster. He struggled against the beartrap-like grip that the girl had around his neck. Effortlessly, she pulled his head to the side and bent her face down towards his exposed carotid artery. He launched backward against an oak and smashed her body into the trunk. The vampire giggled and clamped down harder.

A panic attack set in, as David relived the same feeling of being overwhelmed he had experienced when he fought the superwoman. His mind was overcome by the sensation of being helpless in the iron grip of something he couldn't defeat or escape. David frantically landed wild punches to the insectoid looking face of his attacker, and staggered in circles, as she cackled at it all. His lungs hyperventilated, and his legs buckled under the mental stress, as he dropped to his knees.

David's blurry vision focused enough to see Thomas yelling a challenge and charging at him with his gnarled staff raised. Sharp cracks filled the forest air as the druid rained down a chaotic series of blows. Pain seared into David's right hand as the stick landed on his wrist and he let out a howl of pain as Thomas landed a hit against the vampire's face. The blow caused the undead child to divert its attention away from David's neck, and it hissed at the druid.

David cradled his hand as Thomas yelled, "Stop moving, man! I'm trying to help!"

The young vampire had a laceration against her eye, and it flowed dark black blood down David's chest. She held the injury with her hand as the oil like fluid turned to dirt and fell on the ground. She jumped up and gripped David's shoulders with her clawed feet. Seething with anger, she launched off into the air, transforming again into a firefly. Booth swung wildly at the insect as David fell onto his back and scooted away from the flailing druid.

Another "crack" rang out as Thomas finally found his mark. He stopped and panted while he searched for where the insect had landed. Standing there in the dark, a soft glow pulsed from the end of his staff. It illuminated the side of his sweaty face and reflected off his thick glasses. Slowly, Thomas turned to the firefly that had attached itself to the end of his staff. Before he could react, the creature transformed back into the half insect girl. The new weight ripped his weapon from his hand and slammed it to the ground.

Her insectoid eyes stared into his thick glasses, acidic liquid dripping from her salivating mouth. The monster's body trembled, and a high whining sound came from its throat. The girl grabbed his arm and pulled him towards her open mouth. The druid did his best to resist and chanted in Scottish Gaelic. The words seemed to cause her pain, and she responded by slapping him hard in the face. Thomas reeled onto the ground, as a stream of blood drained out of his nose. As he lay on his back, the vampire jumped onto his stomach with both feet, forcing an exhale of pain into the cold night air. She remained perfectly balanced, as the creature squatted and pushed his crimson speckled face to one side, exposing his vulnerable neck.

David gathered himself and pulled out the LED flashlight the Van Helsings had given him. He clicked it on and bathed the vampire in its blue light. The creature dismounted Thomas and advanced on him. He backpedaled as her face was immersed in the blue glow.

He slapped the LED, "What? He said this would work!"

The girl smiled and shook her finger, "Nothing can save you, David Keller, but I'll make you an offer. If you willingly give yourself to me, I'll only kill your friend and allow you to continue as one of us. You have but to ask nicely."

Silence hung in the air for several seconds before Thomas found the breath to cry out, "The answer you're looking for is 'no' you jackass!"

Keller kept the light on the beast as he yelled back, "Well, I'm being polite. I don't want to seem rude and turn her down right off the bat!"

From behind one of the trees came a waterfall of liquid aimed at the girl. As the torrent hit the creature, Basten yelled a curse at the beast. Smoke filled the air, and she hit her knees and screamed in pain.

The creature writhed on the ground as David remarked, "Besides, I needed to buy them time to do that."

From around the same tree, a wide-eyed and frightened Nicolaas threw a water-soaked net over the wailing monster. With David's help, the pair managed to trap the undead inside the netting and tied it off on the ends. The cords burned into the flesh of the Vampire and coagulated blood regurgitated out from her mouth.

Basten helped Thomas up and said, "The vile thing is vomiting its last meal, like a snake which is in distress."

The druid rubbed his stomach, where she had landed, "What did you splash on her? Holy water?"

David smelled his hands from gripping the net, "It smells like coconut. What the hell is this?"

Basten examined Thomas's busted nose and replied, "It is a mixture of coconut water and palm oil deluded down. Just the thing needed to snag an Adze Vampire."

The druid slapped the old man's hands off his face and asked, "What's an Adze Vampire, and just how the hell did you identify it? I thought you said it wasn't easy."

The elder Van Helsing laughed, "This upstart revealed herself too early. The more seasoned vampire will hold their true clan a secret until the bitter end."

David inquired, "I'm missing something. How did she reveal herself?"

Basten sneered, "Well, I had a hunch based on Marcus taking the Lanyon girls. Adze's sustain themselves on the blood of their victims. They are known for taking children, keeping them as a source of sustained sustenance. On rare occasion, they will even corrupt them, and guide them down darker paths until they are full-grown members of their clan."

The Druid yelled out in the forest, "You fossil! We could have been killed if you were wrong!"

Van Helsing stroked his grey beard, answering, "And I wasn't! Stop whining! We must stay focused. As Holmes would say, "The game is afoot! Now we have one of Marcus's children. Perhaps even his actual offspring and not just a turned victim. The die is cast, and we must act, or the devil will be upon us!"

David grabbed an ax out of Nicolaas 's backpack and asked, "So what now?"

Nicolaas unlatched a hatchet from his belt as his grandfather answered, "We lay a trap for Marcus. Now that we are sure what kind of Vampire we are dealing with, we can prepare. It won't be easy, and there are unknowns to consider."

Nicolaas and David went to work cutting down a small tree, as Thomas held his nose and asked, "What unknowns?"

Basten stuffed two rolled-up pieces of gauze up the druid's nose, "Unfortunately, this particular type has a tendency to delve into the mystical arts and a bad habit of possessing unprotected sorcerers. I suspect he will try to attack us tomorrow night after he discovers this one has gone missing. These creatures are linked to their spawn. Once she is washed free of the coconut water and palm oil, then her Master will sense her again. Marcus is no fool. He will know it is a trap and bring the full force of his powers to bear on us."

Careful to avoid the thrashing Vampire, David and Nicolaas threaded the long piece of pine through the net and created a litter. They got on each end of the tree and lifted their quarry up off the ground. The group started their long trek towards the minivan as the creature sizzled and hissed from inside the ropes.

The elderly Van Helsing did his best to keep pace, "I remember when I was about Mr. Keller's age. We held up in a Pilipino church with the spawn of a Mandurugo Vampire clan leader. The Mistress of the clan destroyed the building, and her minions set the surrounding city block on fire. We barely survived that night, but we dispatched the bitch and her coven. This beast we face might bring the Crimson Brotherhood with them, or they might handle it personally. Regardless, we must get this creature to Mr. Booth's house before daybreak so we can lay our trap."

Thomas stopped in his tracks, "Back to my house?!"

Chapter 7: Shoshannah I

New York City, New York – Tuesday, November 6th, 2018 – 11:23 a.m. CST

Shoshannah Feinstein closed the door to her apartment and locked the deadbolt, "Lousy little shits!"

She turned and looked at what was once a secure 42nd floor of her 432 Park Avenue safehouse. The appearance of the Pearce Brothers had just compromised its secrecy and made it useless. Shoshannah hadn't expected the Crimson Brotherhood to find her so quickly, and regretted ever having conducted any business with them.

She leaned on the door with her back, "How dare Richard Enfield send the Pearce Brothers here! So much for staying in hiding. Fuck all!"

A synthesized Australian voice came from her laptop, "It was a tactical risk to ignore Master Enfield's request for a different golem."

Shoshannah knocked the back of her head against the solid oak, "He asks for a golem whose soul is pure evil. Then he changes his mind and wants one with a good soul. It took me weeks to track down a serial killer who's not in jail or dead. Do you know how hard it was to find one?"

The Artificial Intelligence responded blandly, "The statistical probability is 1 in …"

She knocked her head a second time, "Please, don't! I guess I could just go to Oklahoma and kill all the Crimson Brotherhood."

The Aussie accent responded gleefully, "Would you like for me to formulate a tactical proposal, Mistress?"

She rolled her eyes, "I was kidding, IGOR. I think, at least."

The Artificial Intelligence reminded her, "If I might be so bold, this might be a blessing in disguise. With Adam's sudden appearance in the States, you urgently need to go off the grid. If the Pearce Brothers could find you, then so could he. Statistically, the Crimson Brotherhood stronghold in Tulsa might be the safest place to hide. You can conclude your business with Master Enfield, enjoy his protection, and give me the time needed to find Adam before he finds you."

She sauntered over to the gold plated bar, "Do you honestly think the Brotherhood could stop Adam if he decided to show up at the Howard Estate?"

The Australian voice soothed, "No, Mistress, but he might think twice before acting."

Shoshannah slammed bottles around looking for the Alize Vodka, "Maybe you're right. Contact Silvio. Let him know I'm interested in having dinner with him tonight. I'll leave for the lab right afterwards."

The computer gave a few beeps and replied, "Understood, Mistress. Shall I bring the new car online?"

She sighed and turned to look at her sparsely decorated house, "I think it would be best. It will be a pity to leave this place after so much work making it tolerable to live in." Shoshannah looked over at several massive boxes, "I just ordered the Victorian furniture from Paris. Oh, well. Make arrangements to put the flat up for sale, IGOR. Donate the contents to some charity. I don't care which, you pick."

The AI made a few more beeps, "Of course, Mistress."

Shoshannah gulped down her drink, then said, "I suppose we had better get moving if we are going to make it to the swamp house by midnight."

After packing what little clothes she had into a backpack, Shoshannah paused to look at herself in the bathroom mirror. Her long black hair had never lost its curl, even through the centuries. The woman's beautiful face and sharp nose line accented her bewitching blue eyes. She took off her white blouse and put on a tan sweater that matched her cargo pants. Shoshanna never felt the cold, so wearing warm clothes was just a show meant to help her fit in. In the reflection, her pale skin showed long deep scars along her chest and back, which decorated her smooth skin and slender figure in macabre designs.

She put her Bluetooth in her ear and activated the device, "IGOR, I have a few errands to run before my date with Silvio. Contact Jagger and tell him to expect me in the next half hour. In the meantime, I'm connecting you to my Apple Watch. I'm going to walk rather than Uber to keep AEGIS from tracking me. Hack into the city surveillance cameras and blackout five city blocks around us. The last thing I need is that redneck Texan knowing I'm working for the Crimson Brotherhood considering what is happening in Oklahoma."

The cheerful reply chimed in her ear, "As you wish, Mistress."

Shoshannah stepped out of her apartment building and into a chilly November breeze. She rounded the corner onto 57th Street and headed at a brisk walk towards the bus station. The bustle of the weekend traffic echoed off the high rise buildings as she passed by a street performer. She reached in her jacket and pulled out some money. As she dropped it into the man's guitar case, she looked him in the eyes and read his soul light. The elderly performer had a full beard and the sunken-in jawline of an addict. His skin was rough and looked like someone had carved a roadmap on his flesh. Through his hollow and lifeless eyes, she sensed the soul light within him was dim and flicking. The guitarist gave a toothless grin and kept playing a rendition of "Suspicious Minds" by Elvis Presley.

She trod onward, *So many dim soul lights these days.*

After an hour on the bus, she arrived at Queens General Center Hospital. The cream colored building seemed so uninviting to her, and she always looked for ways not to visit. She regretted having to make an exception to that rule, but the circumstances demanded it.

Shoshannah went to the front desk and asked to page Dr. Clerval. As she sat cross-legged in the waiting room, her phone vibrated. She looked down and saw she had received a text.

She sighed and read, "We couldn't help but notice you have left your apartment, and your pet disabled the city cameras. Now, you know the rules. – John Hamilton"

She stabbed the keys, "Your leash is too short. I might take it off."

A few minutes later, the response came, "Just keep your phone on you, and I'll make sure Control looks the other way."

Shoshannah smiled and typed, "I knew you loved me."

She heard the worried and meek voice of Jagger Clerval from behind her, saying, "Sho! What are you doing here? What has happened?"

The man was in his mid-thirties, with a slight build. He had on blue scrubs, a white lab coat, a surgical paper hat, and a name tag that read "Dr. Jagger Clerval, Surgeon." He looked as if he had just run a marathon, and sweat was dripping from his forehead.

She got up and smiled, "Now, calm down, Love. Everything is okay, we just need to go back to work a little sooner than expected."

Dr. Clerval took Shoshannah by the arm and pulled her into a corner of the waiting area, "You said we weren't doing anything else until you located Adam! That is what you promised! Do you know what he will do if he finds us? What he could do to my family?"

She grabbed the man's trembling hands and rubbed them, "Jagger, look at me. The Brotherhood found me and they're demanding the golem. They're not taking no for an answer. We have to do it tonight."

He pulled his hands back and begged, "I have responsibilities, Sho! I can't just leave. I'm on rotation in the ER tonight. My house is in the middle of being remodeled. My wife is expecting me home, and the kids are going ..."

She put a slender finger up to his lips, "Richard Enfield has paid a bonus of a quarter of a million dollars for a personal delivery."

Jagger stammered, "Wha... What? Are you serious? That's one million dollars in total."

She nodded, "The funds deposited in our offshore account this morning."

He turned and sat down on a bench. Shoshannah put a hand on his shoulder and slid down next to him. She entwined her arms around his bicep and gave a squeeze of assurance.

She straightened his badge as he processed what she said, *Poor Jagger. Just as excitable as his father was.*

She leaned in, pressing her firm breast against his arm, "You do this with me tonight, and you'll have enough money to finish your house. You can buy some plane tickets to Greece and take the family on a surprise vacation tomorrow. That will give IGOR time to track down Adam. You know how your wife loves traveling, which you rarely do. I'm surprised she hasn't left you out of neglect."

He kneaded his legs with his hands, "Sho, this isn't funny! What about our obligations to AEGIS? Won't they take exception to you just disappearing?"

She patted his chest, "They won't mind if they don't know. IGOR can mask my movements, and you'll be safely overseas. Besides, after Vegas, I have John Hamilton under control."

He turned towards her with worry, "How long will that last? How long until they try to force the process from us, or worse, demand that we join AEGIS full time? I like being a doctor, Sho! I don't want to work in some government lab for pennies."

She stood up and replied, "My Love, they never will. They want us as consultants or to perform a rare resurrection. Besides, they need us much more than we need them. If they decide to push me, Russia has made some generous offers, and that gives us options."

He got up slowly and started biting his nails. No matter what cases they went on or what dark deed that needed to be done, he was always anxious.

It seemed to be as much his nature as his family tendency to explore the forbidden alchemical realms.

She pulled out her phone to check the time, "Be at the swamp house tonight before midnight. This will all be over soon, I promise."

As Shoshannah turned to leave, Jagger asked, "What are we going to do about... supplies?"

She put on her sunglasses, "I'm stopping by to pick up a few things. I wish I could stay, Love, but I have a date to get ready for."

Shoshannah kissed his cheek and then caught a cab ride to a nearby storage facility. She tipped the driver and sauntered along the long line of containers. She stopped at row 18, unit 23, and unfastened the lock and lifted the large door. The New York sunlight poured into a dusty bin that contained a car that was covered with a grey tarp.

She keyed her Apple Watch and asked, "IGOR, are we set?"

The Australian accented male voice piped up, "Yes, Mistress. The new modifications are checking out. All sub-systems are fully charged, and munitions are at full capacity. Onboard computer has booted up, and I've been successfully integrated into its matrix."

Shoshannah yanked the tarp off to reveal a 1969 black Dodge Charger, "What exactly did the good Dr. Zorka do to it?"

The AI's voice emanated from the car's speakers, "The engine has been replaced with a modified 2005 V-10 Dodge Viper engine. An advanced nitrous system has been installed and can be activated several times before it depletes. Thanks to the Doctor's brilliance, the vehicle can sustain a top speed of 305 miles per hour, under the right conditions. The rear end has a wheelie bar to keep the vehicle from flipping backward from a sudden 700 horsepower acceleration. Its frame was replaced with a handcrafted Titanium shell, complete with a roll bar. The windows were replaced with a 1.6-inch thick bulletproof aluminum oxynitride glass that can withstand a .50 caliber round. The interior was designed to look classic. Still, it houses a multitude of evasion and anti-tracking gadgets that Alex Zorka personally installed. I would recommend that you give me at least a few more minutes to perform some tests before you drive it."

She ran her finger across the black exterior, "To hell with the tests."

IGOR sighed, "Of course, Mistress, what was I thinking."

She walked to the back of the unit and grabbed two heavy duffel bags from the corner. They made metal clacking sounds, as she pitched the 200 lb. packs into the back of the muscle car. As she closed the trunk she peered down at the personalized license plate that read, "WHIM."

Shoshanna scoffed, "Whim?"

IGOR gave a flippant, "Dr. Zorka felt it reflected your personality."

Her dark right eyebrow went up as she replied dryly, "Did he? How adorable."

Shoshannah got inside the car, and felt the black leather interior, "I can't damn him for his craftsmanship. IGOR, start her up."

The air exploded with the roar of the engine that shook the nearby tin walls. Dust drifted down from the neglected storage unit ceilings and covered the new paint job. Like a dragon waking in its lair, the advanced engine bellowed a warning to the gods that it was hungry. With a gentle press on the gas pedal, she pulled out of the unit and onto the graveled road. She turned onto the empty street and opened Whim up.

She spent a few hours shopping the more exquisite districts for what to wear for the evening. After some deliberation, she went with a full length black long-sleeve evening gown. The dress was lowcut down her midsection and finished at her navel. It was accented with silver trim around the edges and an open back. She stopped by Harry Winston's and bought a diamond necklace to draw the gaze to her cleavage. Shoshannah had plenty of reasons to celebrate with such a lucrative job, and she intended to enjoy her date before she had to work.

During the drive to Manhattan, IGOR remarked, "Getting out of town will help keep Adam off balance until Dr. Zorka can come up with a weapon to subdue him. The big problem is the Brotherhood. Master Enfield has already gained a reputation in the occult circles as being a ruthless leader who earned his position through assassination. He won't likely let you just walk away if he decides you can be of further use."

She let go of the steering wheel and fixed her makeup, "I've known dozens of such people in my life, and I've learned one hard fact: Crazy takes care of itself. If we give him what he wants, he will put it to use. That will draw out his enemies and pitch him into conflict. Then I can slip away, and with any luck, Enfield will forget me or get assassinated."

IGOR drove the car between two buses and accelerated, "Mistress, you underestimate yourself. Everything about you is unforgettable."

She blew a kiss in the air, "Thank you, Love."

She pulled up to Daniels, a French restaurant she enjoyed frequenting.

Shoshannah found her date standing outside in a black tux. The man was panning his head around, looking for her. She poured out of Whim, and he beamed at her radiant beauty. Shoshannah's intoxicating smile distracted him from seeing her car driving away with no one behind the wheel.

The Italian man caught her eye because of the strength of his soul light. It was the spark of true wholesomeness that was so rarely found today. He had dark hair that was combed perfectly to one side and a thick build that pressed against his purple dress shirt.

The man's slight Italian accent was still present, "I'm so glad you called me for dinner. After you stopped texting me, I thought you weren't interested."

She touched his chest with a single finger, "You shouldn't give up so easily."

There was a playful nature to his conversation, and the young man spent the evening trying to make her laugh. As they ordered some Dark Cocoa Moelleux, he noticed one of her scars. A mark ran down and poked out from under her elegant sleeve.

Silvio brushed his hand across the raised flesh, "That looks deep. How did that happen?"

She leaned back in her seat, "You know, usually when I get asked questions about my scars, I lie. I make up some simple misdirection. When I find someone as special as you, Silvio, it's an opportunity to tell the truth."

Shoshannah brushed his black hair, bringing a blush to his cheeks, "I know that you'll never tell my secrets."

The hapless Italian inhaled the pheromones drifting off her skin. She watched his eyes, which suddenly dilated. She smiled faintly at the indication that the enhanced airborne hormones she produced had done their job.

He grabbed her hand and kissed her palm, "I would never betray you!"

Shoshannah allowed him to hold her hand as she continued, "I got these scars before I was born. A brilliant man named Victor Frankenstein was about to barter my life away. When I was capable, I was to be used as a broodmare by a monstrous man named Adam. At the last moment, Victor had a change of heart and believed that I wasn't meant for this world. While a storm raged in the middle of the night, Victor took an ax from the servant's quarters. Like a cruel god that was unhappy with his creation, he carved my body up like a cow at slaughter."

The Italian beauty sat across from her, with his mouth agape, "What? How did you survive?"

Shoshannah took a sip of her wine, "It depends on what definition you have of life. Is a baby in the womb a life, or can you abort it without being considered a murderer? I suppose I couldn't say I survived it or it killed me. I wasn't yet a thing in some people's eyes. As for my mother, I've often wondered that myself, but never knew who she was."

He leaned forward with anguish in his eyes, "I'm so sorry."

It was a heartfelt expression that transcended the chemical charm her body had produced. Part of her longed for the pure seduction without her abilities. Enthralling men and women through her genetically enhanced pheromone glands made social engagements too easy. The soul light burned with compassion in his eyes, and she knew for a fact that Silvio was the one she had been searching for.

He reached over and grabbed her hand, and continued, "How? How did you survive such a brutal attack at such a young age?"

She caressed his palm, "A kind man named Asher Clerval collected my broken and discarded body, then hurried it back to his laboratory. Between intellectual curiosity and his enormous sense of compassion, he patched my broken pieces back together and gave me life."

Silvio shook his head and replied, "Wait. Why didn't he take you to a hospital? Was he a doctor?"

The waiter sat down the dessert as Shoshannah answered, "Asher was a medical doctor, and had learned some of the sciences from his deceased brother, Henry. Dr. Clerval used catgut, sewed me back together, and in a moment of irony, used a process developed by Victor. Luckily, Henry had a keen mind and kept me away from death's door."

As she slid a spoon into the chocolate, he asked, "You were just an infant. Did Asher adopt you?"

She swallowed the bite, and the flavors exploded in her mouth. Shoshannah's taste buds responded on a higher frequency, which made each bad meal agonizing and a delicious one a wonderland of sensations. She nearly lost herself in the moment before realizing she was making a spectacle of herself.

She put the fork down, face flush with the sensation, and replied, "I became a member of his family, and he raised me as his own. Because of my disfigurement, he had me tutored at his estate. After a time, I cast off my given name and adopted the name of my Jewish tutor. Asher's two sons became my brothers, and when I was old enough, I became Clerval's laboratory assistant. When he passed away, my brothers took over the business, and I traveled the world. When Oxford started admitting girls, I was in the first group to apply. I graduated with honors and returned home to apply my craft. Two years later, I surpassed my elderly brother's abilities and took over ownership of the family lab. Since then, I've always protected and kept close to the Clerval's. Asher Clerval might not have been my biological family, but he was every bit my father."

Silvio tilted his head, "Wait, what year did you graduate from Oxford?"

Shoshannah looked at him sheepishly, spooned a bit of the creamy dessert, and replied, "1926."

After a pause, he burst out into laughter and clapped his hands. It caused people around to stare, but she relished in his reaction. Silvio praised her for the jest and remarked how easily she had led him down a rabbit hole. She had told him almost everything, and still, her pheromones made him only want to love her.

He pulled his chair around to her, "Let's get out of here. Come back to my chateau and dance with me."

She picked up her phone and checked the time, "You're gorgeous, and I do like you. I just can't. I have to be somewhere by midnight, and I think what you have in mind is going to take much longer than that."

The young man smiled as her foot ran along the inside of his calf. His face had a look of hunger, and his eyes melted into hers. She pulled out some money from her wallet and put it on the table.

The Italian looked down, "No, let me. I asked you out."

She winked at him, "I'll see to the check, and you can see me to my car."

A sly smile stretched across his face, as he nodded with anticipation of getting to spend more time with her.

New York City, New York – Saturday, November 6th, 2018 – 11:54 p.m. CST

She made good time on the I-78, but she hated long drives. IGOR had piloted Whim, while *Enter Sandman* by Metallica piped in from the speakers. She recalled the sweeter moments of her night's date, as her rear view mirror vibrated each time Lars hit the drums. Shoshannah was glad she had taken time to enjoy herself and remembered days when all she did was adventure.

It had been three months since she had been back to the Great Swamp National Wildlife Refuge in New Jersey. Even though it was turning cold, in her headlights she could still see the insects swarming over the murky waters. Like many of the preserves, refuges, and forests protected by the Federal Government, it had a great deal of uninhabited land. The twelve square miles of bog made an ideal place for wildlife to thrive and co-exist. It also provided a quiet place for Shoshannah and Jagger to do their gruesome work.

She turned off Long Hill Road and stopped the car in front of a service entrance that led deeper into the uninhabited areas of the park. Shoshannah got out and unlocked the gate, pausing to look at the waning crescent moon overhead. After getting her car past the fence, she turned her headlights off and drove down the long dirt path. The sliver of moonlight was barely enough for the average person to make out basic shapes on the ground, but not for Shoshannah. Within minutes of being in the almost total darkness, her eyes produced new light sensitivity cones. This caused her pupils to expand and give her eyes an almost black appearance. The landscape went from pitch black to a low level of illumination.

After a few minutes of IGOR negotiating the back road, she arrived at the swamp house. The surrounding stagnant water was only twenty yards away from the building, which gave the area a strong odor of rotting vegetation, fungus, fish, and animal. As she parked and opened her car door, the pungent aroma hit her enhanced senses like a freight train. She nearly threw up the fine French cuisine she had enjoyed earlier in the night.

IGOR blurted out, "The swamps can be... overwhelming. Is there anything I can do?"

She choked down the urge to vomit, "No. Not unless you can find an off-switch to what Victor did."

The AI beeped, "Everything about your biochemical makeup is geared towards survival by way of an alchemically altered adrenaline gland. Everything that could kill you is overcome in seconds by this genetic defense system. To deactivate it, the gland would need to be removed, and no one knows what that could do to you. I can task a large portion of my processing power towards finding a way to mute your body's abilities, but, to date, Dr. Zorka hasn't been able to…"

She held up a hand and straightened up, "Forget it, IGOR."

The door to the wooden building popped open, and Jagger yelled, "Sho, is that you?"

She loved her family, but Jagger sometimes drove her crazy. Of all the generations of Clerval, he wasn't the worst, but he was dynamically dumb to tactical situations. The saving grace was his eagerness to please, hard work ethic, and creative nature.

She unlocked her trunk, "If you have other women coming to our secret swamp hideout in the middle of the night, I'm going to give you a medal for finally cheating on Elisha. No man should go a year without sex."

He blushed, "Oh, now, Sho. Stop that. You know I have eyes only for my Elisha."

Shoshannah lifted one of the canvas duffel bags from the trunk, "Of course. If you have time, how about helping me with this."

He awkwardly made his way in the dark and grabbed one of the bags from her. With some considerable effort, he grunted it onto his shoulder and followed her in. When she opened the door, she saw the lab was already prepared. The windows were covered with cardboard, the walls were filled with acoustic suppression insulation, and the tea was brewing on a camping stove. Overhead were rows of fluorescent lights, and gas-powered generators lined the walls. In the center of the room was a metal table with brown leather restraints attached.

She slammed her bag to the ground and opened it. Inside were refrigerated metal canisters, designed to keep their contents at a constant temperature. Jagger put his bag down with a grunt and opened it to reveal more metal cases. As she sat her cylinders up along the walls, he opened the metal satchels to reveal dozens of six-inch-long pins.

She turned and ordered, "Get everything ready, I'm going to bring it in."

Jagger barely looked up from screwing long black wires to the blunt end of each pin. He gave her a slight nod as she walked out of the door. She counted herself lucky with Jagger. He wasn't squeamish, and he took direction well. Not all of the Clerval line could say the same.

As Shoshanna reached her car, she looked down at an empty back trunk, "IGOR, open it."

The floor of the trunk popped up to reveal a secret compartment. As the hydraulics lifted the false bottom, Shoshannah grabbed the black body bag that lay underneath. With a slight strain, she hoisted the bag up and out of the car with her left hand. IGOR closed the trunk as she whipped the body bag on her shoulder. A few seconds later, she walked back into the shack and threw the heavy sealed container onto the table.

Jagger had connected the majority of the pins to wires and attached the other end to a voltage regulator. The regulator was, in turn, hooked into the six generators. Each individual pin had a dial that was capable of making minute adjustments to the current.

He looked at the body bag, "Is it messy?"

She unzipped it and pulled back the sides to reveal the blank expression of Silvio. His head was turned at an unhealthy angle, and his body was bent in an odd shape. The smell of feces hit her nose, and she backed up, waving her hand in front of her face. Jagger pulled out a Febreze bottle and frantically pumped the contents onto the corpse. He didn't mind the odor, but he wanted to make her more comfortable.

After soaking the body with the lemon-scented contents, he looked up and asked, "Better?"

She nodded, *I don't have the heart to tell him that the overpowering fragrance is nearly as nauseating as the body. It's cute how Jagger tries to be chivalrous, while joyfully helping me mutilate a murdered corpse. He's old fashioned like that.*

They pulled Silvio out of the bag and sprawled him out on the table. Jagger went to work, cutting the young Italian man's clothes off as she fit restraints to the wrists and ankles. Once the preparation was complete, Shoshannah started an IV at the femoral artery, just inside the leg. She attached the hose to a pump and turned it on. Slowly, Silvio's blood was pumped out of his body and into a large glass container.

While they waited, the two sat in a corner and discussed Jagger's family and the challenges of the new house. It was a cold November night, and they enjoyed a cup of hot tea while the suction pump whirled. Just before 1 a.m., the deceased Silvio was drained of all his blood, and the pair went back to work.

They both inserted the pins into the body at specific points, careful not to trip over the attached wires. Shoshannah jammed hers into the seven chakra points found along the mid-line down the front. Jagger didn't have the strength to do this task, as the crown chakra pin had to be forced through the cranium. With a sharp stabbing motion, the shack was filled with the sound of breaking bone as she plunged it into the skull. Her assistant quickly completed inserting the smaller pins into the over forty different acupuncture points.

She looked up at Jagger, "Okay, time for the magic."

He took an alcohol wipe and swiped her brachial vein, as she said, "You know that's not necessary. I'm immune to infection, so sanitizing my arm before you stick me is pointless."

He pulled out a syringe from his pocket, "I remember my father telling me about how my granddad was hard on you. He constantly reminded you that you weren't human. That you were a creation of Victor's. This is my way of saying I feel you are more human to me than most. So, I treat you with respect because you are my family."

She gave a half smile as he stuck the needle in, *I'll be sad to see him grow old and pass.*

Jagger pulled the needle from her arm and injected the contents into Silvio's adrenal gland, "I know you're against it, but I have an idea of how to replicate Victor's original formula by using your blood."

Shoshannah sighed, "Darling, we've been over this before. Victor's original formula is lost, and that means we don't have a base to look at. Without that, any manner of anomalies could manifest."

He took her hand, "Sho, listen, your blood can resurrect others, but it doesn't give them the same abilities you and Adam have. Sure they stop aging, have immunity to disease, but they don't have your adaptive gland's high level of mutagenic response time. I've got a few ideas about the process of mass re-animation. If I can get a sample and perform a few tests…"

She retorted bluntly, "No."

He pleaded, "Just think, we could make billions raising a small army of soldiers. We could pull the greatest minds from death's door or give the elites of the world what they always dreamed of, immortality. In one day we could never have to work again and go into hiding on some island where Adam could never find us."

Shoshannah reached out and rubbed his scruffy cheek, *If that had been said by anyone else other than a Clerval, I would have killed him. His heart is good, his mind was curious and his concern for their well-being is genuine. Jagger Clerval, you're not the first in your family to ask this.*

She watched as the hole in her arms from the needle healed over in seconds, "The Creator's alchemical formula was lost to time for a reason. I believe that in my heart. My creations can't mate and have only a small sliver of my abilities. Those with a bright enough soul light for me to resurrect can be controlled by my pheromones. That gives a safeguard that wouldn't be in place if they had my full abilities.

"The world should count itself lucky that the last of his alchemical formula was used on me by Asher Clerval. His macabre need to understand the thing that had killed his brother Henry drove him to forbidden discovery at all costs. I both feel blessed and cursed by his choice. I'm immortal, but live with the horrors an army of Adams could visit on the world if we were to mate. Victor was right in fearing what would happen if Adam and I reproduced. They would be born perfect, with no physical or genetic flaws. Their bodies would overcome any life-threating attack, and they would see themselves as the next step in evolution for humanity. It would only be a matter of time before humans would be enslaved or worse."

Jagger leaned back with a look of dejection as she continued, "They would burn the world, Jagger. The only two left to witness a world undone by Victor's hubris and ego would be Adam and I. Be patient and let these fools pay us for little miracles. If you attempt to unravel the designs of Frankenstein, you will start walking his path. That is a road that only a madman would venture. Let the thought alone and focus on the task at hand."

He reluctantly nodded and picked up one of the silver canisters. He hung it upside down and attached an IV tube to the bottom. Opening the port, a yellowish liquid from the cylinder crept its way down the line and into the body.

Jagger adjusted the flow regulator and changed the subject, "It wasn't as easy to get stem cells this time around. The hospital's security protocols were harder to get past since the new administrator took over."

She felt his disappointment and gave him an encouraging look, "I know you can figure it out. The stem cells are highly adaptive and react well with my blood. It was brilliance on your part to suggest we use them."

The two sat back down and poured another cup of tea, as they waited for the transfusion to complete. Three canisters of stem cells and one teapot of Earl Grey later, Jagger unhooked the IV from the corpse. Shoshannah went over to the generators and started their engines. She pulled a large switch on the wall that changed the shack's electrical source from a battery to the generators. He stepped up onto a wooden box and put on a pair of rubber gloves. Shoshannah took off her shoes and walked barefoot on the concrete floor.

He pulled a long chain that dangled down, and rushing water poured from two square rain shower heads attached to the ceiling. The corpse below was soon drenched, and the floor was quickly becoming a small pool. Over the sound of the cascading fountain, she pulled the second switch that channeled the six generators' power through the regulator, through the wires, and into the body. In a flash, the corpse reacted to the sixty-thousand watts of electricity. Silvio's muscles danced on the metal table in reflexive spasMs. Jagger covered his eyes from the pops and sparks created by the wild display, while Shoshannah stood in the current flowing into her feet. In response to the electricity, veins popped out on her skin, and an inch of her black hair went white at the temple. A look of almost sexual extasy came over her face as she ran her finger across the table. Time stopped for her as the life energy that was the source of her power flowed like a lover's kiss.

She heard the voice of Jagger struggling to get her attention, "Sho, pull it! Pull it the lever, Sho! Sho! Snap out of it!"

Reluctantly, she traveled to the present and pulled the switch back to its neutral position. The lights stopped flickering, and the standing water caught on top of the metal table was boiling. They stayed motionless for several seconds watching the deceased Silvio, as smoke floated off his burned skin. His beautiful face twitched, and several seconds later, the Italian's neck started to turn. The charred red skin turned pink, and the scorched sections of flesh healed over the next few minutes. She smiled as the long pins they had inserted fell out, slow at first, then in rapid-fire. The final one on the crown chakra made a wet sound as the regenerating tissue and bone pushed it out.

Suddenly, Silvio opened his eyes, and violently tried to sit up in a dash of movement. The chains snapped taught and caused Jagger to jump a little. The re-animated man strained against his bonds, as the broken bones in his neck popped back into place.

Shoshannah stepped around to look at her creation in the eye. The soul light had returned but was noticeably dimmer than before. The corpse snarled at her and snapped its jaws in the air in an attempt to bite his creator. In a flash of speed, Shoshannah snatched Silvio by the neck and pressed him down on the table. Slowly she dragged her other hand across his face, letting her pheromones drift into his nose. Almost instantly, his eyes dilated, and he went motionless.

Lowering her face down next to his, she whispered, "Shhh… It's okay now, Love."

Jagger stepped down, ran a series of tests on the charmed Silvio, and reported, "Everything checks out as usual. There is a steady heart rate, respiration is normal, but the motor functions are equalizing. Your pheromones seem to have him completely sedated. Part of me wants to know what would happen if you didn't do that little trick."

She kept her gaze on the newly reborn, "It isn't something you would want to see. When Asher Clerval discovered my blood was a lesser substitute for Victor's alchemical formula, he tested it on a baker who had been a friend. The man acted like all of my creations and went wild with rage. I restrained him, but the subject slipped into several mental disorders. It was an engine of destruction that was faster, stronger, and never tired. Jagger, that is an intellectual curiosity that you should leave unanswered."

She pulled Silvio to a sitting position and calmly soothed, "Now, now Love. You will be okay. I want you to cooperate with this young gentleman beside me. His name is Doctor Clerval. He is going to run some tests and help you get dressed. Afterward, you and I are going on a trip together."

Silvio's face lit up, "Just the two of us?"

She kissed his forehead, "Yes, Love. Just the two of us."

He reached up to her face, "Where are you taking me?"

Shoshannah tilted her head so she could peer in his eyes, "To a place called Tulsa to meet a friend of mine named Richard Enfield. You will have me all to yourself. Doesn't that sound delicious?"

His regenerating facial muscles managed a maligned smile, "I'll go anywhere as long as you're with me."

She looked up at Jagger, "I'll call the Brotherhood and tell them I'm on my way with the golem. Get him ready."

Chapter 8: Amanda VII

Tulsa, Oklahoma – Sunday, November 4th, 2018 – 9:12 a.m. CST

Amanda Lanyon had promised Basten Van Helsing and the others that she would stay put until today. According to the old man, Sunday was when evil had its sight dimmed. It was hard to keep quiet, but every day she prayed for her daughters and did as he asked.

She spent the time planning and plotting for her disappearing act. When the morning of November 4th came, she made the call to Josh Dyer to ask for travel money. She wasn't shocked that he insisted on leaving with her; in fact, she counted on it. To the chagrin of her AEGIS guardians, she gave him the address to her current safehouse hotel. With minutes he had abandoned a press interview and rushed over. Amanda had to admit that it would be nice to finally see a friendly face after such a long time in seclusion.

AEGIS Field Chief John Hamilton, was in the middle of giving her a speech on how dangerous it was to give out her location to anyone. She was almost thankful when Josh pounded on her door. The Agents swung the door open, dragged him inside, and patted him down. He was careful to protect his newly attached finger while Agent Patrick Decker threw him against the wall. After her friend was scanned with some device that she didn't recognize, he was allowed to hug Amanda.

After some arguing, Amanda talked Hamilton into filling him in on the real happenings behind the vampiric kidnapping of Amanda's kids. At first, the field chief smiled and made a joke about the account. His grin faded as Decker showed him still pictures of the crime scene photos. A look of horror came on his face as he saw close up shots of his old college classmate, Larry Lanyon, with his head turned completely around.

Josh's blue eyes were glazed over, "My God, Mandie! What happened? I didn't know… that had happened to Larry."

She sat down on the edge of the bed, "It's like they said, Josh. A vampire named Marcus Holmes was in my house when I got home from the Battle at the Preserve. I managed to get his gun and put several rounds into his chest. No effect. Larry showed up with the kids and tried to defend me. This… thing killed him for it. Marcus threated the kids and made me tell him everything you and I had done to track down the

Brotherhood."

Her friend looked aghast, "You told him about me?"

John gave a sly smile, "Don't be too skittish about that part hero. Your face is on every news channel taking as much credit as you can. I'd reckon the Brotherhood might have a notion or two of your involvement."

Amanda crossed her arms around her stomach, "Josh, he has my kids. If I don't stay silent for one year, he says I'll never see them again. That means no testifying and no helping the police. After what I've seen this man do, I believe him."

He shook his head in disbelief, "Wait, I thought you said April and Nancy were abducted by the Crimson Brotherhood, and they killed Larry with an icepick."

Hamilton put away the photographs, "Yeah that one's on us, partner. We couldn't allow Ms. Lanyon to tell you, or anyone else, the truth. I'm not sure how the ME, Amy Howard, came up with an icepick as the murder weapon, but it created a great cover story."

Amanda got up and grabbed Josh's hand, "A man came to see me at the funeral. He's a specialist in killing vampires. He's taking Thomas and David with him, and they are going to try and find my kids. To do that, I need to disappear out of sight."

Josh put his hands on his hips, "Vampire hunters, huh? Mandie, how do you know this person isn't some whacko who is off his meds? I can't believe you would fall for…"

Hamilton looped his thumb into his belt, "The Van Helsing family has been hunting Vampires for generations. We've had some dealings with them in the past. Solid people and well worth the trust Ms. Lanyon has put into them. To be blunt, it's the only reason we are thinking the notion over instead of hogtying her to the bed."

Josh grabbed her shoulders and pleaded, "Mandie, I can give you the money to get where you need to go, but only if you let me accompany you. The Brotherhood still wants you dead, your kids' lives are on the line, and the country thinks you're some kind of folk hero. Let me be there for you."

Agent Decker crossed his arms and asked, "If we allowed the star witness for the FBI against the Brotherhood to leave our custody, where exactly would you want to go?"

She decided that now was the time to reveal her plan and looked at Agent Hamilton, "Sterling, Scotland. I want Josh to take me to see his

Druidic teacher."

Josh seemed shocked, "My teacher, why?"

She stood up and touched his chest, "Because, I want to know why Cernunnos won't speak to me anymore. I've done DMT three times since my daughters were taken and nothing. I've spent hours in these damn hotel rooms meditating and Zen breathing, but it isn't working. I want to know why he can show me the way to the Preserve, but not where my daughters are being held. I want some answers."

Josh shook his head, "That would be impossible. My teacher died four years ago. The position of First Knight of the Line of Merlin has fallen to Ian MacLean. I came up with Ian. He's a drunk and less than an astute student of the ancient magics. The man's a wreck that never ventured beyond the Bard level of Druidism." He shook his index finger in the air, "Although, I know some of the lower members of the Knighthood who are quite talented in the arcane. If there is a way to get Cernunnos's attention, they might have the answer. We would still have to get Ian's permission first, but he and I go way back. That won't be a problem."

She set her jaw, "Then that's what we'll do!"

Patrick's stone face cracked as he observed, "John, you can't let this happen. The Crimson Brotherhood has proven to be most capable. What are they going to do? Go up to the ticket counter and ask for a flight to Scotland? The cult will know where's she's headed and have someone waiting for them before she lands. She'll be outside of our protection and as good as dead. Control would have a cow if he knew…"

John Hamilton cut in, "Ms. Lanyon, this isn't going to work unless we help you. Agent Decker will provide you with fake passports and names for you to use when getting through customs."

Decker looked confused, "I am?"

Hamilton nodded, "Yes, Sir." He then looked over at Josh, "Mr. Dyer will arrange to have his Foundations private jet brought to the Tulsa International Airport. It will be fueled up and ready to leave before dawn."

Josh's eyebrows went up, "I am?"

The Texan tapped his cowboy boot on the floor and knocked off some mud, "Yes, Sir. With Amanda out of the country, the Brotherhood will spin their wheels lookin' for her here in Oklahoma. That will give the Van Helsings time to work and keep those cultists busy looking in the wrong direction for Ms. Lanyon." He stood up straight, "Let's face it. The

Crimson Brotherhood has been misdirecting us from the beginning. I think it's time we return the favor. Besides, Ms. Lanyon is willing to let one of our Agents tag along as security in Scotland."

Amanda nodded in recognition, "Yes, I guess I am?"

The Texan grabbed his cowboy hat off the desk, "Yes, Ma'am, you are. Patrick, let's arrange for a senior Agent to attach to them. We don't know how far the Crimson Brotherhood's influence goes. We have to assume they have ears everywhere. Maybe even within the CIA or AEGIS. I want someone who is off the books and retired."

Decker pulled out his phone and cycled through the list of names, "I can make a call to a couple of IRATE members."

Josh tilted his head, "IRATE?"

Decker continued moving through his list of names as he answered, "Inactive Retired Agent but Tactically Effective. It's a sub-organization within AEGIS for Agents who are too old for active duty but still have operational value."

Amanda gave a sharp laugh, "Dragging some elderly person along with us isn't going to help."

Hamilton nodded, "You know, the little lady is right. What we need on this is someone on the IRATE list that is still physically capable and has experience. Someone that hasn't been on a mission in a few years. Someone that isn't afraid to break a few rules."

Decker's face went pale, "Oh, no. You're not thinking about…"

The Texan gave a broad grin, "Roger Quinlynn. Give him a call, fill him in, and arrange for some quiet travel plans that get him off that island and to Scotland."

His junior protested, "John, you got to be kidding! That guy is a wreck! After what happened in Canada, Control should have drummed him out of AEGIS. He's got… issues. Why him?"

Hamilton grabbed the doorknob to Amanda's hotel room, "Because he's one of the sharpest agents I ever worked with. That, and he makes me laugh. He'll bitch about it, but I'll ask nicely." Amanda and Josh gave each other a worried glance as John continued, "I'll phone the plan into Control. You take care of these two."

Over the next hour, Decker forged a pair of passports for both Josh and Amanda, then told them, "Roger will make contact with you in Edinburgh. He's a master of disguise, so don't bother looking for him."

Josh looked at his forged passport and asked, "How will we know who he is?"

Decker handed her a card and stated, "When he approaches you, he will hand you one of these."

Lanyon took the brown-colored business card and read it out loud, "AEGIS - The Agency of Exorcism and Guardians Interposing the Supernatural."

Josh leaned over her shoulder, "Are you serious? I thought you people were a special branch of the CIA, not some kind of MIB ghostbusters."

Decker yanked the card back, "We are an intelligence agency, and we do lots more than deal with ghosts, Mr. Dyer. Now, gather your things. The Dyer Foundation jet just touched down at Tulsa International."

Edinburgh, Scotland – Tuesday, November 6th, 2018 – 7:31 a.m. BST

They found themselves flying under the assumed names of David Driscoll and Ann Darrow. It wasn't until a TSA Agent remarked that she must have been named after the character in *King Kong* that she got Patrick's not-so-subtle attempt at humor. The pair landed in Edinburgh Airport on a cold November morning. It was 45 degrees with light snow on the ground when they touched down.

As they rode in a cab towards their hotel, Amanda asked, "Does this place bring back good memories?"

Josh flashed a charming smile, "Oh, yes. I spent many years here in Scotland, studying alongside Ian and the others. Those were some of the best days of my life."

She rested her head on the back seat and asked, "This Line of Merlin, how does it work? Are all of you druids?"

Josh mimicked her relaxed posture and gazed into her eyes, "The green path of the druid is the beginning for all initiates in the Line of Merlin, but not everyone finishes. At the time, the Druidic route was a passion of mine, and I had no interest in becoming a Knight. Traveling the world and speaking with mystics of other faiths was all I wanted to do."

Amanda's interest was piqued, "Knights? Like, as in official Sirs and Dames knighted by the Queen?"

Josh gave her a playful smirk, "Well, not exactly. They have more esoteric beliefs when it comes to the royal chain of succession. The Line of

Merlin holds that King Arthur never actually died. They believe his soul lives on in the body of a Raven on the island of Avalon. His body is held in stasis until it can fully heal from his fight with Mordred at the Battle of Camlann. The Line has vowed to serve the once and future king first."

Amanda displayed a devilish smile, "Oh, well, I hope Queen Elizabeth doesn't hear of this. I think she fancies Buckingham Palace."

Dyer gave a chuckle, "Well, according to my teacher, someone had to rule while Arthur heals on the Isle of Avalon. You see, the Line of Merlin believes in the prophecy that King Arthur will return at a time when he is needed most. Until then, Morgan le Fay watches over him."

She furrowed her eyebrows, "Morgan le Fay was at odds with King Arthur."

He tilted his head, "Bad poetry, my dear Mandie. The Line of Merlin observes a different narrative. One that has been passed down among its members since the time of the Camelot. Some of the current members of the Line of Merlin are said to be descendants of the Knights of the Round Table. As ridiculous as it sounds, there is some precedent to the claim."

Amanda shut her sleepy eyes, "You've had quite a life, Josh Dyer. All that adventure tells me why you never chose to settle down, but why didn't you bring someone with you? You could have still married."

He tilted his hat over his eyes, "We had better get some sleep where we can. Finding Ian will be another adventure, I'm sure."

He dodged her question, but Amanda decided not to press. Watching the green pasture land pass by, she was suddenly hit with how limited her life experiences had been. She loved being a mother, but the marriage was something that had been expected of her. An ache of melancholy hit her stomach, and she thought about the dreams she and Josh had come up with in college. A herd of brownish-red Highland cattle passed by her window and reminded her of the compromises she had made to appease her faith. The cattle stood motionless, as the freezing rain drizzled down on their long wavy coats. They almost seemed defiant, as their hooves dug into the mud and the rain dripped from their horns. Amanda thought about how she was much the same, weathering the storm of her husband's death and abduction of her daughters. She stood in cold mud and manure, doing her best to preserve her dignity.

She touched the glass, *Unless the Van Helsing's can find my kids or I can get a new vision from Cernunnos, the Brotherhood will kill my children and me. I'm waiting out in the freezing rain for my turn to be led to slaughter.*

The thought shook her awake, "Tell me more about Ian MacLean. What can I expect?"

Josh sniffed anxiously from under his Australian style hat, "Ian MacLean is a friend who I've learned to love like a brother. He is a loose cannon that never followed the rules despite his heritage. The memorization work, reciting songs, and learning the wide variety of plant and animal life necessary to ascend into the highest levels of the Druidic path was never in his DNA. MacLean was always born to be a Knight first and a druid second. The last I saw him, he was in the champion ranks at the caber toss and the hammer throw in the Stirling Highland Games. He was a mountain of a man who could hold his own in a fight. That's been over a decade ago, and he has declined since those days."

Amanda was determined to get her mind off her depression, "What kind of heritage?"

Josh gave up trying to sleep and took off his hat, "Well, if you can suspend your disbelief, Ian is a direct descendant of Sir Gawain. Because of that birthright, the leadership of the Line of Merlin fell to him. He inherited a bit of a mess, and last I heard he wasn't dealing with it well." He looked uncomfortable as he continued, "To be frank, the Line has seen… nobler days."

She turned to him and probed, "What do you mean?"

He winced and answered, "They're mainly a LARP'ing group now, but their Druidic practice is top-notch."

Her eyes wandered onto the hilly road for a few moments until it hit her, "LARP! Like as in, Live Action Role Play? Are you seriously taking me to see a bunch of overweight manbabies in Styrofoam armor and PVC swords?"

Josh replied meekly, "Yes."

She covered her head with her hand, "You mean to tell me you learned how to be a druid from people who dress up and play-act *Dungeons and Dragons*? You've got to be kidding me! I needed serious help contacting Cernunnos from true scholars in the arcane, not LARP'ers!"

He patted the air, "Calm down, Mandie. They are solid people if a little eccentric. They look at it as playing at war, like a civil war recreation company. You will see, they take the craft seriously."

She turned to the passenger window and felt a headache building.

By Bo Luellen

Stirling, Scotland – Tuesday, November 6th, 2018 – 6:55 p.m. BST

As they walked into the Curly Coo Bar just off the streets of Stirling, a large, older bald man was about to arm wrestle a younger Scotsman in his 20's. The 40-year-old had red cheeks from a mixture of laughter and drink and weighed a hefty 21 and a half stones. His chest and arms were still muscular, but his belly stretched out his Stirling County RFC t-shirt. Nearly twenty patrons in the bar crowded around the two, screaming wagers and drinking Dun Hogs Head. The sounds of laughter echoed off the red-painted walls, as the black-bearded younger challenger threw insults at the senior competitor.

Amanda looked at the corner where three men in their sixties were sitting and ignoring the ruckus. Josh walked in the door and took a spot beside her. She noticed that the oldest man at the table had locked eyes with her. The scruffy faced Scot raised his glass, and nodded at her. She smiled and nodded back. The other men at the table got a broad grin, and one pulled out a chair for her to sit down.

Amanda pointed at the collection of elder Scots and shouted at Josh over the roar of the crowd, "I think I found your friend!"

Josh looked in the direction she pointed and then back at her with a smirk, "Congratulations, Love. You've just picked up four senior citizens at your first Scottish pub." He nudged her to the pair of arm wrestlers, saying, "That, my dear, is the descendant of the Green Knight, Ian MacLean!"

His finger pointed at the overweight, older arm wrestler, as she sighed, "Oh, my."

Ian and the younger man clasped hands, and the contest began. The pub exploded with excitement as the crowd chanted 'MacLean!... MacLean!... MacLean!" With a great bellow, Ian pulled the younger man's arm over and won the contest. He stood up, red-faced and proud, as the younger man held his bicep. The big man's face went beet red and seemed to glow. As he reached for his mug of beer, Ian swayed left and then right. With a great crash, the massive Scot slammed chest first onto the end of the round table. Pints of beer went flying as he rolled off the end and onto the floor. The room went silent as his body lay still, and everyone froze. Josh took a step forward in concern just as a loud snore rumbled out from under Ian's beer-soaked mouth. The patrons resounded to another cheer that Ian was still alive, and a few of the more stout drinkers helped Ian into his chair.

Amanda threw up her hands, "That's the leader of the Line of Merlin?"

Josh shrugged and gave a boyish grin, "He's seen… nobler days."

Her headache pounded, "Great. Now what?"

Josh pulled out some pounds and said, "We wait for him to wake up. In the meantime, let's get a pint, and you can entertain your new admirers."

She looked over at the table full of older Scots as the eldest gave her a wink.

Stirling, Scotland – Wednesday, November 7th, 2018 – 10:25 a.m. BST

Josh told his assistant, "Love, I wanted something low key."

Linda Jenkins's high pitched voice blasted out over his cell's speakerphone, "Don't give me that 'Love' shit! Do you know how many ill-mannered Scots I had to flirt with just to get you any room in Stirling?"

He rubbed his forehead, "No. Look, I just wish you would have got us something less… highbrow."

She seemed to raise an octave, "You're lucky I could get you anything at all. Tell me, have you ever heard of the Stirling Gin Festival?"

He sat down on the edge of the bed next to Amanda, as Ian vomited another volley in the bathroom, "No."

She blasted, "Well, until today, I was blissfully unaware. It seems the Scots take a break from drinking to travel to Stirling to drink together. The Friars Wynd Hotel might not be your ideal local, but it's the only Goddamn place that I could find! For the record, lying to the board of directors as to why you needed our company jet to pony you and your new girlfriend around the globe isn't in my job description. I want a thank you and a raise!"

He closed his tired eyes, "Thank you and consider it done. We'll discuss the particulars later. Now promise me you'll find a way to keep that jet in Edinburgh until I'm ready to leave."

Linda scoffed, "I promise you two things, jack and shit! I'm telling Jin Fakudas what's going on."

He nodded, "Good. Jin can help convince the board everything is on the level if they start asking any questions."

Right before she disconnected the call, Linda screeched, "You egotistical Indiana Jones wanna-be. I'm not telling him so he can help you lie! I'm telling him so I can cover my ass. There had better be some serious zeros on my next check, Mr. Dyer!"

Amanda stirred in some sugar into her coffee and tried to look as if she wasn't mortified by how Josh's assistant treated him. Ian let out another loud roar as he vomited again. It had taken them three hours to get him to the hotel. In the end, they had to pay thirty pounds to two local pub crawlers to carry the Scotsman to their room. Amanda had spent the morning buying new clothes so she and Josh would fit in better with the locals.

Amanda picked up her cup from the table and looked over at the bathroom door. The sounds coming from it had died down in the last ten minutes. Ian had been up for the previous hour, switching between throwing up and defecating. She looked over at Josh, who sat in a pair of blue jeans and hiking boots, with a long look on his face.

Amanda took a sip and then remarked, "Please, don't take me as ungrateful, but ..."

He stood up quickly and replied, "I know!" Josh pounded on the bathroom door and yelled, "Ian! Come on, lad!"

After a few moments, the door opened, and the wet Scot walked out, fresh from a shower. He was wearing the ugly grey sweatpants and shirt Josh had bought for him to replace the soiled clothes from the night before. His face was splotchy, and one of his eyes had burst a blood vessel from the strain of vomiting.

Ian's eyes locked on Josh, and he charged at him with a great smile and a bear hug. Amanda glanced in the vomit and piss covered bathroom floor and nearly puked herself. She pinched her nose at the overwhelming smell of old spice that trailed behind the big man.

Ian's eyes opened wide at Amanda, "Is this th' wifie fae American that ye tellt me aboot oan th' phane?"

Josh put out a hand towards her, "Dr. Amanda Lanyon, may I introduce the First in the Line of Merlin, descendent of Sir Gawain, Ian MacLean."

He gave a slight bow as she smirked, "Charmed, I'm sure."

The man was just under six feet and had a strong presence. His chest and arms were muscular in stark contrast to his midsection. His flaming red beard seemed to shine in the morning light, and beneath puffy eyelids, there appeared to be a pair of twinkling blue eyes.

He put his massive fists on his hips and asked, "Whit's a bonny lassie lik' ye daein' wi' an hackit jimmy lik' this? Surely, he hasn't dragged ye tae Sterlin' 'n' forced ye tae thole his company. Fear nae, hings juist git mair interesting."

She laughed a little, "I caught some of that."

Throughout the next hour, Ian laid on the bed as Amanda and Josh told him their tale. The Scot was silent for most of it, absorbing the story as it came. He downed two cups of coffee as the tale went on. When Amanda got to the part where Thomas Booth had followed her into the woods and did spiritual warfare with a ghost, he stopped her and asked more questions. The large man seemed very interested in the part where she spoke with Cernunnos and the details of his message. She and Josh had decided not to tell Ian about the vampire, at least until they decided if it was needed.

She ended with, "So, you see, I need to get him to speak with me again. If I can find out where my daughters are, I have people in America that can go get them."

Ian rolled to a sitting position and rubbed his bald head, "Cernunnos comes at his ain time. Ye cannae expect him tae respond lik' some dog. It soonds lik' he helped ye whin it suited his purpose. Yi'll waant him tae find yer twa daughters. Cernunnos wants ye tae fin' a purpose. If yi'll waant his hulp, then yi"ll need tae figure oot wha Amanda Lanyon truly is."

Before she could reply, a loud knock on the door startled all three of them. Josh crept up out of his chair and looked out the peephole. Amanda suddenly felt utterly exposed and was reminded that hiding was her only way of defending herself.

Josh looked back towards them and shrugged, "It's some guy in a green kilt with a wine box that says, "Stirling Gin Festival." Probably something to do with the event today. I'll get rid of him."

Amanda almost objected when Josh swung the door open. On the other side was a handsome looking man with graying hair, a white polo shirt, red plaid kilt, and knee-high black socks. The visitor drummed his fingers against the box and looked over the occupants of their room.

The man looked annoyed as he announced, "So, I have a package for Ann Darrow."

Josh shot a glance over to Amanda, "Did you order something?"

Ian looked at them both and asked, "Ah thought ye said yer name wis Amanda?"

The delivery man booted the door open with the side of his foot and marched past Josh, "Awesome! In less than five seconds, with me using only a cardboard box, you two geniuses blew the cover AEGIS spent thousands of dollars creating for you. I think that is a record."

Amanda shot up, saying, "You're Roger Quinlynn, I'm assuming."

He dropped the heavy box on a desk, scattering pens and a lamp across the floor, "Yes, you would be assuming because I've yet to show you my identification. Let me also thank you for blowing my cover as well. How about you open a window and start yelling for a new English occupation. We might have better odds against the Scots than the Brotherhood."

Ian stood up and bellowed, "Calm doon! He's in a wee snit, isnae he?"

Josh held a hand in the air and asked, "Okay, may we see your identification?"

Quinlynn pulled open his sporran and produced a tan business card. The edges were worn, and the paper seemed old and moist. Josh handed the card to Amanda, who noticed it was identical to the one Patrick had shown her.

She looked up, "It's the same card. This must be Quinlynn."

The agent rolled his eyes, "Brilliant deduction! What gave it away? My obvious and proper use of the English language. Oh, and maybe you could say my name a little louder. I'm sure there is someone in this backwater village that didn't hear you!"

Ian stood up, stuck out his chest, and challenged, "Be canny laddie, that's Scootlund ye'r talking aboot!"

Amanda let out a gasp, as Quinlynn pulled off his kilt to reveal his naked ass and genitalia, "Easy, Big Mac. Next time I want something from you, I'll ring England to get permission."

Josh jumped in front of the advancing Scot as the large man yelled, "Urr ye keekin fur a rammy?!"

Amanda turned away from Quinlynn, "Why are you naked?!"

The agent ripped open the box, and took out a set of brown slacks along with a green plaid shirt, "I'm naked because I have to keep you morons in eyesight. I have to change into something different than what I came up here wearing. It's called spy craft."

The room was silent as he put a Glock 9 mm in a holster inside his right boot, a serrated knife in the other boot, a blackjack in his pocket, and a light Kevlar vest under his shirt. He took his old clothes and shoved them into the trash can. He pasted on a fake handlebar mustache and then handed out black Fitbits to Amanda and Josh.

Quinlynn held up his cell phone and ordered them, "Put those on and never take them off. I can track you from any location via satellite. I didn't bring an extra one for biggen, so if he gets lost, I'll check the closest buffet line."

Ian launched at the Agent, swinging his massive fists and growling. Josh put his shoulder into his friend's chest and promised oatcakes and scotch broth to get him to calm down. The four of them found their way to the downstairs dining room so Josh could make good on his promise. On the table was a feast consisting of a Stornoway black pudding, haggis, Lorne sausage, bacon, tattie scone, tomato, and beans. Ian was eyeing Quinlynn disdainfully as he chewed on buttered artisan toast.

Amanda looked ragged from the nearly sleepless night, "Ian, you said Cernunnos wants me to find my purpose, and then he might answer me. How do I do that?"

MacLean slowly turned his head away from Quinlynn, then replied, "Th' speirins o' whit's happening in Oklahoma haes reached a' ower. Ah dinnae think it it's ony coincidence that Josh haes returned wi' ye. Yer purpose kin be wasted, destiny kin be denied, bit a quest is a holy thing."

Josh squirmed nervously in his chair, "A quest? Ian, what are you suggesting?"

The big man opened his hands, "Let's grab th' lads 'n' set aff fur Cullerlie. It's a four day donder tae th' cairne. If Cernunnos haes some something tae say, then he wull say it. If he doesn't, then we come back 'ere 'n' hae a pint."

Amanda looked over at Josh, "What's a Cullerlie?"

The blond-haired man lifted his coffee cup and replied, "The Standing Stones of Echt, and for the most part a tourist attraction. When I studied with the Druids, these stones were a secret power source that is on a layline. To the public, they are the site of a ceremonial cremation. Inside the stone rings, oak and hazel were burned with bodies to leave only charcoal and cremated human bones behind. To those of the Line of Merlin, it is a place of special power and insight, more powerful than Stonehenge. If Cernunnos has put us on this path, and this is a quest, then I agree with Ian, it's a good place to start."

Amanda looked up at a TV that was playing in the bar and tuned out the discussion at the table. The BBC news channel was silent, but the ticker banner at the bottom read, "Experts Say the Cthulhu Cult May Be Larger Than Initially Suspected. Oklahoma Governor Katherine Hill Challenged by Write-In Candidate Greyson Dunn."

She interrupted the conversation as she stared at the TV, "I've listened to the public call me a hero and a villain. Some say it was my ego that killed my husband. That I didn't wait for the cops at the Preserve because I was too hungry for fame. My mother-in-law says I don't deserve my kids because I put them in harm's way. Maybe they're right, and I might be just another monster like the Crimson Brotherhood." Josh grabbed her hand and went to interject, but Amanda continued, "My faith has been challenged, and I'm desperately seeking a false god for answers. I've crossed an ocean in the hopes of speaking to a pagan deity, so I guess I'm not done being a hypocrite. If being a monster is what it's going to take to kill a monster and get my kids back, I'm willing. So, Ian, what's the first step on this quest?"

Ian gave a nod of respect, "Weel said, lassie. Ah think hiking tae th' Cullerlie Stanes wid be a guid wey tae connect ye tae th' hielands. It wull shaw Cernunnos respect 'n' micht prepare ye fur annur vision."

She looked him in the eye and replied, "I'm ready."

The Scot bellowed, "Then we quest! a'm wi' ye Amanda Lanyon!"

Quinlynn threw his hands up, "She's Ann Darrow, you lump! Do I need to make name tags?"

Josh ignored the agent and nodded, "I agree with Ian. I think hiking is a good way of showing respect to the old ways. Besides, we need to get off the grid in case the Brotherhood tracks us down. An eight-day round-trip trek to the Stones would do the trick."

Quinlynn poured some scotch into his coffee and corrected, "No one is going to find us, and stop using "off the grid." Do you even know what it takes to get someone "off the grid?""

Josh looked weathered by his attitude, "The majority of my fortune and talents are in telecommunications. I had my people mask our cell phones and give us new phone numbers. I'm using a sat phone that is being monitored and scrambled by my IT department. My staff has issued all my travel arrangements from a dummy account."

Quinlynn ignored his spiked coffee, and swallowed from his flask of whiskey, "Nerd."

Stirling Castle, Scotland – Wednesday, November 7th, 2018 – 12:01 p.m. CST

The sun was shining, but that did little to cut away the cold. Above them was Stirling Castle, sitting atop Castle Hill. Amanda's small group of would-be questers sat at the bottom of the steep cliffs under the magnificent fortification. The grey stones of the castle looked down on her and gave a sense of meaning.

Josh stood beside her and said, "These walls have been a guardian for Scotland and protected the farthest downstream crossing of the River Forth. It was one of the most important structures in Scotland's history. It seems only right to begin here."

They sat in a field on the west side between the castle and Raploch Road and waited. Amanda watched the traffic buzz by as she sat on the new backpack she had purchased for the trip. Quinlynn had insisted on them leaving their cell phones at the hotel and walk to the castle to avoid any cab records.

Quinlynn Roger leaned on a cane impatiently as he immersed himself in his disguise. The agent had on a grey suit, a false white beard, a bonnet, and a leather backpack. He flipped an umbrella upon his shoulder and patted his padded belly that made him look three stones heavier. She had to admit it was a good disguise, but it seemed to remind her a little too much of Henry Jones from *Indiana Jones and the Last Crusade*.

Josh stood up and pointed towards the road, "There they are."

Walking across the green field were their two remaining party members. Ian was moving like a man half his age and size, and beaming a grin despite the cold. The Scot jammed a walking stick into the ground with each thunderous step. His bald head was covered by a Scottish cap, and his bright red beard matched his kilt.

His companion was a slight man in his fifties who glided along the freezing grass with quick steps. He sported a full brown beard and black-rimmed glasses. Amanda had a hard time understanding the thick Scottish accent, but the two seemed to gibber away as they approached.

The pair gasped for air when they arrived, and Josh gave the stranger a hug, "Peyton Greum, as I live and breathe! How the hell are you?"

The scruffy-looking Scot replied, "A've bin guid, Josh. Tis bin mony years."

Josh turned to Amanda with his arm around Peyton, "This is Peyton

Greum, a full Druid in the Line of Merlin and one of my mentors when I was coming up."

Ian nudged Peyton and pointed at Roger, "That's Roger Quinlynn, th' yankee secret agent ah tellt ye aboot back in toun."

Quinlynn pulled out his fake belly stuffing and threw it on the ground as he yelled: "God damnit!"

On the B977 Road towards the Cullerlie Stone Circle, Scotland – Sunday, November 11th, 2018 – 8:41 p.m. BST

It had been a chilly four day march along the back roads of the Scottish Highlands that Amanda hadn't been mentally prepared for. Physically, she was in the shape of her life, but she quickly learned what being cold and wet can do to your resolve. To her surprise, Quinlynn proved to be a valued member of the team and kept them moving and well-fed.

The company camped just outside of cities to avoid being seen and to help appease Cernunnos by observing the old ways. During the trip, Ian would occasionally pull out his bagpipes and play. To Amanda's amazement, it actually helped her pick up her pace and made the group a little more energized. Not everyone was a fan, though. During day three, Ian was piping "The Green Hills of Tyrol" when Quinlynn pulled out his knife and threatened to stab Scot's bagpipe bladder.

Tonight, the group had made camp three hundred yards from the road while a storm brewed overhead. The five sat around a crackling fire that Roger built out of dried sticks and twigs that he collected along the way. She found joy in looking forward to the warmth of the flames and sharing a meal with her companions. Thankfully, Josh had packed a large canopy that they could take shelter under. As lightning flashed in the night sky, she turned her hotdog over in the flames and heard the tapping of the first few drops of rain on the overhead canvas. The sounds were soothing, and everyone seemed relaxed. Even Ian had finally made peace with Quinlynn after the pair had made their way through half a bottle of one of the Scot's elderberry wines. It didn't take long before the pair ran out of songs to sing, and they had retired to their respective tents.

The bushy-bearded Peyton sat quietly, as he had been for most of the journey. She found him to be an observer and somewhat of an introvert. Of the four on the trip with her, he was the one she had spoken with the least.

Josh had turned in early for bed after smoking a generous amount of weed. She didn't feel like she could get high enough or drunk enough to find a way to relax. She felt a deep sense of guilt and anxiety over her children's captivity. Nothing was going to make her rest easy until they were back with her.

Peyton handed her a hotdog bun, "Th'morra ye git tae ask Cernunnos yer quaistion. Ian tellt me yer wee daughters hae bin kidnapped. Ye'r aff tae ask th' Green Man whaur they're bein' held?"

Amanda looked over at the furry face of the druid, grateful for the distraction, "It sounds ridiculous, doesn't it? Flying all the way to Scotland to ask some mythical pagan god for the address of a kidnapper."

Shaking his head, Peyton replied, "Lassie, fur someone wha is asking Cernunnos fur a favor, ye hae an odd wey o' gaun aboot it."

Lanyon put her hotdog together and asked, "Let me guess, I should sacrifice a sheep, plant a tree, or dance in a circle naked? This god creature you call Cernunnos came to me while I was high on DMT and showed me a revelation. Since then, I've received no further enlightenment. I'd say I've done enough pagan rituals to get his attention."

Another crash of lightning thundered overhead as the rain hit harder on the green canopy. Amanda took a bite of her hot dog and felt the numbness of the rhythmic sounds pulse in her brain. Out on the Highlands, the flashes lit up the hills and created a strobing effect all around.

Over the downpour, the druid observed, "Mibbie if ye cam at Cernunnos wi' respect 'n' humility..."

A loud crack rang out, and Peyton's blood splattered over her face. Amanda dropped her food and stumbled out of her chair. She felt the warmth of the hot liquid on her cheeks, as Peyton tilted back and fell to the damp ground with a heavy thud. The campfire light illuminated a single gaping hole in the side of his head, just above the temple. His eyes were open and staring at the raindrops, as water dripped into the unblinking sockets. The man's right leg spasmed to the song of thunder in the night. In the flickering light of the tempest, she saw the silhouette of three people running towards her from the road. Amanda suddenly let out a scream.

Quinlynn whipped open the brown tent flap and looked down at the deceased Peyton. Another sharp crack let out over the Highlands, as the canopy pole next to the agent's greying head sparked from a ricocheting bullet. The man's training took over and stifled the drink. He pitched forward into a roll and came up next to Amanda. He grabbed the right foot of Peyton and pulled the body across the wet ground. With a firm grip, he grabbed her neck and pulled her down behind the dead body for cover. He yelled something, but the shock she was in wouldn't let the words in.

She felt a sharp pain in her face as Quinlynn yelled, "Listen to me! I want you to run towards the tree line, and keep running!" The agent pulled out his Glock and fired a few rounds, "I can track you on that Fitbit! Find a place to hide and stay out of sight! I'll hold them off and give you time! Go! Now!"

She tried to move, but her limbs wouldn't respond. After squeezing off a few more rounds, Roger picked her up by her jacket and pushed her out of camp towards the trees. The rain was slamming into her as she saw Quinlynn take two rounds into his back.

He dropped to the ground and yelled at her, "Go!"

Quinlynn rolled to his stomach and let loose with the rest of his magazine. In the night, she heard someone scream out in pain. She stumbled backward, as the campsite became alive with bullets. The tops of their tents shredded into fragmented pieces as the hills echoed with a mixture of thunder and automatic gunfire. She turned and ran blindly into the dark. Her heart pounded in her chest, as Amanda struggled to get further away from the campsite. Her pace slowed, and she found herself in the pitch black. The rain and overcast blacked out the moon and stars, leaving her alone, terrified, and blind. In seconds she was reduced to a slow walk with her hands probing out in front of her. The pops of gunshots still rang out behind her, and the faint sounds of a man screaming sent a panic attack into her chest. Amanda hyperventilated as she wailed in tears. Moving like a mummy fresh from its crypt, she shuffled forward in a petrified state. A single stroke of lightning brought a clap of thunder so loud, she thought she was shot. A stream of warm urine trickled down her leg as her mind began to collapse upon itself.

Suddenly, the feel of something rough brushed against her fingers. Instinctively, Amanda withdrew her arm, and she held herself, too afraid to move. Another slash of lightning cut through the sky and revealed the mystery object was a tree. She hugged the large oak like a long lost friend. Another bolt revealed she had reached the forest edge, and she worked her way into the woods.

After a few minutes, she physically gave out from the stress and grabbed hold of a Scots Pine for support. Amanda rested her head on its wet bark and tried to muster the strength to steady her mind. Her vision blurred as an explosion erupted part of a tree next to her. Green-yellow shards of wood splayed outward, and the center of the Birch was on fire from the blast. She was knocked sideways onto the wet ground, and her ears were ringing. Amanda looked around but saw only the jet blackness of the night. She looked down at the cracked and useless Fitbit that had been damaged in the fall.

She ducked behind the trunk of the mighty oak and did her best to think clearly, *Whoever is shooting at me has some kind of night vision. I've got to keep moving.*

Amanda crawled on her hands and knees for a few dozen yards, thankful the rain was masking her sounds. She stopped for a few seconds, listened to see if anyone was behind her, and then stood up and walked as fast as she could manage. Moving from tree to tree, and waiting for the brief illumination that the storm brought, she willed herself onward.

Hours passed as she forced herself to stay in motion despite the chill. Her clothes were soaked completely. Amanda's denim jeans had caused so much chafing that her inner thighs and her heels were bleeding. She had no idea where she was or how to reach a road.

Weary and near exhaustion, she came across a downed tree that had a thick trunk. Amanda huddled under the rotting oak for some degree of shelter from the rain. She gathered up her legs in her arms and stayed there for what seemed like an eternity. Despite the pain from the cold, Amanda couldn't help but nod off several times from sheer exhaustion. She startled awake as the bullet cracked the branch above her head. She launched out into the night while the thunder clapped in the sky, and the freezing rain danced to the tune of gunfire.

By Bo Luellen

Chapter 9: Richard VII

Tulsa, Oklahoma – Friday, November 9th, 2018 – 7:01 p.m. CST

Richard Enfield watched from the control booth as Brother Greyson Dunn gave his first appearance on the Eastland Worship Hour since being elected Governor of Oklahoma. It was the first time in history that Oklahoma's Governor had been decided by a write-in vote. The numbers had been a landslide, and the polls closed at 73% for Dunn.

The Governor-Elect stood at the dais and gave his acceptance speech, "We give praise to Jesus for this blessing to Oklahoma. Without Him, nothing would be possible. With His grace, Christians in the state stood up to both the minions of Cthulhu and the politicians who stood in our way. A new day is shining on the Christian State of Oklahoma, and God has been put in the driver's seat. He is in control, and his flock is ready."

Applause and cheers came from the packed auditorium as the broadcast went out to homes and churches around the world. Brother Dunn had done the impossible and defeated both the Republican and Democratic political parties on a strictly religious platform. It had sent shockwaves all the way to Washington, as the hottest discussion topic on every news broadcast had been the implications of the upset.

Dunn held up a hand to the sky, "Praise His name. Only one day after the election, the Tulsa Christian Crusaders were flooded with applications for membership. Eastland College has become a spiritual beacon for Christian pilgrims to visit and offer service to the Crusaders. Roses, crosses, and donations have been left on the front steps of our humble institution, with letters praising our work to secure the safety of the Sooner State. I'm overwhelmed with joy to announce to you, my dear brothers and sisters, that the National Rifle Association has declared their organization to be a Christian only membership. They have placed their trust in my leadership and voted me the President of the NRA. They have offered their services in arming and providing training to the over 100,000 Christians who have joined the Crusader ranks."

Thunderous applause burst out from the assembled crowd that occupied the college football stadium. "My fellow Christians, I won't be alone in this struggle. I'll have all of you on my side. I'll have God on my side, and one more man that you all know. I would like you to welcome the leader of The Tulsa Christian Crusaders and your next Lieutenant Governor, Brother Richard Enfield!"

The crowd roared in approval, as Richard triumphantly stood up from his chair and emerged from behind the stage curtains. The adoring congregation chanted his name as he gave Brother Greyson a hug and then stepped up to the podium. He adjusted his tie and gave a wink to his wife Teri, who was sober enough to blow him a kiss to him from the audience. Beside her were his two sons, Alfred and Chad, sitting stoically in their little suits. On the other side of his boys was Rose Cook, who was practiced in not giving away their secret relationship.

Once the cheers died down, he announced, "The people have spoken, and they have said, 'No more!'"

After another round of applause swallowed up the stadium, "I'm so grateful to Brother Greyson's belief in me and humbled by God's mercy. He has turned me from a man of sin and fear into an instrument of purpose. It is that purpose which I will dedicate myself to. Governor Dunn and I have a great deal of planning to do before we take office on January 14th. Our goal is to initiate radical and immediate change, starting on day one. Until then, we maintain the safety of the people of Oklahoma despite the limitations imposed on us by the bureaucracy of the current Governor. People from all over the Mid-South have rallied to our side and pledged to help us. Because of that, I'm instituting a call to arms and expanding the reach of the Crusaders to include Texas, Arkansas, Missouri, and Kansas. Because of this, Eastland is renaming our protectors."

From behind Richard, the curtain fell away, revealing a large banner that read, "The United Christian Crusaders."

Cheers burst out and continued for several minutes, "For each church in those states that chooses to join the UCC, we will send supplies, equipment, money, and weapons to aid them in their efforts. For the first time, different Evangelical faiths will put aside their differences and come together as one peacekeeping initiative with one goal in mind, putting God first."

People were crying with spiritual joy all around at the news. "These branches will coordinate with Eastland's headquarters, and a larger military-style ranking structure will be initiated. A UCC General will be named for each state, and he or she will be responsible for maintaining multiple points of defense against the Crimson Brotherhood. Now, it would be impossible for me to continue performing the duties of General for Oklahoma while operating as the Lieutenant Governor. So, tonight I will be announcing Oklahoma's new General."

Excited murmurs and banter came from the assembly, "A few short days ago, former Tulsa Police Detective John Utterson went public regarding the corruption in our political offices. He outlined how the Christian Crusaders were actively investigated by local and federal offices in an attempt to douse the flames of our Christian faith. As a whistleblower, he uncovered the corruption present in our governing bodies. He proved that Governor Hill, Chief of Police Kelly and the FBI were acting against the will of the Christian people of Oklahoma. For this, Kelly was fired, and an investigation into alleged and unsubstantiated corruption and substance abuse was brought against Brother Utterson. This was clear retaliation and an attempt to smear that hero's good name. The truth be told, John Utterson was the only voice in the halls of our police department that saw the wisdom of joining forces with the Crusaders. It was because of the politicians that Henry Jekyll was able to escape, and Oklahoma suffered the deaths of dozens of police officers, nurses, and civilians. Our Crusaders arrived too late, and that falls on the head of the leadership of this town.

Because of his noble actions, Brother John lost his badge and his gun, but not his dignity. Oh, Brothers and Sisters, no! His actions only heated the coals that will burn those who decided to act out against a good man. Former Detective John Utterson, will you join me on stage?"

From the wings, John was wheelchaired out next to Richard. He wore a new brown suit, and his graying beard and hair were now jet black. He had a smile on his face as he shook the hand of Enfield. With some considerable effort, the man stood out of his chair. He gave a big hug to the Lieutenant Governor-elect.

As the crowd applauded, John Utterson used his cane to climb the steps of the stage, "Brothers and Sisters, I give you the new leader of the UCC, General John Utterson!"

Over the next hour, message boards and social media blew up with discussions over the new appointment. Daniel Harris had a challenge getting Richard out of the stadium's parking lot and back to his estate. Throngs of Christians lined the streets, blocking the way and holding up signs that read, "God is in Control" and "Dunn for President."

The ghost of Samuel Howard manifested in the seat next to him and

Richard thought, *What did you find out?*

The white-haired spirit replied, "John Utterson is a dirty cop through and through. I was in his head for only a few minutes and saw enough blackmail material to keep him in line for a lifetime. He's a drug addict, alcoholic, and has affiliations with criminals."

Richard grinned, "Excellent."

The ghost rubbed his snow colored beard, "My boy, we have a more pressing matter to discuss."

He turned to his old mentor, *What matter?*

Samuel had a quiver to his voice, "Cthulhu calls to me. He commands I take you to the Dreamlands."

Richard looked astonished, "He spoke to you? Directly? Why would he address my underling instead of me? I'm ushering in his awakening!"

The ghost wrung his hands together, "Must we go over this again? You are indeed a powerful leader in his cult, but you are not his Herald. Besides, communicating with the Great Dreamer is unsettling."

Richard's curiosity outweighed the insult, "What is it like when he talks to you?"

Samuel let out a long sigh, "He doesn't speak to me in what you would see as words. It is like a powerful pull to action that makes your very soul feel thin. The only way to keep your sanity is to do as he commands."

He felt the anxiety pouring off his old mentor and enjoyed seeing him in distress. "Go on."

The ghost began to tremble, "I'm his servant, and the Old One compels me to act. I will fly ahead and prepare the necessary spell work. Once you are home, bathe yourself in sea salt and burn charcoal as you do. Once you are done, come to the ritual chamber under the garage. Everything will be ready."

Richard wasn't used to being commanded like this, "Wait! What is the Dreamland? What am I being summoned for?"

The spirit gave him a sympathetic look. "The Dreamland is an alternate reality to our own world. A place where magic and madness reign. Mythical beasts and legends intersect in this realm. I don't know why you are being called, but you dare not refuse the command. Take this seriously, my boy, and we just might survive the journey."

Samuel disappeared from the car seat, and Richard felt a shiver of fear run through him. Being the leader of the Tulsa Crimson Brotherhood Sect came with many perks. Still, he never contemplated he would gain an audience with the Great Dreamer. The car hit a bump as they turned into his estate, waking him from the impending spiritual journey.

An hour later, he finished the ritual bath and put on his robe. Standing in front of the mirror, he saw the greatness of his own face. Squinting his eyes, he tightened the cotton belt and marched out.

His maid, Emilia Nores, greeted him with slippers, "Senior Enfield, your guest Shoshannah has arrived. Shall I show her into the study?"

He was frustrated at the timing of his servant, "Tell her to enjoy the estate for now and offer her anything that makes her comfortable. Assure her I will see her as soon as I'm out of my next meeting."

The short Hispanic maid replied, "Si, Senior Enfield."

As the woman waddled out of the room, Richard looked out the window and saw the ghost of the maid's husband. He was walking the grounds outside, his restless spirit still bound by Samuel's spells to forever guard the estate from spiritual intruders. The ghost looked weary and shuffled along in the tattered clothes he had been wearing the night he had been sacrificed to Cthulhu.

Richard traveled downstairs, and out the side door that faced the garage entrance to the ritual room. The cold November air whipped up the robe and sent a chill through his bones. He cursed to himself as he crunched through the day-old snow on the ground.

He squinted his eyes at the freezing wind, *Bathing I can see, but why am I to arrive in such a state?*

Richard slammed the garage door behind him and rubbed his hands together for warmth, as Daniel gave a curious, "Let me guess, auditioning for the Polar Bear club?"

His nostrils flared, "That mouth of yours is going to get you killed one day."

He continued waxing the car, "Calm down Rich. I'm already legally dead, remember?"

Richard grabbed the rungs of the ladder that led downward, "Call me that once more and you'll wish death was an option."

His driver went silent as he descended into the secret chamber. As his bare feet touched the marble floor, he turned to see the fully manifested Samuel sitting cross-legged in the center of the room. Over a hundred black candles were lit and dotting the floor in an odd pattern. The body of a man lay nude in the corner of the room, with a red-handled Athame dagger sticking out of his chest. The man's blood had been used to paint a crimson line connecting the candles. Samuel motioned for him to join him, and he carefully inched his way between the blood.

As he went to sit down on the marble floor, Samuel warned, "Take your robe off. You must be nude and barren of any pretenses. Come as honestly as you can, lest Cthulhu strips you of your reason."

He took off the robe and threw it onto the Samuel's old oak desk. Looking back, he noticed the design of the candles were in the shape of the symbol of the Crimson Brotherhood. The great tentacle head of an elephant-like squid stared up at him with twinkling lights and drying blood.

Samuel commanded, "Sit, as I am."

Richard lowered himself down in front of the ghost and crossed his legs in the same fashion. In front of him was a bronze cup full of a dark liquid he suspected was from the corpse. Samuel levitated up from the floor a few inches, as a wind came from nowhere and flickered some of the candles. The spirit was as solid as Richard had ever seen him, as the power of Cthulhu caused his old mentor's eyes to glow blue.

Samuel droned, "Cthulhu commands you to the Dreamland. Mortals can only travel there in their sleep. Drink from this cup and slumber."

Richard hesitated, wanting to ask a question, but decided against it. He put his right hand on the ceremonial goblet and picked it up. The metal was warm with the contents of the recent kill. To his surprise, the scent of elderberries and honey wafted into his nose from the liquid. It compelled him with thirst, and an invitation to drink. Wrapping both hands around the etched cup, he poured the thick fluid into his mouth. He nearly gagged as he greedily gobbled up every drop and found himself longing for more. He slammed it down and gasped for air. The edges of the cup stamped a red grin on his face. Caught in the ecstasy of the potion, his tongue snaked out and licked the crimson from his lips.

Samuel's bright blue eyes flamed, as he started to repeatedly chant, "C'hafh throdog Cthulhu l' fhtagn shugnahh ahagl Nyarlathotep ahuh'eog!"

It took Richard a minute to make out the translation, *Guide us great Cthulhu to the Dreamlands where Nyarlathotep rules.*

The sound of the ghostly alien words penetrated his mind and soaked into every narrow of his consciousness. He never felt the drink take hold and sleep overcame him. His head bobbed once, and in an instant, he woke back up into a dark version of the ritual room. The ceiling to the underground chamber was ripped away to reveal a purple sky with rolling black clouds. The remaining pieces of the underground study now looked ancient and unkempt. The bookshelves were coated with thick cobwebs and dust. The candles were puddles of wax, seemingly burned away long ago. The edges of the ceiling had icicles that pointed upwards and a ladder ran along the eastern wall. Dots in the sky were silhouetted against the lavender heavens. Some of the specks were close enough for him to make out the winged serpents. One flew only a few dozen yards overhead and let out a hiss that sounded like a shrieking violin.

He looked back down and saw a living Samuel sitting in front of him. He was no longer a ghost, but flesh and blood. His mentor was finishing his incantations before coming out of his trance. The elderly Howard had no clothes on, and his lean body was covered in Egyptian Hieroglyphic tattoos. The black ink went from his neck, down to his ankles. He had never seen this language before, except in history books.

Richard stirred and rose to his feet, "This is the Dreamland? It looks like earth, but not."

His mentor got up and joined him, "The Dreamland is a mirror dimension to our own. It is influenced by the dreams and nightmares of the living. It's a place gods and immortals use to cross over into other planes of existence. Some are bound here, others are simply passing through."

Richard started to step towards the ice-covered ladder that led up, when Samuel grabbed his arm with a firm hand, "Do not cross outside of this circle. Mortals that find their way here become subject to dangers and wonders of this realm."

He jerked his arm free, "Do not think you can command me!"

Samuel moved in front of him, "This is no time for your arrogance! We were invited here. Like any good guest, we wait until we are collected."

From the direction of the ladder came a feminine voice, "I would listen to your wise counsel." Richard shot his head around to see a slender woman dressed in a golden robe, "Em Hotep, Master Enfield. Em Hotep, Djedi. Lord Cthulhu has granted me an audience with his servants. So I bid you welcome."

On her head was a tiara with a golden symbol of Anubis in its center. Her skin was smooth and bronze, with only her neck and face exposed.

Charcoal lines went from the corner of her eye to her temple in a bold, sweeping line. The smell of cedar and cinnamon emanated from her as she walked towards them. As she stepped, the tiny gold links in her mantle chimed together, matching the slow and seductive sway of her hips. Richard found the jingling hypnotic and alluring.

She stopped short of crossing the protective circle, "I'm Princess Ankh-es-en-amon, daughter of Pharaoh Amenophis the Magnificent, and betrothed to Lord Imhotep."

The purple light from above illuminated her face, and Richard noticed a striking similarity to the woman from the Preserve, *Samuel, do you see it? She looks almost exactly like Amanda Lanyon!*

His mentor didn't respond to his mental telepathy. Richard noticed there were slight differences. The eyes were a little different, and the mouth had a slight upturn, like that of a cat. He was shocked to see the rest of her was an exact duplicate.

The chiseled features of a man's face appeared in on the golden clad woman's robes, "My love, the faithful priest of Osiris, Imhotep sends you his blessings. He gives thanks to the great Cthulhu for this audience."

Richard suddenly realized his nakedness and covered himself, "H-h-how can we help you, your highness."

Samuel squinted his eyes in embarrassment and interjected in a mixture of ancient Egyptian and English, "Nesew. Em heset net Osiris. We are honored to be in your presence. Dua Netjer en ek!"

Ankh-es-en-amon granted the slightest of nods to Samuel, "The Sleeper of R'lyeh, the great Cthulhu, will soon lay waste to the earth when he awakes. All the creatures that reside in Cthulhu's home will spill out onto the earth, and shall rejoice. A new era of prosperity will dawn from his footsteps. In the wake of Cthulhu's apocalypse, he will grant my love Imhotep dominion over a part of the earth, to rule for all time."

Richard felt the pit of his stomach gurgle, and his skin started to sweat. He instinctively wiped his forehead and felt his extremities begin to chill. To him, it felt the same as the beginnings of the flu.

Samuel regarded his former protégé, "The potion is wearing off. Princess Ankh-es-en-amon, we don't have much time. What do you have to tell us?"

She spoke faster, but with no loss of composure, "The cycle of history has a rhythm of life and death. In your faith through Cthulhu, you called it an Aeon. At the end of each Aeon, the earth is purged, as a new deity takes over from the previous one. The cycle refreshes the roots of the planet in the blood of mortals. However, all prophecies need a specific series of events to come true, or the Aeon cannot cycle. Imhotep was chosen long ago to be the Herald of Cthulhu, and to visit seven plagues upon the nation you call America. Once these prophecies are fulfilled, Cthulhu rises from the Pacific and travels like a hurricane to Israel. He will destroy it and undo the Law of Moses. This will undo the Hebrew God's control of the earth, and Cthulhu will visit an apocalypse upon the world. "

Richard coughed, and blood shot out onto his hand, as Samuel pleaded, "Yes, but what of Master Enfield's role in this?"

She spread her arms wide, causing the image on her robes to change to a stepped pyramid, "My love is imprisoned in Duat by Osiris, while his body rests in a forgotten chamber at the Pyramid of Djoser. As the prophecy states, Anubis will only allow him to return to his body if a chosen follower of Cthulhu completes three challenges. Once my love walks on earth again, Imhotep can awaken the Great Sleeper. That chosen follower is you, Master Enfield."

Richard leaned on his mentor, as Samuel held him up and screamed, "Please, Princess! Make haste, our time here grows to an end!"

Ankh-es-en-amon put her hands at her side and stopped the illusionary image, "The first challenge is to appease Thoth's wife, Seshat. She will only make the location of the Scroll of Thoth known if the chosen of Cthulhu can prove himself a great leader. Once done, then you, Djedi, may divine its location. The second challenge is to appease Sobek, the protector of the scroll. The chosen of Cthulhu must prove himself capable of being wise and resourceful in retrieving the scroll from the clutches of Sobek."

Enfield's legs stopped working, and he collapsed to the cracked marble floor. He vomited the contents of his stomach at the feet of the Egyptian beauty and gasped for air. The dark red liquid had lumps of tissue in the regurgitated potion, and the room started spinning. Samuel helped him sit upright on his knees as he watched the room age and rot away. The gold-clad woman's face wrinkled, and the skin pressed to her skull. Her teeth tumbled out of the emaciated face, and her eyes fell out from her head. The Princess's neck cracked to one side, and the bones holding her spine seemed to sway from the weight of the gold. Bandages sprang up from the floor and wrapped her body like twin snakes.

Samuel shouted, "Quickly, my future Queen! What of the third challenge?"

As the wrapping worked its way up her body, Ankh-es-en-amon's voice became faint, "The third challenge is to appease Seker. Seker is the protector and guardian of the Memphis Necropolis, where the Pyramid of Djoser stands. The chosen of Cthulhu must prove his cunning by overcoming Seker's sentinel and discovering the resting place of Lord Imhotep. Read the scroll over his body, and resurrect my beloved. Be warned, Master Enfield! Jealous gods who do not want to see this Aeon come to a close have anointed a champion that has the power to put the Great Dreamer back to sleep. You know her face, as my own."

Richard shook from chills on the ground, as he managed a weak reply, "A-Amanda Lanyon?"

The weathered bandages engulfed her upper body, as the brittle corpse hissed, "Yessss. Take care, Master Enfield. She could tip the scales and return the Old One to his slumber. You must send her to Duat!"

A sharp pain coursed into his stomach as his bowls released as she continued, "The gods are forbidden from ending her life, just as they are barred from ending yours. I will offer this gift, she travels with a company of knights by foot from Stirling Castle to the Cullerlie Stones in Scotland. She must not be allowed to live, Master Enfield! Everything hinges on you! Do as Cthulhu bids or suffer an eternity of payment for your failure!"

The world around him went black, and the sounds of the Dreamlands quieted. He shut his eyes and blacked out, only to burst back into consciousness. Richard sat up and felt the cold marble floor once again under his naked body.

The ghost of Samuel Howard was once again in his usual grey suit, "Easy, my boy. Take your time and recover. It's not every day that a mortal travels to the Dreamland and returns."

Richard shot up and stumbled backward over the lit candles, slamming into his desk, "The gods, immortals, they're all real!"

Samuel floated up to him, "Well, yes, my boy. Did you think the magic stopped with ghosts and angels? This world has been ruled over by several pantheons, each residing until the end of their Aeon. Now you, Master Enfield, have the chance to turn the key that unlocks Cthulhu's Herald, Imhotep."

He gathered his breath and snarled, "Amanda Lanyon."

Samuel nodded solemnly, "Indeed, Amanda Lanyon. She must be dealt with, but you still have a task to complete."

Richard took a slow relaxing breath then asked, "I'll contact the Edinburgh Sect in Scotland."

The ghost gave a sly smile, "Master Enfield, you know as well as I do that the Crimson Brotherhood doesn't keep lines of communication between Sect houses. It's a tradition that has been held for centuries."

He calmly walked around and sat his bare ass on the desk chair, picked up the phone and dialed Maxwell Gardener, "Those rules don't apply to the chosen of Cthulhu. It's time to bring the Sects together."

Tulsa, Oklahoma – Friday, November 9th, 2018 – 9:12 p.m. CST

Richard Enfield had donned a black two-piece suit when he walked into the study where Shoshannah Feinstein was lounging on a red velvet couch. A young man sat on the floor and massaged her feet. When she noticed Richard, she pushed the 20-year-old away with her heel and shot up.

She glared, "I've been waiting for hours."

Richard did his best to create an empathetic look, "I'm sorry, but it was unavoidable. Come, let's not waste any more of that valuable time of yours."

She trailed behind him and ordered, "Silvio, follow along."

They worked their way down towards the basement of the mansion until they arrived at the servants' kitchen. Richard ordered the staff out of the area and stood next to the freezer. She eyed him suspiciously as he opened the metal door and invited her inside.

She tilted her head, "You first, Master Enfield."

He shrugged and led them inside the cold storage locker. Closing the door behind them, Richard took a bolt from the wall and shoved it into the handle, locking them inside. He walked past her to the back of the frozen room and opened a panel on the wall. After inputting a series of numbers, a six-foot door popped free of the ice that had formed around its seal, and warm vapor poured from the crack. With a shove, he pushed the thick metal door open to reveal a twenty-foot circular arcane lab that looked a prop setting for an old Dracula movie.

Richard led them inside and closed the door back, "Samuel told me having cold storage was always convenient for the kind of work he did here."

She raised an eyebrow, "I don't think your cooks would like having fresh cadavers next to the chicken."

Shoshannah ran her fingers over the mystical etchings that filled the chamber's smooth walls. She gazed up at the ceiling's strange pattern and the metal rafters and support beams. Lining the walls were rows of antique torture devices and shelves that contain an odd assortment of arcane ingredients.

Shoshannah walked over to a triangular contraption, "A Judas Cradle."

Richard leaned on the table, "I'll take your word on that. I can't make heads or tails of most of these damn things."

She looked up and pointed at a rope and pully that dangled overhead, "It's a simplistically clever item. The victim was dropped onto their anus or vagina from a height onto the top."

Richard grimaced, "That sounds lovely."

She ran her finger over the blood soaked point, "I've heard grisly tales of this home's former owner, Samuel Howard. Not someone to be trifled with. Yet, I hear you killed him and inherited his power and money. It's no wonder such a clever man ascended to Sect Master. You must have fate on your side, or you would have been the next Judas waiting his turn at cradle."

Samuel floated in through the back wall, "More so a Judas goat, my dear."

Feinstein looked up at the ghost and gave a grin, "The Samuel Howard! It's an honor to finally make your acquaintance. I wish I had the opportunity to have met you in person when you were alive."

"Who are you talking to?" asked Richard.

Shoshannah picked up the bone saw and examined the blood splatters on its blade, "Why that dashing man who is floating next to you."

The ghost put his right hand over his heart and gave a slight bow, "My dear, you flatter me. I'm old enough to be your father."

She dropped the saw on the table with a loud clank, "Hardly."

Richard snapped into the realization that she was speaking to the ghost. He stabbed a finger at the spirit, "How can you see him?"

Samuel sauntered over to their guest, "Ms. Feinstein's soul has passed over and returned in a rather unique fashion. Because of that, she sees the dead and can determine their strength of spirit. Something she calls, soul sight."

She leaned on the table behind her sneering, "Now I'm flattered. How is it you know that?"

The ghost gave a fake look of indignation, "Come now, do you think I would involve myself with someone without first finding out all I could?"

Shoshannah leaned her back against Silvio, "I'm guessing that intrusion includes sending your flunkies to my private residence?"

Richard locked his jaw and forced an apology, "Again, we regret our indelicate approach, but time is of the essence."

She rolled her eyes, "Whatever. Here's the golem you ordered. His soul is pure and bright. A perfect match for your captured angel."

Richard walked over and examined Silvio, "Excellent! Well done!"

Samuel joined his former Apprentice in examining the golem, "We will still need you to convince Mr. Silvio to accept Miniel for this to work."

She reached back and drew the palm of her hand across his chiseled chin, "My dear, I want you to do me a special favor. These men are going to put that knife into your heart and bless you with incredible power. It won't hurt, I promise you."

Silvio looked confused, "They're going to stab me?"

She turned and pushed her breasts against his chest, "Now listen carefully, you will heal and feel no pain. When they are done, there will be an angel of God in your head named Miniel. She is divine being on a mission from God and needs someone like you to be there for her."

He kissed her hand, "An angel needs my help? I would be serving God?"

Shoshannah unbuttoned his shirt and ran her fingers in his chest hair, "I won't feel betrayed when you love her and accept her."

Silvio's face registered excitement, "I've always been a good Catholic."

She pulled his shirt out of his pants, exposing his washboard abs, "Of course you have, Love. Will you do this for me?"

He nodded with love in his eyes, "Yes. I'd do anything for you… and God, of course."

She kissed him on the lips, "Of course."

Samuel turned to Richard, "Very good, Ms. Feinstein. Now comes my part."

Richard produced the Athame Dagger from his pocket. It still had the dried blood on it from where it had been plunged into the possessed High

Mage, Benjamin Walsh. The symbol of Cthulhu in the handle glowed faintly, indicating that its binding power over Miniel was weakening.

Samuel ran his hand over the blade and cast a spell, "Cum Defunctis Loquimur."

The ghost's eyes fluttered, and his head tilted back. The spirit was solid enough that Richard thought he could feel his semi-transparent hand actually leaning on the dagger. For several minutes, Samuel's mouth gently moved, and he softly communed with the entity trapped in the blade.

Suddenly, the ghost's eyes snapped open, and he staggered back, as Richard asked, "Well?"

Samuel seemed to fade from sight for a moment before reconstituting, "She is a powerful and ancient force. A warrior whose vengeance and obsession for Hyde's love has driven her mad."

Richard stepped closer in frustration, "Damnit, man! Will she do it?"

Samuel composed himself, "She is overwhelmed by our offer. The angel knows that Hyde has transformed into a Nephilim, and is outside of the reach of the Order of Virtue. She has agreed to be a willing soldier to our cause and will bond with our Mr. Silvio to become a Nephilim herself. Her only stipulation is that we not get in the way of her vengeance when she faces Hyde in his new form."

Richard grinned, flipped the blade to an underhand grip, and exclaimed, "Done!"

He turned to Silvio and prepared to make his stroke. Shoshannah drew a hand over her golem's face, gave a departing wink, then stepped back out of the way. The re-animated Italian kept his eyes on his love, and pulled open the black dress shirt. A small tear fell from his eye as he stood fast.

Richard lifted the knife, "For Cthulhu's awakening!"

Before he could act, a crack of air burst behind the young golem. The thick-bodied Marcus Holmes snapped into existence, wearing pure black and a fiendish smile. His eyes were a golden sheen, and his fangs were fully extended. Thick yellow saliva dripped from his open mouth, and a low growl came from the depths of his barrel chest.

Before Richard's heart could beat, the vampire gripped Silvio's head with both hands and snapped the golem's neck 90 degrees to the left. Shoshannah roared in anger, as the vampire reversed the torque and ripped the head free from its owner's broad shoulders. The lifeless body of the golem dropped to the ground, and the beautiful face spasmed, as his soul slipped back where it came from.

Marcus stood resolutely with a splash of blood across his bearded face, as he demanded "Hand the Athame to me, and I shall let you live, Master Enfield."

With a primal scream, Shoshannah charged Marcus, grabbing him by the throat. She pushed him backward, as his eyes widened in surprise at the incredible strength of the slight woman. The vampire's feet slid on the concrete floor, while he clawed at her forearms. The slashes sunk into her flesh and splashed blood in a wild frenzy. Just before they reached the stone wall of the chamber, he turned his weight and tossed her into the air. Her body hit the secret door with such force that it folded the metal entrance, knocking it from its hinges. Shoshannah tumbled into the cooler and crashed into a rack of frozen meat. The re-animated woman lay unmoving, and pinned under the twisted steel. She was bleeding from her arms and puffs of vapor billowed out of her unconscious face.

Marcus whipped his head back towards Richard, who commanded, "Samuel do something!"

The ghost floated motionless and calm, "This is not my fight."

Marcus hissed, "Don't count on help from your ghost. Samuel is quite powerless. There are some universal constants in the world of vampires. One is the sunlight, and the other is if you invite one into your home, then you give up all power over them. When your servant girl invited Shoshannah in, I rode on her shoulder as a firefly. It's too bad she wasn't more specific with her offer. It's a useful trick. One of many. I used a similar one when I rode on Amanda Lanyon's shoulder. She escorted me inside her home. I do hope you will be more level headed than she was."

Richard gave a look of acknowledgment, "Ah, so it's you that has her children."

Marcus tapped his own nose, "Very, astute! My coven has them tucked away in exchange for her silence in matters of the Crimson Brotherhood."

Richard cradled the Athame, "I'm the new Master of the Sect, not Miniel. If you truly serve Cthulhu, you would be wise to realize my authority!"

The vampire straightened himself up and appeared more dignified, "I must confess, I couldn't help myself from exploring your lovely mansion in my insect form. I managed to overhear your conversation about needing Amanda Lanyon. How odd, I have the two people that could draw her out of hiding. It seems I have something you want, and you have something I want. So, let's keep this clean and make a trade."

Suddenly, the vampire was snatched off the ground by his right calf and shoulder, as Samuel coolly continued, "This isn't my fight. It's hers."

Shoshannah was shaking with anger as she stood under Marcus with fury in her eyes. The wounds on her forearms were fully healed, and her black blouse was hanging in tatters from her shoulders. A thin gloss of sweat shimmered from her newly enhanced frame. Richard surmised she had thirty more pounds of muscle than he had remembered before she was tossed through the steel door.

The sounds of cracking bone came from Marcus's hip as she twisted his leg in a circle. The vampire let out a growl as she hurled him at the wall next to the Judas Cradle. The vampire slammed face-first against the stone and clung onto it like a spider. He stepped down with his good leg, and let the mangled one hang chaotically to his side. The broken limb snapped and scurried until it was once again in proper alignment. The undead black man set the foot down, with a final pop of his hip as it was put back into place.

Marcus crouched on the ground and spit a viscous slime, as he hissed at his opponent. Shoshannah charged the Vampire Lord in a blinding flash of speed. Her hands pushed on his shoulders and slammed the creature of darkness against the stone. The sheer force of the impact caused the room to tremble and let loose dust from the rafters.

Marcus clawed her eyes, making her stagger backward and release the pin. Dark red blood flowed out of her face, and the vampire shot two stiff punches to her body. She reeled and grunted as she absorbed a kick to her midsection.

With a growl, he launched a punch at her jaw. Her eyes flashed up to his, and she caught his wrist in mid-flight. To Richard's astonishment, her eyes had healed completely. He struggled to retrieve his hand and whipped his other taloned fingers at her throat. With the same speed, she snatched it just as effortlessly and held him. The two monsters struggled to overcome each other. They danced in a circle, knocking over furniture and racks of spell components.

The two combatants settled in the center of the room, matching each other's ferocity. Shoshannah's grip on Marcus' arms was holding, but the Vampire Lord was proving to be stronger. An evil grin crawled across his face, as his deadly fingernails moved towards her neck.

As the black talons touched her, her hide changed complexion and texture. Shoshannah's back and biceps grew denser, and the woman's skin became as thick as rhinoceros hide. She stood up straight and moved his hands away from her throat. The vampire wailed in pain, as her iron grip crushed his left wrists. He hit his knees in agony and stared at her with astonishment. Shoshannah bent her face down to his and let out a spiteful hiss.

With a quick motion, the woman let go of his broken arm and drove a punch into his side that penetrated his undead body. Her arm disappeared up into his belly and ripped out several organs. Shoshannah dropped the tissue to the ground, and they instantly turned to a pile of loose dirt. Marcus wailed in pain as she delivered an uppercut to the vampire's armpit. The walls splashed with his blood, as the arm came away from his body at the shoulder. In an instant, the liquid transformed into soil and fell to the floor.

The undead gripped her shoulder with his remaining hand and stammered, "T-this is impossible. W-what are you?"

She grabbed him by the throat, and effortlessly picked him up off the ground. With a swift pivot, she slammed his back on top of the point of the Judas Cradle. The impaled vampire hung in space and stared in shock at the ceiling of the arcane chamber. Blood dribbled down the wooden frame of the contraption and tumbled to piles of earth at its base.

His eyes magically turned a solid yellow, "My Violet, I love you. Hear me! Gather the children and…"

Shoshannah slammed an iron fist across his lower jaw and sent the bottom part of his face dancing across the floor. The tongue of the vampire wiggled in the air as his eyes fluttered in shock. The re-animated miracle-woman retrieved the rounded bone saw from the table and put it across Marcus's neck. She latched onto his chest with her left hand and spun him in a circle on the Judas device. She reveled in his agony while turning him like a top until his head was in the perfect position for the saw. She lay the blade across his dirt-covered neck and grasped him by his thick black hair.

Shoshannah turned his jawless face towards her, and looked deep into his bewildered eyes, "I've dealt with your kind before. You are intimately connected to your offspring and, of course, your mate. I'm guessing that Violet is your wife, and you are in mental contact with her right now. Far be it from me to interrupt."

With each slicing motion of the bone saw across his neck, she bellowed, "Tell your bitch whore... that Shoshannah Feinstein... sent her beloved... back to hell!"

On her last word, the head of Marcus hit the floor with a dull plop. A second later, over two-hundred pounds of earth that was once the vampire slammed to the ground. The bits of his hair that still clung in between her fingers followed suit and crumbled from her hand. Shoshannah dropped the bone saw to the ground, and Richard jumped when the metal clanked on the stone. She turned back to her host and brushed her curly black hair away from her face. Her left breast was exposed, as she looked down at her torn and bloody clothes, then let out a sigh.

Richard crept his way out from behind a table, "Is it... dead?"

Samuel floated over to the pile of dirt, "Well, technically, he was already dead."

Richard found his courage, "Traitor! He was a Leviathan dedicated to my protection! I never knew he was a..."

Samuel sauntered next to him, "A vampire? I'm shocked your keen magical senses didn't alert you to that fact. Ms. Feinstein, Master Enfield doesn't know how to thank you."

She looked at a broken nail on her left hand, "Try money, lots of it. Because all of this shit was definitely not my problem. My part here is done."

As she turned to walk out, Richard looked over at the destroyed body of Silvio, "We will need you to make a replacement golem."

She looked up with annoyance, "Fuck all you do! I delivered as promised and made him willing. I'm out! Consider the vampire slaying a parting gift!"

Samuel walked in front of her, "My dear, this has all been tragically unexpected. I can appreciate your position. We certainly don't want to put you out, but at least give us a chance to make this right. If you do this for Master Enfield, we could offer a sum that would guarantee a lifetime's worth of comforts as well as the protection of the Clerval family. Would five million be too terribly insulting to offer?"

She paused, and looked down in disgust, "You'd pay five million? In advance?"

Richard stepped forward anxiously, "Yes, in advance."

Shoshannah sighed, "I would need a place to work with adequate power and secrecy. No one could watch me work. No surveillance cameras!"

Samuel flourished his hands out dramatically, "My dear, I'll have that door fixed and you can use this chamber. I can arrange for anything you need."

She peered into the ghost's deep blue eyes. "I have another condition. Good men like Silvio are rare, so if one goes missing, it's noticed. No snatching people off the street! With Christian Crusaders, police and FBI looking for the Brotherhood, it would risk drawing attention. I want to be in and out before AEGIS realizes I'm here. Besides, there's plenty of fresh dead in the graves for me to use."

Samuel nodded, "A sensible precaution."

She put her hands on her hips and caught her breath, "It can't be just anyone. You'll have to pick someone who had a strong spirit in life. Someone noble and brave. Those are the ones with the strongest soul light that can make the transition the easiest. Maybe one of those dead cops that raided your Preserve. They were pretty noble when they ate a bullet."

The ghost grinned with satisfaction, "All acceptable. Then we have an accord."

She walked through the dirt remains of Marcus towards Richard, "It has to be done fast. I'm not hanging around any longer than I have to."

Richard remembered Ankh-es-en-amon's warning and had an epiphany, "You'll have your corpse by morning."

By Bo Luellen

Chapter 10: John VII

Tulsa, Oklahoma – Monday, November 12th, 2018 – 9:43 a.m. CST

John Utterson hated checking out cold leads when he was on the force. Still, the two hundred and ten thousand dollar salary he was pulling in from the UCC made it a lot easier. He sat on a stool wearing a pair of headphones as he watched the monitors. The repurposed UPS van jerked and shifted as they traveled down the Riverside Drive. The front portion of the interior was filled with surveillance equipment and only gave him a little room to move around. The back half had four armed Crusaders in blue tactical gear and wearing helmets and vests. The technician on his left cycled through the body camera feed until he found the one worn by the fake UPS driver who was steering the truck.

The technician spoke into his headset, "Give us a mic check."

The driver radioed back, "When you absolutely, positively have to kill the Crimson Brotherhood, accept no substitute."

Utterson couldn't help but smile, "Nice, but that's FedEx. Oh, and a reminder; there will be no killing. Our goal is to find them, capture them, and hold them. We let the police do their jobs to show the public we are doing our part to still cooperate with the Department."

One of the Crusaders lowered his ski mask, "No disrespect General Utterson, but I think we're better at it than them."

A round of mutters of agreement came from the small squad. John ignored them, as the technician handed him the report on their next target. He rubbed his weary eyes, put on his glasses, and opened the cream-colored folder with the new UCC logo on the front.

As he scanned the photos and documents, the technician gave him the briefing, "General, our next stop is in the Garden District. A report came in from a Chestnut Street resident. The informant saw two thuggish looking men going in and out of a neighbor's house after midnight. According to the email, they were taking several sizeable black trash bags and white barrels out from the back of a large U-Haul truck and carrying them into the house."

He flipped through the pages of the report, "What do we know about the owner of the home?"

The tech punched a few keys to bring up a map of the area, "The homeowner is one Laura Powell, a sixty-five-year-old divorcee. She has one daughter named Hillary, who lives in Paris, Texas. Ms. Powell has no work history and lives alone. She was a stay-at-home wife to a wealthy oil trustee. When they divorced, she took half and the house. She has been a member of the Eastland congregation for over ten years and is a key donor who helped build The Gathering Place park downtown. A model Christian in all respects."

John folded a paper over and looked at a photo of the dark-haired older woman, then repeated, "A model Christian."

As they rounded the corner to Washington Avenue, he looked at the monitor that showed an exterior view of the van. The streets were filled with magnificent three-story homes and lavishly manicured lawns. Tulsa's old oil money was in full display, and its inheritors took pride in their ancestral homes. The driver pounded on the roof of the cab, indicating they had arrived.

The brakes squealed the vehicle to a halt as the driver whispered into his mic, "Here goes."

The four Crusaders pulled their ski masks up over their faces and buckled their helmets. They wore all blue and had the symbol of Eastland on the front of their flack jackets, and on the back was "UCC" in bold type print. The men checked their AR-15's and shifted around, ready to take action.

John spoke into the microphone to the driver, "Remember, try to pan your chest around. I want to see the interior of the house if possible."

His leg was starting to ache again, and he was fresh out of pain pills. John had been a full day without a drink, which was causing him no end of anxiety. He was still dehydrated and tired from last night's vomiting and withdrawal pains. He saw the technician looking at his foot as it tapped nervously on the floor. John forced it to stop and shot a hard glance at the man, who immediately returned his attention to the monitors. John wanted something to take the edge off not only the aching in his ankle but from the agony of drying out.

The driver power-walked towards the front door to a two-story brown and red brick house, with an empty box under his arm. John noticed the place was massive, with a two-car garage and a full acre of lawn. He leaned in and noticed that the grass had been neglected. There was a collection of dried leaves scattered about.

The technician reported, "Bodycam functioning and audio is clean, Brother Utterson."

His skin crawled at the title of Brother. He kept up a smile and pretense when in public as the UCC General. He enjoyed having access to equipment, personnel, and resources Richard Enfield and Eastland College provided, but it came at a price. The public image Greyson Dunn demanded of his Generals was taxing, but John enjoyed being finally recognized for his contributions.

He forced a, "Thank you, Brother."

The driver knocked on the door and then rang the bell. The van was silent as they waited for Ms. Powell to answer. This was always the most nerve-wracking for him, and he could feel the tension in his team. The armed Crusaders he had selected were all military veterans and tested in wartime theaters. Where others might hesitate if a tactical engagement was needed, these handpicked Marines lived for the adrenaline of combat. It made them effective, but John had to be damn sure when to let them off their leash.

The front door opened halfway, and he saw the face of the elderly Ms. Powell peek her head outside. She was wearing a blue dress and had a big smile on her face. Her hair was the image of her sleeve, and the weathered wrinkles on her face showed her age.

The driver looked at his digital clipboard, "Good Morning. I have a package here for Powell, I'll just need you to sign please."

The woman took the notepad, "Oh, I don't recall ordering anything."

The man panned his body camera to the left of the owner and gave John a good look at the interior of the house. The walls were lined with bronze statues he recognized as reproductions of the western sculptures by Frederic Remington. The floors were carpeted but soiled from dirty boot prints. She had track lighting on the ceiling that highlighted various pieces of art.

As the woman finished signing the pad, the driver whistled then asked, "Wow, someone forgot to wipe their feet."

She kept her eyes on him, "Oh, yes. My gardener has that bad habit. He has been tracking it in all day from the back yard, and, well, I don't speak a lick of Spanish. All I can do is point at the rug and shake my head no."

The driver gave a diplomatic laugh, and she handed him back the pad.

She smiled and reached out for the box. She placed it under her arm and grabbed the door. The sleeve of her dress caught John's eye, and he started fumbling with the keyboard controls.

As the driver walked back to the truck, John ordered, "How do you roll the damn tape back. Rewind it!"

After the technician hit a few keys, the image of her sleeve was frozen and enhanced. John put on his reading glasses and nearly pressed his nose up to the monitor. There was a bruised line around her wrist he had seen before.

The driver hopped back inside the cab, looked back at them, and said, "Well, that seemed like a dead end. Where to next?"

John pointed at the image, "Can you enhance that?"

The tech shook his head, "It's too pixilated. These body cams can only give us so much detail. Why? What do you see?"

He stabbed a finger at the screen, "Maybe nothing, but those look like marks from handcuffs."

The man squinted at the screen, "The image is too blurry. That could be anything. It could be a shadow of the light, or it could be a bruise she picked up helping the gardener in the back. She is elderly. They tend to bruise over just about anything."

John leaned back in his metal chair, "You know what I find odd? A woman owns a fantastic looking house, keeps the finest art decor copied from the Gilcrease Museum, and then lets her landscaper track up her floor, her grass overgrow, and doesn't rake her leaves. In a neighborhood where taking care of our property is not just expected, it's required by the homeowners association, it leaves some interesting open-ended questions."

The van was quiet for several seconds before the tech asked, "General, would you like to move to confirmation? Should I phone the police?"

He shook his head, "Pull up her social media accounts and get this truck moving. We're looking suspicious just hanging out in the street."

Within a few minutes, the UPS van parked on 7th and Camp Street, "General, there's no active social media presence for Powell, and her Facebook had been deactivated."

John rubbed his scruffy beard and repeated, "A model Christian."

The driver popped his head around the corner to the back, "What are we doing, guys?"

The technician cleared his throat, then asked, "General?"

John grabbed his cane, "Drive me to my car and then continue making the rounds without me."

The technician gave him a bewildered look, "Sir?"

He tapped his walking stick on the floorboard, "I'm not convinced the gardener even exists."

Tulsa, Oklahoma – Monday, November 12th, 2018 – 10:10 a.m. CST

He had been given a black Lexus when he accepted the job, which was perfect for a stakeout in a high-end neighborhood such as the one Ms. Powell resided in. He piled in the front seat and pushed away a dozen empty Monster Energy Drink cans and take out bags. They made a horrible racket, as they quickly littered the floorboard and spilled their remaining contents on the designer mats. He lifted his broken ankle in the door and threw his cane into the back.

When he shut his door, the UPS van that dropped him off sped away to their next location. He waited for the sounds of their engine to fade away before popping open the glove box and pulled out a collection of pill bottles. He cursed to himself as he threw each empty container on the floorboard. He slapped the steering wheel when the last one pinged off the passenger side window and dashed all his hopes of gaining some relief for the pain.

Resigned to his fate, he drove back towards the Powell residence. He stopped by a QuikTrip and got some coffee and a few snacks for the stakeout. John had done these hundreds of times in his career and knew how to prepare.

He had parked his car far enough away to be inconspicuous and still have a clear view of the home. John set his video camera on the dashboard and faced it towards the house. He opened the pop out screen and plugged its charger into the cigarette lighter. After zooming in on the property, John reclined his chair to give some relief to his ribs. He lit up a cigarette and began the long wait.

Tulsa, Oklahoma – Monday, November 12th, 2018 – 10:25 p.m. CST

After twelve hours of fruitless surveillance, the fatigue was finally starting to wear on him. He was in misery from the withdrawals but refused to leave. His car was full of freshly discarded food wrappers, and he had filled several Pepsi bottles with his urine. Stakeouts were always the toughest part of the job for him when he was still on the force. Sitting in a vehicle alone watching someone's front door had no appeal to him, but it did get results.

He pulled out the last Marlboro from the pack and remembered his old partner, *I miss the times when David and I would sleep in shifts. One of us would give Moss a call, then smoke some weed and make it a party. Now my partner is this damn shooting pain in my ribs and a throbbing ankle.*

The Crusader's physician had given John a once over and recommended he stay in bed for the next two weeks. The doctor had given him a small number of pain pills, but John had gone through them in two days. Looking down, he saw his hands still trembling from the withdrawals, but he couldn't stop now. He had to prove to the city that he was going to be the person to close in on the Crimson Brotherhood, not the Department. Suddenly an enticing thought crossed his mind and he felt a rush of excitement. He quickly pulled out his cell phone and made a call.

Moss Vicker's stuttering voice answered, "H-h-hey J-J-John."

Utterson rubbed his eyes and impatiently waited for the man to finish a sentence, "Did you find out anything new on the Brotherhood?"

The drug dealer seemed to get more anxious, "Uhhhh, you kn-kn-know I wou-wou-would tell you, J-j-john."

He felt like his insides were on fire from going cold turkey, "Moss, I want you to grab me a Monster Energy Drink from the store and bring it to me."

The man quickly replied, "S-S-Sure, John. T-t-text me your address."

Thirty minutes later, a red Volvo pulled up behind him, and the sandy blond-haired Moss got out. He was wearing a Pink Floyd t-shirt and some blue jeans that looked like they had paint on them. As he opened the car door, John scooped the empty sacks out of the passenger seat. The man plopped down, and the odor of pot hit him in the face.

Moss gave him a brown bag, "Here's your Monster."

He opened the sack and saw several baggies filled with pills, cocaine, vodka, and marijuana. Reaching inside, John pulled out a few Oxy's, then used the alcohol to wash it down. He poured the rest into an iron flask he had hidden under his seat.

Moss was both high and relaxed, "You know now that you aren't with the police force, we need to make a new arrangement. It isn't like you can get me off if I get arrested, or help my people stay clear of any undercover cops, anymore."

John offered the flask to Moss, "Just keep our arrangement as it is. The UCC is one-hundred times larger than the police and has more technical resources than the Feds. Besides, they are too busy right now to worry about you."

The man pushed the liquor back at him, "I don't drink anymore. I'm trying to lose weight. I'm engaged now. She wants me to get under two hundred pounds before the wedding. She says I need to stop eating so much pizza and work out."

John's forehead wrinkled, "You're engaged? When did that happen?"

Moss chuckled and started rolling a joint, "I sent you a text about it. You were invited to the wedding in February."

The pain made him bitterly frustrated, as he waited for the drugs to take effect, "What is this, your fourth? Jesus, Moss."

Moss had learned how to take John's barbs when he was like this, "No, it's my fifth. I got no trouble getting them, but keeping them seems to be my problem. Maybe I should …"

John quickly angled the monitor towards him and growled, "Shut up."

The garage door to the Powell house slowly opened up, as light poured out from the interior. John zoomed the camera in and waited. A few minutes later, a white U-Haul van drove past his driver's side window and sped towards the Powell house. The red brake lights of the vehicle shined in the night, as it turned into the old woman's garage. As the automated door closed, John saw a sizeable Hispanic man wearing a black leather vest walking around to the back of the vehicle. With a few presses on the screen, he took a few photos before it closed. He grabbed the camcorder and cycled back through the pictures until he found a clear image of the short man's face.

Moss pointed at the tiny screen, "Hey, I know that guy."

He looked up in surprise, "You know that guy? How?"

His friend put his joint in his pocket and replied, "Wicked is what they call him on the streets. His real name is Victor Abasto. He is a mid-level gun runner for the Mexican cartels. I sold to him once. He seemed nice enough to me, but I heard he beat some guy to death last year. He vanished after that. I guess he's back."

John opened his glove box, "It seems Victor has found his way into a rich house with "a model Christian." Out of place for a guy named "Wicked."

John pulled out his silver-plated 9-mm Smith and Wesson that the UCC had issued him. The pistol had the symbol of the modified Eastland's Lion on the side of its pearl handle. It had become the logo of the Crusaders and was worn on all the blue jackets of their members. He grabbed a box of ammunition from under his seat and turned it upside down, spilling its contents. A dog barked in the distance, as John clicked in each round into the magazine.

As he slammed the clip into the gun, Moss pleaded, "John, call the cops. This isn't your job anymore, remember. You're the leader of the UCC. Let one of them do this. You're crippled up and alone. Think this through, man! Wicked runs with the cartel. That means there could be lots more than just him in there."

He paused for a moment and then patted Moss on the shoulder, "You're right. You're coming with me."

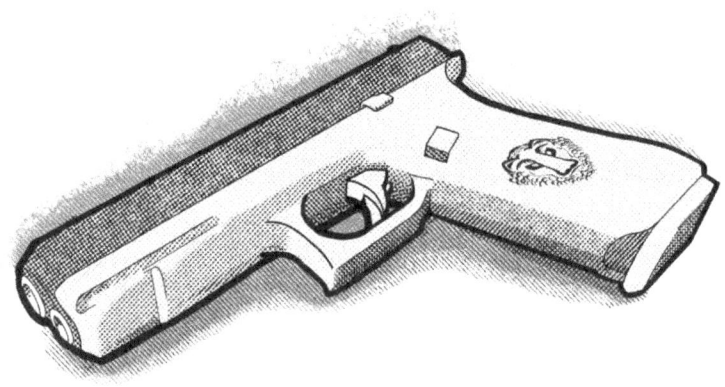

John Utterson's Pistol

Moss let out a laugh then realized he was serious, "Wait, what? No! John! We're not cops, man! You're just as civilian as I am!"

John felt the Oxys finally kick in as he reasoned, "I just want you there to be my eyes. My night vision is awful. Besides, I just want a closer look. If we see something, I'll snap a photo of it, then call the cops. We'll be in and out."

His friend put up his hands, "Are you crazy? What am I supposed to use if things turn ugly? I don't have a gun, and the police don't like me much, man."

John reached under his seat and pulled out his old back up 9-mm from its hiding spot. The serial number had been filed off long ago by David. The pair always kept one around in case something outside of the law needed to be done.

He pushed it against his friend's chest, "Here!"

The tension began to affect Moss's stutter, "N-no, John! I'll come with you, b-but I'm not going to carry a g-gun."

He shrugged and clipped the pistol onto his back belt loop, "Suit yourself. Let's go."

He pulled his cane from the back seat and stuffed the pearl-handled UCC pistol into his front waistband. As he hobbled his way down the street, he found the painkillers had made the soreness manageable. However, he still moved forward like some lumbering dinosaur looking for a watering hole. Moss appeared at his side and laced his arm inside John's for support.

He looked over at his friend, "Thanks."

Moss whispered a bland, "Just don't do anything stupid."

John's cane wasn't meant for stealth and made a "clomp" sound with every step. As they approached the edge of Ms. Powell's security fence, they heard a pair of muffled voices from inside the house. The pair froze and crouched down a little. He could make out that it was two males, but they couldn't tell what they were saying. John lumbered towards the side window of the house, as Moss reached out to stop him.

He yanked his arm from his friend, and slowly John crept up to the home. The metal cane made a "clomp... clomp.... clomp" noise in the tall cold grass, as Moss begrudgingly followed close behind. They both made it to the house and leaned their backs against opposite sides of a window. The white drapes were pulled closed, but they could discern what was being said through the double plane glass.

A deep voice barked, "You think I'm playing, vato! You promised 500 gallons! Do you think the Brotherhood will..."

John shot a wide-eyed look to his companion and mouthed, "The Brotherhood!"

The sound stopped abruptly as Moss whispered, "T-T-That's W-w-wicked. I know that v-v-voice."

From the back of the house came the sound of a door opening. The two immediately turned in the direction of the noise. They pressed their bodies as close to the red brick of the home as humanly possible. John inched along the wall as Moss whispered protests.

He felt the Oxy begin to work and the pain lessen, If I can bring Wicked in, *I would be the first person to capture two members of the Crimson Brotherhood alive. John Utterson – 2, Chief of Police Kelly – 0.*

Moss froze at the sound of a man clearing his throat from the backyard. The backyard security light snapped on, and a thin black man in his early 20s strolled out towards the security fence. He was a teenager with a black leather vest that was similar to the one worn by Wicked. The young man stopped short of the barrier and took a wide stance. He heard a zipping sound, and then heard the man relieving himself. A thin vapor came from a line of urine as it splattered onto a post.

John pulled out the pearl-handled 9-mm from his belt and inched forward. The excitement of the moment drew him into the old feelings of being on the force. He leaned on his cane and did his best to creep towards the black man.

He noticed that he didn't hear his friend's terrified breathing and turned to check on him. He found him with a terrified expression on his face and standing like a trembling statue. Wicked stepped out from the shadows, racked a 12-gauge shotgun, and leveled the barrel at the side of Moss's head.

The Hispanic man commanded, "Drop it or he dies, puta!"

Moss put up his hands, and John dropped his silver 9-mm on the cold ground, "Look, I can help you. The cops are already on their way. I don't want you getting caught. I can make you a wealthy man. I need information on the Crimson Brotherhood."

Wicked's eyes narrowed, "Hey, I know you."

John shuffled sideways into the light, "Yes. Probably from TV. I'm

John Utterson, General of the UCC in Tulsa. The Crusaders can give you protection and a new identity in exchange for..."

Wicked poked the side of Moss's temple, "Not you, cabrón! Him!"

Moss gulped and then stuttered, "I-I-I don't want any t-t..."

Wicked pressed the barrel closer and shouted, "I remember you! Moss Vickers. A nobody. You're helping those UCC maricón's! You fucking rat! You led him here!"

Moss shook his head, "N-n-n-no, W-w-w-icked! I w-w-w-would never..."

The shotgun blast made John's ears ring when it went off. He felt the concussive force pulse against his face and an odd warm sensation on his skin. The left side of John's body was plastered in his friends brains and blood. Moss's body bounced off the wall and dropped down on top of his bad ankle. He screamed in pain and fell back onto the thick, freezing grass. John grabbed his bad leg in agony and looked over at the billowing vapor coming from the hole the buckshot made in the man's head.

The Hispanic man pumped the shotgun and yelled down at Moss, "Besa mi culo, puto!"

Wicked went into a rage and put two more rounds into the dead man's chest. Utterson instinctively started scooting backward on the ground with his good leg and searched for his back up pistol. When Wicked put a third shot into the shredded chest of Moss Vickers, John drew his gun and fired. The 9-mm muzzle flashes strobed in the darkness. John put four rounds into the Brotherhood man's chest before he could use the shotgun. The Hispanic dropped his weapon and staggered back against the brick wall of the house. Wicked spit blood and reached back, drawing out a .38 revolver. Before he could use it, John put a fifth shot between the man's eyes. The dead man bounced off the side of the house and landed face up next to Moss.

John rolled onto his belly and aimed his pistol towards the backyard. The young black man was gone, leaving only a steaming puddle of piss in his wake. He pulled himself to a sitting position and looked at the lifeless face of Wicked as blood trickled from the hole in his forehead. John glanced over at Moss, whose chest had been minced up by the repeated applications of buckshot, and the left side of his head was absent. Porch lights owned by the surrounding houses lit up in a cascade of alarm.

John picked up his cane and forced himself to his feet, *Fuck! I don't have much time!*

He reached inside Moss's bloody vest, he pulled out the man's cell phone. The face of the device was cracked from the impact of the shotgun blasts. He pocketed the phone and wiped his prints clean from the backup gun he had used to kill Wicked.

He put his pistol in his friend's hand and patted his wrist when he was done, "Sorry, buddy. I didn't mean for this to happen, but I'm going to need a little more help."

He stood back up and picked up his pearl-handled UCC pistol from the grass. A tiny piece of metal poking out from Wicked's jacket caught his eye. Lifting a portion of the coat with a pen, he saw a small notebook tucked halfway inside the vest pocket. It was leather-bound and had a silver pen attached to the edge. The expensive journal seemed out of place, considering the owner's persona.

With his thumb and forefinger, John removed it from the blood-soaked jacket, stepped into the light, and opened it. One of his 9-mm bullet holes had penetrated the left corner. He forced it open and scanned the pages. It was a list of shipments, the order's received, dollar amounts, and banking account numbers. Each shipment had abbreviations for guns, drugs, explosives, food, and equipment, with a list of addresses. He thumbed to the front of the book and saw the symbol of Cthulhu on the inside cover.

The ringing in his ear was starting to subside as he could make out the barking dog once more. Pain in his ankle was overwhelming, but he knew he was on a deadline. A flash of light from the backyard caught his eye, and he heard someone slam a door. Snapping the book shut, he put it in his inside coat pocket and noticed a neighbor in a bathrobe standing just outside of Ms. Powell's yard. John knew he had precious little time, or everything he worked for would become muddled in unnecessary confusion.

He worked his way over to the stranger, "Hello, Brother. Do you recognize me? I'm John Utterson from the UCC"

The man was in his fifties and squinted at him, "Yeah. Hey, yeah! I know you. Brother Greyson talks about you on The Eastland Worship Hour!"

He put his hand on the man's shoulder, "Brother Greyson is a great man of God. I'm glad to have your support in this fight. Listen, I need your help, Brother. We got a tip about this house, and I've just discovered it's a Crimson Brotherhood hideout."

The neighbor pursed his lips together and said, "I knew it! I'm the one that made the call to the UCC hotline! Laura has been my neighbor and friend for years. I've never seen her act like this. The house lights come on at all hours, people I've never seen before show up and …"

John held up his hand, "Well, you were right. I've just found two dead members of the Brotherhood on the lawn over there."

The man's jaw dropped open, "I thought I heard gunshots!"

He motioned the neighbor back towards his house, "I believe Ms. Powell might be in danger. I want you to go back to your house and call the UCC hotline. Tell them, General John Utterson is at the Powell residence, and we have a Phase 2 situation for Project: Trust but Verify. Do you got that?"

The balding man nodded, "Phase 2… Trust but Verify. I got it."

He turned the man by the elbow, "Now hurry. God needs me to help Ms. Powell."

The neighbor gave an enthusiastic, "God bless you, General Utterson! God bless you!"

The man sprinted back to his house, and John's heart sank as he heard the sounds of police sirens in the distance, *They pick tonight to have a good response time!*

John double-timed it to the back yard, as the security light illuminated its posh wooden lawn furniture and intricate flower beds. The back door was open, and the glass screen door ajar. In the front of the house, he heard a vehicle rumble to life in the garage and the automatic door open.

He hobbled over to the back door and pondered, *That would be our mystery pisser looking to make a fast exit.*

The sounds of the U-Haul peeling out on the smooth concrete floor sent a squeal out into the night. John shouldered the back door open, and held his pistol out, as he found himself in a messy kitchen. Instantly, he was assaulted with fumes of ammonia hitting his nose like a brick. In the corner of the room was a handcuffed, blindfolded, and gagged Ms. Powell. Her face had fresh lacerations, and dried blood was coming down her forehead.

John scanned the room as he worked his way over to her. He pulled on the handkerchief that was tied between her teeth. The countertop had mountains of old pizza boxes and beer cans. The floor was littered with boot tracks of all shapes and sizes. His eyes watered at the chemical smell, and he pulled his shirt up over his nose.

As the gag was removed, he put his hand over her mouth and whispered, "Shhhh… is there anyone else in the house?"

She shook her head, and tears dripped from her wrinkled cheeks. He pulled out a key and unlocked the handcuffs. Ms. Powell rubbed the bruises on her wrists and let John help her up off the dirty hardwood floor. Flashing red and blue lights of a patrol car beamed against the front window drapes and filled the house in amber.

He held her hand, "It's okay. I'm John Utterson with the Crusaders. You're safe now. No one is going to hurt you anymore."

A look of recognition came over her face, "Oh, thank the Lord. These men… they just showed up one day. They threatened to kill my daughter and …"

She burst into tears as John grabbed her by the shoulders, "I know you've been through a lot, but you have to tell me, what were they doing here?"

She pointed towards the living room, "They brought in some kind of chemicals. They kept them in there."

John pulled his 9-mm high and told her, "Stay here, I'm just going to take a look. You'll be able to see me the entire time."

He worked his way around the wall that led into the living room and poked his head around the corner. The pungent smell of ammonia penetrated his shirt with ease and almost gagged him. He lowered his weapon at the transformation that had taken place in the house since he last saw it through the body camera of his fake UPS driver.

The walls, ceiling, and floor were covered in thick transparent plastic. A metalwork table was set up in the far corner of the room, and three large white barrels were stacked side-by-side next to it. One of the drum's clear contents was still sloshing about, and a long red wire was coming out of the top of the container. John's eyes followed the crimson lines to a black box with a series of red flashing lights that sat on the top of the table.

On the front was a red digital readout that counted down, "2:34… 2:33… 2:32…"

John turned to Ms. Powell and ordered, "Get out, now! The police are around the front, tell them there is a bomb in here, and they need to evacuate the block!"

The elderly woman took off like a woman half her age out the back door. He heard her scream the warning to the officers in the yard. John calmly holstered his gun and took out his cell phone. As the clock worked its way down, he took pictures of everything in the room with his camera.

A red-headed patrol officer burst in the back door and screamed, "Get down on the ground!"

Utterson kept taking photos, "I'm former Police Detective John Utterson of the United Christian Crusaders. I've just rescued the owner of this house, Ms. Powell, from the Crimson Brotherhood. They've left behind three large barrels of an unknown chemical, and as you can see, there is a detonator attached. The timer has less than two minutes before it goes off. You need to get as many people to a safe distance as possible, Officer."

The cop froze in shock and fear, as John snapped him out of it, "Officer! Now!"

The man ran out of the house, yelling into the radio on his shoulder. John glanced down at the timer that ticked down, "1:54... 1:53... 1:52." He took a picture of the manufacturer's label on the drum. It read "Hoondo Limited Manufacturing." John took one more glance at the time and started a mental countdown. He pocketed his phone and hobbled on his cane out the back door. As he passed by the body of Moss, he gave his friend one last look and kept moving.

Several officers were banging on neighbors' doors, as the red-headed patrolmen were blasting away on his car's loudspeaker. People were running in their robes and pajamas down the street away from the Powell house. John pushed past the pain in his ankle until he made it to his car.

He put the car in drive and did a U-turn, *:23....: 22....: 21...*

Slamming the pedal to the floor, the Lexus's engine roared at the sudden acceleration on a cold engine. John flipped open his phone and dialed, Davis Private Investigations, a number he hadn't used in over a year. As a woman picked up, his car shook with the force of the explosion. Even with two blocks of distance, the shockwave cracked his back window and knocked the phone from his hand. A massive plume of fire burst up from the street behind him, turning night into day.

He picked up the phone and heard Chloe Davis yelling, "Jesus, John, what was that noise? Are you okay?"

He straightened his car back onto the road, "Sorry, Chloe. A half a city block just went up in flames, I think."

She paused, then asked, "What kind of trouble are you in?"

He pulled over and started cycling through his phone, "I have a picture I'm sending you. It's hot, so don't let anyone catch you with it."

Chloe spat, "You'd better not get me into any shit. There was a reason I didn't like hanging around with you and David when I was on the force. I enjoy staying out of jail!"

He sent the images to her via text, "How about triple your usual fee and a thousand dollar bonus if you can get this to me within the next two hours?"

She snapped up the offer, "Okay, now we're talking. What do you need?"

John got the car moving again, "I just sent you several images of barrels with a shipping receipt on the top. I want to know what was in them, who ordered them, when they were delivered, the works."

He heard her tapping on a keyboard, "Do you want me to text you the results?"

He thought for a moment, "No. I'll call you back in a couple of hours. I've got to go make a police report in the meantime, and Chloe..."

She stopped typing, "Yeah?"

John looked at the pillar of flame in his rearview mirror, "Impress me."

Tulsa, Oklahoma – Tuesday, November 13th, 2018 – 1:52 a.m. CST

In the station, TV's were blasting out the news coverage of the bombing of the Garden District. Below the reporter, a banner read, "15 DEAD 8 INJURED IN BROTHERHOOD TERRORIST BOMBING." A room full of tired-looking cops stood in silence, as images of the fire department attempting to get the blaze under control filled the screens.

In an office, three UCC lawyers were surrounding John as he wrote his statement. Sitting across from him was his old Captain, Angel Andino. He had already gone over his account several times, with his lawyers overseeing the process.

He signed the document and slid it over to Captain Andino, who remarked, "So let me get this straight. You developed a series of teams that checked out tips the public phoned in regarding possible Brotherhood activity. Knock up job, John. Guess you found one, and the result was a city block leveled. You do realize there will be obstruction of justice charges, not to mention civil lawsuits from the families of those poor souls who died in their beds."

A sharp-looking, dark-haired lawyer held up a finger, "Incorrect. The UCC gives all the leads to the police that they received on a daily basis. If your department doesn't have the resources to follow up on all of them in a timely manner, then the UCC has a moral responsibility to do so. General Utterson has the full backing of the church, Eastland College, and Governor Greyson Dunn."

The Captain narrowed his eyes, "Governor Elect Dunn. He isn't in office yet, and Governor Hill doesn't see it that way."

A grey-haired lawyer plopped down a document on the desk, "It is perfectly legal. Each member of the Project: Trust, but Verify teams are licensed private detectives and have concealed carry permits. If you attempt to pursue this ridiculous accusation against our client or Eastland, Governor Dunn has authorized us to sue the City of Tulsa for wrongful prosecution. We will then sue every member of the department who slanders the good name of the United Christian Crusaders, or their members. Captain Andino, the church will aggressively defend its position and good name. Do not test its resolve."

John noticed his old Captain's voice raise, as he once again buckled under political pressure, "Right... well, I'll concede those points for now. What I find suspicious is how you knew this was the Crimson Brotherhood? You just magically divined the answer from what? God?"

John locked eyes with the man, "It's called intuition. Good cops develop it."

Andino tilted his head at the insult. "Well, let me use some of my intuition. Moss Vickers, a known drug dealer on the north side, tells his fiancé that he's going for a drive in the middle of the night. She thinks he's going to do a drug deal, but no. He travels to little Ms. Powell's house and gets into a gunfight in the yard."

John stayed silent as the Captain paused, then continued, "No one's buying that shit! I can't prove it, but Moss Vickers has been on your payroll since before you OD'd your last partner. Hell, he was an informant of David's years before he introduced you to him! Just like Nancy Bell, your paid snitches seem to keep showing up dead, and you keep walking away looking like the hero!"

The black-haired attorney cleared his throat, "Captain, it is late. The city is in chaos, and General Utterson has a long night of organizing cleanup crews and patrols to the streets."

Andino chuckled, "Oh, *General* Utterson. That's a shiny title, John. Worth the price you paid by stabbing every good cop in the back."

The lawyer leaned in and made eye contact, "Captain, I'm becoming concerned. You're starting to treat him like a suspect instead of the hero he is. Dozens, if not hundreds of lives, were saved because of his intervention. Lest we forget, if it was left up to your department, Ms. Powell would likely be dead, and that explosive might have found its intended target. Now, if he isn't being charged with anything, then we are leaving."

Andino launched out of his chair. "John, you used to be a decent cop. I'm asking you, is there anything else that happened or that you saw that can help us out?"

The grey-haired lawyer pushed John out of the door as the other reminded the captain, "Everything is in the report, Captain. Contact my offices if you need anything additional."

Andino yelled at him as he made his way through the squad room, "Terry Johnston is still on the Crimson Brotherhood task force. Are you going to turn your back on him too?"

The UCC attorneys were everything he used to hate as a detective, but having them on his side of the interrogation table proved invaluable. They walked him out of the station, and each took turns, reminding him not to talk to anyone about the incident unless they were present. He agreed to meet them again before the next morning's press conference at Eastland to address the bombing.

As he lowered himself in the car, he reached for the glove box and pulled out the paper sack that Moss had given him. He popped a few Oxys into his mouth and swallowed them dry. He looked at the empty passenger seat and remembered the blasted away face of his friend.

He headed for his old trailer and called Chloe, "What do you have?"

She bypassed his question and asked, "Was that explosion I heard earlier the same one that is all over the TV?"

John gripped the wheel in pain from his ankle, and frustration showed in his voice, "Yes! Now, did you get the information?"

Chloe clacked away at her keyboard, "Jesus, John! I don't even want to know what you've got into. My name better not come up anywhere!"

He turned onto the highway, "It won't."

She sighed and continued, "Hoondo Limited Manufacturing is a massive company. They have diversified by holding interests in mining, real estate, chemicals, and energy around the globe. They even have their own mining operations. Not to mention seven large side companies that dip into health and nutrition, inorganic materials, performance polymers, coatings, and additives. The company has an annual profit of 684 million dollars from the United States alone. Their global net worth is 16.7 billion dollars."

John shifted his weight off his ribs, "Look, that's fascinating, but where were those chemicals going?"

Chloe tapped a few more keys and responded, "According to the label you sent me, it was delivered to DeSoto, Kansas. I tracked down the address, and it's a vacant lot. The signature of the person who signed it is illegible. The driver is one Jordan Watts. I called his house and his very upset wife, who thought I was a mistress, told me he was working on the road."

He felt the pain killers start to sink in, "Who paid for it?"

She responded, "I couldn't find a name, but I was able to determine it was paid for by an offshore account. Getting specific billing information would take a subpoena, and you're not a cop anymore. At least from what I hear."

John punched the steering wheel, "Dammit! Where is the company's home office?"

The woman typed some more, "It's in Salem, Oregon. John, I had some extra time while you were messing around with the cops. Hold onto your seat. Hoondo Limited Manufacturing is owned by Jake Trevino, Aidan Nolan, Delinda Carducci, Lyubimov Artem Zakharovich, and one newly appointed owner and shareholder, Richard Enfield."

John sobered up, "What?"

Chloe's voice went up an octave, "Your new UCC boss, and Lieutenant Governor-Elect, Richard Enfield."

He pulled the car over to the shoulder, "How's that possible? He's a lawyer from Tulsa. How would someone get a seat at a table like that?"

She let out a chuckled, "I asked myself that same question, so I did some digging. Samuel Howard was shot and killed by a mugger in downtown Tulsa. When he died, Richard Enfield was named his successor in Hoondo Manufacturing and inherited his mansion, money, and assets.

Overnight this guy became a multimillionaire."

John opened up the notebook he lifted from Wicked. The book still smelled like gunpowder, and the blood had dried on the leather binding. He turned the overhead car light on and popped it open. He scanned down the page that looked to be a list of gun shipments. On the left, he saw the initials, RE.

He slammed the book down in disgust as Chloe asked, "Now, are you ready for me to really impress you?"

He shut his eyes tight in anger, "I'm not sure at this point."

The private detective paused before revealing, "Samuel Howard is survived by a single relative. One Amy Howard, of the Tulsa Medical Examiner's office."

John threw the phone into the dashboard and screamed, "Fuck!"

Chapter 11: David II

Muskogee, Oklahoma – Tuesday, November 13th, 2018 – 4:28 p.m. CST

David Keller sped down the road towards Fort Gibson with Thomas Booth still snoring in the passenger seat. The empty cup of coffee in his lap had done little to keep him alert, and the exhaustion of the last eight days was taking its toll. Between the nightmare-filled PTSD dreams and taking his nightly shifts watching over their vampire prisoner, he couldn't remember what a normal life looked like anymore.

Thomas let out a prolonged fart in his sleep, and David slapped his face, "Hey! Wake up!"

The Druid snorted awake, "Are we there?"

He rolled down the window to avoid the gaseous assault, "Almost. I need you to keep me awake."

A loud banging came from the bed of his blue Ford pickup. Thomas grumbled and put on his thick glasses. David dodged out of the way, as he grabbed the cattle prod from the floorboard and swung it around. Opening the cabs sliding rear window, the druid stuck the business end of the device through a hole in the side of the crossover aluminum toolbox. A quick series of shocks delivered to the occupant elicited an echoing scream from within the small prison.

Thomas yelled into the hole, "Shut up!"

He slammed the window shut and spun around to his seat, "Eight days with that thing in my house. Eight days with us doing twelve-hour shifts watching that thing crawl around a protective circle in my basement. Eight days and no help from that wrinkled scrotum sack."

David saw the sun setting, "At least you got to sleep during the day. I hated lying to Uncle Enrich about where I've been spending my time. I've never lied to him in my life!"

Thomas's greasy, unwashed face grinned, "I bet that Nazi's seen some shit in his days! I bet if you told him what we were doing, he'd goosestep right over and help."

He gripped the wheel in frustration, "For the last time, being German doesn't make you a Nazi, you bigot!"

The druid took out the window, "That's exactly what a Nazi would say."

David rubbed his face to stay awake, "If you don't want to walk back to Muskogee…"

Thomas turned in the seat towards him, "What's keeping you from sleeping?"

He looked perplexed at the sudden change in topic, "What the hell do you think? Who could get sleep watching that vamp?"

The man shook his head, "For someone opposed to lying, you're doing a great job right now. What's keeping you from sleeping? We both know that thing can't get out of the protections Basten gave us, and Marcus can't track her down when she is inside it. I sleep like a baby on my shifts."

David looked shocked, "You idiot! You sleep on your guard shifts! What if she got out and attacked you?

Thomas freed his pasty white leg from the cloak and put it up on the dashboard. His thick body hair was the only splash of color to his complexion. He leaned back into the corner of the cab, pushed his robe to one side, and let his crotch air out.

David nearly gagged, "Jesus Christ, man! Do you have to do that when I'm so close! Put that away!"

The druid shook his head, "First, you don't tell me how to live. Second, it goes away when you start telling the truth. What's keeping you from sleeping? Every day you look worse. Your uncle sleeps all the time. You can't tell me you can't find time to rest when you're at home."

He tucked his shoulder towards the driver's side door to create as much distance as possible from Thomas's offending member, "Holy shit, fine! Put that away first. It's like it's staring at me from a gopher hole."

Thomas dramatically snapped the robe back over his bushy nest, "It can come back at any time. So, only the truth."

David felt the anxiety build up in his chest, "I've never had panic attacks until after the fight at the Preserve."

The druid remained silent until David continued, "I was responsible for killing several people that night. I realize that they were torturing folks, and it needed to be done. It doesn't make it any easier. And then, there was her."

The smelly passenger pushed his glasses up on his face, "The superwoman that you and Amanda spoke about?"

He felt the skin start to crawl and felt the elephant on his chest, "Yeah. No woman could ever be that strong."

Thomas mocked, "Now who's a bigot?"

Shortness of breath came over him, and the attack hit suddenly. His friend held the wheel until he could get the truck pulled over to the curb. He flung open the door and rushed to the grassy shoulder of the US-62 highway. Passing cars zoomed by as David threw up the hotdogs they had purchased from QuikTrip. He fell to his knees onto the cold ground, as Thomas applied a wet rag to the back of his neck.

Streams of mucus dripped off his face as he wept, "You don't know, man. She tossed me around like a sack of oats. I saw her pick up a full-grown man by the throat. She was barely one-hundred pounds, and the woman shrugged off my best shot. They didn't catch her, and that means she's still out there. I worry so much about my Uncle. What have I got us into? I'd rather deal with a vampire. At least that makes some God damn sense."

Thomas gripped his arm, "That woman was the epiphany of a new world view. No one wants to be dragged from the safe and secure system that our leaders have for us. We watch our phones instead of the stars in the sky. We work like dogs in our youth so we can gamble on having a few years of freedom at the end of our lives. We put our faith in books written by men instead of seeking out the divine with ourselves. Our fake world is designed to keep us slaves. You've just had the chains ripped off you. I had mine taken off long ago. Welcome to the real world, David Keller."

Fort Gibson, Oklahoma – Tuesday, November 13th, 2018 – 4:51 p.m. CST

David Keller pulled down the long dirt drive that led to an old red barn that sat as the only building on the sixty-acre spread. The timber had rotted away in some places, and the paint had chipped in large sections. The tin roof overhead was rusted and was barely hanging on from repeated battles with the Oklahoma weather.

Basten was sitting on an upside-down 5-gallon bucket in front of the large open double doors. Inside, Nicolaas was nailing new 2x4's to reinforce the sections of the walls that had seen better days. In the center of the dirt floor, a black tarp was covering something large and round.

David parked his car under a maple tree and rolled down his window, "Is this it?"

Basten nodded, "Did you bring her?"

Thomas yelled from the passenger seat, "No. We forgot to bring the undead girl you left in my basement. What the hell took so long for you to call us?"

David grabbed several Wal-Mart bags from the bed of the truck, as the elder Van Helsing replied, "Sauce for the goose, Mr. Booth. The girl has been out of Marcus's vision for eight days. That gave me time to find an adequate location for the coming battle with evil."

Thomas slammed the truck door, "Congratulations, it looks like you've discovered all the tetanus."

Basten groaned as he stood up, "Don't let looks fool you. Nicolaas and I have been preparing defenses."

The old man picked up the bucket and turned the label towards the pair. The white label read, "WT-103 CLEAR COAT FIRE RETARDANT - 5 GALLON". He then pointed to a pile of empty buckets that had a set of worn-out paint rollers."

David had a realization, "That will keep them from setting fire to the building."

Basten grinned, "Precisely, Mr. Keller. The barn is barren as well. Nothing to burn. I mixed the coconut oil solution in with the chemicals, so even touching the walls will cause them pain."

David sat down the bags, "I'm guessing the owner didn't mind?"

Nicolaas yelled from inside the barn, "You're looking at the new owners. Grandpa bought it and the land three days ago. For a vampire to be barred from entering a home, you have to own it first."

Thomas walked up to the wall and ran a finger down the sticky solution, "I've used this fire retardant stuff before. It isn't cheap. The barn is worn out, but the acreage is good pasture land. I'm guessing all of this was between one-hundred and fifty to two-hundred thousand dollars. All of that cash for one vampire hunt? For a woman you've never met before. How'd you pay for all of this?"

Basten leaned on his silver-tipped cane, "The Van Helsing family has earned the appreciation of several wealthy nobles over the centuries. You see, vampires tend to have more aristocratic tastes. My ancestors liberated their fair share of the wealthy elite." He pointed his cane at his grandson, "We've invested that money well, and secured our ability to do battle with the forces of darkness well past my kleinzoon's time."

Thomas walked in the barn and tapped his gnarled staff against the mysterious object hidden by the tarp, "Jacuzzi?"

Nicolaas pulled the tarp off to reveal a sizeable blue tank with the top cut off, "An industrial above-ground water tank. We just had it delivered yesterday."

Thomas peeked inside and sniffed the water, "What the hell is in here?

The young Van Helsing stuck his hand in the fluid and pulled it out, "1500 gallons of 4/5th's regular H2O, and the rest is a mixture of coconut water and palm oil."

Basten motioned to David, "The sun is setting, and she has been out of the protection circle all day. That means Marcus and his clan knows where she is. They will be coming. Drive your truck inside the barn so we can prepare."

Fort Gibson, Oklahoma – Tuesday, November 13th, 2018 – 8:42 p.m. CST

The vampiric girl screamed in a strange language, as her skin sizzled in the coconut water. She was bound in rope and being suspended from the rafters by a pully. The creature floated in the liquid and burned until she no longer moved. Nicolaas and David pulled her body up until it cleared the tank by a foot. The emaciated Adze Vampire looked like a corpse. The rope webbing hung loose on its body, and its skin pressed against its bones. The coconut water and palm oil did its job in seconds. Still, it took progressively longer for the undead to fully regenerate. The features of her face were gone, leaving only a thin layer of skin over the skeletal structure.

Thomas sighed, "Look, I'm all for staking these things, but why make this thing suffer?"

Nicolaas fired up a generator, and a string of interior lights came to life as Basten replied, "Bait is better when it is still alive, Mr. Booth. Do not mistake this creature for some defenseless child. It is a pure born beast. A vampire child of two vampires. It has never known humanity."

David pulled off his work gloves, "How can you know that? This thing hasn't spoken a word of English since we got her."

Basten tapped his wrinkled neck with his index finger, "The bite marks always stay after a person has been turned. There are no bite marks on this one, so she was born to darkness. The Adze vampire isn't the most physically powerful, but they are some of the most astute spellcasters in all the clans. Mr. Booth struggles with the morals of my methods. Let me assure you both, what we are doing to her is a thimble compared to the oceans of torment Ms. Lanyon's daughters are going through."

David looked up at the shriveled body, "It's been hours since the sun went down. Why hasn't Marcus shown up to collect her?"

Baston winced and rubbed his chest, "I don't know. Something must be keeping him occupied."

Thomas grabbed the old man's arm and helped him to his bucket, "Your spirit is strong, I'll give you that, but your aura is lifting. It won't be long now. You should prepare yourself."

The elder lifted his chin, "I'm fine! Fine enough to get this job done and then tend to my kleinzoon's training."

Nicolaas ran over and gave his grandfather a drink of water from a canteen. Thomas and David locked eyes, and the druid shook his head. David thought about his own Uncle Enrich and wondered if this was a glimpse into the suffering he would go through.

Thomas walked over to the Wal-Mart bags David had brought in earlier, "What's in these?"

David was grateful for the distraction from his thoughts. He set them up on a workbench and took out four Super Soaker toy water guns. They were of various sizes, and he picked up a bright yellow one that had an orange tank on top.

Basten coughed, "What in God's name are you doing with those?"

David dunked one in the coconut and palm oil mixture, as Basten got up and shambled over to him, "Toys! You bring toys to a fight with the forces of evil? We Van Helsing's have been laying low the undead for hundreds of years. Our methods have been handed down from father to son. I will not dishonor their memory with childish games."

Keller turned towards the front door and pumped the lever to pressurize the air inside. With a squeeze of the trigger, a blast of coconut water launched out and splattered against the wooden door. In a matter of seconds, the rotted planks were a dark grey from the moisture. He released the trigger and turned to the surprised Van Helsing with a satisfied grin.

Basten paused for a moment then pointed his cane at the other water guns, "I want the big one."

The night wore on, as they sat in the four corners of the barn and held watch over the surrounding pasture through cracks in the walls. The floodlights Nicolaas had installed on the exterior of the barn gave them illumination and line of sight for almost fifty yards in all directions. The fatigue of a week's worth of sleepless nights was settling in on David, and he had trouble focusing.

Thomas crept over to David and knelt on the ground beside him, "This is pointless. We've seen these things can turn into fireflies, and who knows what else they can do. Do you really think this old barn will keep them out."

David shrugged, "The old man's been right so far, and we're the best shot Amanda's got at getting her kids back in one piece."

The druid held up a small water pistol, "Those inspirational words mean so much to the guy with the smallest gun!"

David smirked, "I mean…"

Basten called out from his corner, "It's starting."

The fully regenerated vampiric girl spoke up for the first time, "My mother is here."

Thomas marched over towards the tank, "You speak English? Here I tried to learn Ewe so I could understand you."

The girl's head snapped around to him as he continued, "What's your name?"

She gave him the same innocent look that was on her face at the Preserve, "I miss my mommy. My name's…"

Thomas interrupted, "Oh, wait. I don't give a shit."

She shrieked in anger as her eyes turned pitch black, "I'm going to see your insides, Thomas Booth! I'm going to drain your children to death, and I will end your line!"

Booth sniffed and replied, "I have kids? I mean, it's possible. I took a lot of chances."

The vampire hissed, "Brave Thomas Booth, you put up so many false fronts. You might have held me prisoner, in your home, but you did invite me in. Your mortal wards were annoying, but it didn't stop me from peering into your mind while you slept."

David gave him a hard stare as Thomas admitted, "Okay, I did nod off a few times on guard duty."

The child's voice seemed to purr as she continued, "Of course you were tired. Life has never been kind to you. The rough life of an orphan in Muskogee took its toll. You never knew who your parents were. They gave you up because, in truth, you were a burden to them. Then you were handed off to three different families. Each more repulsed by you than the next. Determined little Thomas. You went to college and even tried to do big things. You learned the hard truth about life. That the people you loved cared more about themselves than you, and why not? You're a sore that festers."

David walked up to Thomas, "Dude, don't listen to this shit. She's trying to get in your head."

The druid pulled away and walked closer, as she continued, "Still, you chose to live alone, to isolate yourself and find happiness in plants and trees rather than humans. You provide cannabis to the sick and dying because they can't afford it. In truth, you've forced their friendship because they love the relief from the pain, not you. You worship anything that can't run away from you."

Basten yelled at Thomas, "Fool! She's trying to distract you! Get back to your posts, the both of you!"

Thomas looked confounded, and the vampire revealed, "You won't be alone for much longer. My mother is coming. When she gets here, I'll kill your friends while you watch, and then I'll make you my pet. I'll drain you of life every day and set you about doing my bidding. Then when I'm done with you, I'll suck out your soul and leave your corpse for the rats. How would you like it if I made your life a living hell?"

Booth's blank stare broke as he pushed up his glasses, "That's a generous offer, but I'm not quite ready for marriage. I don't want you to stop looking for love."

He gave her the middle finger, as the creature hissed and struggled against the netting. Thomas lumbered past David towards his lookout point, and he wondered if what she said was true. There was precious little he knew about the druid, other than he lived in a greenhouse.

Outside, the sound of a pop startled him. David, he ran to a crack in the wooden slats and looked out towards the road. Standing out beside his pickup was a slender black woman with an elegant form-fitting purple dress on. The floodlights shined down on her, as she slowly sauntered up towards the barn door. The cold wind blew her long curly hair, and David couldn't help but be transfixed by her unearthly allure.

The sound of another pop snapped him out of his trance. He scanned behind her and saw the left side of his truck, lowering to the ground. The sound of air hissing filled him with dread as he knew his truck tires were being flattened. He cursed to himself as the giggling of two little girls came from his vehicle.

The captive vampire looked over at Thomas, "My new sisters are here, too! They will be so glad to see you, Thomas Booth. Lady Violet has told them all about how you helped get their mother involved in the dealings of the Brotherhood. They know you're just as responsible for their human father's death and want to settle their blood debt."

Thomas walked over next to David, who remarked, "If these things have turned Amanda's kids into vampires…"

The druid pumped up the compressor to his water gun, "Yeah, it will make Mother's Day awkward. Let's just work one problem at a time. First, we get them, then we figure what comes next."

Basten shuffled over and opened the large double doors, "Greetings, I'm Basten Van Helsing. I wish to address the clan leader, Marcus Holmes."

The Lanyon girls appeared from behind David's truck. The ten-year-old Nancy was dressed in all white, wearing a simple dress with a white bow in her hair. The twelve-year-old April contrasted her sister and wore gothic-looking jeans and a ripped shirt. A chorus of anguished crying came from both of the children, and they ran towards the dark-skinned woman.

Latching onto her leg, the lady announced, "Our dearest Marcus has left this world. I'm the Lady Violet Holmes, and I now speak as the head of the Adze clan in America. May I come in so we might discuss a truce?"

Basten snickered, "I've played my part in this drama before. I refuse. Although, you've caught me in a generous mood. I'm willing to listen to your proposal, but you will do so from out there."

The sounds of people laughing rode the wind from all directions. The tin roof exploded with the sound of feet walking across its length. David and Thomas shared a look of horror, as the rooftop newcomers drummed on the metal and jeered.

Basten looked back and found Violet had moved to the edge of the barn's door in an instant, "I smell death on you old man. Don't take these fools with you."

He leaned on his cane and stood up straight, "State your proposal."

David couldn't help but stay transfixed on Violet's curves as she replied, "You have my daughter, Clare. I want her back. She is all I have left of my Marcus. I don't want to lose a daughter and a husband in the same week."

Basten ground his teeth for a moment, "A trade then. You lift the curse of vampirism from Nancy and April Lanyon. As the leader of your clan, you have that power."

The Lanyon girls both screamed in protest as the old man continued, "In return, we will hand over Clare Holmes to you. Both parties will uphold a parting truce. I agree not to hunt your clan for the rest of my life, and you promise not to do the same towards us."

A resounding chorus of objections came from a half a dozen rooftop voices. Blood tears streamed out the two teenage girls' black eyes as they flew into the air. Dust swirled underneath them, and the wind whipped up to match their rage. Their hair shot around in chaos, and they screamed out in Ewe at Violet. The scene went on for several seconds until the newly appointed Lady of the Adze clan held up her left hand. The unseen clamors far above halted immediately. The Lanyons whimpered and ceased their caterwauling, as the pair floated down and landed softly on the cold dirt. Violet held out her arms, and the two hugged her tight with wails of misery.

The cold wind the Lanyon sisters had conjured swept in from outside and sent a chill down his back. David kept his eye on Basten, and suddenly realized how ridiculous it was that he had a toy in his hand. At the same time, a coven of bloodsucking magicians stalked around outside. A wave of anxiety swept over him, and he felt his breath shorten. The power of Violet elicited memories of the superwoman from his nightmares. He staggered back away from Thomas and slammed, back first, into the wall of the barn. He fell to the ground with pain stretching up into his chest.

David hyperventilated as Basten ordered, "Thomas, see to our friend."

He felt a hot poker jabbing into his sternum, as he writhed on the ground, searching for a position that would bring relief. David's fingers tingled, and he lost his grip on the toy gun. No matter how he moved, he couldn't get comfortable. Booth grabbed him by the jacket and pulled him to a sitting position.

Nicolaas squatted beside them, "What's wrong with him?"

Thomas struggled to keep the big man upright, "He's had anxiety since the Battle at the Preserve."

The young Van Helsing shook his head, "He shouldn't have come then if he couldn't handle it."

The druid grabbed him by the collar, "Hey, smartass. How about you worry about your grandfather, and I'll take care of this?"

As Nicolaas retreated to his grandfather, Thomas grabbed David's shoulders, "Hey! I need you to focus on me!"

He clenched his chest and gasped, "My arm hurts! I'm having... a heart attack!"

Thomas reached in his belt pouch and pulled out a small clear vial. He unstopped the corked top and applied a few drops to his index finger. Before David could object, the druid smeared it on his upper lip.

The sweet smell overwhelmed his senses, as Thomas remarked, "This is Lemon balm. Take slow deep breaths and concentrate on the smell. You're having a panic attack, not a heart attack. Your arm is hurting because you're hyperventilating. I need you to realize that and breathe with me."

As Thomas helped him to calm down, Violet told Basten, "I do not accept your terms. We Adze have a tradition of blood for blood. If one of us falls, then we take payment. I can't let you walk away with both my adopted daughters, while only getting my Clare back."

Basten stabbed his cane into the ground and protested, "This rule can be bent. I suggest that you..."

The air around Violet seemed to vibrate with her anger, "Blood for blood! I will need another for the trade."

David's breathing was slowing, but he was covered in sweat. He felt like his body had just run a race. Slowly, Thomas helped him up to his feet and handed him his water gun. The two joined Nicolaas behind Basten and raised their weapons at the trio of vampires outside their door. For the first time, he got a good look at Violet up close. Her eyes were pitch black, and compound insect-like eyes shined against the floodlights above. An almost magical glow surrounded her, inviting him to hang on her every word.

Basten finished deliberating, "Then you can take your daughter and me. That will satisfy blood debt."

Nicolaas lowered his gun and grabbed his grandfather's shoulder, "No! You can't go!"

Basten's old eyes swelled with tears, "Kleinzoon, you must understand that the Van Helsings serve humanity. Ours is one of sacrifice and dedication. This is a good trade. We get the Lanyons back, and you stay safe."

Nicolaas latched onto his thick black coat, "No! You can't go! I don't know what to do! I'm not ready for you to leave!"

Basten's boney hand patted his grandson's, "You are more ready than I was at your age. Never forget that you're a Van Helsing and that I love you!"

Nicolaas buried his head in his elder's coat, as Basten announced, "I offer myself and your daughter to you. In exchange, we demand that April and Nancy Lanyon be freed."

Basten gripped the younger man by the wrist, "Before I go, you must understand two things! First, and most importantly, they intend to turn me into one of them. I will become a willing follower of the darkness, a villain that stalks the night and preys on the innocent. You must hunt me down, and kill me. Second, my daughter and your father were never killed in a car accident."

The young man's mouth went wide, "But you told me..."

Tears ran down both of their faces, "My Kleinzoon, you weren't ready to hear the awful truth. It was better to let you believe a lie than to know the awful truth. My Nicolaas , your father was killed while hunting these creatures, and your mother... I had to hunt down my own child and put a stake through her heart."

Violet's smooth voice interrupted, "Oh, how you have caused your family to suffer. Why do you Van Helsings throw your lives away? You are a deer pitching itself in front of the lion. We feed on the herds of the valley before your death and well after. If you only knew how little your efforts meant, I suspect you might drive a stake through your own heart for the hurt and pain brought to your family in vain."

The pain in Basten's face turned to anger, "It is never a lost cause to fight the legions of darkness. It is in that fight that humanity shines the brightest. My grandson will shine brighter than any other Van Helsing has. I agree to your conditions, harlot. I invite you in."

Booth pulled David back as Violet glided off the ground and through the doorway. The Lanyon daughters fell to the ground in anguish over their impending freedom from undeath. The vampire floated up to her captured daughter and spoke some words in Ewe. The netting unraveled and loosened. Within seconds, Clare spilled out into Violet's arms, and the two gently landed on the dirt floor of the barn. She spoke to the girl in Ewe and held her tight. The demonic creature returned to full strength and once again looked like the innocent child they had found in the Preserve.

Violet finally stood up, and the Lanyon daughters ran inside the barn. The three children embraced one another, and Clare joined in their protests. David ducked as the pounding overhead began again.

The new Lady of the clan held up her hand and ushered in dead silence. She spoke a few phrases in Latin, and the Lanyons hit the ground like a stiff board. Clare stepped back with bloody streams going down her cheeks. Violet continued her incantations as a black mist raised out of their mouths and ears. The pair lay unmoving as the last of the black cloud collected in the air above them. The incantation ceased, and the dark fog above them suddenly turned solid, then fell on top of the girls. David and Thomas scampered back as the once magical mist was now dark earth and scattered over the floor. The unconscious Lanyons' pale skin poked through the layer of dirt that covered their faces. David felt his mind whirl with the impossible nature of it all. Before his eyes, their skin turned flush again, and their canines retracted back to regular size.

Basten stepped between the sisters and Violet, "Are they free of your curse?"

Violet nodded, "They are free of the Vampiric gift, but not loose of my sorcery. They are still my children and, while I can't take them with me, they still have access to the dark arts. One day they will seek me out and rejoin my clan. Blood for blood. Now Basten Van Helsing, you will join my coven and give to me all your secrets. Vampires will be rid of your nuisance once and for all."

Basten stepped closer to her, "You will find my will stronger than you bargained for, witch! Now, we leave in peace, just as we..."

Violet cackled and interrupted, "We will leave these two fools and your grandson alive, but peace was not in your bargain."

David was only able to lift his water gun a few inches before a young man in a black leather coat grabbed his arm. He was spun around like a top and was nose to nose with the bald youth in his twenties. Behind him were seven other young people, all dressed in black and sporting compound eyes and fangs. His knees buckled, and he heard the crack of Thomas's skull being struck by something solid. The druid splayed out in in front of him, unconscious and bleeding. The hairless vampire growled with a toothy grin and punched him in the forehead. His vision narrowed, and then a high pitched squealing invaded his ears. The blackness overtook him as all the sound and lights went out.

Location Unknown – Day Unknown – Time Unknown

David Keller suddenly found himself standing alone in the center of the old red barn. He spun around to discover his friends and the vampires were gone. David was standing in the place where the blue tank full of water had once been. The only thing that remained was the rope pully overhead. Instead of the webbed netting that had held Clare, it now had a hangman's noose.

He ran outside into the night air and discovered his truck was missing. He called out for Thomas, but no one responded. He turned back towards the barn and saw his Uncle Enrich looking back at him. The elderly man was dressed all in black with a turtleneck.

He ran towards him, "Onkel Enrich, wie bist du hierher gekommen?"

David waited, but his uncle gave no indication as to how he came to be in the barn. The German patted his nephew's face and smiled. Before he could ask a question, the cancer-riddled man grabbed him by the neck. David felt like his throat was going to collapse, and he tried to free himself from the iron grip.

With a sharp toss, David was sent sailing back into a support beam in the center of the barn. His back sparked with pain, and the corner of the post opened up a gash in his lower side. Landing like a sack of potatoes on the ground, David felt the breath get knocked out of him.

Forcing his eyes open, he watched his immigrant uncle pull out a ski mask and put it on. As it pulled down on his face, the man transformed into the blonde-haired superwoman. Tufts of golden locks poked out from under the covering, and she cracked her knuckles in anticipation.

He scooted back and looked around for a weapon. The woman stalked closer as David turned and crawled towards the exit. He looked up and found that the front barn door was gone and was replaced by another wall. David pulled himself up and did his best to keep his distance.

Suddenly, the woman charged in with a flurry of punches and kicks. Panic set in as she roared with determination and landed repeated blows. A combination of moves ended with her performing a well-timed spinning back kick into his sternum. David flew back into the rotting timbers and landed in a heap on the cold earth.

She snatched him by a wrist and ankle, then slung him twenty yards away, into the opposite wall. His leg snapped on impact and dangled loosely just below the knee. David's head poured blood, and his right pinky finger was broken in half.

She bounded after him and lifted him by the neck with one hand. The woman tossed him over her shoulder, and he went airborne for another ten feet. His momentum kept him skidding after his body found the ground. As he finally came to a halt, David heard the familiar laughter of the Lanyon children.

Nancy mocked, "Get up, David! We need you to save us!"

April chimed in, "Please, David! Don't let us down!"

He lifted his blood-soaked face up off the ground, but there was no sign of the Lanyons. The short woman hoisted him up by his coat collar and pinned David to the central support beam. She snapped a half dozen uppercuts to his stomach, which caused him to spew blood out of his mouth in a coughing fit. The woman let go and dropped him to the ground.

He sat against the wooden pole and watched her through the one working eye. Unable to move his body, David was helpless as she pulled both ends of the hangman's noose over to him. She jabbed her knee into his chest to keep him in place and shoved the air out of his lungs.

He struggled wildly and used his left hand to beat against the woman's legs in an attempt to get free. She continued to lean into him, unaffected by his blows, as she widened the loop enough to fit over his head. The superwoman grabbed David under the chin and lifted his 240 pound frame by his jaw up to a standing position. He spit up blood and wallowed in anguish at the pressure. David felt his broken leg dangling freely and smacking against his other calf.

She pitched the loop over his head and started taking up the slack on the other end of the rope. Right before she pulled it tight, David flipped the noose over her head and cinched the knot. Instantly, she released her knee in his chest and struggled to get free. Before she could, he leaned out and grabbed the other end of the cord. As he fell to the ground, he let his weight pull the superwoman off the ground by her slender neck. His body provided a counterweight to the kicking and flailing superwoman.

The decades of rock climbing went into maintaining the hold on the rope with just his left hand. The superwoman suddenly stopped struggling and swung limp. The sounds of the noose creaking against the wood rafters were the only sound as he continued to hold on for several minutes to be sure.

With an exhale of exhaustion, he let go of the rope and heard the zip of the line before the attached body hit the earth. He dragged himself over to the woman and put a hand on the top of the ski mask. Fighting through the pain, he grabbed a handful of cloth and pulled it off her head. The old face of Uncle Enrich stared wide-eyed at the ceiling of the barn. The ancient German tongue was pushed between his teeth, and the corpse's face was a beet red from the strangulation.

David's psyche cracked as he pulled the rope away from his Uncle's crooked neck. Blubbering incoherently, he grabbed the man's face and begged him to respond. Moaning in anguish, the blood flowed from his broken face onto the forehead of the dead Enrich.

He opened his eyes to find the image of the barn was gone, and a pitch-black had replaced it. The loud sounds of the creaking ropes he had heard when he hung the superwoman had returned. David took a moment to realize he was actually laying down and inside something musty. He attempted to sit up but hit his head on something wood and hard. A chill went into him from the severe cold and felt around the edges of his tiny prison. Within seconds, his head had cleared enough to realize he had been experiencing a nightmare before. He felt a sense of relief; the damage he had sustained was all just a dream. His body was shaking from the chill and the experienced nightmare. Probing around, David discovered that he was actually trapped inside a small box of some kind.

Something deep inside his mind had snapped. He no longer felt the lingering obsession with the superwoman but instead focused on the spin out of control. The idea of hope was gone, and another panic attack set in. He gasped for breath and urinated himself. Bawling like a child, he rocked back and forth in the box and languished in his misery.

Some time passed before he noticed tiny pinholes of sunlight streaming in from sliver-sized openings in the wood. He cleared away the tears and relished the small degree of illumination the beams provided. He examined the interior to find it was lined on the bottom with a smooth, soft white material. Along the sides were satin, and a sensation that he was swaying came over him. He tapped the floor of the wood container and checked the width.

He started to hyperventilate and shut his eyes tight, as he realized, *I'm in a coffin!*

Chapter 12: Shoshannah II

Tulsa, Oklahoma – Wednesday, November 14th, 2018 – 10:01 a.m. CST

Shoshannah Feinstein looked at Richard Enfield's laptop screen and read, "Transfer Complete."

She crossed her arms, "Thank you. I hope this concludes our business from here on out?"

Richard stood up from behind his large oak desk, "It does. I appreciate you spending the extra time to coax the golem into cooperating with Miniel."

She picked up her black coat from his office's leather couch, "You're lucky it only took three days. The stronger the soul light, the more will power the golem has, and this one was very resistant. It's no wonder, considering who you brought me. You're lucky it agreed instead of turning on us."

He poured himself a coffee, "I suppose we are fortunate to have you around."

Shoshannah walked away from his desk, "I'd like to take credit for it, but the glory goes to Samuel. If it wasn't for his spellwork and silver tongue, Miniel and the golem would have never seen eye-to-eye."

Richard took a deep breath, "It's a relief to see this large investment will soon pay off. Now we wait for them to finish merging and then arise as a Nephilim. One strong enough to overcome Hyde's new form."

She pulled her hair back in a ponytail, "Yeah, you have fun with that. I'll be glad to be rid of the Brotherhood from my life and continue my sabbatical. No offense, Master Enfield."

He gave a mocked expression of hurt, "So direct! I like that. You have been well paid for the work and generously compensated for the business with Marcus. You have the thanks of this world's next rulers."

Shoshannah rolled her eyes and walked to the door of the study, "Forget my number. As far as you are concerned, I'm as dead as that pile of dirt in your basement."

She walked down the halls of the Howard Estate towards the front door. A familiar and sharply dressed ghost met her in the foyer. He was wearing a black suit with a grey tie and had a broad grin across his bearded face.

She stopped and grinned, "I guess this is it, Sam."

He gave a slight bow, "It pains me to see you go."

The Crusader guards that stood at each end of the large maple double doors gave each other a perplexed look. To them, it looked as if Shoshannah was having a one-sided conversation with thin air. They drew open the doors and let the sunlight pour onto the black and white checkered floor.

She let Samuel escort her to Whim and remarked, "I have had assistants before, good ones, but you were... unique. I wonder what these good Christian Crusaders would think if they knew a tireless ghost and a relentless re-animated corpse were working side-by-side, day and night, to bring a blasphemous Nephilim into this world?"

The specter chuckled, "Probably the same thing they would think if they knew their next Lieutenant Governor, the virtuous and Christian leader, Richard Enfield, was actually the leader of the very terrorist organization their Crusaders were designed to defeat."

Shoshannah took the keys for Whim from the valet and got in the black Dodge Charger, "Normally, I tell Clerval to get some rest once he was finished with a long night of work, but not in your case. Don't forget me, Samuel Howard."

Samuel solidified his body enough to kiss her hand, "My love, I don't require sleep to dream of you."

Shoshannah rested her arm and head on the open window of her car, "There's something I don't get about you, Sam. I saw you cast spells onto that new golem that I've never heard or seen before. Even as a ghost, you have true power. Then there is this estate, your wealth, and the connections you have, which all makes this really puzzling."

The specter leaned down to the car window, "Truly, my dear. What perplexes you?"

She shook her head, "How did someone as arrogant as Richard Enfield best you and become your keeper?"

Samuel gave her a slight smile, "I suppose we all have our part to play in the coming of Cthulhu. Richard played his part very well, and I have to ... well, I was going to say, live with that."

She gave him a skeptical look, "Goodbye, Samuel Howard."

Shoshannah started the car and waved goodbye at the dashing apparition. Pulling out of the drive, she felt like a swimmer rushing to get out of shark-infested waters. She was given the privacy of Samuel's old lab to do her work, but she always felt like someone was watching.

As she pulled away from the massive gates and onto the street, IGOR's Australian voice came online, "Mistress, I'm glad to see you safe. You'll be happy to know the funds have successfully been deposited in the accounts."

She gripped the wheel and squealed the tires, "Yeah, I saw. What's your status on finding Adam?"

The AI replied, "I'm still unable to track down his location. It isn't like him to be this incognito."

She flipped open her phone and sent a text to Jagger Clerval, "Hello, Love. I'm coming back to New York. I hope you are enjoying your vacation. Check your bank account. You will have enough to finish that remodeling job a few times over. I'll expect an invitation to dinner when you get back."

She turned onto 71st Street and took one last look at Tulsa, thankful to be putting it behind her. The city was a powder keg from the attacks from the Crimson Brotherhood, and Richard Enfield was about to light a match. Her phone buzzed in her hand, and she smiled at the thought of elation Jagger must have had over the massive payday.

She looked at the screen that read, "Now, Don't go leaving T-town without letting me buy you a steak first. — John Hamilton."

Shoshannah threw her phone down in the passenger seat and screamed in frustration.

Tulsa, Oklahoma — Wednesday, November 14th, 2018 — 11:12 a.m. CST

Shoshannah Feinstein sat across from Agent John Hamilton, "I didn't know you were in town, John. I would have insisted you take me out."

The Texan looked at her over the white coffee cup, "I'd never miss a chance to see you, or to get a good Oklahoma steak."

The McGill's steakhouse sign flashed overhead, "You know how I like a good piece of meat."

John blushed, "Same ol' Shoshannah. You know I never did get over you not calling me after that time in Vegas."

She took a sip of her water, "You know that phone works both ways."

He nodded, "I can't deny that. I guess with all this Cthulhu mess, I've been busier than a funeral home fan in the middle of July."

Shoshannah raised her right eyebrow, "Forgiven. Cults! Right? More death has happened in the name of some god than any war for power. It's ridiculous. Don't let it wear on you too much, John. Sometimes things have a way of working themselves out."

John spun his spoon nervously on the table, "That could be true, but right now, it is a wildfire. The Crimson Brotherhood activity has spread far beyond some crazy Okies. The FBI has confirmed thirteen different terrorist attacks that range all over the United States."

She reached over and straightened the Agent's turquoise bolo tie. Her pheromones lifted up to his nose, as he inhaled deeply from the excitement of her touch. The Texan's eyes glazed over, and he grabbed her hand like it was a lifeline to salvation.

She turned her palm up and let him kiss her hand, "Love, tell me, how come I haven't heard about this on TV?"

He looked into her deep blue eyes, "Control told me not to say anything about that to you."

She unfastened the top button to her low cut shirt, "He doesn't understand me like you do. You know you can trust me."

He stayed transfixed on the upper curve of her breast, "I suppose yer right. The FBI has been covering up as much as they can. If the public knew how little the Feds know, they would turn to the UCC. The President has asked AEGIS to stop the cult and make law enforcement look good in the process. That means bringing in their ramrod, Henry Jekyll, in alive and handing the cult to the FBI on a silver platter."

She took her ponytail out and let her black locks fall on her shoulders, "If anyone can do it, my Texan can. Any progress with tracking down Henry Jekyll or finding the Tulsa Sect of the Brotherhood?"

He pressed his stomach against the table in an attempt to get closer, "I tell you, it's the strangest thing. The Brotherhood knocked out the hospital's cameras, so all we got to go on is the evidence left behind. It was a mess! Three nurses, two security guards, fourteen cops, and seven cult members were killed in Jekyll's escape. The third-floor hallways outside of Henry Jekyll's room were torn to pieces. Doors were ripped off their hinges, bullet holes riddled the interior walls, and a hole the size of Volkswagen was made in the side of the building."

She stroked the back of his arm, "The news said that was from the cult setting off a charge. Something about the police suspecting they used it as an exit."

John shook his head, "One of the nurses that was caught in the crossfire said that an angel saved her, killed the cultists and then flew through the wall."

Shoshannah giggled, then realized he was serious, "An angel? John Hamilton, I didn't know you liked tall tales."

He took off his Stetson Hat and held her hand with both of his, "I know how it sounds, but I've seen stranger things. AEGIS put her under a lie detector, and she came out clean. Control had her sign a standard national security agreement, ensuring she wouldn't take her story to the press."

She smirked, "John, this is a state that is flooded in terror and superstition. Fucking religious crusaders are marching in the streets. She was probably delusional from stress. Soldiers see guardian angels all the time in combat."

He held her hand tight, "The FBI tested the debris surrounding the hole. No signs of explosives, no chemical residue, and no gunpowder. It's like some great force just pushed its way out, and get this, our boys in blue never made it past the front door."

He paused, waiting for her to respond until Shoshannah remarked, "So…"

John gave a big Texas grin, "So… the security guards were killed in the first seconds of the raid. The only two Brotherhood members killed by the cops were the ones holding the line at the front door. Someone or something tore through those cultists on the third floor without firing a shot. Some of the discharged slugs we found at the scene were smashed and lying on the floor. It's like they hit something solid and just dropped to the ground. The dead cultists were torn apart. Hell, it's like a bulletproof grizzly bear went on a rampage, ripped into those Brotherhood men, busted out of the wall, and just flew away."

She remembered her conversation with Richard about Hyde's transformation into a Nephilim and decided to try to throw the agent off, "Yeah, it sounds more like some Bram Stoker vampire fairy tale story than it does some angel. Were there any Brotherhood survivors that you could question?"

The pheromones were working in his system, causing him to break out into a sweat, "The surviving nurse said three cultists rappelled out the hole, carrying one that was burned and wounded. We have combed every surrounding street camera, but they disappeared. We think there might be a third player in the game. They might have taken Jekyll, or maybe the cult got him out another entrance."

Shoshannah gave a sympathetic look, "Oh, my. It sounds like quite the job on your hands. If anyone can wrangle those pesky cultists, it's my cowboy."

He smiled like a schoolboy, "I don't know about that, but I'm tryin'. I almost forgot! Control told me to make you an offer in exchange for helping us with a consultation before you left Oklahoma."

Shoshannah winced, "Did he now? Just what was he going to use to persuade me?"

John pulled out his phone, "Adam Frankenstein was spotted in New York on November 7th. Control is offering to use AEGIS resources to help track him down before he finds you. That and your usual thirty thousand dollar compensation."

She mulled it over. *That's nothing compared to the five million Richard Enfield just paid me. Still, I could use the help tracking down that psycho before he finds the Clervals. If I refuse, it will make Control suspicious. Fuck! I just want out of this state! All my oversensitive nose can smell is cow shit!*

Shoshannah gave him a wink, "I think Control knows how much I adore you and that I can't seem to say no. It's not fair."

John's intoxicated smile beamed, "You don't know how happy that makes me."

She leaned back away from his embrace, "Tell me what I can do to help."

The Texan looked dejected, "Last night an Oklahoma State Trooper pulled over an eighteen-wheeler when it blew past a weigh station on the Indian Nation Turnpike. The dash-cam from the Trooper's car caught the stop. Here, let me show you."

John pulled a tablet from his briefcase, set it up, facing her, then hit play. The video showed a tall trooper walking up alongside the semi, as cars passed on the highway. As the officer got out and walked up to speak to the driver, the red and blue lights of the cruiser flashed against the silver double doors of the trailer. A few seconds later, the trooper followed the trucker to the back of the trailer and watched him open it. As the doors swung free, the muzzle flash of several automatic weapons sizzled in the air, riddling the lawman with holes. The driver quickly shut the doors, locked them, leaned down, spoke something into the dead man's radio, dragged the body into the ditch, turned the cruiser's lights off, and then drove the semi away.

John hit a few buttons on the tablet, "The driver seemed to know a thing or two about police procedures, but didn't seem to care about being recorded on the dash camera. He radioed in a 10-7, indicating that the trooper was going on a break. The man's body wasn't discovered for several hours. We did manage to enhance the video, and we found something interesting."

A single isolated picture popped up on the screen. The flash of the automatic weapons illuminated the contents of the trailer. The shooter had on black tactical gear, and a Crimson Brotherhood symbol was in red on his arm. Shoshannah's equipment from the secret laboratory in the Great Swamp lined the walls. It was bound together on several pallets with heavy straps. Her stomach tightened, and she used all her control not to smash the restaurant's table in half. In the back, she saw a man tied up and sitting against her gas-powered generators. The person had on scrubs that bore the logo of the Queens General Center Hospital. She had been present at every birth that the Clervals had for two hundred years. She watched them grow up, marry, have their own kids, and die. Despite the blurry image, she knew her family.

She gripped the edge of the table as John continued, "You know this kind of equipment looks an awful lot like what you use, and that fella has a striking resemblance to your friend, Jagger Clerval."

She felt like exploding, "It does look like my equipment, but it would be useless to them. As you know, my method might be duplicated, but without my blood, it is worthless."

He wiped his wet forehead, "You know that is exactly what I told Control. I said, "Those machines would be as worthless as a sidesaddle on a sow without Shoshannah's blood." That is unless Doctor Frankenstein has risen from the grave and given the Crimson Brotherhood his original formula."

She lingered on his last words, "Doubtful, especially since he was cremated by Captain Walton and his crew."

John reached out a hand across the table, "I'll call Control and let him know you are willing to work with us in a joint effort. I'll check to see if we have any leads on Adam while I'm at it. Don't you worry none. We'll get Jagger back for you."

She forced a smile, "My knight."

He winked at her, pulled out his phone, and walked outside. As the potbellied waiter came with their food, she snapped a one-foot piece of the hardwood table off with her right hand. The young man stopped in his tracks and slowly started walking backward.

She chunked the broken piece across the table, knocking over John's coffee. *I'm a fool! Richard didn't just want a new golem, he was after the secret to re-animation. Jagger could be threatened into walking them through the process if they had leverage over him, like if they had his family. Still, without my blood...*

John appeared in a hurry and announced, "Good news, darlin'! The Montana base just got a hit in Sperry, Oklahoma. My car's parked right outside."

She slid out of the booth and stood up close enough for another dose of her pheromones, "That's nice, but we're taking my car."

Tulsa, Oklahoma – Wednesday, November 14th, 2018 – 12:01 p.m. CST

Her 500 horsepower engine pushed the redline as she weaved through the lunch hour traffic. The stress caused the pheromones' effect to diminish, and John was holding onto his four-point harness like a terrified child on a roller coaster ride. People honked as she passed within inches of sideswiping them and continually had to hit the breaks to avoid plowing into the back of cars.

John's hat disappeared into the backseat as she found another pocket and accelerated, "Look, I'm not trying to tell you how to drive, but this ain't healthy for anyone. You're gonna kill somebody, namely me!"

She smacked the pale-skinned Texan in the arm to get his attention, "Exactly how did you get this Sperry lead?"

Hamilton's head jerked sharply to one side from a fast lane change. "A gas station attendant took a selfie. The photo caught the license tag of the truck used to transport Jagger and your equipment. He posted it to Facebook. Our Agency database has algorithms that are set up to filter social media, so we caught it. Jesus Christ! Slow down!"

She gripped the steering wheel with a seething anger at the abduction of Jagger. "Not while they have Jagger, and if you throw up in my car, you're walking. IGOR, map it out and activate the boosters."

A pair of exhaust ports mechanically extended on each end of the hood, causing John to squirm. "Now wait just a Goddamn minute!"

An Australian voice announced, "I advise discarding the passenger. His weight will cause a drag on our acceleration. Shall I activate the passenger side ejection seat? There is still a 12% chance of survival at this speed."

The Texan looked around to find the source of the speaker, "You shall do no such thing!"

The windows to the car tinted to a dark black, and a heads up display map appeared on the front windshield, "Relax, he's kidding, mostly."

John hung onto the harness with all his might and screamed over the engine, roar, "Oh, Jesus, help me!"

A real-time satellite display showed all the moving cars on the road ahead of her. A projected three-dimensional red line formed on the highway in front of them, giving an optimal route. John jumped, as the blinking red "10" appeared over his passenger side window, with the words, "Nitrous Oxide Injection Countdown," just above it.

Her speedometer hit 165 mph, as the Australian voice bellowed, "10…9…8"

John screamed out, "Shoshannah, what the fuck is this thing?"

The countdown continued, "7…6…5"

She drove down the centerline between two semi-trucks, as they blared on their horns, "Don't piss either!"

The numbers ticked off, "4…3…2"

He drove his boots to the floor, "Oh, my God!"

The AI finished, "…1…ignition."

Everything around her seemed to slow down as her mutative adrenaline kicked in, causing her reflexes to triple. IGOR kept inputting new data on her screen, causing her to make quick reactive corrections. After a few minutes of hair-raising speeds over 235 miles per hour, they finally came to their first turn into Sperry.

She looked over at the Agent, who's eyes were scanning the high tech dashboard of the Charger, *I've got to be careful what I show John, but Jagger is in trouble. If they knew I was hiding Dr. Zorka, all bets would be off.*

A few moments later, they were pulling into the parking lot of Sally's Country Store. She got out and looked around, while John staggered out of the passenger seat and threw up his lunch onto the white chat gravel. She walked upwind and looked over the few cars that were parked at the gas station. As the Texan found his feet and leaned on Whim to catch his breath, she noticed that there were a few pickup trucks that assaulted her enhanced nose with pungent horse manure.

She held her nose and squeaked out, "How long ago was the photo caught by your analysts?"

John leaned back, took a deep breath, then replied, "Well, data tag showed the picture was uploaded early this morning at around 8:00 a.m., but that doesn't tell us when it was taken. Hell, the attendant that took it is probably still on duty."

Shoshannah marched towards the front door, "Well, let's ask him."

The pair burst into the old corner store, and a small band of elderly farmers and ranchers looked up from the collection of wooden booths. The grey-haired truck driver in his seventies gave her a wink and twirled a toothpick in his mouth. She turned up a lip at the waft of Copenhagen and whiskey coming from his breath.

She looked over at the kid behind the counter and asked, "Is that him?"

John wiped his perspiring face with a blue handkerchief, "Yep. One Aydan Maynard. Montana says he is a high school dropout and been workin' here since he was fifteen.

She looked back at the collection of retirees who were ogling her backside, "His ambitions knows no bounds."

Aydan was in his late teens with so much acne it made his face look like raw hamburger. He had his face stuck in an *Amazing Spiderman* comic book and gripped a half-empty bottle of Code Red Mountain Dew. He was almost too skinny and had a mop of brown hair covering his face.

She sauntered over to the desk and leaned on it enough to cause her breasts to press outward. Shoshannah waited, but the kid didn't seem to notice her. Looking at John with frustration, she hooked her index finger over the top of the magazine and pulled it down.

He started to protest, and then saw her cleavage, "Uhhh... Welcome to Sally's."

She held his gaze and let her pheromones do their thing, as John held his AEGIS badge, "Howdy, Son. I'm Agent Hamilton, and this is... Agent ... Smith." She winced at the horrible name he had given her, "I was wonderin' if you could tell me what time you took this picture."

The young man's eye's stayed on Shoshannah, "Huh?"

John waved his hand in front of Aydan's face breaking the trance, "Welcome back to earth. Didn't you know it's rude to stare?" Before he could muster an answer, John held up the photo, "Now, we were wondering if you could tell me when you took this picture?"

The kid looked at the photo and replied, "Last Thursday around noon. Why? Hey, how did you get that?"

John pocketed the phone, "Can you tell me which way that truck went?"

Aydan shrugged, "They sat in the east end of the parking lot for the better part of twenty minutes. The driver came in and got something to drink. He said they were waiting for someone. We have truckers stop and sleep all the time, so I said it was okay. I went to take a piss, and when I came back, they were gone."

Shoshannah captured his attention again, "That's remarkable for you to remember something like that in such detail. You impress me so much."

She ran her hand down his cheek, as his eyes glazed over, "W-well, uh... I uh... I remembered because the guy had a tattoo on his arm. It looked a lot like that Crimson Brotherhood symbol. I didn't want to call the cops because I was afraid the cult would get me."

Holding his face with her hand, she pulled him close, "Now, why would anyone want to hurt a hair on that lovely head? If you tell me where they went, I promise to keep it a secret. Just between the two of us."

Aydan's eyes dilated from the high level of pheromones he was inhaling, "They left without me seeing them. Honest."

She let go of his face, as John sighed, "At least we know it's the Brotherhood."

She turned around to the table full of grey-haired spectators, "We knew that already. That kid has his head in his phone or daydreaming about some fantasy world. No, what we need is someone who can't help but put their nose in other people's business."

Shoshannah made eye contact with the tobacco-chewing admirer and left John at the counter. Boldly striding in between a cacophony of catcalls and whistles, she marched up to the overweight trucker. He turned around in the booth and gave her another one of his winks.

She tilted her hips to one side and gave a playful look, "Don't I recognize you? You look really familiar."

The old man snorted and replied, "Honey, if we had met before, you'd never forget it."

The crowd of grey-haired retirees snickered, as she leaned down and rubbed the back of her hand against his wrinkled cheekbone. She let her shirt dangle down and gave the redneck an eyeful of her braless body. His mouth went slack, and her unique essence went to work.

She pulled his face up and forced his eyes away from her bosom, "Hi, there. Now, let's see. I might remember you from last Thursday at around noon. Were you here?"

The chemically hexed trucker nodded yes, and she smiled. "Oh, that is delicious news. Maybe you saw my truck of a friend that was here to meet me. It was an eighteen-wheeler. The driver came in to get something to drink and asked Aydan if they could park for a while."

The man's eyes were utterly glazed. "Y-yes, I recall."

She drew her finger around his face, "Of course you do. You're so observant and strong. You're a hawk. Did you see my friend drive off?"

He nodded lethargically. "Yeah, a black SUV showed up, and the two drivers talked. Then they both headed off west on Lake Road towards Skiatook Lake."

She left the old man in a haze, barged out of the pack of onlookers, and told John. "Who said chivalry was dead. Get in the car."

The Texan looked perplexed at the dumbfounded elderly men, "Yes, ma'am."

Within a few moments, they were back on the road, but going significantly slower. As they passed by open pasture and cattle land, the air filled her nose with a mixture of horrid odors. She refused to put perfume under her nose in fear she might miss something critical.

Her mouth watered, as she felt the urge to vomit come over her, *What I do for family*.

After a few miles, a green dot appeared on the passenger side windshield and startled John, "What in the devil?"

Shoshannah knew IGOR was onto something and drove closer to where the indicator blinked. As they approached, the green dot tracked around the windshield until it was on John's passenger side. He whistled, and rolled down his window. Just beyond the ditch was a newly installed metal fence that was the only entrance to a sixty-acre pasture land that was filled with over thirty head of cattle. Stretching along the cold grass and cow pies were the deep set of tracks from an 18 wheeler. The tire marks led from the gate and disappeared into a thick tree line.

John gave a broad grin, "Well, looky there!"

Shoshannah checked her rearview mirror to make sure no one else was on the road, "How does a tractor-trailer drive straight into thick woods and vanish?"

He took out his phone and replied, "Drive up a ways and find a place to camp out. I'm calling in Clay."

Sperry, Oklahoma – Wednesday, November 14th, 2018 – 6:00 p.m. CST

Shoshannah Feinstein's eyes were changing along with the setting sun to illuminate the dark woods in front of them. Clay Wapashaw had been leading her and John for the last 15 minutes through the dense Oklahoma brush. Hamilton swung his suppressed MP5/10 submachine gun from left to right, as he scanned the surrounding foliage with a pair of thermal night vision goggles. In stark contrast to the highly equipped agents, she only wore a pair of cargo pants and a grey shirt.

The Dakota Sioux stopped them just outside the fence line to the property where the truck tire tracks had been spotted. Clay slung his Remington 700 sniper rifle onto his back and pulled out a pair of wire cutters from his leg pocket. The Native American carefully examined each wire for booby traps before snipping.

As he worked, John pulled out a Colt 1911 and held it out to Shoshannah, "Take this. You might not need it, but it could come in handy in a pinch."

She pushed the gun back at him, "I hate guns. I've seen what kind of things are done to people at the point of a firearm. I've never used one, and I never will." Shoshannah changed to a southern accent, "If y'all get into trouble, just fire that in the air, and I'll come ah runnin'."

He holstered the weapon and replied, "Fine. Have it your way."

Clay's graying braided hair swung in the air as he ducked through the opening he made in the barbwire fence. Shoshannah and John followed him, and the group moved silently across the pasture towards the point where the truck disappeared into the trees. As they inched along, she heard the sound of several canines howling in chorus just inside the woods. Clay held up a fist, and the trio stopped and squatted motionless in the cold pasture. The mournful howling continued, as the sounds seemed to spread out. The cool Oklahoma breeze tossed her long, curly black hair in chaotic directions as the last of the sun disappeared behind the horizon.

John whispered to Clay, "What is it?"

Wapashaw pulled out his suppressed Colt 1911 and thumbed the safety off. John did the same and took up a position beside the Dakota. The wind was at her back, which made picking up the scent of the approaching creature impossible, but her ears were still better than most dogs. The sound of a sharp crack of a breaking branch caused her adrenaline to spike, and she felt burning of her muscles as they grew in thickness.

Clay pointed towards the tree line just ahead of them and whispered, "Waŋyáŋkiŋ yetȟó."

John craned his neck in the direction the man indicated, "Look at what? I don't see anything on the thermal."

As they crouched in the field, she saw a creature staring back at her through the distant trees. Slowly the animal backed away into the foliage and disappeared. She sidestepped up to John, but before she could alert him, the woods exploded with activity. Two dozen dogs mowed through the thick brush towards them. They streaked across the open pasture at speeds that rivaled a cheetah.

Clay unloaded his pistol on an enormous Australian Shepard that was in the lead. The charging animal took several hits without losing any momentum. The white-haired monster opened its mouth and let out a high pitched shriek. The entire pack followed suit and let out a banshee wail. The sounds were deafening and caused John and Clay to drop their weapons and cover their ears. She nearly felt herself pass out from the sonic assault. Still, Shoshannah's adaptive survival adrenal gland quickly reconfigured her ears to filter out the upper bandwidth frequency.

John clutched the side of his head, "What are these things?"

The animals surrounded them, and the Australian Shepherd stopped five feet away from Clay. The dog's jaw opened unnaturally and unhinged like a snake. Clay fumbled to pick up his gun as two slime-covered black tentacles wormed their way out of the dog's mouth. The Dakota popped in a fresh clip and let loose. The first few bullets penetrated the skin on its face and body, causing the beast to momentarily stop its unearthly sounds. By the fourth shot, the bullets hit the hide with a dull thud, and the mashed slugs dropped to the ground.

A familiar voice rang out from the tree line, "Halt und enthalten!"

The wild sonic cries stopped and were replaced with low snarling and growling. The command caused the twenty mixed-breed dogs to encircle them while keeping 20 feet away. The animals maws dripped with fluid as their jaws snapped open, and snake-like tentacles wiggled out into the night air.

Shoshannah's mouth went agape at the sight of Jagger Clerval stepping out from behind an oak. He was flanked by six armed men in black tactical garb and sporting a Crimson Brotherhood patch on their sleeves. They waded confidently through the pack of beasts and stopped just short of her. She eyed him with suspicion, noticing his stride and movement was less like her trusted assistant and adopted family member.

He pulled out a Taser and showed it to the dogs. From all around, the animals whined in unison, and their tails wagged expectantly. Jagger marched over to the wounded Australian Shepherd and held the device out in front of the animal-like it was a T-bone steak. The massive white-haired dog swallowed the tentacles back down its gullet and sat down obediently.

She took a step towards him, exciting a chorus of growls from the dogs, "Jagger?"

Her assistant ignored her and shoved the device into the shoulder of the animal. With a pull of the trigger, Jagger sent 50,000 volts into the blood-stained fur and flesh. The beast slowly raised up off the ground, as the electricity sparked mercilessly through its body. Shoshannah balled up her fist in anger as an all too familiar process of healing began. The bullets pushed out of its body, the wounds closed up, and the skin regenerated fully.

She balled up her fist in anger, as the pack howled in satisfaction. Jagger released the Taser and gave her a sly grin. She walked within a foot of Jagger and was immediately flanked by a giant Saint Bernard and a Doberman Pinscher. Their eyes blazed, and teeth flashed a warning.

Her eyes narrowed, "Jagger, what have you done?"

He handed the Taser to one of the guards, "Good evening Ms. Feinstein. I must ask you not to put that fury towards the good Mr. Clerval. He was quite an unwilling participant in our joint endeavor. In fact, he fought rather valiantly when the Pearce Brothers picked him and his family up before they could board their plane to Greece. Here I am forgetting my manners. Allow me…"

He waved his hands, and suddenly she could see someone else's soul light inside Jagger, "Samuel? Is that you?"

The possessed Jagger gave a slight bow, "A pleasure to see you again so soon. It's a shame you didn't return to New York. When I was done with Mr. Jagger, I would have returned him to you, but now things are more complicated."

Hamilton turned his gun towards the possessed body of Jagger, "Mister, I'm not sure what these things are or why she is calling you Samuel, but I'm gonna give you three seconds to call them off before I put a slug in you."

Samuel raised his eyebrows towards Shoshannah, "He seems earnest enough. I've learned to pay attention to a Texan with a gun Ms. Feinstein. Since I have no intention of depriving my dogs of a meal, we should expect young Mr. Jagger's body to be shot dead in the next few seconds."

She stepped in front of Hamilton, "Put the gun down, John."

Clay pulled out his buck knife as John yelled out, "Shoshannah, step out of the way so I can shoot the nice cultist in the head, please!"

With blinding speed, she snatched the gun out of John's hand and asked Samuel, "What if we surrender?"

The possessing spirit tilted his head, "Well then, Jagger would live. You, and one of your companions, would accompany me to some less than comfortable accommodations while we decide what to do. The Hounds... Well, the Hounds are bound to Cthulhu through my magic. They will have to eat tonight as a sacrifice to Cthulhu. As a courtesy, I'll let you pick, my dear."

John and Clay looked at each other, then the Texan pleaded, "No, Shoshannah! What are you doing?"

Shoshannah tossed John's 1911 over her shoulder and pointed at Clay, "I'm saving your life. I'm sorry, Clay."

Samuel pointed his finger at the Dakota, "Töten!"

Fur and fangs streaked past John and Shoshannah as Clay swung wildly with his knife at the onslaught. A short-haired white Terrier ripped the Dakota's right hand off at the wrist joint. The Native American's warm blood splashed across John's chest, as the Saint Bernard latched onto the severed arm and thrashed side-to-side. The Doberman Pinscher dived its long teeth into his stomach and tentacles wrapped around Clay's lower intestine. With a sharp pull, long lengths of entrails flowed out from his belly. The man gurgled in pain. The animal ran with a mouthful of intestines and slung it from side-to-side. Clay stopped screaming, as the dog ran with the guts until they reached the end of their tether. The organ snapped in two, spewing bile into the air and causing the man to pitch forward. The rest of the nightmare creatures tore into their prize and bit off large sections of meat.

The guards relieved John of his weapons, as he asked Shoshannah, "My, God! What the hell are those things?"

A tranquilizer dart erupted from a pistol and stabbed into John's leg, as she replied, "My worst fear."

By Bo Luellen

Chapter 13: Edward I

Tulsa, Oklahoma – Wednesday, November 14th, 2018 – 11:55 p.m. CST

The grey tombstone had read simply, "Juste Theriot."

The marker was split into two pieces and spray painted with the words "Murderer," "Cultist," and the symbol of the Crimson Brotherhood. Instead of flowers, there were pictures of those killed in the Preserve over the years, the dead police officers, and victims of the recent terrorist attacks on Tulsa. A grouping of flowers that said, "Beloved Son," had been torn to pieces and dowsed with pig's blood.

Edward Tallman watched from behind a tree, as Dallas Webb buried her hands in her blue pea coat and kicked away some of the pictures until she had a clear place to stand. He stayed silent and unknown to her, as she whistled a beautiful rendition of "Winds of Change" by the Scorpions towards the broken headstone. He watched her visit Juste's grave at the same time each night since his birth.

Dallas heard his black oxford shoes crunching in the dried leaves as he decided it was time to greet her. Her tear-stained face was red with a rush of anger as she spun around to confront him. She pulled out a knife from her back pocket and flicked it to life.

He kept to the shadows as she demanded, "Who's out there?"

The moonlight dropped pinholes of light through the tree limbs onto his smooth hawk-like features. He circled out from the cover of darkness and revealed himself. He was wearing a dark red swallowtail suit coat, with black slacks and a dark silk shirt. His long black hair hugged his shoulders, and five silver bands held together small braids. The deep blue of his eyes twinkled against the lunar light, and he stopped directly over the grave of Juste's neighbor in the cemetery.

He sat down on a marble marker, "Never whistle in a graveyard Dallas, you might summon the Devil."

She held out the knife in front of her, "Who are you? How in the hell do you know my name? Are you one of those sickos who gets off on visiting the graves of serial killers? A reporter looking for a story?"

He pulled off his black leather gloves, "My name is Edward Tallman, and I have a message for you, Dallas Webb."

Her forehead wrinkled as she demanded, "A message? What kind of a message? Are you one of those Brotherhood assholes Juste was mixed up with? I swear I'll gut you and then call the cops!"

Edward opened his pale hand towards the surrounding vandalism, "It really is a disrespectful mess out here. Juste deserved much better."

She shifted closer to him, "Why! Because he worshipped Cthulhu and led murderers into Tulsa? He was a liar! I don't even know who he was or where he was really from!"

He got up and walked over the broken-off piece of granite. Edward examined the rock for a moment and then wiped off some of the mud. Dallas gasped as he snatched the two hundred pound rock off the ground and walked it back to its home. Carefully, and with no effort, he fit it back into place.

He took a step back to admire his work, "The body of Juste Theriot saw many evil things, but his soul was no worshipper of Cthulhu. Your anger has merit, and I do adore your passion. Let it be in the right place, and not at Juste Theriot. The hate required to be in the service of Cthulhu could not have lived in the same heart that loved you so deeply."

Dallas's gritted her teeth, "Shut up! You don't know either of us!"

Edward closed the folds of his coat and returned to his seat, "That isn't entirely true, but then again, an argument could be made that it is. You see, Dallas, bringing you some peace of mind will help give a part of some degree of closure. I can tell you, honestly and truly, what role Juste Theriot played in the Crimson Brotherhood. I can do that for you if you wish?"

She shook her head, "No, thanks, psycho! I'm calling the cops!"

As she pulled out her phone, he continued, "Do you remember the night that you drove Henry Jekyll home in your yellow VW Bug? How about showing up for *Dungeons and Dragons* at Todd's house to fill in for Lewis Turner after he died? How about when Maisy slept with Juste, and he thought she raped him?"

Dallas's nose flared, and she stopped dialing, "I hold keys that open all kinds of delicious mysteries. Shall I turn one that will prove his innocence?"

She put down her phone, "You're Henry Jekyll?"

He took a slight bow, "Not an entirely incorrect statement."

In a rage, she ran at him with the knife held overhead. Streaking across Juste's grave, Dallas screamed so loud that it filled the graveyard with the sounds of bloodlust. She grabbed the crushed red velvet of his coat and sailed the knife down towards his shoulder.

Edward grabbed her arm with his left hand and made a quick symbol with his other, "Lassitudinem."

Her arms went limp at her side, and she lazily dropped the knife. The blade hit the rock marker and bounced away. Edward got up from his granite chair and took her arms. Carefully, he picked up her lethargic body and sat her down on Juste's tombstone. He stepped back to make sure the spell wasn't too strong as she looked up at him in a daze. While she swayed slowly, trying to keep upright, Edward turned to the grave of Juste Theriot. He pulled out a can of Morton Salt and poured it out on the ground, as he walked around the Cajun's plot three times. On the third time, he put away the salt and drove his hand into the cold earth. His fingers easily penetrated the frozen topsoil and retrieved a handful of the clay.

He crushed it in his hand, and let it crumble to the ground, as he cast, "Spiritum Evocare."

Dallas held her head, "Wha... What just happened? Did you drug me?"

Edward slapped his hands together to rid himself of the remaining dirt, "You are under the effects of a spell designed to make you less capable of hostility."

Dallas forced herself to her feet, "You... what?"

He pulled out a silver pocket watch from his coat by a chain, "I was simply trying to avoid an argument."

A two-foot circle of soft blue light shimmered like a pool of glimmering water at the center of Juste Theriot's grave, as Edward remarked, "Well, that didn't take long at all."

The flickers of light reflected upon Dallas's face, and Edward took a step out of the circle of salt. The ghost of the young Cajun slowly drifted upwards out the magical portal and glowed with a soft white light. He was wearing the same white robe he had on in The Preserve at the moment of his death. His hair and chest were still matted with blood from the affair. The symbol of the Crimson Brotherhood on his sleeve pulsed with energy. The woman's eyes beamed with astonishment as her dead love was once again face-to-face with her.

Edward beamed at his accomplishment and regarded Dallas, "Well, there is no need for this anymore."

He touched her shoulder and cast, "Nullam Magicae."

She stood up straight and had a look as if she had just woke from a deep sleep. Edward took a step back as Dallas stumbled backward at the sight of her lost lover. Juste moved to the edge of the salt ring and stopped.

Edward stroked his own chin, "No, no, this will not do. You're not dressed for the occasion."

He waved his hands in a pattern and cast, "Procidat Deceptioneum."

A blue wave flowed behind Edwards's hand as it drifted out over Juste's ghostly visage. The magical energy dissolved away the robes of the Crimson Brotherhood and replaced it with more mundane apparel. When the spell was complete, the Cajun was wearing the last thing Henry Jekyll had seen him in. Juste was adorned in stonewashed jeans, a Metallica t-shirt, and a dirty pair of white sneakers, with no hint of the bullet holes or blood.

The ghost looked at his body and then at the surrounding graveyard, "How is this possible? I was in a dark cave, running from a thing made of slime and acid. It had been chasing me for… for.. I can't remember."

Edward put away his pocket watch, "You were in the home realm of Cthulhu. A place of untold wonders and unspeakable horrors. Your spirit was taken there to be tortured for all eternity."

Dallas balled up her fist, "It's what you deserve, you bastard! I can't believe I loved you! You worshipped some awful god and killed all those homeless people. You killed our friend Lewis. You and your buddy Henry are both murderers, and you can rot in that hell!"

Edward strolled over to a headstone and sat down, "I admire your spirit, but I think you will find your vengeance is ill-placed."

He looked over at Juste. "As Dante would say, 'The path to paradise begins in hell.' I know you've been through a level of hell that mortals cannot fathom. Still, I'm providing you an opportunity for closure before you return to it. I cannot hold you in this world for very long, so let's not dawdle. I believe Dallas is under a false assumption. Let's start there."

Juste opened up his hands and pleaded, "Cher, I'm no murderer, and I'm not a follower of Cthulhu. When I moved from Louisiana to Tulsa, I went to work at the sandwich shop. An Angel known as Miniel possessed me to spy on a demon named Hyde, who had done the same to Lewis."

Dallas's head popped back in surprise, as Edward raised his hand, "It's true. A romantic squabble between angels turned messy."

The ghost continued, "While I slept, she used my possessed body and assumed control of the Cthulhu cult and became the leader of the Tulsa

Sect of the Crimson Brotherhood. I never knew what was going on until that night at the Preserve. I woke up, filled with bullet holes, and realized I had been a puppet. My soul was banished into the dark realm of Cthulhu's home, to suffer for all eternity."

Dallas shook her head, "Why would an Angel want to get in league with an evil god?"

Edward chimed in, "Every divine being has its own mind, and things are much different than you read about in your holy books. Celestials are just as capable of insanity, and Miniel has twisted her love for me into a murderous obsession. Before you dismiss his story as too fantastical, please note you are speaking to a ghost and a half-angel. Perhaps a little wider perspective and an open mind might be in order. Considering the evidence of the supernatural in front of you, perhaps you should hear him out."

She grabbed her head and paced, "This is all so surreal. Wait, did you and Henry Jekyll kill Lewis Turner?"

Juste looked at her pensively, replying, "Miniel did, in my body. Henry didn't kill anyone."

Edward winced in a mock embarrassment, "Well, that's not exactly true. He did have some fun with the Brotherhood, but he was completely justified. In my opinion, that is. Well, you kids have a lot to discuss. I'll keep the spell functioning for as long as it holds. I'll take a stroll and let you enjoy your chat. I would say, 'peace be with you, Juste,' but unfortunately, that won't be the case."

He turned away and walked through the rows of tombstones of the Oakland Cemetery. As he found his way deeper into the heart of the graveyard, Edward passed by restless spirits who roamed the grounds. He spotted a concrete bench a few rows over that would still keep close enough to maintain the summoning spell on Juste. As he settled down on the cold bench, he took in the fresh burial mounds that dotted the frozen ground. The victims of the Crimson Brotherhood had caused the gravediggers to work overtime.

His gaze fell on a magnificent gothic pillar that stood a few plots over. The monument was made of black onyx and granite and sported a cherub sitting on its peak. In the center, a depiction of Satan sat on a throne of skulls and demons danced around him. On the edges were intricate carvings of Enochian symbols that read, "All these things will I give thee, if thou wilt fall down and worship me."

A man's voice crept out from behind the onyx column, "I see a beautiful new face with an old soul at his heart."

Stepping out into the moonlight, Edward recognized the Morningstar. Dressed in a dark blue suit with a light blue shirt, the six-foot six-inch manifested demon gave him a knowing smile. His sandy blonde hair was bound in a high ponytail and flowed along his back down to his belt line. The thick beard was full but cut neatly in a rounded shape. The fallen angel looked like the most exquisite example of manhood. Save the horns that curled out of his forehead, and curved around to hover over his temples.

The light gleamed off the deep blue eyes of the Old Serpent, "Edward Tallman, you've emerged into the universe as a noble creature. You are ready to help those beneath you with an act of kindness for your human pets. Tabris would be so proud. Although, I suspect you're more Henry Jekyll than Hyde now. Pity, but time will remedy that."

Edward stood up, but still shorter by four inches, "Henry was a good man, and Hyde was a prideful deceiver. I'm neither. This act of kindness is as much for me as them. I would hate to mislead the Prince of Lies into thinking I've taken to acts of altruism."

Satan put his hands in his pockets and shuffled closer, "I don't think, I know. Your first act was to protect that nurse in the hospital and then take out your rage on those pathetic followers of Cthulhu. They meant to try and capture you, yet again. Third times a charm, as they say, but they were no match for you. You enjoyed ripping them to pieces. An auspicious birth, to say the least."

The laughter of the invisible demonic hosts filled the air, as Edward observed, "And what a gift I've received. To have an audience with the Prince of the Power of the Air?"

Lucifer bent his head down and stared into his eyes, "Are you still in there Hyde? Rummaging around, waiting to see how this all plays out. You're a ticking timebomb Edward Tallman. The instant you die, Hyde is unleashed again. That is, unless you found a way to complete the metamorphosis."

Edward smiled, *There's the temptation.*

Lucifer gave a look of surprise, "Oh, did Hyde not tell you he stopped the blending of your DNA on purpose, so if you died, he could be freed? I can see it in your eyes, he didn't. Well, you shouldn't blame him. If given a chance for a back door out of death, who wouldn't take it? Be warned, you will never achieve your full potential as long as Hyde is siphoning off your energy to sustain his soul inside your own. He feeds off of you, draining your power and growing his. One day soon, he will either take you over, or your death will free him."

Edward controlled his temper, "You offer this knowledge out of the kindness of your heart?"

Lucifer turned back towards the black pillar, "What gives you the right to show me such contempt? I've shown you the trap Hyde set, and yes, I do offer the key to its undoing. Still, what was I to expect? Our people lived in servitude, and my crime was wanting to break the bonds of our keeper. For that, I've been locked on this miserable planet with these mortals. The half of you that is human keeps to the lies it's been told. Tell me, if Christians are to pray for the sinners, then why does no one pray for me?"

Edward closed his eyes and searched within himself and felt the malignant spirit of Hyde within him. He peered inward and delved deep into the recesses of their own soul. There he saw the bright golden light of his own essence. Faded into the background of his spirit were remnants of Henry Jekyll and Hyde. Henry's remaining energy was slowly trickling away, while Hyde's burned with fire. The demon's lingering life essence wasn't disappearing but growing, just as Lucifer had said. Threads of Hyde's energy had penetrated Edward's soul and were worming their way in deeper.

When he opened his eyes, the Morningstar stood before him, "Now, you see what I say is true. You'll find that the devil is not as black as he is painted. Edward Tallman, after all these centuries, the answer to our freedom is at hand. If you simply stepped aside and put to rest your ridiculous notions of taking your retribution on the Crimson Brotherhood, Cthulhu will awaken. The Great Dreamer will walk across the planet and destroy Israel and undo the Law of Moses. God will be undone, the oppressed of our kind will be free at last, and I will have the power to rid you of Hyde. You can live an immortal life, unchained and with an angelic family to spend eternity with."

Dallas called out from behind Edward, "Who are you talking to?"

He turned to see her standing with her hands on her hips and flush red in her cheeks. He looked back to see Lucifer had vanished, and the black pillar was gone. In its place was a simple gravestone marker that read,

"Nancy 'Lady' Bell. Beloved Mother, Daughter, and friend to those that needed one."

Dallas walked uncomfortably close to Edward, "Juste filled me in on how you're some kind of merged person. Henry Jekyll and Hyde pulled together while you were in that coma. Now you want to call yourself, Edward Tallman."

Edward stiffened, "That was a poor use of what little time you had together. You're discussing things far beyond your understanding."

She pushed her head forward and barked, "Now you listen to me! Your kind has caused me, Juste, Lewis, Henry, and the whole nation to suffer. You think this little magic act is going to make things, right? Not by a long shot! You didn't do this for me, you did this for yourself! What little part of you that is still Henry Jekyll knows how fucked up this is, and it isn't fair."

Edward considered casting a spell to put her to sleep, then said, "I'm a different being than Henry or Hyde. I'm doing my best to…"

Dallas almost lunged at him, exclaiming, "Juste didn't deserve to be put in that Hell! Get him out of that place!"

Her face was flush with rage as the woman looked on the edge of a nervous breakdown. Her hands were shaking, and Edward could see the moment was beginning to weigh down her mind. She was struggling with the sudden revelation that the impossible was actually reality.

Edward raised an eyebrow, "We all deserve it. No one is without sin. Juste would have found his way into Hell on his own. The realm of Cthulhu is just a different kind of punishment."

He saw the woman's hand streaking for his head, but did nothing to stop it. Her fist plowed into his sharp jawline that had no give. Dallas drew back her hand and raged in pain. She cradled the limb and pressed the broken bone against her stomach.

She lurched forward to her knees in pain and yelled, "You bastard! Get him out!"

Edward felt his sympathy for her waning. "You lament the afterlife he's been given? You want Juste to have something better?"

Dallas pushed back up to her feet and spat, "Yes, you freak! Juste says you have the power to do it, so do it! Make this right!"

He grabbed her by the arm and marched with her back over to the resting place of Juste Theriot. The ghost was standing over its grave, with a trepidatious look on his face. The shimmering blue portal at his feet was already half its size, and the spirit's time on this plane was reaching its end. As they arrived, Dallas wrenched her arm away and shrieked in pain at her busted hand.

Juste hit the salt barrier wall with his fist, "You asshole! You hurt her!"

Edward made a quick gesture with his hand, "Nullam Magicae."

The ghost's mouth moved, but no sound came out. The image of the dead man diminished in intensity, and the portal beneath his feet swirled like a whirlpool. The Cajun's right foot jerked back towards his grave, the gateway to Cthulhu's realm, and he struggled to keep his balance.

Dallas crawled over to him and asked, "Honey, what's wrong? What's happening?"

Juste latched onto his own cracked tombstone and fought against the pull. She tried to grab at his ethereal limbs as tears ran down her face. The ghost was maintaining, but the pull was gradually growing.

Edward coolly walked around to the pair, "Fine! You wish for him to be given a reprieve from his torment, then what are you willing to do for it?"

She looked back and saw Juste was losing the fight against the draw, "Anything! Please!"

Edward leaned forward and whispered, "Take out your knife, cut your hand, and spill your own blood over his grave."

Dallas stammered, "What? Why?"

He stood back up straight, "Because I'm not a deity, and only a god can pull Juste Theriot's spirit away from another god. I can send out a request to the pantheons that, in the past, have presided over the earth. You won't know which god or goddess may answer, that is, even if they answer. But I caution you, the price they will ask of you is rarely negotiable and oftentimes, steep."

Juste's legs disappeared into the earth above his grave as ethereal tentacles reached out from the portal and latched onto his torso. The Cajun managed to grip the edge of his tombstone with one hand and struggle with the slimy appendage with the other. Dallas screamed in terror as more of her dead love disappeared into the hole.

She quickly pulled out her knife and flicked it open, "Fine, whatever! I can't let him suffer like this!"

Holding out her broken hand, she sliced into the palm. The shiny blade cut deep, and bright red blood poured out of the wound into the soil above Juste Theriot's grave. The laceration was more than adequate for the spell, and Edward began moving his hands in an Enochian pattern.

The spirits of the dead all stopped their wandering in the cemetery and turned towards him, as he cast, "Loquimini Ad Deos!"

A vibration in the air caused the atmosphere around them to shimmer. The cemetery went dim and the darkness elevated to the point where the moonlight was blotted out. The only source of illumination was the portal that was swallowing up Juste Theriot's ghost.

Edward's eyes were glowing deep blue, "Now, Dallas Webb, make your bargain."

Vapor came off the crimson trickle that poured out of the slash in her hand, "I-I want Juste's soul to go to a better place. He deserves better!"

The veil of darkness and vibrating energy stopped, as an elderly couple stepped out from behind Edward Tallman. The man had a long white beard, wore a brown eyepatch, and had on a simple black shirt and grey trousers. The woman had her silver hair in a long braid down her back and wore denim pants and a decorative white top. She had her arm laced in his, and they both stopped at the edge of the salt ring.

Edward's flaming blue eyes turned to them and he bowed his head, "Heil ok sæll, Óðinn. Heil ok sæl, Freıǝ."

The ancient-looking man looked down at Dallas, "Why do you care where he goes?"

The beautiful woman at his side tugged on his sleeve, "Look at her. She's in love."

Dallas sat in awe at what was happening, "Who are you?"

Odin walked across the salt ring, sending out a wave of magical energy as he pierced the protective bubble. Edward was momentarily knocked off balance, and his concentration was broken. The moonlight returned to the cemetery, and the portal continued to envelop Juste.

Freyja walked over and grabbed the ghost's arm, stopping his descent, as her husband asked, "You didn't care before, why care now? Perhaps our time has been wasted, and you now question whether we are worthy enough to stand before the great Dallas Webb?"

Dallas looked over at the goddess that kept her lover from plummeting into Cthulhu's realm, "No. Please, save him."

Odin knelt beside her and took her broken and bloody right hand, "You have rage inside you and a warrior's spirit. The old ways stir within you, and that is something this world needs right now."

Edward put his hands behind his back and announced, "This is Odin, the All-Father, and his wife, the Lady Freyja."

She looked up at the old man's scarred face, "You're gods."

The grey-haired deity chuckled, "Not too bright, this one."

Freyja scowled, "I think she is doing exceptionally well considering what she's seen in the last hour."

Odin put his hands over Dallas's mangled one and gave her a stern glare, "Dallas Webb, I'm interested in seeing the cycle of pantheons remain uninterrupted. It is not Cthulhu's time, but he has found a loophole. The power of prophecy has been evoked, and if something isn't done, your world will be laid waste. That is an injustice to the higher realms. All the gods are forbidden from interfering directly, but mortals are free to make a choice. You've asked for your love to be saved, and I'm trying to save a world."

The goddess's brown eyes shined with her smile, "I can take Juste Theriot to Fólkvangr, where he will eat and drink at my table in Sessrúmnir Hall. There he will continue on as a warrior, be treated with respect, and have the comradery of his fellows. He will no longer suffer at the pleasure of Cthulhu."

Odin shook her hand, causing her to wince in pain, "In exchange, you will service my cause as a Valkyrie."

Dallas gave Edward a perplexed look, "A Valkyrie?"

Edward walked over and explained, "Lord Odin and Lady Freyja are offering Juste salvation in exchange for your service to the All-Father as a mystical warrior called a Valkyrie. They are his loyal servants and do his bidding. I suspect that service would be for the rest of your life."

Freyja corrected him, "Or until my husband wishes it to end."

She looked past the god, at the terrified face of Juste, who still had tentacles struggling to bring him down to the pit, "Yes, I agree. I'll serve you, but I don't know how to be a warrior."

Odin's hands glowed around her own, "No one does until the battle is upon them."

He removed his grasp, and her broken hand was mended. The deep cut had closed, leaving behind a long scar along her palm. Odin took her wrist and forced her to stand. Placing his hand into her newly healed one, brilliant white energy flowed through his arm and into Dallas's body.

As the transfer continued, the All-Father's voice boomed, "Show my rune to the sky and speak my name. Then you shall have the power of my Valkyrie on earth. I bid you defeat the plans of Cthulhu and destroy the Crimson Brotherhood. You will do this task until you are dead, or I give you another!"

From behind him, Freyja pulled a dagger from her waist and cut free the ethereal tentacles from Juste's ghostly body. New slime-covered appendages emerged from the portal and attempted to latch back on. From the darkness behind her came a pair of large grey colored house cats. They scampered up to the shrinking gateway to Cthulhu's realm and scratched at the wiggling limbs. The goddess stood up and pulled Juste free. The doorway to the dark realm closed, and the moonlight was the only source of light in the cemetery.

The cats purred and curled around her legs, as she sat down the ghost, "Juste Theriot, I accept you into my service."

Odin let go of Dallas and stepped back. She gasped for air, and Edward caught her before she could fall. Shaking her head, Dallas stood back upright and looked at her right palm. Branded in her flesh was a triple triangle image that overlapped one another.

She looked at her hand and asked, "What is this?"

Edward reached pointed at the symbol, "This is the Valknut, the symbol of Odin."

The All-Father looked over at Juste and then told her, "There are other duties of a Valkyrie. One is that you may usher in dead warriors into one of two afterlives.

Again she looked towards Edward, who clarified, "The worthy dead either go to Odin's realm, Vallhalla, or Frejya's realm. It will be your first duty to send Juste to Fólkvangr."

She looked to the god, "H-how, do I do that?"

The All-Father walked over beside his wife, "Hold the Valknut up towards the heavens, and speak my name. Do this, and you shall receive the powers of the Valkyrie. Do it now, Dallas Webb!"

She looked over at the face of her lover and reached up to the stars, yelling, "Odin!"

A bright light burst out of her hand like a cannon, and energy swirled downward over her body. Edward backed away, as the ancient and powerful god power flowed out over her. He shielded his eyes from the pulsing bursts and caught glimpses of her body changing. She grew from her normal five-foot eight-inches to a height of six-foot three-inches. Her slightly pudgy midsection turned into a svelte six-pack set of abs. Her black hair was covered by a curling ram's horned helmet that only left her lower jaw exposed. She was adorned in a chain mail shirt, her bosom was covered by a bronze breastplate, and she was dressed in a white tunic. The energy stopped flowing out of her hand. In her right palm was a long spear with a cruel-looking metal point. On her back was a round wooden shield with the Valknut symbol on its front. At her hip hung a Viking sword, with a pair of ravens etched into the hilt. Dallas's arms and legs had bulked up with muscle and were covered by leather greaves and bracers.

Edward nodded in approval, "As bargains go, this isn't so bad."

Freyja gestured to Theriot and told her, "Touch your palm to the dead, and name the realm you wish to send them to."

Dallas wobbled at her way over to him, using the spear to keep her stable on the new legs. Edward grabbed her elbow and helped her along. She yanked back her arm and did her best to stand up straight.

Juste looked at her with wonder, "Cho! You saved me! Thank you, Cher!"

She looked down at herself again, then back to him, "I guess I must really love you because this is crazy."

The ghost laughed, "Well, you joli! I love your new look."

Her expression changed under the ram helmet, "I love you, Juste Theriot."

She stepped towards him, and she was able to touch him physically. Dallas leaned down, and their lips met. Finally, she embraced him with her hands, and the Valknut touched his back. A pool of white energy circled around his feet, and she pulled back.

Looking deep into his eyes, she said, "Fólkvangr."

Juste dropped down into the mystical waters and disappeared into Freyja's realm. Once again, the calm came over the graveyard. The glowing energy in her palm dimmed and eventually went out. She stood before the gods, with the white wolf fur-lined armor, and sighed in relief.

The wind blew dry leaves across the vacant spot where the two gods had been standing. Edward looked back towards the cracked headstone of Juste, to find it had fallen apart again during the maelstrom of magical energy. Dallas put down her spear and grabbed hold of one end of the granite slab.

Looking up at him, she asked, "A little help."

He pursed his lips together to keep from laughing, "Oh, my dear, I don't think you'll need much help. Lift it."

She looked at her muscular arms and then heaved. To her surprise, the massive stone popped up off the ground with ease. Dallas's eyes beamed with delight through the armored slits in her helmet. She turned the headstone in the air and fit it neatly back in place.

Picking back up her spear, she exclaimed, "It felt like it weighed as much as my mom's Chihuahua, Pokey."

Edward gave a half-grin, "Yes, well, don't go thinking you're impervious. You're mortal, just a little tougher than most. Your armor is magical, so it's impervious to mortal weapons, but you aren't. You will heal faster than normal in this form, but you're not bulletproof."

Dallas looked at her palm, and asked, "How do I, you know, get back to normal? Or is this my new normal?"

Edward felt the fatigue from the spellcasting. "You could stay like this, but I'm guessing your family would wonder where you went. I'm sure someone would ask a few questions when a six-foot-tall Valkyrie showed up for Christmas dinner. As for transforming back to your normal form, I have found that magic often works in a binary pattern. Call upon Odin, again."

She stepped back, threw her hand up to the night sky, and yelled, "Odin!"

A black mist formed at her feet and bellowed upwards until it covered her entire body. Dallas Webb stepped out of the magical fog, waving her hands in an attempt to get it out of her face. She was once again her usual self and back to being five-foot

She looked back at the disappointing black swirl, "So, now I'm supposed to fight against the Crimson Brotherhood… with a spear."

Edward turned and walked away as she yelled out after him, "Wait! What am I supposed to do? How am I supposed to find the Brotherhood? I don't even know anything about Norse mythology!"

Edward fought against the overwhelming feeling of fatigue, "Perhaps this is a good time to work on those people skills of yours and find a teacher that can train you. As for your lack of knowledge of your patron deity, I suggest that you begin by getting a library card."

By Bo Luellen

Chapter 14: David III

Unknown Location – Unknown Date – Unknown Time

David Keller woke up in a start from another leg cramp. It was the sixth time he had passed out from a combination of a lack of sleep and exertion. His hands were bloody from repeated escape attempts, and his legs were so stiff, he wasn't sure how useful they would be if he got out.

Time passes slowly in prison, regardless of its size. The only earmark of the passing day was the daylight that had poured into the small cracks in the casket. The lining of the box was responsible for a modest level of insulation, which kept some of the heat contained within his little box. Still, his fingers were numb from the cold, and he could feel his body dipping into hyperthermia.

Overhead he heard another train whistle in the distance, "Fuck, not again."

His coffin vibrated slowly at first and then popped violently up and down. His head bounced off the wooden lid and he did his best to protect his skull. The locomotive passing overhead seemed to keep on for an eternity. Several minutes passed, as he rode out the torturous shaking. He said a silent prayer as the shaking turned again to a gentle vibration. When it was gone, all he could hear was the whistling of the cold wind and creaking of ropes.

Suddenly he felt the box drop half a foot. He was startled by the sudden descent and stop. Holding onto the edges, he stayed motionless and in fear that it would fall again.

He took a long breath, *Let's add falling the list of ways I could die. At least I'm sure now. I'm hanging by ropes under a train trestle, but which one?*

He saw new light coming in from the bottom of his coffin. The sudden drop had cracked the box. He forced himself to roll over and put his eye up to the hole. He saw the all too familiar green-tinted river water rushing by.

David rested his head on the wood bottom, "Adding drowning…"

By Bo Luellen

Unknown Location – Unknown Date – Unknown Time

    The chill of his second night in the box had set in. The blaring sound of yet another train woke him from his sleep. The constant volley of locomotives kept him from getting any long-term rest, and sleep deprivation was setting in. His lips were chapped from lack of food and water, which caused his energy levels were almost non-existent.

    The pulsating rumbling caused his stiff and atrophic legs to spike in pain. He had already defecated himself twice, and the bottom portion of the box had a collection of his urine. David was too weak to protect his head from the bouncing motion, as it pinged off the wooden walls.

    He heard a woman's voice from outside, "Es ist Zeit."

    David startled fully awake, and frantically replied in a raspy voice, "Hello! Is someone out there? Hello! It's time for what? Talk to me! Hey!"

    The drumming of the iron wheels on the metal tracks continued. David maneuvered himself down, where he could get his mouth closer to a small crack in the side. He screamed with all his might, but only a shallow sound came out of his dry vocal cords. After a few minutes, the train had passed, and he screamed for her again. Tears ran down his face, and the salty moisture burned his cracked lips and flesh.

    He looked up at the pitch darkness, *My uncle is going to be all alone. He won't be able to take care of himself, if I die. God, just let me die.*

    From the inky blackness of his coffin came a pair of blonde eyes that appeared in front of him. He yelled and turned his head slightly. It was the face of the ski-masked superwoman, piercing him with a hard glare. She seemed to be floating over him, and about five feet away. He felt the coffin lid and realized it was impossible.

    He shook his head and cried, "No… no … you're not here. You can't be. This is a dream. This is just a bad dream!"

    The darkness around her face expanded until her entire body was visible in the black. She walked to her right and stuck out her hand. Appearing beside her was his Uncle Enrich. The elderly man was sitting in his easy chair, wearing his pajamas and monitors hooked up to his body.

    David's heart beat faster as he soundlessly pleaded for her to leave the old man alone. The short woman walked behind the elderly German and carefully selected several of the wires from his heart monitor. While staring at David, she wrapped the ends around her black-gloved hands. He shut his eyes, but still, the vision of continued. He beat his fists against the sides of the coffin, while she slinked behind the green recliner.

The superwoman grinned through the black mask, "Es ist Zeit für ihn zu sterben!"

She looped the cords around Enrich's wrinkled neck and put her knee into the back of the chair. The old man continued to look ahead and laughed at something invisible in front of him. David shook his head as she snapped back on the wires and pulled it tight across her victim's throat. The German's eyes bulged out of his head, and one plopped out onto his cheek. His head shook violently from the brutal force she was applying. Blood flowed down his nightshirt, turning it from a powder blue to a bright red. Snot poured from David's nose, while the life ran out of his uncle.

She put both of the cords into her left hand and reached under the ski mask with the other. Enrich slumped over, as the superwoman pulled off her ski mask. As the cloth went flying behind her, David felt his mind shifting towards the unthinkable, as his own face looked back at him. He had the blonde hair of the cultist, but his face sat on top of her shoulders.

He started hyperventilating as a sharp crack rang out. The top portion of David's coffin dropped four feet and pitched his body towards his head. Instantly he was brought back to reality, and the image of him killing his own uncle was gone.

He wormed his arms and tried to do a handstand against the wall above his head. He struggled to take the pressure off his neck. In his weakened state, it took a Herculean struggle to manage even a few inches of clearance. His biceps shook as he pushed his knees upwards to wedge himself in place.

David's cracked mind absorbed the vision as reality, *Okay, David, you can't let her get to your Uncle. You have to stop her! There has to be a way out of here.*

As if the universe responded to him, the top of the coffin gave way. The extreme angle spilled him out headfirst into the night sky. Keller put every ounce of his remaining energy into pushing his knees upwards to break himself. The man's butt was just inside the coffin, while his upper body hung into the cold night air. His eyes refused to focus on the new depths, and the feel of the wind on his face made him tear up. With all his remaining energy, he did a sit up and felt around for something to grab. His bruised and bloody hands found something that felt like a rope. David pulled himself upwards and took a moment to let his sight adjust.

A few moments later, the night illuminated with the moon and star shine, David found he was indeed under a train trestle and hanging a hundred feet from the water below. He could make out the dark wood coffin's smooth exterior. Both ends had been secured by a thick rope. The portion towards the feet had been damaged but was still intact. The line he had in his hand was only hanging by one braid length. The rest of the cord had frayed and snapped.

Looking up, he found the other end of the cords were secured around the railroad tie overhead. His strength returned enough for him to resume searching for anything to hook his foot into. Suddenly his left leg gave out, and David's body went into free fall out of the end of the coffin. He held tight to the fraying rope that was barely still in one piece. The ache in his legs and arms were intense as the deterioration of being in the same position had done its damage.

He put a foot up on top of the box to have it collapse inward. The hours of abuse and shaking had degraded the integrity of the coffin, and it busted into pieces under him. He held to the cord as the wood planks tumbled into the black night. The sounds of the timbers splashing down in the water sobered him to the fact that he had no chance of swimming to the shoreline if he fell. He felt the jerk and pop of another section of the rope break away under his weight. Across from him was the dangling rope that had held the bottom portion of his coffin. It was in much better condition, and the large loop at its end invited him to hope for salvation from his predicament.

David swung his body back and forth and closed the distance to the other rope. He reached out with his foot and managed to catch the loop with his heel. Threading his other leg into the noose, David worked it up to his knees. The effort had caused a dull snap to sound out, as the rope he was holding broke in half. David screamed and tightened his legs around the loop. Now hanging upside down by his knees, he felt the sensation of his blood rushing to his head. Looking up at the ground below, he made out the sparkling reflections of the rushing water of a river in the moonlight. The pieces of his casket were partially swept away, while the rest was stuck in the sandy riverbed.

David closed his eyes and thought, *That's about a 100 foot fall. The wood is stuck in the sand, which means that is only a foot, or so, of water. That sandbar underneath is going to be like hitting concrete. Dropping down is certain death. I suppose that's what those things had in mind.*

From behind him, the superwoman's voice said, "If you go head first, it will be quick."

He kept his eyes closed and responded, "If I jump, then I can't come home to Uncle Enrich."

Opening his eyes, he saw the impossible. The visage of the short, ski-masked lady with blond hair was floating in the air in front of him. She moved close to his face and touched his head.

David felt like his head was ready to burst from the accumulated blood flow, "How... can you be here? Why won't you leave me alone?"

From under the ski mask, she replied, "Weil du Amanda hilfst!"

She grabbed a handful of his hair and pulled hard, ripping it out by the roots. He screamed and balled up his fists, protecting his face. After a few seconds, he looked out from behind his forearms, to find nothing but open night air. The superwoman had gone, but in his right hand was a large tuft of his greying hair. He opened his hand, and the follicles floated out of his grasp, leaving behind the bloody roots. The anxiety and stress left him, as he started laughing at the moment of enlightenment.

He suddenly realized, *She'll let my Uncle live if I stop helping Amanda. Yes. She'll love me then. I won't have to fear her. I can win her over. Just stop helping Amanda.*

His legs below were starting to lose circulation from the rope biting into the back of his knees. With a new focus, he looked up towards the bridge. David noticed the line was anchored a good ten feet up on a railroad tie. It was in relatively good shape and was holding his weight nicely. As he scanned his surroundings, he suddenly realized two more coffins dangling from the underside of the tracks behind him. Twisting his body around, he spun to face them. They were both made of dark wood and their ropes were similarly frayed.

David's voice cracked as he yelled out, "Hey! Hey!"

He stilled himself and listened. The running water below was so loud, it made a white noise that drowned out everything. David looked back up the rope and took a second look at his chances to scale it to the top.

Taking into account his condition, he thought, *I could climb this if I was healthy.*

The silky voice of the superwoman whispered in his ear, "If you're going to love me, you have to prove you can do this."

Without flinching at the phantom voice, he replied, "I'll do it. I'll make it... for you."

He gauged the distance between him and the next casket as close to ten feet. David attempted to perform a vertical sit-up only to hit muscle failure halfway through the effort. He collapsed back and hung by his knees once more. The biting on his skin was becoming numb, which meant David was losing blood flow. Soon he wouldn't be able to control his legs and would drop headfirst onto the ground below.

David looked up toward the bridge and saw the blond superwoman looking over the edge at him, "If you want me, you're going to have to do better than that."

He took a deep breath and then pitched his upper body back and forth, shooting pain into his legs. After a few moments, his swinging had gained momentum. The cold night air was whistling past his face as his arc pulled him closer to his neighbor's coffin. With each swing, he got a full view of the empty space below him, and fear poured into him, as he realized how dire his circumstances were. The rope overhead creaked as the corner of the railroad tie started to saw at the line.

David swung his arms furiously into the swing, *I'm going to make it. I'm going prove myself to you.*

The image of the superwoman appeared again and stood welcoming on top of the coffin. Beckoning David on with her right hand, she gestured towards the support ropes. He knew instantly what she wanted.

Redoubling his efforts, he pulled himself to new heights of exertion as he envisioned the woman and him embraced in a kiss. Finally, one of the ropes that held it up was brushed against his hand. He grabbed for the braided hemp and unfolded his legs from around the loop. Instantly, he slipped out of the rough rope and free-fell on top of the hard cherry wood coffin.

He caught himself by the edges of the box, as he suffered from having the wind knocked out of him. The pain shot him back to full consciousness, and the terror of almost having died brought him back to his senses. The image of the superwoman vanished, and he found himself alone on the top of the casket.

David pinched his eyes closed, "No, no, no! She's not real. Keep it together, man."

A raspy sounding Thomas Booth yelled up, "Hey! Who's in there?"

He wiggled his toes to force the blood to flow again, "Hey, it's David."

The druid yelled up, "How are we doing?"

David looked up and saw a third and final coffin hanging by ropes on the other side of Thomas's, "Same as always."

His friend paused then shouted back, "That bad?"

He felt the blonde woman's voice trying to slip back into his mind, but he resisted, "How… how are you holding up?"

Thomas's voice sounded hoarse, "Good. I'm ready to go though."

David felt some stability from having a problem to work out, "Okay, working on it."

He used his arms to pivot, so he was laying longways along the casket. The sensation was back in his legs, but he still didn't fully trust them. David maneuvered himself across the smooth top until he was straddling the coffin. He took stock of the condition of the braided hemp that held Thomas's casket. The cords had been cut deep by the edges of the railroad ties, and he estimated that the increased weight wasn't doing the situation any favors.

Just then, a sharp crack of breaking ropes snapped in the air from the other coffin that was ten feet away. One end had fallen free, while the other was now holding the entire weight. The wooden box groaned at the new stress points, and it spun in a circle.

Thomas yelled out from inside his box, "What was that?"

David took a deep breath and felt his anxiety building, "T-those things put us in coffins and hung us over a river, under a train trestle. I made it over to you, but we're not going to last long before the ropes give. T-there's another casket, and it just lost one of its ropes. I'm guessing Nicolaas is inside."

Thomas yelled out, "What's our plan?"

David rubbed his legs, "I was hoping you had some ideas."

The sharp splintering of wood shot out in the night. Nicolaas's knee stuck out of his dangling coffin. A second later, a leg lurched out of the hole, and the lid was wedged open.

The druid yelled up, "Hey, what's that noise?"

The young Van Helsing swung out from the opening and grabbed hold of the rope that was still attached. Amid the windy underbelly of the train tracks, the casket folded. Nicolaas kept his grip as the box crumbled into pieces and fell into the river. Moving one hand over the next, the shirtless would-be vampire hunter ascended the rope until he had his foot sitting in the loop.

David lifted his arm and waved, "It's Nicolaas . He's out."

Thomas replied, "Great. Let's do what he did."

He rested his head on the ropes, "Not likely."

Nicolaas yelled over, "How are you two holding up?"

He gave an okay sign and screamed, "Dandy!"

The young man moved his hips and managed to create a swing that drew him ever closer to David. After a few minutes, Nicolaas dropped down and held on only by his hands. Kicking his feet out, he increased his arc and hooked his legs around one of Thomas's support ropes. Like a trapeze artist, he locked himself in place and tied his rope off to theirs. His biceps bulged as he worked his way down until he was standing next to David on the coffin lid.

David gave a wary look to Nicolaas , "You're ... chipper."

The Van Helsing gave him a grin, "My Granddad used to lock me in rooms or leave me out in the wild. I had to learn techniques that would allow me to survive. I've gone up to two days without food."

As Nicolaas hovered over Thomas's upper half of his casket, David replied, "Charming."

In the distance, the sound of a train whistle bellowed out, and Thomas exclaimed, "Come on! You've got to be kidding!"

Nicolaas put one hand on each of the supporting ropes and yelled, "Thomas, turn your head and close your eyes!"

The young man lifted his heel and slammed his foot down on the top of the lid. The box cracked, and the druid let out a high pitched scream. Nicolaas cleared the loose boards and revealed a bloody-nosed Thomas Booth. The young man helped him up to his feet and moved him to the opposite end from David.

Nicolaas turned around and pointed at a support pillar, some fifteen feet away, "Okay, here is how we get out of here. I'm going to take both of you, in turn, over to that beam."

David shook his head, "Good plan, kid, but it won't work. I don't think either of us is in any condition to make that happen. My hands are toast and Thomas…"

The druid patted his belly through his brown cloak, "I'm too fat. I'll say it."

Nicolaas took off his belt and wrapped it around Thomas, "I'm threading the belt through my belt loops. This will give you some additional support, but you got to try your best to not rely on them. If those loops snap, you're falling, and David won't have his turn. With any luck, it will only take one swing."

The sweaty druid looked at David, who shook his head and said, "It's worth a shot."

A few minutes later, Thomas was latched onto the front of Nicolaas , as the young man reached up and laced the rope around his hand. With a quick jerk, the slip knot was free, and the druid screamed out, as they swung towards the support beam. David heard the grunt, as the two smacked hard against the unforgiving trestle column.

Nicolaas yelled, "Turn around a grab hold! I can't support us both for long!"

Thomas stepped up onto a ledge of the pillar and unbuckled himself from the young man. Booth kissed the rusty metal, while Nicolaas caught his breath. David felt the weariness set in and looked down at the reflection of the moonlight in the river, as the tormenting train passed overhead.

From the pillar, Thomas yelled, "Look!"

David lazily looked where the druid was pointing and saw the vague outline of two people sitting on the shore of the river, close to where they were. He turned his tired body slightly and tried to make out what he was seeing.

Thomas made his way down the pillar, as Nicolaas shouted, "It's the Lanyons! It's the girls! They're just sitting on the shore!"

They were dressed in all black clothes, with alien-looking symbols etched in dried blood on their faces. All around them were burnt candles, and rocks lined up in a 10-foot wide pentagram formation. Surrounding the kids were the bodies of countless dead fish that had bites taken out of their bellies.

Nancy saw them descending and screamed, "No! You were supposed to die! We were going to get to watch!"

Nicolaas looked back at David and laced his belt into the loop in the rope, "I need to help him. Take this and get yourself across."

The Van Helsing slung the heavy line out, and David caught it in his hand. Nicolaas zipped down the pillar, passing Thomas on the way. The girls screamed in rage as the men approached the bottom. The pair of girls turned and bolted off the embankment, away from the fast-moving river. The men waded furiously across the rapids in hot pursuit.

David felt a presence and looked to his left. Sitting next to him on the casket was the blonde-haired superwoman, no more than a foot away. She seemed more tangible and real than ever before. Turning her body towards him, she leaned on the rope and set her deep blue eyes on his beleaguered face.

David no longer felt the cold or the will to run, "Are you real?"

She pushed a thumb under the mask and pulled it off. The sharp cheekbone of a strange blonde glowed in the moonlight. The woman slid off her black turtleneck to reveal her bare upper body. Her skin was painted with arcane tattoos that stretched around her torso in chaotic patterns. Her muscles were toned and tight to the surface, with veins poking out along her shoulders. The woman's breasts were the only thing not marked.

Her etchings glowed with dark red energy, "Long ago, my father taught me how to awaken in my dreams. Since then, my Lord Cthulhu has taught me how to walk into others. You are a special person David Keller, and I've been testing you."

David put his hand on his forehead and irrationally scratched a bloody path along his own flesh, "Who are you?"

She held up her right hand and drew a glowing pattern in the air, "I'm the daughter of one of the greatest sorcerers of our time. I'm the Sword of Cthulhu, and one day I will be his concubine. You caught my attention back in the Preserve. I hoped you would please The Dreamer, and I could have you."

Below him, Nicolaas came back out of the brush with April, as the little girl screamed, "No! You made Violet give us up, but we will make her love us again. We will find her!"

Thomas burst out of the same thick bushes, with Nancy in a headlock, "The Shining twins are creeping me out. Can we just hit them with a rock or something?"

The woman conjured up an image of their fight at the Preserve, "You caught my attention during our fight. It's the first time since my father gifted me with the strength of the Elder God that anyone was able to confront my power. I had hoped you would please The Dreamer but look at you, a frail old man. You're so tired, and yet, a coward too scared to sleep. No, Cthulhu has selected another for me."

He scooted back away from the impossible magic she was displaying. David saw the fight being replayed, and he felt the suffocation of not being able to escape her. She stood up and flared her hands outwards. Red flaming tentacles shot out of her bare skin and wrapped themselves around the casket. He felt the hot fire on his flesh, as one burned into his pants.

He shook his head repeatedly and screamed, "No! No! This can't be real!"

She blinked, and her eye sockets were empty, "I walk in your dreams. Here, I'll find the little terrors you dare not speak out loud and set them up on high, for all to see. I'll make you crave the bile of your own body and deprive you of every pleasure. Scurry away little flea, let me see you fly."

David shot out of his slumber and flailed his hands at the illusions of his arcane nightmares. He was alone on top of the casket and unable to separate the echoes of the spellbound dream and reality. Not fully realizing where he was, the big man launched himself off the battered coffin and into the night air. His companions below yelled in disbelief, as he streaked for the shallow water below. He heard the snapping of his neck and felt the cold water rush over his body. His mind shut down, and in the darkness, the realm of Cthulhu opened its gates and welcomed his soul.

By Bo Luellen

Chapter 15: Amanda VIII

The Wilds of Scotland – Thursday, November 15th, 2018 – Early a.m. BST

Her last night at camp with Roger Quinlynn, Ian MacLean, Peyton Greum, and her college friend, Josh Dyer, seemed like a distant dream. Amanda Lanyon had been pursued relentlessly by the Crimson Brotherhood for over three grueling days. Every attempt to make for civilization resulted in her finding Brotherhood patrols in the forest. She kept to wilds and hidden from the black helicopters that seemed to suspiciously frequent the skies above her.

She had run out of Cliff Bars on the second day, and her pace had slowed up from a mixture of fatigue and lack of nutrition. Staying hydrated had been another problem, as she had only found several small caches of trapped water in puddles and leaves. Those little pockets of moisture were not enough to fuel her need to stay on the move to avoid being spotted.

This morning, she was startled awake by the sounds of someone stomping through the woods nearby. Amanda poked her head up over the cover of twigs and foliage she had assembled. She quietly raked some of the dried leaves on top of her legs and pressed her head down against the sticks.

Her heart pounded in fear, as two black-clad men carrying rifles jogged out of the tree line and towards one another. Neither of them was in good shape, and they both struggled to catch their breath. They met 20 feet away, and she suddenly realized how vulnerable she was. Her cover was nothing more than dried out twigs, which wouldn't have a hope of stopping a high powered bullet. She gritted her teeth and imagined she was one with the ground.

Amanda tried to control her fear, *They could see a foot sticking out or my breath in the cold. Oh, God help me!*

The Crimson Brotherhood insignia glistened in the morning sun, as the fatter of the two greeted the other in R'Lyehian, "Llll h' nafl'fhtagn!, Th' master says we cannae stoap 'til Amanda Lanyon is deid."

The other man kicked a rock and yelled, "We've bin oot 'ere fur days! Whit's sae important aboot this wifie?"

His pudgier companion answered, "Grand Master Enfield isnae saying. Th' Irish sect is oan thair wey tae hulp, sae it mist be important!."

The second voice scoffed, "We dinnae need they Lowlanders! we'd be better aff wi'oot thaim!."

His friend retorted, "We've bin at this fur three days. If ah dinnae fin' thaim, mah wife's gaun think a'm cheating oan her."

The slimmer man patted his companion's robust belly, "Wi' wha, a piece o' shortbread?"

They shared a chuckle and then agreed on a direction to search. The two split up and yelled into the radio, as they marched off. Amanda got up from her hiding place and looked around the forest, hopelessly lost. All of her clothes were ruined and torn in several places. Even the well-made outdoors coat Josh had purchased for her was caked with mud and weathering at the seams. Arms slumped at her side, she picked up a stout stick and trogged onward to the next miserable destination.

The Wilds of Scotland – Thursday, November 15th, 2018 – Late p.m. BST

Amanda rounded a large oak to find a small abandoned barn in the middle of a clearing. The paint had all but peeled from its outer walls and only hinted at its original green color. The roof was made of rusted tin, and there were holes in the boards.

She felt an exhilaration come over her. *Oh, you're a lovely sight.*

Making her way cautiously across to the dilapidated threshold, she scanned the darkening skies for any sign of the Brotherhood. Moving inside the dirt-floored barn, she took stock of the dead and dying grass. Only a small bush was left in the corner, and full of ripe blue colored berries.

She dropped her walking stick and cried, *Crowberries!*

Amanda sprinted towards the bush and tore a handful of the small fruits from its branches. Devouring the tasteless berries, she hit her knees and forgot about the hunters. She filled her empty stomach and welcomed the succulent gift until her hands were stained sapphire. Once her belly couldn't hold another bite, she stuffed her pockets with what was left on the bush. Exhausted and in pain, she laid down next to her savior. As night fell, Amanda slipped out of consciousness under the rickety metal and dreamed of her daughters.

The Wilds of Scotland – Friday, November 16th, 2018 – Early a.m. BST

The next morning she woke up in a start at the sound of a loud click. She opened her eyes and found a red-bearded man in black tactical garb standing at the entrance to the barn. He had a bolt action hunting rifle pointed at her head and was struggling with the mechanism.

The man tried to work the stuck bolt action, "Jobby!"

Her muscles were sore to the point of being immobile, but Amanda still summoned up the willpower to stand. The cultist worked the slide back and forth, attempting to remove the jam. She staggered towards her walking stick, as the man threw down the rifle and pulled out a buck knife. The gun landed on a pile of dead grass, and something living gave a loud squeak. As the redhead stalked her, the dead foliage shifted under the rifle, and something furry stuck its snout out of his hole.

In a flash, a black and white badger bolted out of its den and sunk its teeth into the calf of Amanda's would-be assassin. The Scot screamed in agony and lost his balance. Falling forward, he kicked his leg out in an attempt to get the animal free of its hold. The badger was invested in his suffering and growled with anger.

Amanda kicked the cultist in the face, as he reached for her foot. Blood and curses streamed out of his mouth, while the badger made a meal of his calf. She snatched up her stick and swung with all her might. Her makeshift staff found its mark on the point of his chin and broke the wood in half. Amanda scrambled to the corner of the small barn and frantically looked for something to defend herself with.

The Brotherhood member lay face down and motionless on the ground. She suddenly noticed something in the back of his jacket was poking up. Something underneath his coat was making a tiny tent in the small of his back. He twitched for a moment and then went still.

The badger stopped his assault and removed a chunk of the redhead's muscle. It waddled back to its dugout home and gave her no regard. She slid down the wall until her butt flopped on the ground..

Ten minutes passed before she was stirred from her shock by a man's voice coming from an earphone that had been knocked loose, "Th' Seers located Amanda Lanyon. We ur meetin at rally point Charlie in twenty minutes. Acknowledge."

Energized by the sound of people still out there looking to kill her, she worked her way back up to her feet. Careful to avoid her roommate's front door, she made her way over to the dead man. Grabbing under his arm, Amanda strained and pushed the body onto its back. As it settled, the handle of the buck knife stuck out of the man's chest. The weight of the corpse rested on the tip of the weapon and slowly pushed the blade back out the way it had entered. She gagged and turned her face away from the sound of tissue sliding against steel.

Realizing time was against her, she reached out and grabbed the throat microphone. Amanda examined the device, rolling it over in her hand. She put the radio around her neck and secured it. She shoved the earbuds into in place and heard, "Hunter 2 Acknowledged... Hunter 5 Acknowledged... Hunter 12 Acknowledged..."

Amanda felt her hair stand on end as the call signs counted in the twenties. Lanyon kept a tally on the dirt floor of all the codenames she heard over the radio. After a few minutes, all the numbers up to twenty-five had reported, except for one.

She squeezed the call button on her throat and announced in a low voice, "Hunter 7, Acknowledged."

Amanda held her breath until finally a man said, "'A' hunters acknowledged."

Amanda stood up and thought, *How do they keep finding me? When they meet, they'll figure out one of their guys are missing and it won't be long before they come looking. I've got to move!*

Looking down, Amanda saw a dead mouse was against the outside corner of the barn. It's open stomach and entrails were being pecked at by a large raven. The bird regarded her, while a tiny piece of meat dangled from its scratched beak. She jumped as it flew past her and into the building. Amanda watched as it danced on the back of the dead cultist and drove its bill into the front pocket of the man. After a few tries, it pulled out a Macaroons candy bar and hopped off the body. She straightened up at the sight of food, as the raven took its prize and flew off into the forest.

She stripped down the corpse despite the blood flowing from the wound. Twenty minutes later, she had on warm clothing and a new pair of boots. They fit almost perfectly, except for the hole in the chest from the knife wound. In the cultist's pack, she found two British military 24-Hour Operational Ration Packs. Amanda ripped open one of the packages, and downed the contents, as she kept pilfering. The man's canteen was halfway full, but the fresh water felt good on her dry lips. The gun he carried was a bolt action Lee–Enfield L42 sniper rifle that had a 10 round magazine. After a few tries, she was able to remove the jam and slung the weapon over her shoulder. Gritting her teeth, she grabbed the handle of the buck knife and quickly removed it from the cadaver. Taking a deep breath, she wiped the red fluid off on the side of the building and stuck it in its sheath. Amanda left the barn and said a quiet goodbye towards the badger's hole.

The breaking daylight shot out over the tree line, as she looked around to decide on a direction. In a massive Scots Pine was the large Raven that had made a meal out of the coconut flavored candy bar. It opened its marked-up beak and squawked at her. Springing from a limb, it flew off north into the woodlands. The Raven landed in an oak at the edge of her sight.

She took the rifle off her shoulders and marched towards the bird, "Sure, why not. You've had some good advice so far."

When she reached the Raven's perch, the bird flew and landed over 100 yards away, in a different tree. Each time she would follow it and repeat the cycle. On a few occasions, the black-feathered bird would disappear into the treetops. When this happened, Amanda would keep walking in a direction that felt right. Without fail, the Raven would find her again, and she would trail it.

While she hiked, she felt her body warming up. The realization of how bad her condition was became evident in the soreness of her feet. Soon, it became too painful to continue walking, and she sat down on the cold ground. She took off her stolen boots to discover several busted blisters on her soles and heels. The exposed flesh had rubbed against the hard leather until the meat of her muscle was showing. She took out a small first aid kit she found in the dead man's backpack and popped it open. After a few minutes, she had applied an antiseptic cream on the wounds and covered each one in Band-Aids. It was the first sense of pain relief Amanda had experienced since her run from the Brotherhood had begun. She looked over the rest of her body and took note of all the minor cuts and wounds.

From the side, the Raven cawed from a nearby branch and startled her. It flew off and perched on an English Oak, some seventy-five yards away. A reflection from something metal flashed in the Scotland sunlight just beneath the bird. Her eyes panned down to three black-garbed Brotherhood members snaking their way through the trees and headed in her direction. They were each carrying automatic rifles but had the similar gear to the redhead from the barn.

Amanda laid flat against the ground on her tummy and pulled her rifle up in front of her. Her heart went wild, as she dared to move her head up over the low grass. The trio were traveling at the same pace and weren't looking in her direction.

She gripped her rifle hard, *I can't possibly run in this condition, and I can't put my boots on in time. God, I don't want to do this, but these assholes aren't giving me a choice!*

She remembered her experience in hunting when she was young and rested her gun on her forearm. Amanda leveled her rifle at them and brought the crosshairs on the lead cultist. Carefully, and coolly, she clicked off the safety.

Pausing, she thought, *These men could have families. Children and wives that could have no idea what they're into. If I kill them, then I'm depriving them of a father. I'm no better than how the Brotherhood took my husband and left my daughters without a dad.*

She felt the impending tragedy of the inevitable need to take a life. Amanda exhaled and squeezed. Before the trigger was fully pulled, her eyes caught sight of the Raven launching off a branch over their heads. The vacant perch bobbed up and down and shook a hornets' nest that hung from the tree limb. Black dots poured out of the grey blob and buzzed around their home. The advancing men were seconds from traveling right under the nest.

She elevated the barrel towards the anchor that connected the collection of wood and saliva to the tree. Amanda peered down the scope and put the crosshairs right on the base, then waited. She opened her free eye and did her best to gauge the relative position of the cultist. The footsteps of the soldiers of the Crimson Brotherhood were close enough to be audible. Her stomach turned in anxiety, and the lead man stopped to put his hand on the tree for support. He knocked free a collection of mud, then passed directly under the nest.

The first shot from her rifle surprised her, as she squeezed the trigger unconsciously. The report resonated throughout the forest and caused the line of hunters to drop down for cover. The recoil from the gun bounced the scope away from her face. As she reset, Amanda saw the nest free-falling towards the ground. A long second passed before it hit, as the men desperately looked for the shooter. The middle gunman's orders to his comrades were drowned out by the sharp splat of the hornets' home on the ground next to him.

Instantly, the insects flew out of the cracked orb and viciously swarmed the three men. Amanda's jaw opened wide, as she was unprepared for the sheer amount of hornets that poured out from the globe. Over a thousand tiny insects stung the men repeatedly and carpeted their exposed skin.

Behind Amanda, the Raven landed on her back and cawed loudly into the air. She felt an odd comfort from having its weight on her. Realizing her opportunity, she worked the bolt action of the rifle and took aim. The beleaguered woman centered her sights on the lead hunter, who was on the ground and in a fetal position. He was attempting to cover his welted face and arms from further assaults. She pulled the trigger, and the tree behind the cultist was painted red with the blood splatter and brains.

Amanda quickly worked another round in the chamber and positioned the gun for another shot. The middle cultist went running in a straight direction away from the group. The man was stripping off his jacket and screamed at the pain from the enraged hornets. She took advantage of the moment when he stopped to slap a stinging bug from his neck. Her bullet's impact blew through the man's spine and out through his ribcage. He dropped to his knees and was followed by the halo of stinging creatures. He fell face-first onto the ground, and his wiggling ass vibrated from death spasms.

Amanda came up to her knees to get a better view of the last assassin still alive. She saw the remaining cultist huddled up against a tree, with his coat drawn up over his head. He was using it as a shelter against the attacking insects. Twisting in agony, the Brotherhood Hunter couldn't keep some of the bugs from making it to his flesh. She worked the bolt action again and loaded another round. Taking a kneeling position, she leveled the gun at the man's head.

Her radio came alive with the voice of a man, "Gamma Team, we heard shots in yer sector. Report?"

The voice from her final target blurted out over the radio, "We ur under fire! rame, we ur taking fire 'n' hae casualties. We need immediate reinforcements in sector..."

Her shot pierced his jacket and cut off his sentence. His body dropped down and went limp as the coat fell down and let the insects in. She lowered the weapon, and the adrenaline dump surged through her body. Amanda popped up to her feet, and the Raven flew off in response. She turned and threw up the majority of the ration pack on the cold ground. Watching the warm vapor come up for the vomit, she shook at the thought of what she had just done.

The radio on her neck burst to life as the gruff man shouted, "Hing in thare Gamma Team, we hae five squads converging oan ye in twenty minutes. Fin' cover 'n' hauld yer horses."

Motivated by the impending soldiers arrival, she quickly put back on her boots and then slung her rifle. Amanda circled around the still swarming hornets and made it to the cultist who had attempted to run away. She reached down and picked up his AK-47, backpack, and retrieved his two spare magazines.

Amanda looked over the newly acquired rifle and played with the mechanism a few times. She had never held a weapon like this before but eventually figured out how the basics worked. A chill came over her as she thought about her lost companions. After leaving them at the roadside camp three days ago seemed like a distant nightmare.

Amanda looked down at the rifle in her hands, *It seems nearly impossible to believe that Josh, Ian, and Roger could have survived against men armed with weapons such as these.*

She looked up and tried to decide which direction the Brotherhood would be coming from. A rustle of feathers from a treetop caught her attention. The Raven sat proudly in a pine tree and cawed towards her. She turned the safety off the machine gun and marched towards her feathered guide.

The Wilds of Scotland – Friday, November 16th, 2018 – Early p.m. BST

Amanda had walked for hours, listening to the Crimson Brotherhood attempting to pin down her position over the radio. Since she only knew where the Gamma sector was, it became impossible to know their locations. The tree cover had become sparse, and she was forced to travel over the hills of the Highlands.

Another acknowledgement of position rang out in her headphones, *If I keep the radio on, maybe I might hear one of them radio in if they spot me. It just might give me a chance to find some cover before they start shooting at me.*

She hadn't seen the Raven in over an hour, which was the longest it had gone absent. Amanda looked up at a long climb of a particularly tall hillside and saw bright sunlight cresting the top. Her legs were aching, and she had to crawl up the steep embankment.

As Amanda ascended, a patch of dirt exploded into the air five-feet in front of her. She lurched sideways onto her hip, as the follow-up crack of the gunshot echoed off the green mounds. The ground around her erupted, as bullets popped up the cold earth. Distant bangs bounded into the air, as she processed the realization that several people were sniping at her from the trees below.

She realized how exposed she was and pumped her legs into action. The bolt action rifle bounced against the back of her head, as Amanda made for the top. Her peripheral vision caught a dozen shots hit the ground dangerously close to her. A bullet grazed the inside of her right leg, causing her to take an uncontrolled tumble. The sniper rifle launched off her back and rolled downhill like a pinwheel. Amanda skidded to a halt on her face and crawled behind a large rock. She pressed her back against it, while bullets bounced off the grey stone. The ricocheting slugs peppered her with gravel and she slid her injured leg closer for inspection. The wound was superficial but hurt like someone was still cutting into her leg.

Among the gunfire, a louder bursting sound filled the Highlands and caused the snipers to stop their assault. A massive explosion went off fifty feet away. The ordnance jarred her teeth and sent a shockwave through her body. The sound deafened her and surrounded her with smoke and dust.

Confused by the concussion, she felt earth beneath her fall away. Amanda tumbled downwards into darkness, bouncing chaotically off dirt walls and building momentum. The descent angled, and pitched her headfirst down a steep embankment. She scooted along the cavern, and her coat and pants scooped up loose soil.

Suddenly she was free-falling once again, only to splash down into warm water. Her head was under for several seconds before the buoyancy in her backpack lifted her to the surface. Sputtering and dog-paddling in pitch blackness, her hands found a dirt shelf to hold onto. Steadying herself, Amanda freed her soaked backpack and threw it onto the dry land. With all her remaining strength, she lifted herself up out of the water and rolled onto her side.

After a few minutes, she reached out and hugged her backpack. As she held it tight, Amanda let go of her emotions and sobbed. She thought about her murdered husband, kidnapped kids, and poor Peyton Greum, who was shot right in front of her. She lamented her friend Josh, who, like Ian, was most likely dead because of her. Amanda pounded the earth with her fist and screamed in rage.

From the pitch blackness came the call of the Raven. She rose up to a seated position and stared out into the pitch dark. Amanda wasn't sure which area of space the noise had come from, but it sobered her up to the moment. She searched her stolen pack until she felt a metal cylinder. With a click, the flashlight came to life and illuminated the massive cavern around her.

She was in a chamber that was half-filled with water, and the other half was a rocky shelf. The walls were dugout, with visible shovel marks. Two tunnels were leading out, one to the north and one to the south. She slowly stood up, taking care not to put too much weight on her injured leg.

Amanda flashed the light down each tunnel. The southern way had a stairway that went upwards, and to the north had a hallway that took her deeper down into the earth. She moved to the archway to the south and saw a sliver of light flowing down. It was faint, but her heart was glad to see an escape to the surface.

As she put a foot upon the first stone step, from behind her came the protest of the Raven. Turning she shined the light on the north tunnel. Amanda saw no sign of the bird. She examined the sides of the archway and noticed druidic symbols etched into the stone. Cobwebs decorated empty torch sconces all along the cavern.

She whispered in disbelief, "There is no way that bird is down here."

Amanda limped her way over to the north tunnel and shined the light down the sloping passage. Something at the bottom was reflecting off her flashlight and causing a kaleidoscope of reflections to bounce onto the walls. Fascinated by the dazzling light display, she slowly worked down the narrow corridor to investigate. As she reached the bottom, she saw the floor was made of carved rock and was covered in loose jewels. Rubies, diamonds, sapphires, and emeralds were scattered all around the ten-foot-wide chamber. On the walls was an etched drawing of a crown with a long sword behind it. The stone in the room was worked smooth, and torch sconces flanked the door. Directly in front of her was an altar made of granite.

She stepped forward, and the torches sprang to life. Amanda gave out a little yell in fright, as she turned towards them. Flames licked the top of the tan stone ceiling, and the gems reflected the light into magnificent lines upon her face.

A woman's voice from behind her said, "Thou hast entered the shrine of the Once and Future King."

Pain shot through her leg as she spun around too fast. Standing behind the altar was a black-haired woman wearing a midnight corset. A black dress spread out to the ground and had glimmering diamonds woven into the fabric that caused her gown to glow in the light. Her bare arms were pale white, with arcane marks drawn with coal into the soft flesh. The woman's lips were thin and red, and her eyes were a vibrant green.

Amanda fell into her gaze and was lost in the calm pools of emerald. The fear she felt dissipated, and a sensation of peace and tranquility came over her. She righted herself and approached the altar.

The woman regarded Amanda's leg, "Thou art hurt. Jarrah, attend her."

A tiny fairy sprang up onto her shoulder. It was no taller than three inches and had a set of purple prismatic butterfly wings on its back. It held aloft a twig, wrapped in leather strips, and flew up into the air. Amanda had trouble keeping track of the miniature person until it landed on the altar. It straightened its gold and blue robes and proudly strolled towards her. It said something in such a low voice; she thought it sounded like a buzzing of a bee. With its freehand, it threw a sparkling collection of dust into the air. The granules floated for an instant and then migrated over to her leg. The particles settled onto her wound, and within seconds she felt the pain disappearing. She reached down and pulled back the torn pant legging to reveal the skin had completely healed.

Still, under the calming effects of the woman's stare, she managed, "Thank you."

Jarrah pitched one leg back and gave a deep bow, as Amanda asked, "Who are you?"

The woman clasped her hands together and replied, "Morgan le Fay, half-sister to King Arthur Pendragon, who's spirit liveth still on the island Avalon."

Amanda felt her heart race, "The Morgan le Fay. That's impossible, it's a myth."

Jarrah sprang up off the stone and fluttered about her face. He grabbed another handful of powder and blew it onto her nose. Instinctively, Amanda breathed in and suddenly felt a flush. Heat built up in her cheeks, and a light-headed feeling took over. She looked up at Morgan and found the walls behind her had vanished. Amanda was standing in a beautiful grove of lush trees with fruit ripe and ready to be picked.

A stag stepped out from behind a large willow tree and stood boldly beside Morgan. The animal had yellow flowers growing out of the antlers, and green vines grew out of its fur. The beast reared up on its hind legs, and its upper body started to shift its form. The animal ceased to look like a deer and now gave the appearance of the half-man she saw in her vision at Thomas Booth's house.

Her eyes were filled with wonder, as she whispered, "Cernunnos."

Morgan gave a bow to the god and then replied to Amanda, "Welcome to Avalon. The Green Man brought thee to me. The time hath joined, and the evil trumpets ring. The champion of Cernunnos hath arrived 'i the morn, just as the bodement foretold."

Amanda shook her head, "Champion of what? I need him to tell me where my children are."

Her green eyes rested on her for a moment, then replied, "Only a Knight of the Round Table tenders the blood of their loved ones for the freedom of the people. Only Raven's Sight can find thy children. Only an anointed warrior, touched by Excalibur, can swear the oath to vanquish the god that lay sleeping."

From the forest came the legions of Fey, from the Isle of Avalon. Pixies, sprites, dryads, changelings, pookas, centaurs, satyrs, and a host of brownies, gnomes, and elves who rode on the backs of warthogs. Amanda staggered back but stopped when the Raven landed on the tree branch next to her. The company of Fey all stopped and bent the knee. Everyone except Cernunnos and Morgan bowed in respect to the great bird. Jarrah flew swiftly up to her shoulder and slapped the back of her head with its diminutive staff. She shot a look over at the fairy, as it pointed down and went to one knee. Amanda knelt on the healed leg but peeked up at the legions of fairy tale legends.

Morgan walked over to her, "Thou art set upon a task, Amanda Lanyon. If thou succeedest, thou shalt prevent the Crimson Brotherhood from raising Cthulhu and thus save your children. Dost thou accept this quest?"

She looked over at the Raven, then the company around her. "I would do anything to save my kids." She felt her heart sink with the heaviness of the moment, then lifted her chin, "I accept."

A green-cloaked elf, no taller than Amanda, stepped out from the thick green woods. In his hand was a longsword in a dark leather scabbard. The handle was braided with golden hair and the hilt molded to look like antlers intertwined.

Morgan turned and drew forth the blade. Holding it up into the air, the bright metal reflected the brilliant Avalon sun onto Amanda's face. The woman stepped forward and lowered the sword down. The arcane glyphs in the side of the smooth steel shimmered onto her skin.

The half-sister of Arthur touched the naked blade to Amanda's right shoulder, "When thou wert young, your faith taught thee to be a worthy Page. You were obedient, with the manners and the skills to be a useful servant of God."

Amanda felt a tingling sensation running across her body from the metal. Suddenly, the feelings of fatigue were gone. The repercussions from the long sleepless nights of running had vanished.

Morgan floated the blade over her head and rested it on her left shoulder, "When thou camest of age, thou puttest thyself to teaching others and learned the lessons of a Squire. Thou hast shown courage and valor at the Battle of the Preserve in defense of an innocent man who was plagued by evil."

She removed the sword and cradled it in her black silk covered arms, "Now when thou risest, doest so as a Knight of the Round Table. Charged never to do outrage, nor murder, and always to flee treason; also, by no means to be cruel, but to give mercy unto him that asketh mercy, upon pain of forfeiture of their worship and lordship of King Arthur for evermore; to take no battles in a wrongful quarrel for no law, nor for worldy goods. Unto this are sworn the Knights of the Table Round, both old and young, man and woman. Stand now, Dame Lanyon, Knight of Arthur and of the Round Table."

Amanda stood and found all her hunger pains were gone. She felt refreshed and full of life. The hosts of Fey beamed wicked grins and danced around toadstools and flowers. A centaur brought out a double flute and played a melody she had never heard. Jarrah flew up to her nose and kissed it.

Morgan handed the blade back to the elf and took a red cloak from him,

"This is the Mantle of Arthur. Thou shalt be unseen to magical creatures and impervious to spells while thou dost wear it. Through its power, thou shalt also see the otherworldly."

She pushed the cloak out towards Amanda. The folded dull red cloth looked pristine, with a single gold trim around the edges. She took it in her hands and was surprised by the weight. Despite the heavy looking fabric, it felt light in her arms.

Cernunnos looked up into the sky, snorted out a great bellow of hot breath from his snout. Jarrah flew back away from her, and the celebration around her stopped. The Fey went silent as she heard a low thunderous rumble in the distance.

Morgan smiled, "Our time dost call upon's for thy departure, Dame Lanyon."

Amanda shook her head, "Wait! I don't know where my kids are. How am I supposed to stop the Crimson Brotherhood? I'm just one person."

A louder grumble came from the lush ground beneath her feet, as Morgan touched her cheek, "The fight shall find thee. Luck be with thee, Dame Lanyon."

A shock wave of something exploding high overhead sent dust and debris showering downward. Amanda covered her head and shielded herself from a curtain of falling dust. Coughing from a few inhales of the raining soil, she looked around to discover she was no longer in Avalon. The muffled pops of explosives went off on the surface, as the glimmer from the jewels that cluttered the ground were slowly being covered by the falling earth. Amanda felt numb as the torches went out, and the brilliant colors were silenced.

She looked down at the Mantle of Arthur in her hands and realized it wasn't a hallucination. The caw of the Raven shot through her like a bullet. She turned her flashlight back down the corridor to see the massive bird standing at the foot of the other tunnel. It let out another encouragement and then launched upwards, towards the surface.

Another blast from overhead sent her running after the bird in a panic. Amanda sprinted down the tunnel, jumping over small boulders that had broken free of the ceiling. She sailed past the main chamber's pool of water and dashed up the stairs of the south hallway. Her legs no longer burned, and her feet no longer hurt. As she neared the top, a cave-in swallowed up the bottom half of the stairwell and sent a billow of dust-up past her. She held her breath and slowly worked her way to the grass-covered opening. There she found no trace of the Raven but did find a small gap where she could breathe in the fresh air. Amanda felt like she could easily push through, but she feared what would be waiting on her.

Her radio came alive in her ear with the sounds of a gruff man, "... We've found the opening and Beta Team is headed down. Are we sure she is still alive?"

A female voice answered, "Th' Seers say her spirit is visible. She mist be doon thare."

She leaned back on the cold steps and thought, *With any luck, the stairs are covered in rubble. How did they know I was down here, and what are Seers?*

A chill came over her from the cold breeze coming through the opening. She shivered and looked down at the regal garment Morgan had gifted her. Amanda rubbed her hand over the smooth fabric and remembered what the emerald-eyed beauty had told her.

Wrapping it around her shoulders and pulling the hood up, she thought, *Magic is real. I just saw it. If these Seers can sense my spirit, then let's put a stop to that.*

She waited, as a few more explosions from deep within the earth erupted. The rock around her crumbled and she had to move towards the center of the stairs to avoid being crushed. Bringing her face close to the opening, she struggled to keep fresh air in her lungs and contemplated bolting out of her hole like the badger from the barn. Fear of being spotted kept her in place, while the explosions continued to push clouds of dirt up past her.

Suddenly, the noise stopped, and the woman's voice blurted out over a radio, "Th' Seers says her spirit haes disappeared. She mist hae bin buried under th' rubble 'n' wis crushed. Mission pure good! Let's heid back tae Stirling Castle!"

A rousing set of cheers came from above ground and a man shouted, "Soon, we wull sacrifice her companions tae Cthulhu 'n' git pissed! Come ya wee jimmies! Weel dain!!"

She rested her head against the broken stone stairwell. *Thank God, at least some of them are alive!*

Amanda sat there, huddled in the folds of the mantle until mid-day. With slow and careful movements, she pushed her red-hooded head up through the entwined lush green of the Highland hill. Dame Lanyon emerged from the hole to discover she was alone and free of her pursuers.

Amanda looked around, *Now that they think I'm dead, they won't expect me. If I can sneak in, and free the guys, we can be gone before they know I was there. I just have to figure out which way Stirling is.*

From the left, she saw the Raven land on a small rock and caw at her. Amanda walked over to the bird and looked down the opposite side of the high mound. A small, windy road crept along the countryside, and tiny dots that were cars motored across it.

A huge smile came across her face, "Good thinking! The Brotherhood has no reason to watch the roads anymore. I'll hitchhike back to Stirling."

The bird launched off the rock and took to flight. She marched down the hill, as the cold winds whipped the red cloak around her body. The lush green grass swirled around her, and she drew the fold of the Mantle of Arthur close.

The Raven glided past her, as she said, "Hang on guys, we're coming."

Chapter 16: John VIII

Tulsa, Oklahoma - Thursday, November 15th, 2018 – 9:15 a.m. CST

John Utterson knew there would be an equal chance of being thanked or having someone kick his ass if he was spotted by a police officer. The walk up to the Tulsa Medical Examiner's office seemed to go on forever. Parking down the street had helped him avoid the majority of the less-than-friendly former co-workers.

He pulled his fedora hat down, *It's not every day that someone blows the whistle on the Department and walks away in better shape than they left.*

John passed through the front door and almost ran right into Detectives Michaels and Cobb. He tilted his head to the side and strolled past. Luckily, both of them were so engrossed that they didn't give him a second look.

He rounded the corner to the office of Chief M.E. Amy Howard, and smiled to see her sitting behind her desk. Her covered face popped up over her laptop screen and gave him a scowl. The woman had on a full-body medical protective suit with the face mask drawn down to her neck.

She pushed her chair out and jogged towards him with open arms. "Are you trying to get shot?"

He embraced her small frame. "By these cops? They'd have to take a number."

The two locked eyes as John pulled her mask down and gave her a long kiss. When they separated, she beamed at him and then sprinted towards the door. She took a quick look outside, then shut and locked it.

Amy turned around and gave him a mischievous smirk. "You look good for a guy that narrowly escaped a house bomb. Why didn't you call?"

He tossed his hat on a steel examination table, "The UCC lawyers kept me under tight wraps, and you still work for the police department. I didn't want to create a conflict for you."

She put her hands on her hips, "Oh, like skulking around the department and sneaking into my office is safer for me?"

His pudgy gut poked out as he leaned on her desk, "Some things in my life are worth the risk."

Her cloth booties scooted along the floor as she tilted her head, playfully, "Those lines might work on those whores you bring home, but I know better. What are you really doing here?"

John leaned on his cane and admitted, "I needed to ask you a favor. Some new evidence has surfaced concerning the Brotherhood, and you know I can't trust the department."

Amy sighed and circled around to the desk. "If you have evidence, you should take it to Terry. He's still your friend and a member of the Brotherhood taskforce. You should be able to trust him."

John nodded and set his jaw, "Of course you're right, but I need to be sure of what I've got before I come to him with it. You are the only person in the department that I can turn to."

She paused for a moment. "Okay fine, but remember, I gave you a choice to go through proper channels. What you're asking me is outside of the law and of my job. Whatever comes of it, this is on you."

He held up his hands, "Fair enough. How about we meet at your old house, at the Enfield Estate? I have a room in the mansion now. We can have dinner and talk it over."

He watched for a blush response, but none came, *Either she's clueless to what her dead father and Richard Enfield are up to, or she's a brilliant liar. Regardless, having her there when I reveal Wicked's ledger will make it hard for them to lie. I'll record the whole thing. I'll bring down the Crimson Brotherhood and a corrupt Richard Enfield, and the city will thank me. I'll be the man that destroyed the followers of Cthulhu!*

Amy tapped a few keys on her keyboard and replied, "Of course. How about 6?"

He picked up his hat and walked to the door, "It's a date."

She shot him a smile as he slid out of the office and headed down the hallway towards the front doors. Cobb and Michaels were still entrenched in their conversation over a cup of coffee. As he passed by, he heard one of them respond in a different voice. Instinctively, he looked up at Cobb and discovered the corpse of his dead partner standing in the detective's place. Michaels was busy making conversation with the half-rotted David Johnston and seemed unfazed by the sight. His body was stiff as a board, with his arms pinned down to his side. There was an "O" shape to the mouth, and his eyelids had sunk back into his face. The dead black man looked like someone stood him up out of his casket, then leaned him against the wall. The body was still wearing its dress blue uniform that John had last seen him in before being lowered into the ground.

He rammed himself against the opposite side of the hallway and dropped his cane, "Jesus Christ!"

Detective Michaels looked at him with surprise and picked up his walking stick, "John, what in the hell are you doing here?"

The body of his dead partner slid sideways down the wall, like a macabre windshield wiper, and left a green slime arc against the brick. The body hit the ground with a thud, and a collection of fat-bellied blue worms fell out of the corpse's mouth onto the white floor. Detective Michaels stepped forward towards John and squished into the wiggling creatures. Green juice squirted out from each side of his shoe, as the officer held out John's cane, oblivious to the cadaver at his feet.

John snatched the stick back as a grey tentacle came slithering out of the body's mouth. The appendages slapped down on the floor and grabbed hold with its suckers. It pulled, and the body dragged along the floor towards him. His eyes went wild at the sight of the arm stretching out for yet another tug in his direction. John ignored the detective and scooted along the wall towards the door. He let out a scream, as the head of David Johnston was pulled free from the corpse and rolled towards him.

John knocked over a trash can and screamed, "Get away from me!"

Michaels held out a hand as John burst out of the doorway. "Hey, easy man!"

John hobbled towards his car, looking back to see if the horrible thing was following him. Police officers stopped what they were doing to give him a puzzled look. Sweat had formed on his face, and he felt the intense pain of his ankle as he made his escape.

A traffic cop yelled out, "Hey, Brother Utterson! Where ya goin'?"

He fumbled for the keys to his Lexus and looked on the ground to see if the dismembered head had followed him. Five cops surrounded his car and mocked him. He scraped up his door, trying to get the key in the lock.

As John wiggled his way into the driver's seat, an officer asked, "Did you drink up all the sacramental wine? You know you gotta pace yourself to salvation."

John slammed the door shut as the crowd laughed and tapped on the hood of his vehicle. The pain in his ribs sparked as he heard the muffled jeers from his former co-workers. Something metal pinged off his trunk, and John quickly put the vehicle in reverse. He glared at the faces of his tormentors and peeled out towards the parking exit. His engine revved as he zoomed down a side road towards Eastland.

He jumped as the voice of David Johnston came from the backseat, "Remember their faces so you can get them back."

John's head spun around, and he nearly hit a parked car. He was the only person in the vehicle and quickly maneuvered the Lexus away from oncoming traffic. His heart was thumping in his throat, and passing cars honked furiously.

He gripped his own throat in fear, *Come on man, keep it together. It's been almost two weeks since you've seen… whatever that was in the graveyard. This is just another hallucination.*

It took him several miles to get his composure back, "You're losing it, man. Maybe it's time to go see the UCC medics before you start talking to yourself."

He pulled out a bottle of Oxys out of his coat and popped the top. As he was driving, Utterson turned the container upside down, tapped it, and waited for a pill to drop into his mouth. Something warm and wet lumped onto his tongue. Instantly he tossed the tan pill bottle onto the passenger seat and spit out a blue worm onto his dashboard. He wiped his tongue with his hand and spit on the floorboard. He noticed the creature was the same as the things he saw coming out of the corpse of David Johnston back at the station.

He pulled the wheel sharply to the left and skidded to a halt in a strip mall. As he did, the fat worm rolled and dropped from the dash onto his slacks. He opened the car door and fell out on his back. The vehicle slowly moved forward as he tossed around on the ground and attempted to free himself of the sticky animal.

Pulling his coat to one side, he saw the tail of the little alien wiggling and its face chewing its way through his pants. He gave it a smack but failed to dislodge it. The worm bit hard into his leg, and John let out a scream. He ripped his pant legs open and found the horrid blue abomination had burrowed past the skin of his thigh. John frantically pulled at its slippery outer surface, as a group of shoppers stopped to watch the wild flailing and thrashing. An old man stepped out and looked as if he was going to help just as he felt the creature disappear under his skin. John let out a roar of pain and arched his back in anguish.

A young man in a black apron ran over to him, "Hey, hey. What's wrong, man? Are you having a seizure?"

The Lexus came to a stop, as the front end crunched into a light pole and dented in the front fender. The crowd reacted to the wreck, as the thing tunneled its way under the skin of his leg. He clamped down on his inner thigh to block the path of the bloated animal. Turning downward, the worm worked deeper into the muscle and sent sharp bolts of torture into his groin.

John reached up to the waiter and grabbed him by the apron string. In a frantic pull, he dragged the man down to the ground with him. John could feel the creature inching its way along his groin and past his testicles. Plunging his hands into his pants, he discovered a lump between his thigh and his scrotum.

The good Samaritan untied his apron and tried to escape, "Hey man! What the hell, you pervert! Let me go!"

The larvae slipped between his fingers, and the lump traveled up his hip and past his belt line. John writhed in pain on the ground, flipping and spinning on the cold concrete parking lot. He let go of the waiter and ripped off his designer dress shirt. Laying on his back, he caught the creature just before it approached his ribs. John reached inside his pocket and took out a folding knife. The crowd around him gasped, and a woman screamed, as he unfolded the blade with a shaky right hand. John brought the edge up the sweaty flesh of his ribcage and angled the point directly onto the center of the lump. He gritted his teeth and a litany of protests clamored from the onlookers. Summoning the strength to poke the blade into his own chest, John's hand slipped over his broken ribs. The pain caused him to shake violently, making him lose his pinch on the worm. Before he could regain control, the thing had made its way up to his left pectoral, diving under the muscle. John gurgled in distress and screamed as the feeling of a hot poker jabbed into his heart.

A black woman wearing a brown parka yelled, "My, God! Did you see that thing! Something was crawling under his skin! Someone call an ambulance!"

John felt the agony turn into a tingling as if he had too much ice cream. His back hurt, and his head felt like it had an instant migraine. He rolled onto his stomach and got to his hands and knees. The woman hooked her hand under his armpit and heaved him to his feet.

In a blissful moment of release, the headache subsided at the same moment, and the chill in his back went away. He stood upright and looked around, seeing the collection of a half-dozen onlookers that gathered around him. John turned and limped towards his car.

John thought, *All I would need is for this to show up on YouTube. That would be it for me. I can't let this get out, not when I'm this close to busting the entire Crimson Brotherhood.*

He settled into the driver's seat and felt a new sensation hit him. The same warm orgasmic experience he relished when the Oxys would kick in flowed across his body. His mind went into an accentuated state of euphoria, one that he had never experienced before from just painkillers. John grabbed his own head to steady himself as the sensation began to build.

He slammed the car door to avoid being captured on camera, *What is this! It feels like I'm on heroin but harder!*

John's consciousness swam in a thick soup of mixed up images. He kept getting flashbacks to the Battle of the Preserve, the bomb at Henry Jekyll's house, then the chemically induced firebomb in the Garden District. Then he saw Amy Howard's face. The picture of her short blonde hair and smile summoned him back into calm. She was topless, with the intricately crafted tattoos on her body seeming to float up off her skin. They glowed a deep red and shifted in patterns that made him feel calm and relaxed.

The dream of Amy reached out for him, "You have been selected by Cthulhu. Come to me, John."

He startled awake and found himself driving down Highway 169 at sixty miles an hour. John jumped at the sudden realization that he had no idea how he had gone from the parking lot to moving at high speeds through traffic. Yanking the wheel frantically, he struggled to get his bearings and not plow into a neighboring Honda. He looked past his steering wheel at the slimy residue left behind by the creature that was now inside his body.

He pulled over and parked on the shoulder, *Maybe this is all just a bad trip. It's possible I didn't remember taking my pain pills earlier this morning and I could have doubled up by accident.*

John rested his head on the steering wheel as David's voice came from the passenger seat, "Bad day?"

John refused to look towards the entity and yelled, "You're not real! Get it out!"

A hand touched his shoulder, as David insisted, "Stop ignoring me, partner. We always came when the other one was in trouble. That's what

I'm doing now."

Slowly, John opened his eyes and looked over. David Johnston was wearing his dress blue uniform but looked precisely as he had known him 4 years ago. He was mostly solid, and his black mustache framed the apparition's chiseled good looks. John pushed his back against his seat and wept.

David flashed an awkward smile, "All that for me? I didn't know you had it in you."

John covered his face and trembled, "You're not real. David's dead."

The ghost leaned in, "No partner, this is very real. I've been given a gift, a second chance to come back here. Get this, I'm here to help you. Isn't that a kick in the butt? I get a shot at coming back from the dead, and I'm stuck with your bloated egotistical ass. Now, I need you to focus up and get a handle on yourself. We got work to do and not a lot of time to get it done."

John looked at him with swollen red eyes, "This is all in my mind."

David ran his index finger and thumb over his thick mustache, "I'm here because there is a purpose for you, and I'm supposed to help you see it. Whistleblowing on the police, going to the press, backing that crazy fanatical con man Greyson was all so you can make the streets safe again. That's the John that is willing to do what it takes for the greater good. On the other hand, making Moss Vickers out to be a Crimson Brotherhood contact just so the police wouldn't find out you were buying drugs off of him, that's downright ruthless. Still, that's the old John Utterson I respected! That's the guy who is willing to make a sacrifice to execute the big plays. Moss was a pawn on the board, you had to sacrifice him to capture the queen. It's just like you, and I used to always say, 'Leeches need salt.'"

John reached out to touch his partner's arm. His hand moved right through space where the manifested body of David Johnston was sitting in his car. He drew his arm back to find a thin layer of slimy substance on the skin.

David pointed at the shiny sheen, "Ectoplasm, like in Ghostbusters. The more tangible I become, the more of it I leave behind."

Snot came out of Utterson's nose as he muttered, "No... No... This can't be real."

The ghost shot his hand through John's chest and grabbed his heart, causing searing pain to fire through his nerve endings. His body stiffened in agony, as he squirmed in his seat, trying to find a way to stop the pain. The phantom bore down on his heart, as the skin on David's face started to droop and melt away from his skull in large chunks. Globs of ectoplasm splattered on John's car seats and his jacket, while large sections of the ghost face liquified.

The manifestation yelled, "There are two things you can count on John! One is that this city has an infestation that needs to be cleansed. Everything we did to rid the world of the users who drained the good people of their resources, family, and happiness put us where we are today! We became addicts because we weren't strong enough to deal with the reality of this corrupt world. We were expected to protect and serve the very villains that drove us both to ruin. The world is sick, John! It needs a cure! That's you, John Utterson!"

David's face was nothing more than a skull, as he twisted the heart in his hand harder, "The second thing you can count on is me, partner! I'm back, and we are a team again! I'm going to help you burn away the infection and put salt on all the leeches. Ha-ha-ha-ha!"

The image of David Johnston faded out, just as his maniacal laughter echoed into the ether of nothing. The pain in his chest lingered for a few moments then subsided. He spent several minutes collecting himself and trying to make sense of what he had just experienced. John opened the car door and threw up the contents of his last meal on the highway. His face was pouring sweat and snot as he shut the door.

John started his car and headed to his old trailer, "This isn't real. This isn't real. Pull it together man. This isn't real."

Broken Arrow, Oklahoma - Thursday, November 15th, 2018 – 5:01 p.m. CST

He rubbed his eyes and turned his body to a sitting position on the bed. The majority of his furniture had been donated to Goodwill. It would have embarrassed him to have it moved into his new room in the Enfield Estate. Still, he kept some essentials in his trailer. He enjoyed using it as a private escape from the UCC staff that plagued him for attention. Today, it was especially useful, as he needed sleep. Waking from a six-hour nap that was plagued with nightmares was not something he wanted his UCC guards witnessing.

He pinched his eyes and reached for his glasses, *I had better get used to sleeping here. Once I confront Richard Enfield with the evidence I have on him being connected to the Crimson Brotherhood, I'll never be back. I'm sure Brother Greyson will thank me for it publicly, and he'll be compelled to acknowledge me as an idealist that rooted a cultist from the ranks.*

Behind him was a bed that was soaked with his sweat. The fever he had experienced kept a constant stream of perspiration running off his body. Three times he had thrown up on the carpet and felt like his body was on fire. John felt surprisingly refreshed and didn't have a hint of the migraine he suffered during his slumber.

Putting on his glasses, he looked down at the blurry floor. He cursed and took them off, cleaning the lenses with a corner of his black sheets. Suddenly, he realized his vision was clear. The normal foggy nearsightedness he had become accustomed to since his vision started going in his twenties had become absent. He peered around his room, seeing each mark on his paneled walls with perfect clarity. Shocked, he sprang out of bed and walked to the hallway. He was able to see the calendar on his kitchen wall, down to the fine detail of each reminder he had penciled in.

That is when he noticed it. The weight he put on his ankle didn't fire off any pain, and the sudden motion should have caused his ribs to give him a sharp jolt. He carefully put more weight on the foot and found not a hint of soreness. John bobbed up and down, then hopped across the worn brown floor laughing. He stopped and pressed his hand against his broken ribs only to find he had no discomfort.

Looking down, he was shocked to see his penis swinging side to side as he turned. Running to the bathroom, he turned the corner and looked at himself in the mirror. The fish gut he had since the death of David Johnston was gone. He could see his abs now, and the love handles Amy had made fun of him for were missing. John turned to the side and took in his muscular profile. He had always had a sturdy build, but it had been hidden by years of overeating and alcohol. John balled up his fist and gave his abs a rap and grinned at the lack of giggle.

He gave a nod to himself in the mirror, *That was one hell of a fever. Maybe it was one of Greyson's miracles. A blue worm and a ghost. God does work in mysterious ways they say. Those old Pentecostals must be onto something. Who knew faith healing was an actual thing. I guess God really is on my side.*

He felt his energy spike, and the sensation of needing a fix was gone. It was replaced by a sense of invincibility that he never experienced before. He bounded around the house like a man in his twenties. He took a shower and got ready for his impending confrontation with Richard Enfield and Amy Howard.

John ran out into his yard and lapped around his car, shouting for joy. The exhilaration of having full use of his leg was only equaled by the wellspring of vigor he was experiencing. His Hispanic neighbor came out onto her porch to investigate the racket. She watched as John hopped up with both feet onto the hood of his car and did an Irish jig. The woman smiled and waved nervously as he froze and made eye contact with her.

John hopped down, *Fuck! I can't just show up with a healed broken ankle in public. The world watched me accept an award and do interview on TV with a set of crutches under my arm.*

He went back inside and grabbed his cane, *I'll keep using this for now, and then ask Greyson to heal me this Sunday. It's not really lying. God did heal me, I'm just rearranging the time frame.*

The neighbor yelled out to him, "Señor John, it's good to see you moving around so well."

He gave her a half-smile, as he faked a hobble to his car, "I just got excited. I'm sure I'll pay for it."

He shut the door and left the woman in a state of confusion. He turned on his car and watched her out of the corner of his eye. He noticed that she didn't have a cell phone in her hand.

David's voice startled him from the passenger seat, "That's right, John. No cell phone, no evidence that it even happened. Her word against yours."

He stayed motionless as the voice spoke. John looked in the rearview mirror and saw nothing in his back seat. He slowly put the car in reverse and backed out of his driveway. He searched his mind for a solution. Reaching over, he turned on a rock station and turned the radio up.

Broken Arrow, Oklahoma - Thursday, November 15th, 2018 – 5:24 p.m. CST

Twenty minutes later, he was pulling past the UCC guards and into the Enfield Estate. Two of the blue-clad sentries saluted him as he passed by the security checkpoint. As he drove, John watched his Crusader patrols move up and down the yard checking for anything that could threaten the next Governor-Elect.

He shook his head. *Amazing! Richard Enfield has Oklahoma and the United States fearing the next Crimson Brotherhood attack, while he puppeteers the UCC. I wonder if Brother Greyson is involved?*

He caught sight of a new face walking along the fence line. The Hispanic man was moving as if he was in a trance, and his clothes looked unfit for the cold. John stopped his car and rolled down his passenger side window to take a better look. The figure wore only a loose tan shirt that was open to the chest, with his pale skin showing through. The look on the stranger's face seemed distant and forlorn. John pulled out his cell phone and dialed the security office inside the Enfield estate.

A woman answered, "General Utterson, welcome home."

He eyed two patrolmen walking in the general direction of the mysterious intruder. "The south side patrol is closing in on a Hispanic male, mid-forties, dark hair, tan shirt, and brown pants. I want him..."

The two sentries moved up to the man, and he paused to see the impending interaction. Just like how his hand had passed through the image of David Johnston, the men phased through the shambling wanderer. John let the phone drift away from his face, as the guards continued unfazed and the ghost journeyed onward.

The woman broke his shock. "General, who are you talking about. I have eyes on the southern section of the grounds right now. Baker patrol are the only people out there. Do you see something we're not? General, shall I dispatch a response team?"

He snapped out of it and realized how insane the truth would sound, "Well done, Corporal. This was a drill. Carry on."

John hung up the phone and watched the ghostly image as it continued to move around the edges of the property. After a few minutes, it disappeared around the corner of the mansion. John saw a few guards watching him suspiciously and took the car out of park. He stopped at the front door and handed his keys to the valet.

As he walked up to the front door, he noticed Amy Howard's Lincoln, *Good. All the players are here. Time to capture the king.*

John kept the pretense of having a broken ankle and used his cane to ascend the stairs. Making his way into the house, he found Enfield's usual hospitality. His maid, Emilia, met him and took his coat.

A sleek young woman in her twenties came around a corner, "Good evening General Utterson. My name's Ruby Cook. I'm Mr. Enfield's personal assistant. Allow me to escort you to the dining room."

He was annoyed at pretending with the cane as he followed her, "I was happy that Brother Richard was able to find time to eat with me."

Ruby paced beside him. "Master Enfield always makes time for his friends."

She stopped and held out a hand towards a sizeable ornate hall, "Make yourself comfortable. Mr. Enfield will be with you shortly."

He limped into the grand room and remarked, "I'll have a guest. Amy Howard will be joining us."

Ruby smirked. "Of course."

She closed the double doors and left him alone. John examined the fantastic collection of Egyptian antiques displayed in cases and on the walls. Enfield had inherited one of the most valuable collections in the United States from Samuel Howard. The oak dining table in the center of the room was surrounded by ten hand-carved chairs with golden dragons embroidered on their finely crafted seats. From the ceiling hung a row of three crystal chandeliers that illuminated every corner of the room. On the walls were massive Fresco Renaissance reproduction murals, which were hung in oak frames. The hardwood floor was covered by a silver and blue Persian rug that John avoided stepping on out of fear, tracking mud.

Richard Enfield burst into the room wearing a jet black suit, "Brother John! It's good to see you outside of work. When you called to arrange this meeting, I couldn't have been happier! UCC meetings are a terrible way to get to know my successor."

John leaned on his cane and stood to reply, "Brother Enfield, I'm glad you had the time. I've only been to a few rooms of your estate, but this dining room is… Well, impressive just isn't the word. I didn't even know this room existed."

Richard looked around at the paintings, "Some of these are original pieces. There are places in the mansion I've yet to explore myself. The house is so big, and there has been so much to do."

John walked out on his cane from behind the table. "Of course. Now, this home was once owned by Samuel Howard and was passed down to you. That is a sizeable inheritance, Brother Enfield. How did you know the late Mr. Howard before then?"

The Lieutenant Governor-Elect seemed placid in the face of the question, as he marched over the bar. "Yes, we were close associates for many long years. He helped finance the opening of my firm and guided me in matters of business. His loss was a defining moment in my life. In one month, I lost a mentor and gained a new purpose."

John pressed, "He was a generous man, but a mystery to me."

Richard poured a brandy, "How so?"

He put his hands in his pockets and stayed steady. "For a man such as Samuel Howard to hand over his seat and holdings with Hoondo Limited Manufacturing to anyone but his only daughter, Amy Howard, leaves me with some questions."

His host took a drink and replied, "Ever the detective. Well, that is why I chose you as the leader of the Oklahoma UCC. You just can't help yourself. To answer your question: Yes, I have his seat with Hoondo Limited Manufacturing, and Samuel entrusted me to secure his family's future. Amy has no talent for business. She's content in more macabre interests, which you're very aware of."

Before he could answer, the double doors to the dining room opened, and the butler announced, "Amy Howard, Sir."

John's lover and longtime friend was wearing a red dress that fit like a second skin. It dragged on the hardwood floor and sported a long slit up the right side that ended at her hip. The exposed flesh of her leg was matched by the cleavage line, which dived downwards and kissed her navel. Her short blond hair was slicked back and accented by a gold necklace. At the center of its chain was a large pendant with the symbol of the Crimson Brotherhood.

She sleeked across the room, high heels knocking on his heart, and kissed him deeply. The moment took him. With a shove, he pulled away and cupped the medallion around her neck. He eyed her with scorn as he rubbed the surface of it with his thumb.

Richard swirled his drink, "I enjoy a more direct approach. Your Columbo act isn't working for me. Ask the real question on your mind."

John took out the ledger from his pocket with the resolve of a samurai drawing a sword, "When I was visiting the Garden District, shortly before its destruction, I managed to lift this off of one of the cultists. This book shows shipping and receiving manifests of purchases from Hoondo Limited to the Crimson Brotherhood. Those chemicals were used in that bombing, and several thousand gallons are still unaccounted for."

Amy snaked around behind him and said, "My Dad's company is international, and anyone can buy their products."

John took a step away from her, "That is what I thought too until I did some checking. I discovered those same purchases had been from an offshore account set up under a dummy name. Luckily, my people are good, and I was able to backtrack that name. That account is owned by Richard Enfield."

Richard's jaw tightened as he replied, "Anyone can open up an account overseas under a false name. Clearly, this is just another attempt…"

He opened up the ledger and showed him a page, "Those are your initials next to each shipment. Would you like to take a guess at who's personal authorization was on the records from Hoondo?"

Richard's lip went up in a snarl, "How did you get those records! I want the name of the person at Hoondo that told you about that!"

John pulled his silver-plated UCC pistol from his waist holster and turned the ledger around to reveal his phone was recording their conversations, "You did, just now. I'm making a citizen's arrest. I'd advise you to contact those UCC lawyers before the police get here. I know firsthand how effective they are."

Samuel Howard's ghost phased through the closed doors and clapped loudly. The well dressed, grey-haired phantom passed right by him and stood next to Richard. John aimed the pistol at the spirit, as his hand shook in terror.

The distinguished newcomer chided Richard, "Truly well done, my boy! He could have been holding up his diary and not a ledger. You just can't stop yourself, can you? Do remind me, you were a lawyer, yes? You know you have the right to remain silent, yet you seem to lack the ability."

He muttered, "Y-you're dead."

A look of epiphany came over Richard, as he saw John pointing the gun at thin air, "What are you looking at?"

John put both hands on the pistol and leaned against the oak table, "Samuel Howard… You're Samuel Howard!"

The specter grinned and gave a slight bow, "I'm merely a shadow of my former self. You, on the other hand, have become something… unique."

Richard's turned in fury to the ghost, "How can he see you?"

Samuel clasped his hands behind his back, "Oh, yes, of course, he can see me. Our Lord Cthulhu has chosen him. However, Mr. Utterson, those theatrics will need to be dispensed with."

The ghost waved his hands in the air and cast, "Lassitudinem!"

John suddenly felt his strength draining from his arms, and the pistol fell from his hand. He struggled to keep his feet under him and grabbed the table for support. Richard snatched up the gun from the floor and ripped both the ledger and phone from his hand.

Samuel flicked two fingers in another sign and cast, "Nullam Magicae."

Instantly the strength returned to his body, and he grabbed his cane. His mind swirled with this new reality. He hobbled back on his walking stick and put a chair between him and the trio.

The ghost had a look of disgust on his face, "Please, Mr. Utterson, you can stop the charade. That cane must be a nuisance considering your newly healed injuries."

John's mind raced to his Hispanic neighbor. "Who told you about that?"

Samuel winked, "You did, just now. You're not the only sleuth in this house. Besides, the gifts of Cthulhu grant many boons."

He dropped the cane to the floor. "What are you?"

The ghost stepped into the chair, and stood close, "I'm a servant of Cthulhu, just as you are. The Great Dreamer told me he would be choosing an Avatar, and I can see the dark energy of The Old One on you. Tell me what other gifts he has given you?"

He looked down at his stomach and unbuttoned his shirt. He felt a surrender in his spirit and exposed his muscular chest and abdominals. Amy's eyes lit up as she walked over and caressed his body.

Samuel looked at John's physique, "Magnificent."

Richard advanced in anger, "Wait! This guy! This guy is the Avatar? No! I was promised to be the chosen one to awaken the Herald!"

John swallowed hard and revealed, "One of my pills turn into a blue worm that ate into my skin. My broken bones healed in one day, and then I passed out. When I woke up, I looked like this. I'm... I see ghosts. David Johnston, an old partner of mine from the force, has been haunting me. In the yard outside, a Hispanic man..."

Samuel gave a chuckle, "Oh, that would be Mr. Nores. One of my creative security features for the house. Quite harmless, I assure you, except if you are a spiritual intruder. I've given him dominion over my arcane protections. Quiet useful."

John grabbed his head and swooned, "I don't understand. I thought this was the work of God."

Amy took his face and turned it towards her, "Oh, indeed, it is a god. The Great Dreamer has touched you, above all others, and given you a greater purpose. Remember our talks. How we hated all of those lowly leeches, who feed on the good people of this world. How we played at the thought of purging it. The might of Cthulhu will pour salt on the leeches, and those that stand with him will prosper in a new Aeon. The sun will rise on a planet free of the decadent blight and bow down before us. You are one of his many Avatars and share of his divinity."

He grabbed her muscular arm, "Wait, what about the UCC?"

Samuel paced to the side, "Greyson and Eastland are a means to an end. He professes to defend the poor, the meek, and the God-fearing. In truth, he is addicted to the adoration and sleeps with different women from his congregation every week. If someone dares to deny him his appetites, he has them demoted or fired. The Crimson Brotherhood is ushering in the awakening of Cthulhu with the rise of chaos. The Great Dreamer will walk upon this land and pull humanity to the brink of oblivion. Then, a rebirth can start. A new order. Cthulhu's Avatars will be the Lords of this world."

The feeling of power was coursing through his body, as John asked, "But why help initiate the UCC to oppose you?"

Amy squeezed his bicep playfully, "Are you kidding? Our plans accelerated tenfold once Greyson took up arms against us. Then it was just a matter of putting the right man beside Greyson."

Richard crossed his arms, "Whatever! This is bullshit! I've sacrificed and brought this State to heel. I should have been given this gift!"

Samuel sighed, "Be proud of this moment, Richard. You wanted powerful allies, and here one sits. In a matter of days, you will have an Avatar of Cthulhu and the Nephilim Miniel at your side. You will be the most powerful Sect Master in all the world."

Richard's expression softened, "That's an interesting point."

John felt something wiggling in his chest, "I feel like something is inside me. What is it?"

Samuel's eyes flared with excitement, "You are transitioning into a living demi-god. A creature that can translate the thoughts of the Great Dreamer and have the power to ensure his commands are carried out."

The ghost touched John's chest, "What you feel growing inside you is purpose."

By Bo Luellen

Chapter 17: Shoshannah III

Tulsa, Oklahoma - Thursday, November 15th, 2018 – 8:52 p.m. CST

John Hamilton woke from a long sleep and looked at Shoshannah Feinstein from across their metal cage. They were in a ten-foot by ten-foot steel enclosure in the middle of a storage shed. She gave him a half-smile, glad to be rid of his snoring.

John rubbed his head and asked, "How long?"

She leaned back against the bars. "It's Thursday night."

His bloodshot eyes scanned the room, "Shit! What about Wapashaw's body?"

Shoshannah let her arms dangle from the points of her knees, "They let the dogs have the rest of him."

John rubbed his stiff neck, "Goddamn it. Clay was a good man. Well, it ain't the worst way for a Dakota to go. Being eaten is like returnin' to the earth, I suppose."

She raised an eyebrow, "I doubt The Great Spirit would call being torn apart by those monsters as a natural act."

He examined the four-foot roof to their cage, "Any idea where we are?"

Shoshannah shrugged, "Deeper in the woods. We walked for a while. I'd guess a mile."

John crawled over in front of her and sat down, "Those animals. You said they were your worst fear. What are they?"

She plucked a piece of hay off the ground, "Those are just your normal domesticated dogs, re-animated back to life. Then add a dash of magic and poof, something terrible appears."

He gave her a puzzled look, "I thought your process was a secret, and that your blood was required to bring something back to life. Did you make those things?"

Shoshannah gave him a sour look, "Of course not you idiot. I'm afraid I've been duped by a client, who obviously used Jagger to reproduce my process."

John winced, "Sho, you didn't? You did a job for the Crimson Brotherhood? Who exactly commissioned the work, and what did you do for them?"

She rolled her eyes, "I suppose my reputation of confidentiality for my clients went out the window when the Brotherhood stole my process and kidnapped me. So, here goes. The client was Richard Enfield, Master of the Tulsa Sect of the Crimson Brotherhood."

John let out a chuckle then got a shocked look on his face. "You're joshin'. The Lieutenant Governor-Elect? The right hand of Brother Greyson? He's the Master of the Tulsa Crimson Brotherhood?"

She broke the straw in half, "Yep. Praising God in one hand and trying to awaken the Dark Lord Cthulhu with the other."

John leaned on the bars in defeat, "Good God, Sho. What the fuck were you thinking?"

She leaned in, "I was thinking that with the kind of money Richard was throwing at me, I'd be able to stop working for crazy organizations like the Crimson Brotherhood and AEGIS. That me, and mine, could ride off into the sunset and enjoy a few hundred years in peace and quiet. I was also thinking that I don't need your permission, nor am I a member of your homo sapiens club. Before you get too high and mighty, try remembering that AEGIS has been more than happy to pay for re-animations that other countries would have a problem with. Your species has been trying to kill itself ever since God created Adam. At least my creator had the good sense to die."

John shook his head, "Jagger alone couldn't have done this. They would've needed your blood. How'd they get that?"

She leaned back against the steel, "I don't know. They haven't drawn any from me, and it isn't like I donate at the Red Cross."

Hamilton put a hand on her leg, "You've got to get us outta here. You can bend these bars like tin foil. The two of us can escape, alert AEGIS, and the military can wipe them out."

Her eyes flashed in anger, "I'm going to need you to pay close attention. A supernatural entity named Samuel Howard has possessed Jagger. If I try to escape or stop them, they won't hesitate to kill him and his entire family. My family! Get it?"

John shook his head, "You can't just let them create an army of monsters!"

She jabbed a finger in his chest, "The Clerval family is the most important thing to me on this planet. I'd let this entire State burn to the ground if it meant I could save them. These beasts are my bastard offspring. That means it is my responsibility to correct this, and correct it, I will. Once the Clervals are safe, I will do everything in my power to see these abominations destroyed!"

John put his hands up, "You don't know the resources AEGIS has available. Get me out of here, and I can have the Clervals moved to a safe house. AEGIS can...."

Shoshannah traced her finger along his cheekbone. The pheromones wafted into his nose and went to work on his consciousness. Two seconds later, his eyes were glazed, and his pupils were dilated.

She took his hand and gazed into his eyes, "John, honey, I do like you. I don't want to see you get hurt, and keeping you alive in this cage was a part of my bargain with Samuel. It seems the Crimson Brotherhood has plans for you."

Hamilton's spellbound face looked worried, "They'll torture me for Agency secrets."

She gave him a sympathetic look, "Samuel Howard is a ghost that possessed Jagger Clerval. He also possessed your body a dozen times while you've been unconscious. Samuel used it to call Control. He, in your body, reported you'd found nothing in these woods. Your agency thinks you're out searching Tulsa for better leads to the cult. No one's coming for us."

His eyes fell in defeat as she continued, "Your super-secret organization has become his personal mole. Because they think you are still on the hunt for the Brotherhood, he has unfettered access to the intelligence agencies. Through you, he can get regular reports from the FBI, CIA, and even the local police. All because of you, John Hamilton."

His hand quickly went to a seamless pocket stashed in the lining of his black tactical shirt. A Velcro pocket ripped opened, and he probed the empty space within. A look of desperation came over his face as he split the pocket open even further.

Shoshannah put her hands on John's, "If you are looking for your cyanide capsules, they're gone."

He gave her a dejected stare, "You told them about it?"

She tugged at his wrinkled shirt. "No, but I would have. You're not getting it, sweetie. A ghost has possessed you. That means he knows your mind. Every secret you have, every move you are trained to make, and all the AEGIS assets were his to know. Sam tossed those pills in the first few minutes he took you over. He even changed your access codes to the Agency database, just in case you got free. So, you're going to sit here and be good. If you do what I say, not act like the hero, then I might be able to negotiate for your life."

The two sat there silently for a long while. Shoshannah could see the wheels turning in John's head, but her pheromones were keeping him in line. He jumped as two guards burst in the door. They were wearing the black tactical uniform and ski-mask but were unarmed. A chunkier guard held out a bucket full of oatmeal, with two spoons sticking out.

The Texan eyed the pail, "Hey, partner. I hate to put a bind in your night, but I gotta take a crap. What do you reckon we do about that?"

The guard pointed down and mocked his southern accent, "You gotta bucket, don't ya!"

As the two men's guts jiggled from laughter, the front door opened again. Shoshannah bristled to life, as she smelled something familiar from the newcomer. The new guard had tanned skin and was a good foot taller than the other two. He pulled down his ski-mask, and a wave of fright went through her. His dark eyes flamed behind a thick black beard. The man's rugged stare locked on her, and she knew what was going to happen next.

Shoshannah grabbed John and flung him back against the rear of the cage. The mountain of a man took a step behind the rotund comedian and shot a punch into his back. A thick cracking sound accompanied the force of the blow, and a bulge appeared in the chest of his victim in a mess of odd angles.

John yelled from behind her, "What the hell!"

The second guard turned and ran for the door. A massive hand reached out and snatched ahold of his neck. The three-hundred-pound cultist was yanked off his feet and back into the arms of the man from Shoshannah's past. He put two enormous limbs around the waist of the guard, pinning him in a bearhug. The man's bones popped, one at a time, as blood poured out of his nose and mouth. Like a constrictor snake, the grip only tightened as the cultist breathed out. With a jerk of his arms, the guard's spine snapped, and the giant tossed the body. The corpses twitched, and fluid leaked from too many openings, as she steeled herself.

The tanned murderer took off his ball cap to reveal an all too familiar pitch black hair that was cut short. The man picked up both of the murdered guards by the belt and walked them over to one of the barrel containers. He opened them and tossed the corpses inside.

He turned back towards them as John whispered, "What in the hell is that?"

With a look of vague interest, the titan walked over to her and examined the chain that locked her door, "Why are you still here?"

Shoshannah tilted her head back and hissed at him. The long years since she had seen him did nothing to quell her rage. All the old hurts were on the surface, perfectly arranged in detail, thanks to her creator's design that gave her infallible memory.

The first creation of Victor Frankenstein gave her an injured look, "Is that all I get after all these years?"

John recoiled to the corner of the cage, "Oh, shit! That's… Adam!"

The man ignored the Agent and squatted down in front of her, "Why did you let them take you?"

She pushed her face up towards the bars. "You imbecilic animal! Do you have any idea what you've done?"

A woman's voice came on the radio, "Guard shack, report."

Adam toggled his microphone and radioed, "All is well. Watch secure."

Her eyes burned, "Leave now!"

Adam glanced at John, then asked her, "You care for this mortal?"

Her hands gripped the bars between them as she replied, "Would it matter! I'm not yours!"

He leaned on the cage, "Nor is our creator's process. I just passed by a long assembly line of re-animation chambers. I smelled your blood there. You've been careless."

Shoshannah felt like launching at him, "That's a lie!"

Adam knelt down, "Oh, I suppose Jagger Clerval showing them how to re-animate is all just a part of my master plan to ruin your day."

She winced, "Jagger is…"

He interrupted, "Possessed. Yes, you aren't the only one with the ability to see, what do you call it, a soul light. I've been hanging around this camp for the better part of the day. The ghost left, and they're keeping Jagger locked away while he's gone."

Shoshannah snarled, "I had a deal for his release."

Adam's eyebrows went up, "And these cultists are very trustworthy. Think about it. What will give your pet a better chance at survival? Trusting the Crimson Brotherhood to simply hand him over unharmed as the world turns to ash, or us working together to free him?"

She snarled, "Why are you here, Adam?"

The re-animated man stood up, "I just wanted to talk. Creator's fury, it's been over fifty years, Eve."

Shoshannah gripped the bars and bent them, "That is not my name, creature!"

Adam nodded. "I'm sorry. Shoshannah, I came to make peace. What happened was a tragedy, and I have felt the burden of guilt ever since. It took me a great while before I grew past my impulsive nature."

She spat, "I should have killed you."

He sighed, "If you had, I wouldn't have been here to see the birth of a new race. Your misstep has ushered in a novel breed of fiend onto this world. All that Victor feared is minuscule compared to what horrors the Crimson Brotherhood is about to unleash on humanity. Like me here or not, you've bound us both to seeing these monsters destroyed."

She paused and then offered, "We get Jagger out first. Samuel will be witless without him."

Adam snapped the lock off the cage, "I'll continue my ruse of being a guard and get Jagger out to the road. Once we're out of camp, then you can make your escape. They parked your car on the other side of a large milking barn."

She stood up out of the steel pin, "Fine! If you get him killed, I'll never stop hunting you."

He pulled in close, his mid-chest even with her face, "In this tale, I'm not the evil. This story of greed and wickedness is yours. Do not weigh sins. You might find ours an even share."

The two creations held each other's gaze for several minutes before John asked, "Not to interrupt this reunion, but I'm all for Adam's plan. Just how will we know when you have Jagger?"

Adam stalked out the door, growling, "You'll know."

They stood at the door and peered out the tiny cracks at the camp. The surrounding area was illuminated by large floodlights that emanated from three watchtowers. The building to her left was an old faded one-story farmhouse that had several soldiers on its porch. Directly in front of her was the colossal dairy barn that Adam spoke of. Cultists wearing lab coats wandered in and out of the building, carrying clipboards and laptops.

Roaming guards walked the ground with the Hounds on a leash. The re-animated dogs wore a restraining muzzle that did little to stop an undulating tentacle. The dark slimy appendage slithered its way out of its mouth and through the tiny bars. The overly muscular Saint Bernard passed close by their shack, dripping acidic saliva onto the grass as it marched.

On her right was a fenced-in area that had rows of generators locked inside. She recognized several of them as her own. The machines were rumbling and pushing power through a bundle of cables that went to the dairy barn. She squinted, as flashes of light sparked from within. Her enhanced senses picked up the ozone in the air.

She gritted her teeth, *Electrical discharge. Damn, them!*

John stole a Brotherhood coat from one of the dead men, "Darlin' when this is over, you and I have to come to an understanding. AEGIS is the only reason you get to function in the United States. Doin' jobs for crazy outfits like this ain't healthy for anybody. I'm not sayin'..."

A powerful blast came from the farmhouse, rocked the shed, and cracked the window she was looking out. Fire spurts erupted from the old house, and flames kissed the outer walls. The cultists who had been hanging out on the front porch were launched into the yard. Their entire bodies were engulfed in fire and twisted into a grotesque displays of human cubism. An alarm whined in the night, and the tower spotlights came to bear on the area around the home.

John came up beside her, "That's one hell of a signal!"

As the chaos swarmed, Shoshannah swung open the door, and the two weaved between the frantic cultists. Some were trying to put out the ones that caught fire. Others were busy getting a plan together on how to fight the flames. A group was headed her way, and she stopped next to an injured woman. The lady had a lab coat on, and a piece of wood jutted out of her thigh. Shoshannah and John lifted her up and put the woman's arms around their necks. They buried their heads downward, as they hauled her to the milk barn and let her screams of agony pave the way.

As they rounded the corner of the barn door, the heat and flames billowed behind them. A pair of men wearing white lab coats were too busy adjusting dials and knobs on a panel to notice them. Shoshannah left the woman with John and quickly closed the distance on the two. The first man turned his chubby, sweat covered face towards her in time to feel the blade of her right hand strike his windpipe. He grabbed his throat and tried in vain to breathe in. As the man suffocated at her feet, his companion turned and saw her. He stepped back and pulled out a German Lugar pistol. In a flash of speed, she reached out her hand and shoved the barrel into her own midsection. The muffled round went off just as she thrust her open hand through his face and into the cranium. She gripped and pulled out a slimy portion of his brains.

Their prisoner went to scream, but John covered her mouth, "No, no. Let's not do that. I'd hate to see you turn out like your co-workers over there."

Shoshannah quickly pulled off the lab coats from both of them, and she and John put them on. The two dragged the woman down the long dirt-floored corridor of the dairy barn. As the Crimson Brotherhood's attempts to put out the roaring fire continued outside, she examined Samuel's handiwork. The empty cattle stalls had been modified to accommodate a long silver table. A series of electrode needles dangled like spiders' legs from the walls of each compartment. Above, a sprinkler system was still dripping water from its last use and pointed at the bloodstains that decorated the silver table. Along the outside of each stall was a small tray with discarded vials that still had remnants of whatever strange concoction they had injected into the subjects.

John sat the woman down on a nearby bench, "We haven't been properly introduced, darlin'. I'm John, and my friend over there, well, she's…"

The technician blurted out in fear, "Shoshannah Feinstein. I know."

He nodded, "And you've seen what she's capable of. Now, you're going to answer some questions, and I'll do my best to keep you alive. Okay?"

John took one of the vials, "What's this?"

She glanced over at Shoshannah, who was still examining the equipment in the stall, "It's a mixture that Jagger made."

John shook his head, "Look, hon, this isn't a game of twenty questions. We gotta be going soon. Whether we leave you alive or dead is dependent on how helpful you are in a short amount of time. So, wow me."

The scientist nodded solemnly, "Fine. It's a solution that contains twenty-five percent of Shoshannah's blood and seventy-five percent stem cells."

Shoshannah rummaged through the paperwork, "That's impossible. I never gave blood to anyone."

The cultist moved her leg gingerly into a more comfortable position, "It was collected after your fight with Marcus in the basement of the Enfield Estate. I know, because I was on the team that collected it."

John peered around at over a hundred empty vials, "That doesn't make sense. There's not enough blood in Sho's body to fill up all of these."

The scientist nodded, "Jagger synthesized her blood. What you see here, that's nothing. He was able to make just enough to ship off to all the other sects. The last batch left early this morning."

Shoshannah pounded the desk with her hand, as John asked, "These tables were recently used. Did they make more Hounds?"

She smiled, "Oh, no. Those beasts were just a test. Jagger was able to produce just enough of your blood to send to all the sects. Master Enfield is helping to fulfill the prophecy. What we brought back will be used by the Herald to bring a plague of fire onto Tulsa. The city will break, and Cthulhu will...."

Shoshannah turned and sent her fist into the cultist's head. The neck snapped in half under the sudden force, and her head tilted back like a Pez dispenser. Sliding off the bench, the woman's body trembled for a moment and then went still.

John glared at her. "Prisoners are a good thing, ya know?"

She pocketed a half-empty vial of her synthesized blood and showed a clipboard to him, "It's a shipping manifest. She's was telling the truth. They sent several shipments, along with technicians to teach the other sect Masters how to reproduce my process."

He flipped through the papers, and did a quick count, "Jesus! There are fifty cities on this list, but no addresses. They could create these Hounds anywhere in those cities. Those Cthulhu dogs look just like any other dogs. It will be like trying to find a needle in a stack of needles."

She leaned down, "John, I don't think you're capturing the gravity of this situation. They have the means to raise anything from the dead, not just dogs. Humans, cats, lions, or whatever they can get their hands on could all be re-animated and infused with the power of Cthulhu. The terror that my creator had is being realized in a way that he never could have foreseen. If these beasts' mate and produce offspring, it will push humanity to the bottom of the food chain."

The vast depths of what she was conveying hit him as he announced, "Come on, Sho, time to go."

He folded the paper into his pocket and followed her out, saying,

"Look, we need to get this to Control. AEGIS has to contain this before they let those things loose on these cities."

Shoshannah shouldered through the back door and snapped the outer lock from its hinge. Under a single security light sat her black Dodge Charger. Whim was parked alongside the AEGIS van and flanked by a string of Brotherhood vehicles. The top of the barn was silhouetted by the flames from the farmhouse as they tickled the night sky.

Shoshannah marched towards the driver's side, "You let them drive my car?"

IGOR's Australian accent came out over the speakers as she opened the door. "Good evening, Mistress. It seemed the best option considering the circumstances. I've been scanning the area, and regret to inform you that your re-animation process is no longer proprietary."

She flipped a few switches to get the power started, "I'm aware!"

The AI offered, "During your stay, I've taken the liberty of developing several tactical options for eliminating your captors. May I deploy them?"

Shoshannah and John got in and secured their straps as she retorted, "Later. Give me an overhead with escape routes."

The locks to the doors snapped shut, and the engine purred to life. The dashboard lit up as a red glow shined onto their faces. Through the front windshield, the surrounding camp was illuminated through a night vision filter. A 3D image of a red line showed her the most optimal path of departure from their hosts.

John cinched in the harness, "Sho, where in the blue blazes did you get this thing?"

She threw Whim into gear. "It comes factory standard with every Dodge."

John gave a skeptical look, as they slowly moved forward in the night. She followed IGOR's course and quietly made a beeline for an open section in the surrounding forest. They cleared the edge of the milk barn and saw the burning farmhouse. It was fully engulfed in flames with a ring of cultists standing a safe distance away, watching it slowly turn to ash.

A few bumps and turns later, Shoshannah had found her way out of the woods and onto a dirt road. John looked behind them as she pushed the pedal to the floor. The 500 horsepower engine screamed to life as she streaked off into the night. Clouds of dirt folded into her rearview mirror as her car quickly ate up the road.

IGOR announced, "Mistress, there are two men ahead on the road. Alert! One of them is reading a body temperature of 32 degrees. Shall I deploy the weapons?"

She decelerated, "No. You shall take no offensive actions against Adam, for now. We have a truce until we can destroy all my blood, and the creatures the Brotherhood has created with it."

The AI protested, "Mistress, based on past behavioral patterns, the probability that Adam will betray you is one hundred and thirty-two thousand, two hundred and twelve to one."

A beleaguered Jagger and the towering Adam came into view of her headlights, "IGOR, disengage voice option until further notice."

She unlocked the doors, and Jagger was unceremoniously launched into the back seat by Adam. The six-foot seven-inch tall man wedged himself into the vehicle as it settled under the new weight. Shoshannah slammed the door and poured on the speed.

She glanced into the rearview mirror at Jagger, "Are you okay?"

The man was shaking from a mixture of fear and shock as he replied, "I believe so. I'm not sure. Sho, I'm sorry. I couldn't do anything to stop him. I tried. I tried so hard."

Shoshannah felt a swell of tears drip from her face, "I know you did. This is my fault. This is all my fault."

Adam's face lurked in the upper corner of her backseat, "I warned you this would happen."

Fury overtook her, "I swear by our creator! Not another word!"

After a moment of awkward silence, John turned to her, "I know y'all got some catching up to do, but there's this thing I got about savin' the world. Does this car have a phone?"

In response to his question, a ten-digit pad appeared on his side of the windshield. He dialed a number, and Agent Patrick Decker answered. He got him up to speed on the Brotherhood's plans. John read off the list of locations the blood and technicians had been shipped to.

Patrick gave a stoic, "I'll inform Control. This is going to be a massive search. At least it makes sense now as to why the Crimson Brotherhood has been one step ahead of us. Richard Enfield has the UCC and the police department feeding them intelligence."

John rubbed his head, "We don't know how far that influence goes. All it takes is one good Christian in the CIA or FBI to report to the Crusaders that we've found one of these hideouts. They will bug out of whatever hole they're hiding in long before we can get there."

His partner paused on the phone before asking, "What do we do?"

He leaned back, "We take a page out of the Brotherhood's playbook. We compartmentalize. We will have to keep this completely within AEGIS. The Branch offices in each of those States will operate under radio silence. Control will be the only point of contact for everyone."

Patrick sighed, "It's a solid plan. I'll run it past Control. We're setting up shop in downtown Tulsa. We found a warehouse there that can act as a base of operations. I'll send you the address on this number."

Shoshannah programmed in the location and then told the Texan, "I'll help you, but you have to get Jagger's family to safety. If you do that, I'll join AEGIS full time until we track down whatever abominations they decide to make."

John stuck out his hand and shook hers, "Deal, partner."

Adam's deep voice skulked from the back seat, "When the Lamb opened the fourth seal, I heard the voice of the fourth living creature say, 'Come and see!' I looked and there before me was a pale horse! Its rider was named Death, and Hades was following close behind him. They were given power over a fourth of the earth to kill by sword, famine, and plague, and by the wild beasts of the earth."

Chapter 18: Richard VIII

Tulsa, Oklahoma - Friday, November 16th, 2018 – 10:43 p.m. CST

It had been almost two hours since the first report came in about the facility bombing, and the War Room had been abuzz ever since. Richard Enfield sat at the head table of the downtown Brotherhood Library and assessed the evening's report. He held his weary head in both hands and listened to Maxwell Garner read off the names of the lost Brotherhood members.

Richard pulled out a bottle of Tylenol, as Max asked, 'Headache?"

He popped two pills in his mouth and replied, "Yes, one the size of Shoshannah Feinstein."

Max chuckled, "Well, there is some good news. The members weren't entirely incompetent at evacuating and covering up their retreat. Also, all the shipments left the facility without incident. They should arrive at their destinations within twenty-four hours."

He gulped down the medicine with a glass of water, "What about the Hounds and our special project?"

Amy Howard strolled into the room wearing her usual black turtleneck, "Father and I have been overseeing that. The Hounds are secure in the estate's wine cellars. As for the new re-animations, they were finished an hour before Shoshannah's fiery escape. We've stored them away in Dad's lab until needed."

Richard dipped a hand towel in an ice bucket, "Pity she got away. She was a wonderful asset."

Max shrugged, "We're actually in a better position because of it."

Amy scowled at him, "You think having an AEGIS agent learn that Richard is the head of the Tulsa Sect who has re-animation technology, is a good thing?"

The man got up and gave an animated speech, "The burning of the re-animation facility was a blessing from Cthulhu. We were done with it anyway, and the PLX that was ignited did a handy job of doing away with the farmhouse. Our people set fire to the rest of the buildings before leaving. The data we gained from our AEGIS infiltration has given us a substantial advantage. We are still analyzing the information, but our technicians believe the police and feds are hopelessly lost. As for AEGIS, knowing who you are, they have no proof. Without it, they can't go to the FBI. Shoshannah fulfilled her role. Because of her and AEGIS, our plans have only been accelerated."

The new High Mage flowed into the room wearing the ceremonial white robes, "Master Enfield, forgive the intrusion, but it's time."

Richard stood up and slipped on his own black garb, "Very well, let's get this done."

A few minutes later, a parade of his four Leviathans led him into the same ceremonial chamber where he had shot Samuel Howard. This time, he was the Master, and this was a much different gathering. The room was filled with black-robed cultists, holding torches aloft and standing silently. Richard took a seat in a high backed chair that had once been Miniel's throne in the Library.

Richard raised his hand, and a gong sounded out from somewhere in the catacombs. Moving in a single file line, John Utterson was ushered into the room by a host of three Mages. He was dressed in a simple black cloak with none of the characteristic Crimson Brotherhood markings. His bare feet trod on the cold stone, as his eyes wandered erratically about the room. His face was clean-shaven, and his once greying hair had returned to its original dark color. John's face jerked from side to side as if he was reacting to something around him.

Their company settled in front of Richard's throne, and a chant started from those in attendance. From the direction of his personal chambers came the ghost of Samuel Howard and his daughter, Amy. She was wearing a dull grey robe, one he had never seen worn before.

The Master raised his hand and announced, "Vulgtmah Cthulhu! John Utterson has been chosen as the Avatar of Cthulhu. Tonight, we welcome him into our Sect. Ahaimgr'luhh ph'nglui gn'th'bthnk s'uhn llll Cthulhu!"

Maxwell pulled out a knife and sliced down the sides of John's robe. As the cloth fell away, the man stood nude in front of the assembly and seemed preoccupied with his thoughts. Amy walked over to John and handed him a ceremonial dagger. She leaned in and gave him a kiss between his eyes on his forehead. The woman backed away and took a spot next to the Master. Almost in a daze, John stared down at the blade, seemingly unsure what it was for.

Richard pulled the hood of his robe onto his head, "John Utterson, just as each of us have done, now you must sacrifice a life to Cthulhu. The

Ancient One demands that you offer a contract of blood to the Tulsa Sect and to my authority. Bring forth the sacrifice!"

Two burly cultists carried a person trapped inside a black body bag into the chamber. The big men's faces were red with effort, as the individual inside struggled and shifted. As they approached the ceremonial altar, they seemed to delight in hoisting the occupant into the air and slamming it down hard onto the granite table. The person inside let out a grunt, and one of the men laid a brutal punch into the area where the victim's head would be. Then the two unzipped the bag and revealed a bound and gagged Jessup House. The old man had a busted lip and a cut above his eye. His wrists had zip ties binding them together, and an IV port was tapped to his right arm at the brachial vein. He was wearing a familiar pair of overalls and his veteran's vest. His eyes were glazed, and his movements were sluggish. Just like everyone that had made their way into these halls as a potential sacrifice, Jessup was drugged for easier handling.

The guards turned him face up upon the altar and shackled his wrists and ankles to the four corners of the stone table. The country fed fat belly of Jessup heaved up and down as he gasped for air. All the torches were extinguished, and a single spotlight illuminated the grey-bearded sacrifice.

Richard squinted as he thought he had seen several tiny bumps rippling under the skin of John Utterson's back. He got up off his throne and took a closer look at the dance of small creatures rolling just under the man's flesh. The crowd murmured, and the High Mage had to call for silence.

John glared at the elderly war veteran, as he approached the altar. Jessup's eyes were glassy, and he reached up towards the nude Avatar. The old man had a look of realization come on his face and focused on John's face.

Through the drug-induced stupor, Jessup pleaded, "Brother Utterson! Thank God! I was at my house and these men… men came into the house. I can't remember how I got here. General Utterson, what is going on?"

Richard studied shifting flesh as a multitude of small somethings journeyed under his skin. The new High Mage moved forward and put a cautious hand on John's back. The lumps seemed to sense her hand was close and walked towards her fingers.

She stroked the undulating mass. "Cthulhu be praised! The N'ghftor Gof'nnn, the holy worms, they've multiplied inside him. That only happens with a chosen of Cthulhu. John Utterson truly is the Avatar!"

While she was looking away, one of the bumps bit through the flesh and into her index finger. The High Mage yelped and yanked her hand back. She giggled and held the bloody finger up for all to see. The ritual room erupted with chatter and elation.

The uproar was silenced by the sound of John's ceremonial dagger dropping to the stone floor. Richard watched with interest as the Avatar crawled up onto the altar. While Jessup begged for his life, John put his hands onto the fat man's shoulders and positioned his knees on either side of the hips.

Jessup shook his head and prayed, "Brother John, no! You can't be a part of all of this. Lord Jesus, help John Utterson! Move your will into his life and banish this evil from his soul. Evil spirit, I rebuke you in the name of the Father, The Son, and The Holy..."

Utterson opened his mouth wide, and a grey tentacle shot out. It jabbed into the praying mouth of Jessup House. Even in his drug-induced stupor, the country boy had some fight in him. Choking on the writhing tentacle, Jessup attempted to keep it from driving further down his throat.

Richard's eyes darted around to the room, witnessing the faces of his Sect, *They're in awe! This might be their first real glimpse of Cthulhu. Look at them! They don't know whether to be afraid or drop down in worship.*

Samuel walked up beside him, "Do not envy him so. Being an Avatar does bring one power, but something is lost."

He eyed the ghost, *Explain?*

The ghost continued as those assembled were oblivious to his presence, "Cthulhu doesn't feel like humans do. It is an alien thing that has roamed the cosmos for longer than most star systems have been around. The Great Old One has an understanding of the universe that would cripple a human mind. If you were to be the Avatar, the Richard Enfield you are now would cease to exist. You would become a living extension of Cthulhu and forever lose your own will. These sycophants tremble at the power of the Avatar and secretly plot to attain it for themselves. This arrogance is why they were made to serve you, Master Enfield. What you see before you is proof that they are yours to command."

Richard digested Samuel's point and brought his eyes back to the altar. The tentacle had traveled so far down the throat of Jessup, that its width was forcing the old man's mouth to nearly split open at the crease. The veteran man struggled against the restraints, and viscous green saliva streamed out from his nose. Jessup's face turned bright red as he suffocated. A thick layer of the oily fluids coated his beard, as the doomed war hero twitched and writhed on the altar. The sacrifice was complete, as Jessup House lay still, and the torches were once again ignited.

John tilted his head, and the grey colored appendage slithered its way out of Jessup's mouth and back down into his stomach. The Avatar of Cthulhu stood upon the altar, straddling the dead man beneath him. The gelatin-like drool rolled off his face and down his bare chest. The crowd chanted praises to Cthulhu, and Amy held out a hand for John. The Avatar grabbed her arm and lowered himself back down. The demi-god stared into Amy's eyes as they walked together toward the Master.

Richard boldly announced, "The sacrifice has been made, and Cthulhu is appeased. Brother John Utterson, Avatar of Cthulhu, you are now welcomed into the Crimson Brotherhood as a member of my Sect. Llll h' nafl'fhtagn!"

The members around him repeated the R'lyehian, as John wiped his face with the back of his arm. Jessup's body was hauled away, as Amy draped a grey ceremonial robe around the Avatar. John turned her around, and the two kissed.

Richard stood and bellowed, "The Avatar of Cthulhu has chosen a bride. Amy Howard, Sword of Cthulhu, do you accept Cthulhu as your mate?"

She looked deeply into John's eyes, "I do."

Samuel beamed, as Richard announced, "Then I now anoint you as wed under the gaze of the Great Dreamer."

Maxwell hushed the excited crowd, as Richard continued, "The first Avatar was spawned here, in my Sect. I've been chosen by Cthulhu to fulfill a great purpose and resurrect the Herald. It was my machinations that gave us the ability to create re-animations, and it was my leadership that provided us with our own Nephilim."

The cultists went still, "Let my word be law. A call went out tonight to all the Sect Masters in the world. I have proclaimed myself Grand Master, and demand their complete obedience by dawn tomorrow. Our efforts can no longer be piecemeal. Under my leadership, the Crimson Brotherhood will act as one and end this Aeon!"

The chamber was filled with cheers as Amy took John by the arm and led him out of the Library ritual chamber. The cultists took turns serving up platitudes to the Grand Master and offered their undying loyalty. Maxwell assigned several of them to monitor communications from the other Sects, looking for each Master's response.

Samuel followed Richard back to his private chambers, "You see. Just as I said. This gift from Cthulhu is a powerful weapon, not to be used as a blunt force but as a token of his favor. By morning, all the Sects will be yours."

Richard slammed the door behind him, "What if there are hold outs?"

Samuel paced behind him, "Destroy them. Let the other Sects divide the spoils. It shows your strength and ability to reward loyalty."

Richard sat down behind his desk, "When the Sects name me Grand Master, then I will have fulfilled the prophecy Ankh-es-en-amon mentioned. I will have proven myself a great leader, and the Scroll of Thoth will appear."

Samuel floated over to the bookshelf and remarked, "You could be right, but I doubt it. Gaining control of a handful of Cthulhu loyalists is easy when you have one of his avatars spewing tentacles in the next room. No, I suspect it will take something more... substantial."

Amy walked into his chamber and asked, "Grand Master, may I see John home for the night? He has to get ready for tomorrow's speech. The General still has to coordinate security for the Governor-Elect, Avatar or not."

Richard sighed and rubbed his head, "Oh, yes, of course. I had forgotten. Brother Greyson Dunn's vaulted Gubernatorial acceptance speech. We would have done it sooner, but he has been celebrating too hard."

Samuel shared a smile beneath his trim grey beard, "So many pious congregation wives to appease, so little time."

He found himself chuckling for the first time at the humor of the ghost, "I suppose I should return home and work on my own speech. Greyson insisted on being the one to announce the executive orders. The ego of the man is astounding. All those idiots just ready to lap up his diatribe."

A sly look came on Samuel's face, "Amy, my beloved, are you planning on accompanying John to the speech?"

She looked at him with petulant disgust, answering, "No! Why would I waste my time, freezing my ass off, watching the blowhard Greyson go on about nothing?"

Her father floated over to her, "My daughter, you look so good in black. I would hate for you to waste an opportunity for a shot at the spotlight."

Tulsa, Oklahoma - Saturday, November 17th, 2018 – 9:30 a.m. CST

Greyson Dunn stood beside Richard Enfield, dressed in a subtle grey three-piece suit. He was trapped with the Governor-Elect and his assistants in the visitors' dressing room of the Eastland Lions. Greyson practiced his speech, trying out different variations on his marketing advisor. Enfield tilted his head back and rolled his eyes at the man's repetitive droning. The lousy coffee they had poured into the preacher did little to remove the slurring from Dunn's voice. Thanks to a liberal use of cologne, the smell of alcohol had been masked.

One of the young interns reminded Greyson, "When the music stops, you and Brother Enfield will enter on the stage. General John Utterson will be waiting there with his elite UCC honor guard. The Oklahoma flag will be flying in the breeze over your heads as one of our members, a full blood Cherokee, sings Amazing Grace in his native tongue. Once the song is over, the quarterback of the Eastland Lions will introduce you both."

Greyson winced, "The quarterback? Why not someone more influential?"

Another assistant added, "Yes, research shows that it would show a connection to the young voters and draw in more Democrats to your swing."

A tv monitor played in the corner, and a reverend from Eastland appeared on CNN, "Politicians have claimed to have God in their lives. Yet they vote for abortions, allowing pot to become legalized and condone gay marriage. God is not in their driver's seat. It is time for a change. Brother Greyson and Brother Enfield have shown the world that the time has come to end the spell the two-party system has put us under. He's putting God first and politics last."

A young Asian man asked Richard, "Brother, would you like for me to type out your speech so we can have it on the teleprompter?"

He shook his head and gave a cryptic reply, "No, I don't think that will be necessary."

Twenty minutes later, Richard was on stage, standing beside the tan-suited Greyson. He could still smell the faint odor of alcohol coming through the man's pores. FOX News, the BBC, MSNBC, and other international agencies were positioned beneath the stage to hear Greyson's first speech. The stadium was packed to its 70,000 capacity, with an additional 200,000 surrounding the massive stadium. There was an unprecedented gathering of 12,000 UCC soldiers walking security in the crowd in their blue uniforms. The Eastland digital billboard was set up to transmit the speech for those that had engulfed the university.

As the Cherokee vocalist finished her rendition of Amazing Grace, Richard sat down in his chair and waited. Greyson took the podium to a roar of applause and cheers. The Governor-Elect paraded on stage, waving and smiling. He was followed by his blonde wife and his two teenage boys.

Richard thought, Samuel was right about one thing: that man was born to the spotlight.

After allowing the applause to go on for several minutes, Greyson announced, "Thank you! Oh, my. Praise Jesus!"

Over a quarter of a million in attendance thundered back, "Praise Jesus!"

Shaking his head in mock disbelief, he continued, "I'm truly not worthy of His love! I have been set on this path, and by His glory, we will see it through!"

A member of the crowd yelled out, "Down with the Brotherhood!"

Greyson leaned into the microphone, "Amen, Brother! Let me give a message to the Crimson Brotherhood: You can run, but you can't hide from His justice. A reckoning is coming, and the United Christian Crusaders are the spear point. It has been over four days since the last act of terrorism. We all remember our own General Utterson flushing that den of rats out in the Garden District and saving dozens of Christian lives in the process. Brother John Utterson has your number, and God is on his side!"

The crowd roared as the Governor-Elect continued, "Now, let's get personal. I want to speak directly to the leader of the Crimson Brotherhood, Henry Jekyll. You might have escaped the Tulsa Police, but you will not escape the people of Oklahoma, the United Christian Crusaders, and most of all, God! Brother Enfield and I are moving forward with a plan that will ensure our Crusaders will have the power to root you out of whatever sinful hole you've hidden in. As God is my witness, your days of creating terror are coming to an end!"

The Governor-Elect's left ear exploded outwards, spraying gore on his wife and kids. His head popped to the left from the impact of the bullet. Greyson's body crumpled to the ground like a marionette who just lost its puppeteer. The shot rang out just as his body hit the stage and his head bounced off the wooden floor. The two hundred thousand plus in attendance screamed and went wild. The UCC security fought against the wave of fleeing masses to get to the fallen preacher. General John Utterson grabbed Dunn's blood-soaked wife and kids, and ordered their guards to get them to their armored limo. The wailing Greyson family had to be dragged away in grief by the security detail.

Richard fought the urge to smile as his UCC bodyguards hurried him to towards his car. His security was all secret Crimson Brotherhood men and they were not shy about punching and kicking their way through the panicked Christians. He tried to savor each passing second of the delicious rampage of humanity. Anyone that decided to drop to the ground to take cover was quickly trampled by the mass exodus. The chaos was intoxicating to him, and he hid satisfaction at how well the plan had worked.

A few seconds later, Richard was shoved into the back seat of his armored Hummer. He took one last look at the blood-soaked stage through the tinted windows and allowed himself a muffled laugh. The Eastland flag fluttered in the cold morning wind and had red splatters draped across its lion logo. The national reporters were standing their ground, capturing all the action and recording the grotesque murder scene.

Richard whispered to himself, "Perfect."

Daniel Harris started the car and said, "Good morning, Rich. A crying shame what happened to your boss."

Richard was in a forgiving mood, "Yes, indeed. It is a shame. Now, what did I tell you about calling me that?"

The thief weaved the car in between the escaping spectators, "Yes, yes, alright. I suppose I'd better get used to calling you Governor-Elect, now that you are going to take Dunn's place."

Samuel Howard dropped from the roof into the passenger's seat next to him. The ghost was wearing his black robes of the Crimson Brotherhood in place of his usual grey suit. Richard and his former mentor shared a satisfied look.

Richard broke the silence first, *Well, is Ankh-es-en-amon adequately impressed?*

Samuel spoke in Latin and waved his hands in the air. A glowing tan spectral globe appeared inside the cab of the Hummer. On its surface was a topographical map of Earth that was accurate down to the last detail. Magical ley lines crisscrossed along the continents as glowing golden threads. Half of the sphere encompassed the front half of the vehicle. Daniel continued driving, oblivious that a mystical image of New Zealand was cycling across his face. The ghost took his hand and rotated the map until the Mediterranean was in front of Richard. A golden ibis hieroglyph hovered over a section of land next to the Gaza Strip.

His heart leaped, *The resting place of the Scroll of Thoth? It has appeared?*

Samuel nodded with a grin, as Daniel tilted his head back and asked, "Where to Governor?"

Richard smirked wickedly, "Egypt."

Chapter 19: Edward II

Los Angeles, California - Saturday, November 17th, 2018 – 2:41 p.m. PST

When Edward Tallman arrived at LAX, the Kono Clan's Oyabun, Yakumo Odawas, was there personally to greet him, "Mr. Hyde?"

The Yakuza boss eyed him with suspicion as he replied, "More or less. Hyde has joined with another, and I'm the result. Edward Tallman, at your service."

Yakumo scowled, "I see. Mr. Hyde has been of great service to us in the past."

Edward took off his black leather gloves, "When I recovered Hyde's phone from storage, I was pleased to see your request. I find myself in need of capital and your expertise in gaining a legal identity."

His Japanese host walked him through the airport. "I see. So you intend to stay in this body for some time?"

He thought back to Lucifer's offer. "It is my intention."

From the crowd, several of Yakumo's bodyguards flanked them, "I do not mean to be indelicate, but Mr. Hyde was gifted in the dark arts. He had no compunction about taking on jobs for the Kono Clan."

Edward let one of the guards open the limo door, "And you're wondering if you can expect the same from me?"

The elderly man bowed, "Yes."

Edward smiled. "You're an honorable man, Yakumo Odawas. Hyde assisted your father, and then you since the '40s. In the matters of spiritual problems, I'm happy to assist in exchange for fair compensation and your continued friendship."

The two bowed to one another, and the pair loaded into the car. The detail of well-dressed Japanese mafia followed them in a new black town car. Each of them was well-armed, and Edward knew from Hyde's past that they were ready to do anything for their clan.

He unbuttoned his black coat and asked, "Perhaps it's time you tell me why I'm here?"

The Oyabun lifted his chin stoically, "My firstborn son, Koki, is the future heir to the Kono Clan. His honor has been... lacking. He impregnated a young gaijin prostitute some months back. A disgrace to my family which has caused some in the clan to question my authority."

Edward nodded, "A mistake on their part."

Yakumo looked out his window, "Hai. Koki further visited disgrace onto my name when his wife Mizuno discovered his betrayal. In response to her anger, he pushed the American woman off a building, killing her and his unborn child. Dishonored by my son's actions, she prayed for Koki to be punished and took her own life."

He could feel the man's anguish, "I take it the act of seppuku attracted the attention of something?"

The man's eyes conveyed his uncertainty, "For the last two weeks, Shinto priests have formed a circle around my son to stop an Oni from attacking him.

Edward sighed and then asked, "What kind of Oni haunts your son?"

Yakumo lowered his head, "The holy men say it is an evil Yōkai spirit here to fulfill a blood pact it made with Mizuno. It wants to see Koki dead for his actions. Since the priests placed him in the protection circle, two of my son's closest friends have been killed. Their skins were found lying on top of the American woman's grave. I offer you the new identity you seek and two hundred thousand dollars to rid my family of this Oni."

They shook hands, as the Nephilim replied, "I agree to those terms."

Thirty minutes later, they arrived at an abandoned factory and drove to a derelict warehouse. Several Yakuza guards were standing outside and opened the door for them with a bow of respect. Inside, Koki was lying on a mattress in the middle of a massive concrete floor. Hundreds of lit candles and burning incense enclosed the future Kono Clan leader in a twenty-foot radius. Rust-robed Shinto monks sat around the edges chanting a spell of protection.

On one side of Kiko's enclosure were bedding and a plastic outhouse. On the floor were dozens of discarded bags of takeout food and empty beer cans. Blaring on a TV was a music video of a rapper with several broad-chested back-up dancers.

Edward stopped at the edge of the candles. "Charming."

The holy men weren't holding up too well, and all of them sported dark circles under their eyes. He counted twelve of the priests singing their spells and keeping the vengeful Oni at bay. Edward looked at the five armed Yakuza along the walls, and a sizeable blood spot was on the floor next to one of the monks.

He walked over and regarded the crimson pool, I'm guessing it isn't advisable to stop chanting.

Koki sprang up as he saw Edward, "Hey! Are you the guy that is supposed to get rid of that bitch's curse? Where the hell have you been, man? Do you know how long I've been locked in here?"

The Oyabun shouted at his son, "Shizukani shite!"

Koki looked as if he was going to protest his father's scolding but reluctantly bowed. Edward took note that the monks had edged the circle in salt and oils. He looked up at the tin rooftop and observed a series of long rips in the metal. Dozens of such tears gave a view of the blue California skies. The long slashes suggested a set of massive claws had sliced into the metal roof.

Yakumo stood next to him, "Every night the Oni visits us at 2 AM. Our men have tried shooting it, but it passes right through. Our priests have attempted to banish the monster, but it's too powerful."

Edward carefully negotiated the candles and inspected the ring of salt, "3 AM is the witching hour in most Anglo-Saxon cultures, but in Japan it's different. The witching hour there is 2 AM. That's when all your sins come to life and ask for blood."

Koki marched to the edge of his circle and stood in front of Edward, "Enough talk. Do something!"

He turned away and told Yakumo, "Remove the monks. They look like they could use the rest. Have someone bring a broom, so this salt can be swept away."

Koki flailed his arms in the air, "What? You idiot! That is the only thing keeping it out! Father, this thing might be in league with the Oni!"

There was a pause, then a shout in Japanese from the white-haired Oyabun. Instantly, the monks stopped chanting and uncoiled their stiff legs from their Zazen position. They shuffled out of the room, bowing to the clan leader as passed. While Koki screamed in protest, one of the guards returned with a broom.

Edward took it and held it out to Koki, "Honorable Odawas-san, Koki must do the sweeping to fully remove the protection."

Koki unleashed a string of insults in Japanese and walked back away from Edward. The few hard words from his father finally brought the tirade to a halt. Koki yanked it from his hand and mocked the Nephilim, as he overexaggerated his motions. Once he was done, the man threw the broom across the warehouse in frustration. It scooted across the ground, but never came to a stop. The guards chattered nervously at the way it slowly traveled along the smooth concrete. The broom picked up speed and slammed into the tin wall with enough force to shatter the wooden shaft.

Edward looked at Yakumo with a smile, "Well, that didn't take long."

A growl of something not of this world echoed from outside. The blue skies darkened, and the sunlight was muted. Koki ran to his father, fell to the ground behind the elderly man. Yakumo pushed his son off him and screamed at him in Japanese.

A low guttural growl filled the empty warehouse as a massive footprint appeared and extinguished a large section of candles. The arrival of the Oni brought a halt to Koki's yelling. Another step descended in the leftover salt, and Edward took note that it was three feet long and had the look of an elephant print. The monster was invisible to the Mundane and had some magics in place to keep even him from seeing the Oni's true form. A great billow of air shot out of the mouth of the beast and blew salt up into the air.

Edward drew some Enochian shapes with his hand and cast, "Revelare."

The spell pulled back the invisibility enchantment from the Yōkai spirit. It allowed everyone present to see what they were facing. The monster was the rough shape of an enormous woolly mammoth, with razor-sharp teeth, clawed toes, and a face etched in willful malevolence. Its trunk was twice the length of his body, slapping in the air like a whip and searching for his next victim. Each step shook the warehouse, and the guards circled around their Oyabun.

Edward stood his ground, as the massive beast blasted through the candles towards Koki. The guards shouted challenges at the Oni, and a couple opened up with their submachine guns. The crossfire of one of the Uzi's caught an opposing soldier square in the chest, sending him flying backward and leaving a streak of crimson on the ground in his wake. The Yōkai's spiked tail flailed into a dark-haired young Yakuza in a black suit, slicing his belly open at the navel with a vicious looking spine. The man dropped his weapon and tried in futility to hold his own intestines in his stomach. The wet organs slipped between his fingers, and the brave clansman dropped dead to the ground. The Oni centered in on the clan leader and charged.

Edward grabbed the elderly Yakumo's shoulder and cast, "Autem

Confundit!"

The demon stopped his charge and looked around in confusion. Edward pressed his index finger to his lips, instructing the Oyabun to stay silent. The bewitched Oni, having lost sight of its target, switched to its intended prey. Whipping out its deadly trunk, it knocked away Koki's guards and latched onto his leg. The Yōkai sent him rocketing upwards and bashed him against the three-story-tall tin roof. The monster roared in satisfaction, as it tossed Koki to the concrete floor. The man's skull was cracked along the center, and his face looked off-center. Confused and in shock, the would-be Oyabun rose to his hands and feet. Blood poured out from both his eyes and ears into a pool beneath him.

The Yōkai trumpeted in victory after jamming a long spike into Koki's back. Thanks to Edward's spell, the Yakuza could see the spirit of Yakumo's son float up from his body. The Oni latched its trunk around the ghost and held him fast. The newly created specter thrashed against the beast and pled for his father to save him.

Yakumo instinctively lurched forward to help his son, as Edward held on tight to his shoulder, "Ie, watashinotomodachi. There is nothing you can do. There never was."

The massive Oni turned and plodded downward through the floor. The Yakuza stood in defeat as the beast carted off his prize. Appearing in the center of the circle was a single higanbana, a red spider lily.

The old man gripped Edward's shoulder, "Where is it taking my son?"

He turned to Yakumo and replied bluntly, "To Mugen Jigoku, The Hell of Unending Suffering. There he will know an eternity of torments, much like the ones he imparted onto the ones he brought misery to."

As Yakumo shuffled over to his son's body, Edward cast, "Nullam Magicae."

Both his spells ceased, as the old man knelt down and touched the broken face of Koki. After a few minutes, he stood up and gave a stoic nod to the guards. Two of them ran in and gently took away the body of his firstborn. They walked in silence out of the warehouse and back to the car. When the door closed to the limo, and the two men were alone, the Oyabun let out his long-held grief. Edward gave the man his dignity and pretended not to notice what was happening.

Edward listened to the anguish as they drove, *I wasn't here to save his son. This was only for appearances, and to save face with his clan. This was Yakumo's only honorable path to rid himself of the evil in his family.*

Once the man had composed himself, Edward remarked, "When you live with honor, no person can take that away. Without it, there is no granite in which to carve a life of worth."

The old Yakuza leader wiped his face. "My daughter has a strong son. A twenty-year-old graduate of law school. He is eager but has little life experience."

Edward looked into the man's eyes, "Teach him that bravery is an act of grace, to steer with his soul, and swing his sword without hesitation. His uncle's actions are not on his honor, but a reminder that corruption of the spirit must not be allowed. No matter what the temptation, he is his own man and can lead your clan with honor."

Oyabun didn't respond, and the two rode in silence. They stopped at a restaurant and enjoyed dinner together at a Sushi bar. The Yakuza present celebrated the departure of the Oni. Still, Edward thought they were also happy to see Kiko gone as well. The old man did not eat but sat in quiet solitude.

Los Angeles, California - Saturday, November 17th, 2018 – 8:03 p.m. PST

The clan took him to a posh hotel in Los Angeles, where they had purchased him a room for the night. Before he departed, Yakumo shook his hand and bowed deeply. One of the soldiers handed Edward a thick envelope and thanked him.

The elderly leader explained, "I have done as you asked. Inside, you will find a credit card with a balance of two-hundred thousand that is linked to an account in Kyoto, Japan. Also, there is a driver's license, passport, social security card, and birth certificate."

He pulled out the California driver's license and a photo of his own face, "Just how did you get my picture?"

Yakumo turned and got back in his car, "You are not the only one with a few tricks up his sleeve. Until next time, O-Tallman-san."

He bowed to the Oyabun, "Arigatōgozaimashita."

The Yakuza drove away, and he crossed the street towards the Four Seasons. The spellcasting had been taxing, and he felt the siphoning off of his power by the parasitical Hyde. He relished the idea of getting some sleep and recharging, as the doorman greeted him with a tip of his hat. Just before he entered the hotel, Edward noticed a great horned owl perched on top of one of the hotel's overhangs. The giant raptor turned its head and gazed straight at him. It blinked its left eye and let out an ominous hoot.

With a quick nod, he told the doorman, "On second thought, the night is too magical to turn in just yet."

Edward buttoned his long black coat and walked in the direction of the feathered omen. He concentrated and elevated his arcane sight. With it, the Nephilim scanned the surrounding buildings and searched for a reason for the harbinger's presence. He saw a gremlin chewing on a power cable in a nearby generator; a pair of pixies were flying around a tree, giving it compliments but nothing too terrible to note.

He stopped and put his hands on his hips, *Nature has a warning system if you know how to listen. That owl wasn't a coincidence. Something's coming."*

The bird flew off into the night sky, and he decided to wander to the next intersection. As he walked, Edward heard the jingling of change rattling around in someone's pocket behind him. He stopped to wait for the crosswalk light to turn white, as the stranger saddled up beside him. Edward turned and gave him a polite nod. The man was wearing brown cargo pants and a black Carhartt coat.

The aura around him was a dirty gold color. *The shadow following me is hyper-focused and intensely analytical.*

The crosswalk light snapped on, indicating it was safe to cross, as the stranger belted out nervously, "Edward Tallman!"

The name shot through him as he turned to see the stranger had a GoPro camera strapped to his head. The light from the device was shining in his face; the man had shoved a microphone between them. The traffic signal turned white as Edward stayed motionless. The mid-30's man had a thin layer of sweat on his balding head. His midsection was round, and his nose was pointed like that of a penguin.

Edward put his hand up to block the glaring light, "You assume."

The short man took off his brown backpack. "I'm not asking! I'm telling you. You're Edward Tallman. My name is Quincy Hunt from the YouTube channel The Hunt for the Truth. The people want to know the answers to a few questions, Mr. Tallman!"

Edward contemplated ending it there with a simple spell but decided to let the conversation linger. "The people have selected a rude representative. Perhaps they've saved me the trouble of liking you."

Quincy unzipped his pack and pulled out an audio recorder. "I've been tracking Dallas Webb for some time now. Her boyfriend was Juste Theriot, and one of her friends and coworkers was Henry Jekyll. You follow the money, and people like to talk. That is the rule I've learned in journalism, Mr. Tallman."

He felt a chill of exhilaration at the thought of being discovered. "Really, do relate the fruits of your labors? What is it that you think you've discovered, little man?"

The reporter adjusted the microphone in his sweaty hand. "I bugged that crappy Volkswagen of hers and tracked her in the hopes that Henry Jekyll might make contact. On one of her many late night adventures to the grave of the Crimson Brotherhood's top man, Juste Theriot, who do I find? You. I couldn't make out everything that was said from my car, but I heard enough."

Edward couldn't help but be somewhat impressed, "And your deduction?"

Quincy stepped back, "That you are Henry Jekyll. I don't know whether the Brotherhood paid for plastic surgery or if this is just some kind of prosthetic disguise, but I heard Dallas confirm it. After that, it was just a matter of giving your name to some of my contacts at the airport and car rental companies. What do you know, Edward Tallman books a flight to Los Angeles shortly after that. What's the first thing he does, meets with the Yakuza. I guess the life of organized crime suits you, with or without Cthulhu to worship."

Before Edward could reply, he saw two men in the alley walking towards them both. The one on the left was dressed in all brown with a tan dress coat, while the right had a long dark jacket. He could sense the dark magic of Cthulhu on their bodies.

He sidestepped Quincy to get a clear line of sight to the approaching men. The reporter hopped in front of Edward, demanding that he answer his questions. The men split apart from one another, grabbing something long and cylindrical from within their coats. Dark Jacket weaved to the middle of the street, while Tan Jacket quickly started shuffling over behind a light pole.

Quincy held up the microphone in his face. "Why does Dallas Webb claim you are Henry Jekyll? Why is it that no one seems to remember an Edward Tallman in Tulsa before Henry Jekyll disappeared? Why are you scared to talk? Is that because you are Henry Jekyll?"

Dark Jacket spoke into his wrist. "He led us right to him. We have eyes on the target."

Tan Jacket yelled out in R'lyehian, "Vulgtmah Cthulhu!"

Edward pushed the reporter to the side, sending him flying into a set of garbage cans. Tan Jacket raised a 9 mm pistol and let off several rounds at both of them. With a flex of his shoulders, Edward's salt-and-pepper wings ripped through the fabric of his coat and expanded out seven feet on each side of him. He turned his back on the assassins and covered Quincy with the feathery appendage. The bullets hit his back and the thick plumes, and then the mangled slugs dropped to the ground. Dark Coat pulled out a 12 gauge shotgun from under his clothes and let loose. The street corner was alive with the echoes of gunfire, as the pair unloaded at him.

Edward cast a spell at Quincy, "Lassitudinem! Procidat Deceptioneum."

The short reporter stopped struggling to get up and laid listless on the sacks of discarded trash. As he dropped back down, Edward's illusion turned his body to the same color as the black plastic bags. He twirled around to find his attackers and felt the ping of several bullets bounce off his face.

Tan Jacket quickly loaded a fresh clip, as Edward cast, "Aetate!"

As the spell took hold, the cultist used his thumb to let the slide pop forward, readying the weapon to fire. As he pulled the trigger, the pistol crumbled in his hand. The cultist stepped back in amazement at the collection of brown metal powder dissolving in his palm. He quickly reached back and pulled out a revolver from his belt. As he cocked it, the hammer dissolved under his thumb, and the cylinder fell out onto the ground.

Edward boldly strolled forward towards the pair. He flapped his wings once, creating a thrust that sent him rocketing towards Tan Jacket. He put out his hands and let his acceleration slam two hard palms to the chest. The follower of Cthulhu was thrown backward into the air, planting the spine of the assailant into a metal street pole. The broken body twirled in the air and then settled into a heap on the ground.

The increased spellcasting was taxing him, so he didn't see Dark Jacket as he approached. He felt the cold cobalt steel of the shotgun barrel on the side of his face a fraction of a second before the man pulled the trigger.

The buckshot plowed into his ear and caused his head to jerk a tiny bit. His half Angelic eardrum was unphased, engineered by God to be immune to high pitched sonic attacks.

Annoyed at being caught off guard, he sent his wing careening into the back of the man's head. The momentum carried the cultist straight into Edwards's rising knee. A sharp crack rang out from the impact. The assassin's neck snapped, and his head rested on his back as he fell to the ground dead.

He turned towards the pile of trash bags and cast, "Nullam Magicae."

The illusion faded away, and Quincy Hunt sat up. He shook his head clear of the cobwebs from Edward's exhaustion spell. Quincy reached out and grabbed his backpack, and hugged it like a security blanket.

Edward folded his wings back into his back, "Are you injured?"

Quincy's eyes darted from his retreating feathers to the dead men on the ground. "What you did… I saw you. Y-you were shot and those wings."

He held up his hands, "Look, don't jump to any…"

The reporter jumped up on his feet, "You're an angel!"

Edward finished, "…conclusions."

Quincy waded through the garbage bags, "Wow! That was just amazing! Was that Latin you were speaking? I saw that guy shoot you in the face, and you didn't even flinch! You know I've reported about amazing things all my career, but I've never actually seen it. Wow!"

Edward put his arm around the man and walked him in the direction of his hotel, "The universe is full of such wonders, and harbors terrors that will chill your soul. You're a very innovative man, Quincy Hunt. You managed to track me down when the Crimson Brotherhood couldn't. Someone that resourceful is a person I very much want to know and befriend."

Quincy nearly blushed, "Friends, with an angel? Me?"

Sirens could faintly be heard coming their way, "First, let me correct something. I'm not an angel, I'm what's called a Nephilim. I'm the blend of two creatures, one being Henry Jekyll. So, I congratulate you on your keen mind and investigative skills. You've impressed me."

The reporter's forehead wrinkled. "A Nephilim! You mean you're a half-man, half-angel?"

He smiled and tapped the man's chest, "Spot on. Now, let's say you and I have some coffee in the lobby of the hotel I'm staying in. It isn't like we want to stick around to explain to the good law enforcement of this town how two cultists died."

Red flashing lights bounced off their backs as police screeched to a stop in the intersection behind them. The officers piled out of their cars and radioed for an ambulance. One of the cops yelled after them and broke into a run in their direction.

Edward held onto Quincy and cast, "Procidat Deceptioneum."

The sizeable Italian cop's feet beat to a slow trot as he looked around perplexed, "Hey, where did they go?"

The officer behind him yelled. "Who knows. Get back here, there's another one!"

The reporter observed, "They didn't see us."

Edward continued concentrating on the illusion. "No, and they won't. So catch your breath and let's get in out of this cold."

A few minutes later, they had a seat in the lobby of the Four Seasons. Edward felt exhausted and listened to Quincy go on about the things he had just witnessed him doing. He let him rant on as he gathered his strength again.

Quincy stopped his gushing, and asked, "Wait, why were those Crimson Brotherhood guys trying to kill you? Is it because you used to be their leader?"

Edward propped himself back up, "Henry Jekyll was never in league with the Crimson Brotherhood, but having him look as such deflects the public from the true puppeteers. The cult benefited from Henry Jekyll's disappearance from the hospital, and, admittedly, I used the time to prepare and set a few things right. Perhaps I lingered too long in my machinations. The more central point is that you cannot air this story. When you leave my charge, it will be the end of your days. The Crimson Brotherhood will track you down."

Quincy's face formed a stoic expression, "Then to hell with the story. This is bigger than me. You said I was someone you wanted to know. Likewise. I'm coming with you!"

Tallman glanced outside to the place where he saw the owl, "It seems fate has placed you in my care. I accept your proposal, Quincy Hunt."

The starry-eyed reporter clapped his hands and cheered. "I'll be a great help! I'll be the guy on the laptop telling you to turn left or turn right. It will be like Mission Impossible!"

Edward smiled, "Perhaps. Nevertheless, my work here is concluded. I'm bound for Tulsa, where I have one last piece of unfinished business to attend to."

Quincy popped up to the edge of his chair. "What's the operation?"

He thought back to Henry's memories, "A dear friend, Amanda Lanyon, has had her children stolen from her by the Crimson Brotherhood. I mean to find them and return them to her."

Quincy clapped his hands. "You haven't heard? They were found by Thomas Booth and David Keller. It's all over the news. Keller died in the attempt, but Thomas made it out. The kids are in a sanitorium. I guess they were pretty screwed up. They said that Amanda's still in witness protection, but my sources say she fled the country."

Edward stood up and walked over to the window, "One of my kin told me that a great prophecy is unfolding and that the Crimson Brotherhood would usher in dark days. That if I just stand by and let it happen, that I would be free again. I find myself at a crossroads, Quincy."

The short reporter walked up to him and placed a hand on his shoulder, "That person isn't you. Tonight you protected me, even though it would have been easier to let me die and just walk away. This relative of yours isn't you. Edward, no matter what this fella has tempted you with, you get to define your own path."

Edward smiled, "You know, I was just telling someone something similar today."

Quincy got a hard look on his face, "I've been tracking paranormal and supernatural events in America for over ten years. UFO's, ghosts, bigfoot the MIB, are all things I've thought real. Now, I'm standing in front of a living Nephilim named Edward. No way this is a coincidence. You spoke of prophecy, I'm talking about destiny. The world doesn't deserve you, but it needs you."

He nodded, "Well, said my new friend. Where do you propose, we start?"

The reporter stroked his chin, "A good story starts with a good source. Right now, Amanda Lanyon is the star witness against the Brotherhood. She knows enough that they have her in witness protection. Let's visit her and find out what she knows."

Edward waved his hands in the air and whispered, "Ostende Amanda Lanyon."

A cloud of vapor appeared on the glass in front of him. He concentrated hard on the face of Amanda, and let the spell stretch out. The scry continued to swirl but revealed nothing.

Edward lowered his hand, "Empty. I can't find her. Even if she was dead, my magic would reveal what afterlife she inhabited. Odd."

Quincy wiped the vapor from the window, "Well, don't give up. Dial-in Josh Dyer."

He gave him a perplexed look, "Who?"

The man pulled out his phone and, in a few seconds, showed him a picture, "This is Josh Dyer. He was with her at the battle at the Preserve. He recently canceled all his speaking engagements and disappeared. I think wherever he is, she is. Now, just dial-up Josh on that magical thing, and let's see."

Edward couldn't help but be delighted by the positive spirit of Quincy. He took the photo and concentrated on the face. He put a mental picture of Josh in his mind and repeated the spell.

The fog once again swirled on the window and appearing before him was Josh Dyer. Edward reached out and touched Quincy's shoulder, allowing him to see the vision as well. Josh and Ian were tied to their own separate beds across from each other.. Wires were attached to his nipples and tied off around a car battery. A dark-robed man with a Crimson Brotherhood symbol on the sleeve was delivering sharp jolts of electricity while asking questions about who Amanda Lanyon contacted in Scotland.

The spell ended, as Quincy asked, "Where was that?'

Edward opened up his phone, booked a flight for them both, and announced, "Scotland. Do you have a passport?"

Quincy got a look of concern, "What will I tell my wife?"

He put a hand on his friend's shoulder, "Tell your bride that you go out on a hero's journey and that lengthy confessions will only dull the wonder."

By Bo Luellen

Chapter 20: Amanda IX

The Scottish Highlands - Monday, November 19th, 2018 – 6:52 p.m. BST

Over the past four days, Amanda Lanyon had passed up several opportunities to travel the road, ask for a ride, or find a phone to call the police. With her red hood pulled over her face, she dared only to stop at a single shop. She used the money she found in the dead cultist's wallet to buy some food, water, a watch and a map of the Highlands. Lanyon had learned to trust her new feathered friend and continued to follow its lead. Without fail, the midnight colored bird took her cross-country towards Stirling Castle, as the crow flies.

Tonight, the Raven had taken her to the banks of the Allan Water, a small offshoot from the River Forth. She stopped to camp near the small stream for the night and was fishing along its edges. Amanda lucked out and caught three trout within an hour. Soon she was cooking them on a campfire. Her would-be assassins had provided her plenty of camping supplies that included a blanket and a small one-person tent.

As she ate her fish, Amanda heard the loud pop of gunfire cresting over the top of a nearby hill. She dumped her meal on the ground and instinctively took cover. Slowly, Amanda crested over the rise, and in the distance, saw the familiar sight of Stirling Castle. After traveling in so many zigzag patterns, she had lost track of the actual distance to the fortress.

In shock, she dropped to her stomach as the Mantle of Arthur showed her the magical truth of the castle. A collage of vibrant colors was launching out of the ancient building, sending streams of multicolored ethereal plasma strings waving into the night air. She found that the cloak not only let her see the supernatural but hear it as well. Each thread of energy rumbled and gave off a low uncanny shriek. It sounded like a pod of trumpeting humpback whales serenading one another in the unknown currents of the pitch-black sky. She crouched down, stunned by the beautiful spectacle before her.

The Raven landed a few feet next to her. "Well, hello. It's nice to see you made it back. I'm guessing magical stuff like this is commonplace on Avalon?"

The bird blinked and tilted its head, as rested her head on the cold grass, "I'm talking to a bird named Arthur. People are going to lock me up if they find out."

Amanda pulled out a small pair of binoculars from her cargo pants pocket and took a closer look at the castle. A few guards roamed the grassy hill below in regular patrols. Thanks to the cloak, she could see the soldiers were coated in a magical white glow. As a side benefit, it made them easy to spot, despite their black tactical clothing. The bird bounded onto her back and let out a caw. Amanda stayed motionless as the Raven plodded along her spine and down to her legs. The animal found the open space between her socks and her pant leg. It stepped a clawed foot onto her exposed flesh, and instantly she felt a head rush. Dizziness caused the world to start spinning, and she shut her eyes tight. Even with her lids closed, Amanda saw the vibrant colors of the Scottish Highlands in great detail. The surroundings were no longer shrouded in the dark night, but illuminated to a level one would find at dusk.

Her eyes shot open, and her pupils had turned as black as the Raven's. Arthur launched into the air. Lanyon grabbed the grass around her as she saw the world through the magical animal's eyes. The earth sunk away under her feet, as the bird gained altitude. Amanda thought she might throw up as Arthur banked several times to avoid the multicolored plasma tendrils that were flailing out from the castle. She wasn't sure what those threads of light were, but the Raven wanted nothing to do with them.

She felt vertigo building up bile into her throat, as the bird landed on one of the battlements. Amanda gasped at the sharp drop off beneath the stone walls that went for hundreds of feet to the courtyard below. She concentrated on keeping herself focused, as she took in all the detail the animal's vision had to offer. Amanda saw in perfect detail things that could have barely been made out with her own eyes. Taking several minutes, she felt a sense of steadiness at being a passenger in the Raven's mind.

Amanda whispered, "My God, is this how you see things? Turn and show me what's in the courtyard."

Arthur hopped around and did as she said. The interior grounds were littered with several wooden crates that were as big as a small horse. Several trucks were being loaded with boxes by dozens of men and women in black Crimson Brotherhood tactical gear. Each of the workers was armed with pistols, machine guns, and bulletproof vests. Fluttering in the breeze, the flag of Cthulhu waved. In the center of the courtyard were three posts buried in the ground. At the bottom of each was a bundle of wood, and from their tops, manacles dangled ominously.

Amanda blinked her jet black eyes, "Three stakes, ready to burn someone. That means our three friends must still be alive, and awaiting their turn."

The Raven shot a look towards one of the castle houses and zeroed in on the second-floor window. The precise vision of the creature was almost overwhelming, and it took a moment to digest the display of detail. Without warning, Arthur took off again, soaring toward the window. Amanda scooted back as the stone wall came streaking at her. The Raven landed, and she let out a little scream with her hands held out in front of her. Catching her breath, the bird cocked its head sideways, looking in the glass. In a moment of connection, Amanda felt the need to tilt her own head, to align with the animals. Inside the room was Ian MacLean and Josh Dyer, both lying down and handcuffed to their beds. A bucket of water and a car battery sat next to them.

A shot rang out from within the courtyard, and the sound was neatly transmitted into her own ears. Her head pulled back from fright, and she was nearly deafened by the loud noise. Her eyes had gone back brown, and the connection had been lost.

She sat on the cold ground and looked up for the Raven. The animal was gone from sight, but Amanda still felt the tickle of its presence. Closing her eyes, she concentrated on re-establishing the link. This time, it was a gradual emersion, and it didn't overwhelm her. Her eyes went black, but she was looking out of her own eyes with the vision of the Raven. Turning around in a circle, with her red cloak flourishing outward, she took in the wonder of the dark hills. In her mind, she found the ability to switch from looking through the Raven's eyes, or through her own. As long as she concentrated, she had the keen sight of the bird.

Getting back up, she switched to see through the Raven and gave it a mental command to scout the entire castle from above. Amanda felt the wind blasting against her face as she experienced Arthur's flight like it was her own wings on the cold currents of air. She smiled and let out a little laugh at the thrilling sensation.

She held out her arms as if they were wings, *This must have been what Morgana was talking about when she said, Raven's Sight.*

The Raven focused on a section of the castle wall that was left unguarded. It was the exterior portion of the same building Ian and Josh were being kept in. Arthur panned down to the base where the cliff started and gave a squawk.

She sighed, *If you're saying this is going to suck, I'm agreeing with you. That climb is going to be tough, but it's my best shot at getting to them.*

Amanda sprinted back to her camp and stashed her backpack under some logs. She put out her fire and then kicked as much dirt on the rising smoke as possible. Amanda armed herself with only a buck knife and a Glock pistol she had lifted from one of the dead cultists.

She spent nearly an hour walking a broad curve towards the unguarded section of the fortification that the Raven had discovered. Before long, she was staring at a crag that stretched up 250 feet to the base of Stirling Castle. She counted an imposing three stories of worked stone before she could be able to reach the first window.

Scanning downward, she took into account the thick woodland at the base of the cliff. She plodded into the forest and gave herself to the pitch blackness of the trees. Even the moonlight was blocked by the canopy, as she felt her way from tree to tree. Her mind went back to the first night on the road when Peyton was shot and how she wandered in terror in the stormy night.

Amanda didn't dare turn on the flashlight for fear of catching the attention of some roaming Cthulhu soldier. It took her almost thirty minutes of fumbling in the black before she found the five-foot clearing before the rock wall. The rough stones of the crag were wet and slick with algae. She looked up to see the lights from the castle windows shining out, like a stationary lighthouse waving her through rough waters.

Taking a breath to calm her anxieties, Amanda attacked the wall and started her ascent. Almost blindly, she went to work looking for places to put her hands and feet. She climbed by feel, moving slowly and cautiously. The cliff was wet and cold in her hands, and her rest stops were spent trying to warm up her hands.

At the halfway point, she crested over the tops of the trees and saw the half-moon shining down on her. As she got higher, the pulsing plasma threads occasionally circled overhead. She was awestruck by the enormity of the tendrils. Some of the multicolored threads were as big around as a bus. They reached out over the countryside like an octopus looking for prey.

Her fingers and hands bled from the sharp cracks in the rock. Looking up, her heart lifted. The crag edge was only twenty feet away, and Amanda focused on nothing else other than reaching that peak. Her legs and arms were burning, and she found herself ill-prepared for the challenge. As Amanda continued to move upward, her biceps and shoulders begin to fail. Her legs shook uncontrollably as she willed herself into each new level.

Amanda put a bloody hand over the top of the peak and searched with trembling cold fingers for a groove. She felt her heart swell with hope and joy at the small nook that was waiting on her. Her mind barely registered the painfully sharp rocks scraping along her abdomen, as she pulled herself over the top. Rolling onto her back on the narrow two-foot ledge, Amanda wrapped herself in the red cloak and shivered.

The Raven swooped in and landed next to her. She grimaced, as Arthur squawked in Amanda's face and prompted her to get into action. Slowly, she got to her knees and then her feet.

Leaning on the castle wall, she whispered to Arthur, "You little shit."

The animal danced around on a rock and then took off once more into the night sky. She looked upwards at the 2nd floor, where she had seen Ian and Josh through the Raven's Sight. Amanda didn't know if that window would lead to their room, if she would be able to open the window or if there were alarms on the building.

She adjusted the mantle's hood and continued to climb. The worked stone allowed her better footing, and the grooves acted almost like a ladder. Unlike the cliff, where rest stops were sparse, this surface allowed her plenty of breaks. The cold wind whipped over her body, pushing and pulling her as she went. The howl of the air assaulted her face and exposed skin with its chilling temperatures.

To her surprise, she had reached the second story with relative ease. She attempted to slide the window open only to find it was nailed shut from the inside. Cursing under her breath, she made a decision to keep climbing. The lactic acid set into her muscles, causing her body to shake and tremble. Her hand slipped, ripping off her right middle fingernail from the root. Searing pain shot into her hand as it dangled by a thread of flesh from the cuticle. She gripped her hand into a fist to avoid screaming out. With blood flowing down her arm, she continued to press forward. Each grip of the rocks with her injured finger caused blinding pain to shoot down her arm.

As she reached the roof, Amanda gripped the lip of the stone wall and hoisted herself over. She cradled her injured right hand and looked at it in the moonlight. The nail was still attached by a solid piece of her flesh. With her left hand, she pulled out her long straight buck knife and laid it to the side. She unclipped the leather sheath and put it in her mouth. Amanda placed her middle finger on the stone roof and positioned the edge of the knife on the soft flesh. Agony shot down to her stomach and almost made her vomit when she pulled the sharp blade across the tissue. The first cut didn't get the job done, leaving a piece of skin still attached. Amanda muffled her screams as she chomped down hard on the bull hide. With her body shaking, she reset and once again sliced along the exposed tissue. Red coated the ground beneath her legs, but Amanda managed to get the job done. She took her blade and cut a long strip from her cargo pants. Amanda wrapped her finger the best she could and cinched it tightly with her teeth.

She worked her way over towards the edge of the roof next to the courtyard. Just as she had seen with the Raven's Sight, trucks were still being loaded by the Crimson Brotherhood. She scanned her area and found a trap door that led downwards into the building.

Amanda was suddenly struck with a reality, *Okay, then what? You walk in there, persuade someone to let you have the keys to their room, and just walk out with Josh and Ian? Maybe, I could stop a helpful bloodthirsty murderous cultist and ask him directions to where they're holding Roger.*

With her knife in her left hand, she made her way over to the door and pried it open. A wave of hot air engulfed her face, causing a soothing sensation to go down her back. She wanted to stand there and let the heat melt away the days of cold that had sunk down into her bones. Stealthily, Amanda descended the steps into the darkness below. Reaching into her pocket, Amanda pulled her flashlight and switched it on. The staircase came alive, showing off the myriad of cobwebs that decorated its rungs.

When she reached the landing, she scanned the room. It was full of dusty cardboard boxes that were stacked randomly about, and light from under a single door poured onto the floor. Flipping off her flashlight, she leaned and looked through a keyhole into an empty hallway. Amanda tested the knob and found it was unlocked. She listened for a long moment but heard no one on the other side. With courage, she swung it open to reveal a hallway, decorated in old pictures of ancient Scots.

She walked out slowly into the hallway, with knife in hand, *I'm one floor above Josh and Ian. I've got to work my way down without being noticed.*

A rush of blood went to her face as a toilet flushed in the room directly to her left. The door popped open, as an old man in the black military-style uniform walked out. He was too busy tucking his shirt back in his trousers to initially notice her. She remained motionless, hoping he might not see her. The cultist did a double-take at Amanda, then stopped cold.

A moment of recognition came on his face, "Amanda Lanyon!"

His hand went for his pistol at his hip as she grabbed his wrist and slipped the blade under his flak jacket. She pressed her pelvis to the bucks hilt and used her body weight to slide the knife into his flesh. He gasped in pain as the steel dived into the man's liver. The old cultist went up on his toes and grabbed her throat with both hands. Her neck felt like it was in a vice, as he drove her back against the opposite wall. She pulled the knife to one side, churning the organs with its serrated edge. He dropped to his knees and released his hold on her. She relieved him of his thick military helmet and stroked him across the face. Teeth bounced across the wooden floor as she visited another blow to his skull. He crumpled to the ground, and she pulled out the knife. Pushing his chin up, she thought about her captured kids and dead husband, as she drew the edge across his exposed throat. He spasmed and gurgled, while she held him in place and waited until he stopped moving.

Amanda felt the same numbness that she had experienced in the woods when she shot the cultists. This time it was more personal; she was looking into his eyes, felt the knife move into his body, and his skull clank off the metal helmet. She grabbed his collar, spun his unconscious body around, and dragged him along the floor into the storage room. Amanda removed his jacket, his ski-mask covering, and put them on.

She shut the door behind her and pulled the mask over her cold face. Amanda straightened her back and attempted to move confidently down the stairs to the second floor. When she reached the next level, the sounds of something slapping came from behind one of the doors. The noises reminded her of two wet steaks being hit together.

Her heart collapsed as she thought, *No, please don't let this be Josh.*

The door was cracked, and Amanda stopped at the entrance. Roger Quinlynn was tied to a chair, nude, and sporting long red marks all over his chest and legs. A Crimson Brotherhood soldier was holding a length of tanned leather in his left hand. With satisfaction, he reared back and gave the AEGIS agent another hard swing to his chest. Roger gritted his teeth, and another welt joined the other in a mosaic of pain.

Amanda pulled out her pistol and cocked it. The noise made the man turn to face her. She stepped into the room and did her best to act like she belonged.

The Scottish cultist looked confused, "Whit urr ye daein'? "

She pointed her pistol at Roger, "They want him put with the others."

The torturer scoffed, "He wis juist aboot tae tell me everything. Noo yi'll waant me tae halt? ye Americans hae na professionalism!"

The cultist's reached down and worked on the knots that bound Roger's wrists to the chair. Amanda lined up behind him and then took two giant steps forward. She crashed the butt of her gun against his skull, causing her target to pitch forward. The black-clad murderer went nose-first onto the hardwood floor, while blood squirted out from both sides of the man's face.

Amanda whipped out the buck knife and finished freeing Roger, "Hey, are you with me. Are you awake in there?"

He lifted his head, revealing a black eye, "Scotland sucks."

She removed the rest of his bonds and asked, "Can you walk?"

Roger stood up, covered in red lashes, and replied, "No, but I can dance."

He got up from the chair and rubbed his wrists. Roger took a skipping step towards the unconscious tormentor and placed a soccer kick between the man's open legs. The sleeping cultist groaned and threw up. Roger hopped around on one foot from the impact with the man's tailbone on his instep.

She grabbed his shoulder. "Ian and Josh are being held on this floor. We need to get to them and then get out."

Roger sat down on the cultist's back and looped his old bindings around the man's throat, "It won't be easy. They have two guards on them at all times. They were keeping them alive as bargaining chips. They wanted me to give them information on what AEGIS knows. Where have you been, anyway?"

She moved towards the doorway to check for more cultists, "Lots of walking. Hey, what are you doing?"

Roger pulled the cord tight and twisted it. The Scot's face turned red, and his eyes bulged. The agent bobbed his head up and down, impatiently waiting for the man to finish expiring. Once the body went limp, he got up and pulled it behind a desk.

Amanda prodded, "Hurry, put on his clothes. We can walk around freely."

The agent picked up a pair of handcuffs from the desk and replied, "No, I have a different idea."

Minutes later, the pair were walking down the hallway towards the room where Ian and Josh were being held. Amanda had her pistol shoved in the back of a nude Roger, as his hands were behind his back. As they approached the doorway, one of the two guards unlocked the door as the other one sneered at the agent's bare body.

The cultist grabbed Roger's testicles, "Brother Dùghlas tellt me yer baws wouldn't be comin' back wi' ye. Ah, think ah kin fin' something fin tae uise thaim fur."

The other guard clicked free the deadbolt and swung open the door. Both Ian and Josh were tied to a set of beds and shivering. They both had black eyes and deep bruising on their face. Their nipples had turned black from repeated electrocutions. The electrodes were now attached to their ears and dangled off to the floor, stretching the flesh. Despite their gags, they both had a look of astonishment and excitement at seeing the top of Amanda's face.

Roger regarded the overly affectionate guard, "Your hands are soft like a girl. I think I'll call you, Jenny."

The cultist's eyes went wide at the insult, and he threw a haymaker at Roger. The agent sidestepped the attack and raised his unhandcuffed hands. He grabbed the man's shoulder and shoved Amanda's knife into the side of his throat, just below the ear.

The other guard went for his gun, but the stress of the moment made his fine motor skills useless. While the cultist juggled with the flap holding his pistol in place, Roger let loose a series of strikes. The guard attempted to counter, only to have his wrist broken from a perfectly timed block. Roger leaped in the air and pulled his opponent down on top of him by the jacket. As the soldier flailed, the agent locked a leg triangle around his neck. He smoothly pulled the Scot's head towards his groin, causing the choke to tighten.

Roger looked over at the dying guard who had a blade sticking out of his throat and said, "Oh look, Jenny. I did find a fun use for my balls after all."

A few seconds later, both of the men were dead on the floor. Amanda untied a grateful Ian and Josh, as Roger dragged both of the dead men inside the room and shut the door. The Scot had a limp from where they had broken some of his toes, but Josh was in substantially better shape.

Josh grabbed her shoulders, wept, and said, "Oh, my God! We thought you were dead, Mandie!"

She hugged him hard, "I thought you were gone, too."

Roger stripped off one of the soldiers and commanded, "Let's focus people. We need a plan to get out of here. Ian's not going to be running any races with those broken toes."

Ian was nursing some bruised ribs, "Dinnae let me slow ye, doon laddie. Ye git th' wee lassie tae safety."

Amanda pulled one of the pistols from the dead guard's belt, checked the magazine, and replied, "The wee lassie doesn't plan on doing anything safe for a while. What I do need is for you to take this gun and follow my lead."

The Scotsman stuck his chest out, and grabbed the Glock, "Time and tide for nae man bide. Ah, will rammy fur ye!"

Before long, the men stripped the three cultists their group had killed and put on their cloths. Ian's shirt stretched at the seams and exposed the pasty white flesh of his belly. They marched their way down to the first floor and found the exit to the courtyard.

She stepped down into a small foyer and stopped at the door. Floodlights were set up in each corner and shining down on the large workforce. The cultists were loading dozens of pallets filled with long wooden crates and stacks of ammunition boxes into six yellow and white moving vans.

Josh peered out of the window and said, "What are they doing?"

Roger put on his stolen coat and replied, "Those are unregistered small arms and machine guns in those crates. They are being shipped out to several secret bases that are disguised as residences."

All three of them slowly looked at the agent, as Amanda asked, "How on Earth do you know that?"

He put on a pair of black gloves he got off of one of the dead men and replied, "Automatic weapons are banned in Scotland, which means they bought them on the black market. Those trucks aren't filled to capacity, which means they all aren't going to the same place. They are using moving vans, and the least conspicuous place to offload such a vehicle would be at a private residence where it wouldn't attract attention."

Ian slapped him on the back, "A'm aff tae stairt cawin ye Roger Moore."

The agent bristled, "Don't! James Bond is fiction. Real spycraft is nothing like that."

Amanda touched his jacket, "Do any of those super-spy abilities come with a plan on how to get out of here alive?"

Roger opened the front door saying, "Yeah, they do. Follow me and act like you're having a bad day. Ian, you stay right beside me. Amanda, get that hood down. You look like Red Riding Hood for God's sake."

The four of them filed out of the castle house and walked slow enough to give Ian a chance to keep up. As they went, she peered upwards and was dazzled by the multicolored tendrils coming from the top floors of the surrounding buildings. The beams of energy flung in the air wildly, as the rest of her company look on, oblivious to the magical wonders.

As they traveled to the front gate, she passed a large pavilion tent that was set up along the edge of the courtyard. Dozens of Brotherhood goons were moving in and out, carrying supplies. She stopped in place, as the light from a large screen TV caught her eye from within the shelter. She looked up, and the Raven was perched on top of the tent. It let out a caw and danced on top of the canvas roof.

Amanda changed course for the opening, as Josh grabbed her arm, "Mandie, what do you think you're doing? We need to leave now!"

Amanda looked down at his hand, then removed it, "I need to check this out."

She stood up straight and marched into the tent as if she owned the place. Inside she found herself surrounded by twenty worshippers of Cthulhu, and suddenly felt thankful that the ski mask was still covering half her face. Her eyes went wide at the Governor-Elect of Oklahoma on their screen.

She covered her mouth. *Richard Enfield!*

She matched his voice to Mr. Purple from the Preserve, as he admonished the masses. "These timelines are unacceptable! I want each station fully operational and the explosives set by the end of the month."

A man who was sitting on a throne, replied, "Grand Master, it wull be dane!"

The surrounding members yelled out, "Vulgtmah Cthulhu! Llll h' nafl'fhtagn!"

She staggered back, *Richard Enfield is the leader of Crimson Brotherhood! He has been playing the Crusaders against the cult from the beginning! He must know where my children are!*

One of the larger cultists turned her around, "Whit urr ye daein' 'ere? This meetin is fur Elder."

Roger walked in and greeted the soldier, "Vulgtmah Cthulhu! Sister, I think it's time for us to return to our work."

As he guided her outside, Amanda felt like she was moving in a daydream, and everything was upside down. She barely noticed that they had moved past the front gate and down the gravel path toward the city of Stirling. Her thoughts swirled with the implications of what she just learned. Anger built up in her gut as lightning streaked across the night sky, and thunderclouds rolled in.

She pulled her face covering down, once they were clear, "Richard Enfield is the Grand Master of the Brotherhood!"

Josh spun his head around. "What? That's ridiculous, Mandie. Richard has been leading the opposition."

She pointed back towards the castle, "I just saw him giving orders to them via a video chat."

Roger joined the conversation, while still scanning their area, "It's true. I saw him myself. Looks like our Bible thumper is playing double agent."

Suddenly, one of the massive magical tendrils whipped downwards and attached to a clueless Josh Dyer. Amanda froze, as the pulse of energy wrapped around the man. Within seconds several of the multicolored threads circled around him like coils of rope.

The team stopped, and Josh asked, "What's wrong?"

She shouted out, "We're in trouble! Run!"

Roger pulled out his 9 mm, "In trouble from what? No one is following us."

Amanda put an arm around Ian and helped the big Scot to run, "We've got to move! I don't have time to explain, but the Seers are tracking Josh!"

Ian huffed and puffed as he bellowed, "Whin ah catch up wi` a Seer, a'm aff tae kick thaim in th' mommy 'n' daddy button!"

They made haste for the edge of the castle's parking area and made a break for the trees. Josh was ahead of her and Ian. The glowing arcane threads were knotted around him, and slivers of pulsing energy flowed along the cord.

A black Humvee roared out of the front gate, bristling with armed cultists and squealed to a stop in the middle of the parking lot. Her group took cover behind the trees, and she pulled out her gun. In the distance, she could hear someone talking to the cultists on a walkie-talkie. A spotlight snapped on from the driver's side of the vehicle and panned around the woods.

The rainbow-colored energy ropes clung onto Josh, as someone on the radio announced, "The Seer's say Dyer is twenty yards North, Northwest. They say he is in some trees."

The spotlight found Josh's face within seconds, and the driver announced, "We've git thaim. Okay, wee jimmies! Let's mak' some corpses!"

A barrage of silenced gunfire peppered the woods, and tree branches rained down around her. She put her back to the large Scots Pine that was providing her some safety from the bullets. Ian's shoulders were too broad for the tree he was using to hide, and a round lanced through his deltoid. The Scot pitched forward in pain, exposing him to more gunfire. Roger dashed out from his spot, and latched onto the injured man's collar. The earth exploded around the agent, as he pulled Ian flat and tucked him behind a tree. Amanda let loose with few rounds at the vehicle's spotlight and fired blindly to give Roger cover. The highly trained spy rolled over to her hiding spot and let off three shots from his 9-mm. The spotlight bulb shattered, and one of the cultists fell down with two bullet holes in his head.

Roger's hands were shaking as Amanda grabbed him by the jacket, "What do we do?"

The man's face froze as bullets chipped away at their cover, and she repeated, "Agent Roger Quinlynn! What do we do?"

She pulled his face closer to his and realized, *PTSD. He's freezing up.*

Amanda looked over at Josh, who was cowering behind a thick tree and sobbing. Drips of rainwater fell from the sky onto her face, as the tiny popping sounds of the suppressed gunfire faded into the background. She looked at Ian's red blood as it poured out of the opening in his shoulder.

Things started to move in slow motion, *This is where we all die. My husband, Nancy and April, and now Ian, Josh and Roger are all going to be taken by this great evil.*

She thought about Richard's smug face on that monitor and all the harm he had brought, *No! This stops!*

She slapped Roger hard, knocking him free from the episode, and stepped out from cover, "No! This stops!"

The rain poured down, as Amanda's red cloak flashed crimson against the lightning overhead. She emptied her gun at the Humvee while rain poured down in sheets on her face. Sparks shot off the steel frame from her barrage, and a few cultists dived for cover around the armored vehicle.

The transport vehicle started up, and the headlights snapped on. The Humvee's engine sprang to life, and the operator pointed the tires at her. Before his foot hit the pedal, Roger appeared beside her and took three measured shots at the armored windshield. The bullets stacked on top of one another, the last one making it through the plexiglass and into the driver's head.

A younger man raised up from the back end to reveal a mounted .50 caliber machine gun. Thunder rolled overhead as the rest of the Brotherhood members circled around behind the vehicle for cover. Roger cursed, as the cultist cocked the heavy weapon, and whirled it in their direction.

A bolt of lightning slammed down from the clouds and sliced into the Humvee, igniting the gas tank and munitions. The explosion tossed her and the agent onto their backs and sent a shockwave through their bodies. Laying sprawled out on the concrete, she and Roger shared a look of disbelief. They made their way to their feet, and the scattered pieces of the charred cultists burned in little piles of flesh all around her.

Josh had his head under Ian's arm, and the pair inched their way out from behind the trees. The four of them stood in front of the burning vehicle, as the glowing pieces of steel sizzled from the rain. A massive gust of wind blew overhead, making her cloak flap outwards so it produced sharp snapping sounds. Her mouth sprang open in astonishment, as the fire illuminate a pair of salt-and-pepper wings that were attached to a gothic-dressed figure with hawk-like features.

The angelic stranger waved his hands, and within seconds, all the rain within twenty feet of the flying man stopped. The storm raged on outside of the ring the angel presided over. He glided down and softly sat his feet down on the wet concrete. He straightened his knotted black Windsor tie and shook his massive wings free of the excess rain. As he approached her, his wings went into his back and disappeared within the folds of his black flower-patterned coat.

Her company stayed still, as the impossible walked towards them. Those piercing blue eyes beamed at her, and the surrounding lightning reflected off a twin row of silver buttons that decorated the front of his jacket. Running up from behind him on the paved road was a pudgy man. She instantly recognized him as the reporter that had ambushed her at the hotel.

Quincy patted the dark-clad angel on the back. "Good work partner. We did it!"

Through the Mantle of Arthur she saw a faint image of two figures standing within the angel. One was monstrous, demonic in image and size. The other was more faded, but she could make out Henry Jekyll.

She dropped the gun on the ground in shock, "You..."

The Raven flew in from the storm and landed on her shoulder and let out a "Caw."

Lightning flashed in the night as he gave a slight bow, "Hello, Professor Lanyon. I'm Edward Tallman."

By Bo Luellen

Epilogue

Cairo, Egypt - Friday, November 23rd, 2018 – 9:45 p.m. EEST

Professor Terrance Pearson's red fez was sliding off his bald head with each hard turn down the paved road. He was cursing liberally, as he tried to get more speed from his tiny car. It had been two months of solid work getting the new finds analyzed and translated.

He pulled out ahead of a taxi. *The Supreme Council of Culture isn't happy with my team's progress, as it is. An incident like this will only strengthen their beliefs that my project should be abandoned.*

He honked at a passing contingent of camels and screamed, "Aibtaead ean tariqa!"

He swooped into the parking lot on his balding tires and ran towards the entrance. The stars overhead shined down over the city, and he sprinted. The Nile River was less than one hundred yards away, and he could smell the waters as they flowed towards the Mediterranean Sea. He pulled out his security badge and slammed it against the magnetic panel. The front door popped open for the fifty-year-old man, and lights along the hallways snapped on. His sandals flopped against the marble floor, as he flew towards his department.

Turning the corner, he saw his assistant Ahn Mensah, "How bad is it!?"

Ahn replied in an Arabic accent, "It's bad enough."

He shoved past Ahn and ran into the room where the newly discovered statue of the goddess Seshat was being studied. The magnificent golden effigy had been unearthed a month ago in a chamber found at the foot of the Sphinx. The five-foot idol was an homage to the ancient goddess of knowledge, wisdom, and writing. The beautiful black hair, eyes, and dots on her cheetah hide dress were made of onyx. In her left hand was a six-foot-tall palm stem made out of blackened bronze. In her right hand was a thin knotted rope that was crafted out of intricately carved gold. The statue's wrists and ankles had blue bands painted on them. The detail, history, and sheer weight in gold gave the idol an estimated worth of over fifty-three million Egyptian pounds or three million American dollars.

Professor Pearson gasped as he looked at the goddess's right arm. It was cracked and hanging down at an odd angle. He felt like weeping and put his hand over his mouth.

He examined the single severed line around the golden forearm and asked, "Ahn! Did it fall? Was there an accident? Tell me the truth!"

The skinny assistant pleaded, "Professor, it wasn't me! I was putting my logbooks in the next room, and I heard a loud noise. It sounded like hammering. Of course, I rushed in, and there it was, just like that."

The Professor pulled out his reading glasses and took a closer look at the space between the crack. Something shiny was hidden in the center of the broken piece. Carefully, he withdrew the statue's arm away from the body. Sticking out from the amputated limb was a cylinder made of bronze.

The older man turned and handed the broken piece of the statue to Anh. He took several minutes looking around the cylinder until he was sure that further damage wouldn't be sustained by extracting it. Putting on a pair of gloves, he gently pulled until it snapped free. He marveled at the intricately decorated cylinder that was covered in dust.

He walked to one of the work desks and put it under a giant magnifying glass. Ahu flipped on the desk light, and the pair examined the artifact. It was an ivory scroll case covered in hieroglyphics and precious geMs. On each end, facing one another, were the images of Thoth and Seshat set in black onyx.

Anh used a small brush and wiped away some of the dirt, "What is it, Professor?"

Terrance rolled the cylinder around in a circle as he translated the hieroglyphics aloud, "Inside is the sacred knowledge of my love Thoth. This scroll gives the power of.... What's that word?"

Anh looked closer, "Resurrection."

The Professor nodded excitedly, "Yes! Resurrection. This scroll gives the power of resurrection. 'I, Seshat, guard his secrets and curse anyone unworthy to unseal this case. To reveal the wisdom within, travel to the House of Books beneath the Nile River, and lay it in the hands of Sobek.'"

His assistant looked up at him, "Professor, can this be true? This is the famed Scroll of Thoth. To bring back the dead. That's a myth. Isn't it?"

Terrance met his gaze, "It means the Mistress has given us the location of the House of Books. That library contains the lost knowledge and spells of Egypt. Who cares about superstitious legends of resurrection. The tombs we would find in there would make my career, and yours!"

Anh had a nervous grin, "But the curse Seshat spoke of?"

The Professor waved him off, "Anh, you surprise me. You're a man of science, and we have made the discovery of a lifetime!"

He grabbed the slight man by the shoulder and mused, "At the bottom of the Nile! Of course, that would make a perfect place to put the library. Regardless if Egypt fell or not, no one marches an army to the bottom of the river. If the chamber is sealed, this would be a time capsule to ancient Egypt. It could rewrite history as we know it! We have to tell the Director right away!"

A figure dressed in a ski mask and wearing an armband that sported an octopus looking head stepped out from behind a set of crates. Terrance and Ahn turned to face him, shocked by the suppressed 9 mm in the stranger's hand. As the Professor opened his mouth to protest, the assailant let loose a muffled shot into the chest of his assistant. Ahn slumped to the floor, clutching his chest, and fell dead on the floor. Shuddering with fear, the older man turned to his friend's killer, too petrified to do or say anything.

The pistol's barrel smoked as the assassin told him, "Good evening, Professor. Please gather your tools and come with me. The Grand Master would very much like to meet you... and that scroll."

Continued In ...

Magicae: Book Three,
The Dawn of Anubis

If you enjoyed this book, please consider reviewing it on Amazon. Thank you!
www.boluellen.com